ECHO

ECHO

Jack McDevitt

ACE BOOKS, NEW YORK

THE BERKLEY PUBLISHING GROUP
Published by the Penguin Group
Penguin Group (USA) Inc.
375 Hudson Street, New York, New York 10014, USA
Penguin Group (Canada), 90 Eglinton Avenue East, Suite 700, Toronto, Ontario M4P 2Y3, Canada
(a division of Pearson Penguin Canada Inc.)
Penguin Books Ltd., 80 Strand, London WC2R 0RL, England
Penguin Group Ireland, 25 St. Stephen's Green, Dublin 2, Ireland (a division of Penguin Books Ltd.)
Penguin Group (Australia), 250 Camberwell Road, Camberwell, Victoria 3124, Australia
(a division of Pearson Australia Group Pty. Ltd.)
Penguin Books India Pvt. Ltd., 11 Community Centre, Panchsheel Park, New Delhi—110 017, India
Penguin Group (NZ), 67 Apollo Drive, Rosedale, North Shore 0632, New Zealand
(a division of Pearson New Zealand Ltd.)
Penguin Books (South Africa) (Pty.) Ltd., 24 Sturdee Avenue, Rosebank, Johannesburg 2196,
South Africa

Penguin Books Ltd., Registered Offices: 80 Strand, London WC2R 0RL, England

This is an original publication of The Berkley Publishing Group.

This is a work of fiction. Names, characters, places, and incidents either are the product of the author's imagination or are used fictitiously, and any resemblance to actual persons, living or dead, business establishments, events, or locales is entirely coincidental. The publisher does not have any control over and does not assume any responsibility for author or third-party websites or their content.

FIRST EDITION: November 2010

Library of Congress Cataloging-in-Publication Data

McDevitt, Jack.
    Echo / Jack McDevitt.—1st ed.
        p.   cm.
    ISBN 978-0-441-01924-3
    1. Human-alien encounters—Fiction.   I. Title.
    PS3563.C3556E35   2010
    813'.54—dc22
                                2010028545

PRINTED IN THE UNITED STATES OF AMERICA

10 9 8 7 6 5 4 3 2 1

For Ron Peifer,
always the man of the hour

ACKNOWLEDGMENTS

I'm indebted for advice and technical assistance to David DeGraff of Alfred University, Walter Cuirle of the U.S. House of Representatives Page School, and Michael Fossel, author of *Cells, Aging, and Human Disease*. Thanks also to Ralph Vicinanza, for his continuing support. To Sara and Bob Schwager, for their suggestions. To my editor, Ginjer Buchanan. And to my wife, Maureen, who has to read the early version.

Lost in the wind was the last dying echo of who we were.

—JOSHUA KILBRIDE, *DOWNSTREAM*

PROLOGUE

LATE WINTER, 1403, RIMWAY CALENDAR

Somerset Tuttle's AI announced that Rachel had arrived. *"Do you wish to admit her, sir?"*

"Of course, Jeremy. Tell her I'll be right there."

Rachel had been upset when she called. That was utterly out of character for her. Sunset, she'd said, verging on tears—he loved being addressed by the nickname, intended by his rivals as a commentary on his career, but which nevertheless had an adventurous ring—I have to see you. No. Tonight. Please. Whatever you're doing. No, I don't want to tell you over the circuit. Are you alone? Well, get rid of them. You won't be sorry.

When he'd suggested they meet over dinner, she'd all but come apart. *"Now, Sunset. Please."*

He liked Rachel. She said what she thought, she had a good sense of humor, she was smart, and she was beautiful. Soft brown hair and penetrating blue eyes and a smile that lit up his life. He enjoyed having her with him when he attended social functions because she was inevitably the most beautiful creature in the room. The nitwits who thought he was crazy because he'd invested a lifetime trying to determine who else might be out there—the most important question of the age—could only watch enviously as he escorted her through the crowd.

She worked for World's End Tours, where she took people sightseeing among the stars. And over on your right is Anderson's Black Hole. And straight ahead is the Crab Nebula. He smiled at the image and kept the smile in place to reassure Rachel that, whatever was bothering her, it would be all right.

His great hope was that one day he would introduce her to someone not born of human stock, someone other than the idiot Mutes, of course, who'd been around so long it was hard to think of them as alien. That they would sit down over lunch with a true Other, fill the wineglasses, and talk about purpose, design, and God. That was what mattered.

Tuttle had been looking for over a century, sometimes with colleagues, more often alone. He'd examined literally hundreds of terrestrial worlds, places with running water and bright sunlight and soft winds. Most had been devoid even of a blade of grass or a trilobite. A few possessed forests and creatures that scampered through them, and seas teeming with life. But they were rare.

Nowhere had he seen something that might have been able to appreciate who he was and where he came from. Something that, on occasion, might have looked at the stars.

He didn't look forward to Rachel's upcoming hysterics. He couldn't imagine what it might be that had rattled a woman he'd considered, until this moment, unflappable. But he didn't want to get involved with what was clearly a sticky personal situation. It sounded like a problem with her boyfriend, but surely she wouldn't bring that to *him*. What then? Trouble at work? That had to be it. Maybe she'd gotten caught in some sort of compromising situation with one of the passengers. That was prohibited, for reasons he'd never understood.

She'd needed fifteen minutes to get there, a stretch of time that had seemed endless. Now she stood in the open doorway, staring at him with red-rimmed eyes. Sunset straightened his shirt and opened his arms to her. "My dear, come in. What's wrong?"

The door and entryway were glass, and the snow-covered grounds

behind her gleamed in the sunlight. Rachel's sculpted features were frozen. The animation that fueled her loveliness was gone.

"Sunset." It was all she seemed able to manage.

She was wrapped in a light jacket, too delicate for the weather. He
took her by the shoulders and started to embrace her, but she pulled
away. "Rachel, it's good to have you back. Come in and sit down. Can I
get you something?"

She shook her head, holding back tears.

He led her into the sitting room. "Can I get you a drink?"

"Oh, yes, please." She collapsed into a chair while he got her favorite
liqueur, Margo's carousel, out of the cabinet. He poured two glasses,
walked back, and handed her one. She'd taken off the jacket, and he was
surprised to see that she was wearing her uniform. It was dark blue, and
a captain's silver stars rested on her shoulders. But the collar had been
pulled open.

"Now what seems to be the problem?"

"Sunset," she said, her voice barely more than a whisper, "I need help."

She'd been gone three weeks. He hadn't expected her back for another
few days.

"Of course, love. What can I do?"

She looked up at a mural of the Milky Way, which dominated the
west wall. She stared at it, sighed, shook her head, wiped away a tear.
Then she picked up the glass and took a sip. Her eyes went back to the
mural. "You've been looking your entire life, haven't you?" she asked.

"Yes, I suppose so. I got hooked when my father took me out on one
of his missions."

"He never found anything, either."

"No. Rachel, nobody *ever* finds anything. Except Melony Brown."
Melony had come unexpectedly upon the Ashiyyur, the Mutes, centuries
ago, while she was measuring solar temperature ranges. She was the lady
for whom the river had been named. "Did something happen on the tour?"

"Yes."

My God, she'd been caught in flagrante on the ship with one of the
passengers. It would be the end of her career. "So," he said, keeping his
voice carefully level, "what happened?"

She looked at him and suddenly he knew. It hadn't been a tryst.

There were stories all the time. Somebody saw lights out at Ringwald 557. Somebody else intercepted a strange communication in the Veiled Lady. A couple of people on a once-in-a-lifetime vacation came across ruins on Sakata III and came back claiming to have made the discovery of the age. Except that the lights never showed up again, the communication was never traced, and the ruins were five thousand years old, all that remained of a settlement lost to history. Just ordinary people from Flexnor, maybe, or Vikoda. Nobody knew for certain. When you've been running around the Orion Arm for thousands of years, history gets lost.

A million systems that had never been looked at lay within reach. But the impulse to explore had gone away a long time ago. People had looked for centuries and found nothing more advanced than monkeys and dolphins. Somehow, for reasons still not clearly understood, the evolution of mental faculties did not generally exceed a fairly low level. Maybe it was that there was no clear survival value in drawing pictures on walls or writing poetry. Something almost unique must have happened with humans.

"Sunset," she said, "I saw something you'd be interested in."

Tuttle was accustomed to it. *Aliens* was a popular topic on the science talk shows, so he got a lot of invitations, and everyone knew who he was. To his colleagues, he was a man who'd wasted his life, chasing dreams. But to the more imaginative members of the general public, he was the guy they came to when they had, or dreamed they'd had, a strange encounter. They were inevitably mildly deranged. He'd expected more from Rachel.

"So what did you see, love?"

She started to reply, but her voice caught. She was wiping her cheek again. "It's not good," she said.

"Tell me what happened."

Finally, the tears came.

PART I

The Tablet

ONe

1431, TWENTY-EIGHT YEARS LATER

"Chase, I may have found something of interest." Alex's voice, over the internal comm system, sounded dubious. Maybe he had something, maybe not. I was just getting ready to tackle the morning's work, which consisted primarily of calculating charges for our clients and getting out the monthly billing notices. It had been a good year, and if current trends continued, Rainbow Enterprises would experience breakout earnings.

Interest in antiquities tends to move in cycles, and we were currently riding a wave. People wanted not only ordinary stuff, lamps and furniture from the last few centuries, but they were getting in line for rare, and sometimes unique, items. We'd just moved a chair that had belonged to E. Wyatt Cooper for a quarter million. Cooper had departed the scene more than a century ago, after a writing career that had appeared undistinguished. But his reputation had grown since his death, and today his vitriolic essays had become a staple of the literature. One who took mockery to the highest levels could expect to be defined as "cooperesque."

Jacob, who'd started life as the house AI for Alex's uncle, Gabe, had noticed the chair when it was put up for sale by a young woman who had no idea of its value. We'd intervened, getting to her before anyone else did, informed her of its value, and managed the subsequent auction. And, if you're wondering, yes, we could have bought it ourselves at a price that would have constituted virtual robbery, but Alex never took advantage of anyone, except those blowhards and would-be cheats who deserved it. But that's another story. Suffice to say that Rainbow Enterprises did not want to be perceived as disreputable. Our income resulted from putting clients in touch with one another. And our clients tended to be generous when they made twenty or fifty times what they'd expected for a hand mirror or a bracelet. It was essential to the business that they trust us.

Jacob had a long history of locating valuable antiquities amid the junk offered daily at the Rees Market, BlowAway, Ferguson's, and other online sites.

"Take a look, Chase," Alex said. *"You'll probably want to follow up on it."*

"Okay."

"Let me know what you decide."

I asked Jacob to show me what he had. He produced two pictures of a pale white stone tablet, taken from different angles. The tablet was rounded at the top, not unlike some of the markers in the cemetery adjoining Alex's property. Three lines of symbols had been engraved across the front of the object. *"Actual size,"* Jacob added.

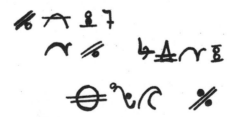

It was a bit less than half as tall as I was, an arm's length in width, and a few millimeters thick. "What's the language?" I asked.

"I have no idea, Chase. It looks a little like the Late Korbanic period, but the characters don't really match."

"Angle it a bit."

The bottom wasn't smooth. Someone had used a laser to cut it loose from its base. *"It appears to be a clumsy effort,"* Jacob said, *"to reduce the size in order to make it fit somewhere."*

"Or to remove it from the original site. Who's the owner?"

"Madeleine Greengrass. She's a tour guide at Silesia Park."

"What does she have to say about it?"

"Not much. She says it's been a lawn decoration at her house as long as she's been there. She's giving it away. Wants to get rid of it. Haul it off, and it's yours."

"See if you can get her for me."

I went back to the billings, but I'd barely started when a small, light-skinned woman appeared in the middle of the room. Her blond hair was cut short, and she looked tired. She wore a park ranger's uniform and was in the process of straightening her blouse while simultaneously drinking from a steaming cup. The scent of coffee came through. *"What can I do for you, Ms. Kolpath?"* she asked, putting the cup down.

"I'm interested in the tablet."

"I'm at Rindenwood," she said. *"You know where that is?"*

"I can find it."

"Good. Gold Range, number 12. It's on the front porch."

"Okay. We'll be over later today."

"It's all yours. But you'll need a couple of guys to haul it out of here."

"Ms. Greengrass," I said, "where did it come from?"

"It was here when I bought the house." She looked away. I got the impression she was checking the time. *"Listen, I'm running late. Take the tablet if you want it, okay? I have to go."*

Alex was seated in the conference room, studying the pictures, which had been blown up to make the symbols clear. Behind him, an overcast sky pressed down on the windows. It was the first day of autumn. Despite the threatening weather, a few sailboats were out on the Melony. "Wish we could read it," I said.

"If we could, Chase, it wouldn't be half as interesting. Jacob, get me Peer Wilson." Wilson was an expert on all things Korbanic.

Jacob said okay, he was already on it, and Alex wondered aloud how old the tablet was.

"*We have a recording,*" Jacob said, and played it. It was audio only: "*This is Dr. Peer Wilson. I am currently unavailable. Leave a message.*"

"Peer," Alex said, "this is Alex Benedict. Give me a call when you can, please."

"What do you think?" I asked. "Is it worth anything?"

"Hard to say, Chase." I knew what he was hoping: That it would turn out to be a remnant from some forgotten colony world, seven or eight thousand years old. Something from the very beginning of the Great Emigration. "Where's she been keeping it?"

"It's on her front deck now."

"I mean, where's it been the last few years? It looks as if it's been out in the weather."

"In the garden, I guess. She said it was a lawn decoration."

He sank into a chair. "Even if it *is* Late Korbanic, it's only going to have minimum value. Unless it turns out to be Christopher Carver's gravestone. Or something along those lines."

Carver, of course, was the Korbanic hero who'd gone missing three centuries ago while walking in a park. "It looks like a grave marker," I said.

"I was kidding."

"I know. But it *does* look like a marker."

"All right. Let's get the stone."

"Jacob," I said, "get Tim on the circuit."

The lifting would be done by a couple of guys from Rambler, Inc., which provided a variety of services for Rainbow. Its manager, Tim Wistert, was a quiet, reserved guy who looked more like a bureaucrat than a mover. "*Two guys?*" he said.

"It looks heavy."

"*Okay. But we won't be able to get over there until late this afternoon.*"

"What time?"

"*About four?*"

"Okay. I'll meet them there."

Peer Wilson might have been the tallest man in Andiquar. He'd been around a long time, probably more than a century. His hair was beginning to lose its color. But it was stiff like prickly grass, and stood straight up, making him seem even bigger. He had a neatly trimmed mustache, and he made no effort to hide the fact that he disapproved of the way Alex made his living. Wilson, like many in the academic community, considered him a glorified grave robber.

Alex had signaled me when Wilson's image showed up, and the conversation had already begun when I walked into the boss's office in back.

"—*not Late Korbanic,*" Wilson was saying. He was seated in his office, behind a nameplate, awards prominently posted along the wall behind him. Northern Linguistic Association Man of the Year. The Gilbert Prize for Contributions to Historical Research. The Brisbane Award for Lifetime Achievement.

"Peer," said Alex, "you remember my associate, Chase Kolpath. Chase, Professor Wilson."

"Yes. Of course." He smiled politely. *"I believe we've met somewhere, haven't we?"* Then he plowed on, not waiting for an answer, which would have been *Yes, several times.* *"No, there is some slight resemblance to one of the Korbanic codas. But it's purely superficial."*

"Professor, do you have any idea what language it might be?"

"May I ask where this object is at the moment?"

"At the home of a client."

"I see. Doesn't he know what it is?"

"The owner is a young woman. And no, she seems to have no idea."

"Yes. Well, I wouldn't get too excited about it, Alex. I assume you'd like me to research it for you?"

"If you would."

"Ordinarily, I'd expect a consultant's fee. But as it's you—" His lips parted in a contemptuous smile.

"Nitwit," Alex said, looking up. "Chase, I've been checking on the previous owners of Gold Range number twelve."

"And—?"

"At one time it belonged to Somerset Tuttle."

"Tuttle? The guy they called Sunset? Who was always out looking for aliens?"

"That's the one."

"He's been dead a long time, hasn't he?"

"Twenty-five years. Give or take."

"You think the tablet was his?"

"Maybe."

"If it was his," I said, "the language probably doesn't make any difference."

"Why is that?"

"If he'd found it in an archeological site somewhere, and it had any value, he'd certainly have known about it. I doubt it would have ended its days as a lawn ornament."

"That would certainly seem to be a logical conclusion. Still, it seems like an odd thing to keep around the house. Let's look into it."

"Okay, Alex, if you say so."

He smiled at my skepticism. "Stranger things have happened, young lady."

"How did he die, Alex?"

We were still in his office in the back of the country house. A light symphony was playing on the sound system, and he was splayed out on the lush sofa he'd inherited from his uncle. "Sunset Tuttle enjoyed sailing. He used to go out on the Melony. One day he sailed into a storm. The wind caught one of the booms, swung it around, and clipped him in the head with it. He was alone, but there were witnesses in another boat. They got to him as quickly as they could, but—" Alex shrugged. "He had a reputation for being preoccupied. Not paying attention to what he was doing. He was 139 years old at the time. I wonder if it's possible—"

"If *what's* possible, Alex?"

"That the tablet is from an alien site."

I laughed. "Come on, Alex. There aren't any aliens."

"How about the Mutes?"

"The Mutes don't count."

"Oh? Why's that?"

I gave up. Alex likes to think he keeps an open mind, but I was thinking how sometimes it's *too* open. "So what are you saying?" I asked.

"Well, I don't know. It makes no sense. He spent his life looking for aliens. If he found them, Chase, either living or otherwise, any evidence at all that they existed, he'd have put it all over the media."

Alex keeps a couple of tabitha plants near the window. He got up, inspected them, and got some water for them. "His colleagues laughed at him. Lectured him for wasting his life. If he'd found the slightest evidence, he would not have held it back, believe me." He finished with the plants and sat down again. "Maybe it's time we talked with the great man himself."

"Jacob," I said, "does Tuttle have an avatar?"

Jacob needed a moment. *"No, Chase. He was apparently a very private person."*

"I guess that's a result of all the ridicule," I said.

"How about his wife? Did *she* have an avatar?"

"Which one?"

"How many were there?"

"Three. India, Cassa, and Mary."

"Can we reach any of them?"

"They've all passed away. The last of them, India, died just last year."

"So which ones had an avatar?"

"India does."

"Okay. Which years were they together? He and India?"

"From 1380 until 1396."

"Did they have any kids?"

"He had one child. Basil. And before you ask, he seems to be still alive."

"Good. Can you connect me with him?"

"Unfortunately, Alex, I have no link. Or address. His last known residence was in Foxpoint."

"On the other side of the continent?"

"No. Not that Foxpoint. This one's out in the desert in the southeast. But he moved several years ago."

"Okay. See if you can track him down." He smiled at me. "Somebody has to know something," he said. Then back to Jacob: "Get us through to India."

Moments later India Beshoar blinked on. She had lush brown hair, a good smile, a great body, and deep green eyes. Of course, everybody looks good in avatar form. You ought to see mine. *"Hello,"* she said. *"Can I be of assistance?"*

Alex introduced us. Then: "India, you were married to Sunset Tuttle."

"Yes. That is correct." Her expression did not change. No happy memory there.

"Were you together in the house at Rindenwood?"

"We were. Why do you ask?"

"What was he like?"

"Sunset? Basically, he was a decent man."

"But—?"

"He lacked some social skills."

"May I ask, in what way?"

"This is difficult for me, Mr. Benedict."

"I'm sure it is. India, Chase and I are trying to do some historical research, and that sometimes requires us to ask personal questions we'd rather leave alone. But it really doesn't matter now, does it? Since you've both passed on."

"I guess not." Those green eyes looked my way for sympathy. *"He didn't take his vows too seriously."* I nodded. You can't trust guys, I was telling her. We all know that. *"The best way to describe our marriage was that I always felt alone."*

"I'm sorry to hear it."

"I'm sorry to say it. But it was my own fault. I knew what he was before I married him. I thought I could change him." She shook her head. *"I was old enough to know better."*

"What did he care about?" I asked. "Other than the hunt for aliens, what was important to him?"

"Aliens were all that mattered."

Alex showed her an image of the tablet. "India, do you know anything about this?"

"No," she said.

"Could it have been in the house, or in the garden, when you were there, without your knowing about it?"

"How big is it?" Alex expanded it to actual size. *"No,"* she said. *"I would certainly have known. Why? Is it valuable?"*

"That's what we're trying to determine," he said.

She shrugged. *"Wish I could help."*

TWO

There is no more critical question before us than that which seeks to determine our place in the universe. We now know that intelligent life is extraordinarily rare. So we are not simply one species among a number of equals, as we had once expected to be. Rather, we are the climax toward which the universe has been evolving for twelve billion years. We are the part of the cosmos that observes, and senses, and grasps the magnitude of this incredible place we call home. What a waste it would all be were it not for the presence of the Ashiyyur, and of us.

—Somerset Tuttle, "Breakfast with the Aliens"

We did a search on Tuttle. *"I am sorry to report,"* said Jacob, *"that there is no comprehensive record of his flights."*

"How about a log?" said Alex. "Or a notebook?"

"No, sir. Nothing."

"A journal? Anything at all?"

"I can find no account anywhere that would indicate where he has traveled."

It was an inauspicious start because there wasn't much else of substance. No one had ever done a serious biography. Accounts of other explorers existed, containing some details about Tuttle's missions. And a few interviews shed light on destinations. But even there, only a few were precise. Mostly, we saw attacks launched by his colleagues, who used him as an example of the results of wishful thinking and a refusal to face the hard facts of life. His name became a verb, to *tuttle*, which meant to persist in an endeavor with no hope of success.

We discovered a few tributes, which came from enthusiasts and true believers who had followed his lifelong effort to find an alien intelligence. There were some laudatory comments on his charity work. He'd been born wealthy and had been a generous contributor to numerous causes. During his final years, he'd sat on the board of governors of the Belmont Foundation for the Underprivileged. We also found a handful of interviews and presentations. And there was a collection of essays.

For more than thirty years, he'd ridden the *Callisto* around the Orion Arm in his fruitless quest. During most of that time, he'd been his own pilot, and he usually traveled alone. He claimed to have found more than six hundred biozone worlds, of which only a handful had actually been home to living things. The vast majority were sterile. But none, not *one*, had contained, as he put it, anything that had waved back.

At the time of his death, he'd been a member of the Gibbon Society. For those unfamiliar with it, it's a group that thinks our best days are behind us. That we're decaying, and that, unless we get hold of ourselves, the end is near.

"It's one of the reasons we need to find an alien intelligence," he said in an interview with talk-show host Charles Koeffler. *"We need something to challenge us. To bring us back to life."* Koeffler asked whether he was speaking about a potential military threat. *"No,"* he said. *"Of course not. But someone to remind us what we might achieve if we ever really get off our front porch."*

"What," I asked, "does he think the Mutes are?"

"They've been around too long," said Alex. "I'd guess he perceives them as part of the natural world he lives in."

Jacob threw himself enthusiastically into the search. *"Korchnoi University invited him to speak to its graduates in 1400,"* he said. *"They took a fair amount of criticism for it because he wasn't perceived as a serious figure in the academic world. The school became the butt of jokes. They were said, for example, to be granting graduate degrees in alien psychology. And to be debating the ethics of cutting down talking trees. You will, I hope, pardon me, but I fail to see the humor."*

"As do I, Jacob," I said.

"I have the Korchnoi address. Did you wish to see it?"

"Sure," said Alex.

It's always hard to be certain about physical size when you're looking at a hologram, but Tuttle appeared to be a small, unimposing figure. He had gray eyes, a weak chin, and he smiled too much. He didn't strike me as a guy who could be passionate about anything. At least, not until he finished the preliminaries, talking about the value of education in general, how it was for the benefit of the individual student and not for a prospective employer. Then he caught his breath, came out from behind the lectern, and told his listeners—about two hundred students and a handful of professors—what it meant in modern times to be a professional of any stripe.

"Your advisors will tell you," he said, *"how to handle profit and loss statements. How to be prudent about your career. How to make more money than the person sitting next to you. But your education is for you, and not for anyone else. If you choose to be an anthropologist, as I did, they will recommend that you invest your time hunting down lost ships and forgotten settlements. Find a city somewhere whose builders have dropped out of the history books."* He raised a clenched hand and waved it in the air. *"That's how you make your reputation. But it's not where the real prize is. Anybody can do that. And who really cares what kind of plumbing systems they used on Machinova IV two thousand years ago?"*

Alex adjusted the image, bringing Tuttle closer. The gray eyes had caught fire. *"There's only one reason the human race left its home world, and it had nothing to do with establishing settlements along the Orion Arm. That was strictly a by-product. We came out of the solar system because we wanted to look around. We wanted to find someone else. Someone like ourselves, perhaps. Or maybe someone entirely different. But in any case, someone we could talk to. It was an adventure, a mission, not a real-estate investment.*

"If you read the books written during the early years of the Technological Age, especially the fiction, you won't find very much about founding outposts in the Aldebaran sector." Something in front of him caught his eye, and he grinned. *"What's your name, son?"*

Alex adjusted the angle, and we saw the person he was addressing, an athletic-looking young man with blond hair and a suddenly sheepish expression. *"Colt Everson, sir,"* he said.

"Colt, you look skeptical."

In fact, Colt looked uncomfortable. *"It's hard not to be, Professor Tuttle. I can't believe people ever seriously thought they'd find aliens. I know that's what we always say, but how does anyone really know that?"*

"Read their books."

"Well, the fiction talks about it, about aliens, but if you read the science abstracts of the period, I don't think you see much."

Tuttle looked around the room. *"Anybody want to respond to that?"*

A young woman raised her hand. *"It's because scientists are supposed to be ruled by the evidence. During the early years of the Fourth Millennium, there was no evidence."*

Somebody prompted her: *"The* Third *Millennium, Carla."*

"Whatever. Their reputations were on the line, as they always are." Like Colt, she looked uncomfortable. She wanted to say more, but she smiled shyly and sat back down.

"You're wondering about me, aren't you, Carla? Has my reputation suffered because of the work I do? Let me point out that I was invited to speak to the graduating class at Korchnoi." A few in back began to applaud, and it caught on and spread through the room. Tuttle waited until it had subsided. *"At the risk of ruining their reputations, I think I can state unequivocally that Professor Campbell and Professor Baryman are sympathetic to the work."* More applause. It was easy enough to pick the two named persons out of the crowd. Both nodded acquiescence. *"I've been looking for other civilizations now for more than a century. Most of my colleagues are convinced I've wasted my time. But, if nothing else, I've left a track for whoever comes after. He, or she, will know, at least, that* these *worlds are empty. Don't look* here. *It's not what I would have preferred to do, but maybe it's the only way."*

"Professor?" A young man in the rear stood. *"May I ask a personal question?"*

"You may ask."

"If you had it to do again, would you go in a different direction?"

"Oh, yes. Certainly. Absolutely."

"What would you do differently?"

"You asked if I'd go in a different direction. And of course I would. I didn't find anything in the direction I took. But if you're asking whether I'd spend my life digging up Fifth Millennium kitchen utensils from a dead city on a world we forgot about two thousand years ago, the answer is no. Certainly not. I'd rather fail at a world-shaking effort than succeed with trifles."

"That's strange," said Alex.

"What is?"

"He talks as if he left a complete record."

"You know," Alex said, "the tablet is going to turn out to be a joke. Something somebody gave him for his birthday. But I guess it doesn't cost us anything to look."

"How long did Tuttle live in the Rindenwood house?" I asked.

"He was born and died there, Chase."

I was watching the time. I'd be leaving in a few minutes for the place. "It seems odd," I said. "A guy who spent his life exploring the stars but never really left home."

Alex was wearing a frumpy University of Andiquar sweater. He noticed it was hanging crooked, unbuttoned it, and fixed it. "Take a contract with you," he said. "If Ms. Greengrass isn't at home when you get there, park on her doorstep until she shows up and get her signature. Give her a nominal payment."

"How much is nominal?"

"Twenty-five. No. Make it *thirty*-five. Just make sure we have every-thing in writing." He got up and started for the door. "Chase, I don't have to tell you—"

"I know," I said.

I prepped a contract and got moving. A light rain had begun to fall as I came out the side door and hurried down the walkway to the pad. Alex keeps saying he's going to put a roof over the walkway—Andiquar gets a lot of rain—but it never happens. The skimmer lit up as I entered, and said hello.

It would be a sixteen-minute run to Greengrass's place.

Rindenwood was a moneyed area. Some houses looked like Greek temples, others incorporated Aurelian domes and Sanjo towers. No false modesty here anywhere. And not a place where I'd expect to find a government worker. Number 12 in the Gold Range was conservative by local standards, but it was a luxurious place by mine. It was a plastene two-story structure with decks on both levels and a cluster of evergreens out front. Broad lawns opened onto the Melony, where Madeleine Greengrass had a pier and a boathouse.

I descended onto the pad, sending a passel of spindels fluttering out of the trees. Alex always claimed it was a sign of bad driving when you couldn't land without scaring the birds. It was pouring by then. I got out, made a dash along a brick walkway, and climbed three or four steps onto the front deck.

There was no tablet. I stood in front of the door, and the house asked if I needed help.

"My name's Kolpath," I said. "I'm here to pick up the tablet. Ms. Greengrass is expecting me."

"I'm sorry, Ms. Kolpath. But the tablet is gone."

"Gone? Gone where?"

"Someone came for it."

"She was supposed to hold it for me."

"I am sorry. I guess there was a misunderstanding somewhere. But someone else called, and they came right over."

"Can you reach her for me? Ms. Greengrass?"

"Is this an emergency?"

"It qualifies."

"What does?"

"Let it go. Do you know who it was? Who took the tablet?"

"Yes."

"Can you tell me, please?"

"I'm sorry, but I'm not really permitted to give out that kind of information."

"Is Ms. Greengrass home?"

"No, she isn't."

"When do you expect her?"

"She will probably be in at the end of the day. After six o'clock."

Tim's people were descending onto the pad as I started back out to the skimmer. They set down beside it and climbed out. There were two of them. One was Clyde Halley, with whom I'd worked before. I didn't know the other. Clyde was a big beefy guy, and so was his partner. "Problem, Chase?" said Clyde.

"It's gone," I said. "I guess we brought you guys out here for nothing. Sorry."

"It happens," he said. *"You're sure you don't need us?"*

"Not at the moment, Clyde." I tipped them both. Then I turned back to the house: "Would you get a message to Ms. Greengrass?"

"I can put it on her board."

"Ask her to call me as soon as she can."

"Very good, madame. Is there anything else?"

"Can you tell me anything at all about the persons who took the tablet?"

"I'm sorry, but that would not be ethical."

Alex was not happy. I can tell because he always starts telling me not to be upset. "This Greengrass should be able to let us know who took it, and we'll just make an offer."

"Sounds good."

"We should be able to track it down easily enough."

"Maybe whoever took it is thinking the same thing we are."

"You mean that it's an artifact? Not likely."

"Why not?"

"How many academics do you think scan the Rees Market every morning? No, I think somebody just likes white stone and decided it would make a nice garden decoration."

Jacob broke in. *"Pardon me, Alex,"* he said, *"but Ms. Wellington would like to speak with you about the Ivar vase."*

The Ivar vase had stood in a prominent place onstage during the turn-of-the-century hit *Showstopper*. The problem was that Ms. Wellington, its new owner, had encountered an "expert" who was telling her that her vase was only a duplicate. That the original had been broken during the next-to-last performance. All the paperwork was in place, but Ms. Wellington needed to be reassured she had the original.

Alex signaled I should go back to work while he got on the circuit with his client. I went down to my office, finished the billing, did some inventory work, recommended to a couple of clients that they not participate in planned trades, and eventually it was time to go home.

I called Madeleine Greengrass again.

"Ms. Greengrass is not available. If you wish, leave a message."

Well, I wasn't about to leave the building until I'd found out what the situation was, so I settled in to wait. Alex came down after a while, told me to go home, and promised he'd call as soon as he heard something.

"It's okay," I said. "If you don't mind, I'll hang on for a bit."

He suggested it was pointless. "It's much ado about nothing, Chase. Don't waste your time. Go home and entertain Mack."

Mack was my boyfriend of the hour. Alex didn't especially like him. He was an archeologist, he disapproved of what we did for a living, and he made no effort to hide it. "Years from now, Chase," he had told me, "you're going to look back on all this vandalism and grave robbing and selling off antiquities that should be in museums, and you're going to regret it."

Mack was a charmer, and that was the reason he was in a temporary status and not gone altogether. I hoped he might eventually arrive at a more reasonable point of view. At least that was what I kept telling myself.

I stayed on at the country house. We sent out for sandwiches. Then Alex got caught up in a conference with two people who'd just come back from an excavation at a thousand-year-old military base in a star system I'd never heard of. Of course, there was nothing unusual about that. If you haven't traveled much off Rimway, you probably have no idea how *big* it is out there.

I was sitting in my office, finishing what was left of a pot-roast sub, when Jacob indicated we had a caller. *"It's Professor Wilson. He wants to talk to Alex, but Alex is busy. Did you want to take the call?"*

Wilson appeared to be at home, relaxing in a large fabric armchair. I couldn't see much of the room, but it had dark-stained panels, and the lighting was subdued. A trophy case guarded a doorway behind him, placed so that it was visible to callers. Concert music rumbled through the background. Heavy stuff. Barankov or somebody, I thought. But the volume was turned down. *"Ah, Chase,"* he said. *"I was calling for Mr. Benedict."*

"He's busy at the moment, Professor. I can have him get back to you, if you like."

"No, no. I've looked again into the tablet engraving. It's definitely not Late Korbanic. Which is not a major issue. But there's nothing like it anywhere in the record. I have found a few similarities to other systems, but nothing close enough that would give us an identification."

"What about the Ashiyyur? Could it be a Mute artifact?"

"Possibly. We don't have complete information on ourselves, let alone on them."

"So we've no idea where this thing might have come from."

"None. I'd say it's either a hoax, or you have something quite valuable on your hands. What does Alex think?"

"I don't know. I'd guess he's on the fence."

"Well, let me know if I can do anything else."

That evening, I finally got through to Greengrass. "Madeleine," I said, "the tablet was gone when I got there."

"I know. Stafford told me."

Stafford? That would be the AI. "We think it may have some intrinsic value."

"Too late now. It's gone, Chase." She had a laid-back manner, probably a result of doing presentations for the visitors at Silesia Park.

"Can you tell me who took it?"

"No idea."

"You don't know?"

"*I think that's what I said.*"

"They didn't give you their names?"

"*I didn't give my approval for anyone to take it. A couple more people called after you did. I thought I told them it was no longer available, but there might have been a communication breakdown. I don't know. I just wanted to get rid of it, okay? I've no idea where it is now, and I don't particularly care. I apologize, though, that you made the trip for nothing.*"

"I was hoping you could help us retrieve it."

"*How valuable do you think it is?*"

"We don't know yet. Maybe a lot."

"*Well,*" she said, "*it's only money.*"

"Ms. Greengrass, I'm not promising anything, but it might have bought you another house."

"*You're not serious.*"

"As I say, we don't know yet. Is there anything you can think of that might help us locate it?"

"*Well, I wish I could. But I just don't see anything. I don't even know who those people were.*"

"How about if we take a look at what your AI has. We might be able to identify whoever took it."

"*Hold on a second,*" she said.

I waited. After a minute or so she relayed some images to me, and we watched two men and a woman walk up onto her porch. The tablet was sitting there, between two chairs. "Madeleine," I said, "don't you log skimmers?"

"*Yes, we do. Stafford?*"

"*They came in a Sentinel, Madeleine.*" Late model. White, split-wing.

The woman had dark hair. She was wearing athletic gear, but she looked like money. She knelt to examine the tablet. After a minute or two, she looked up at the others and nodded. The two men, dressed in the same sporting style, moved the chairs out of the way.

One was big. Broad shoulders, lots of muscle, built close to the ground. He had a black beard and a bald skull. The other male looked a bit thin to be moving rocks. But they took their positions on either side of the tablet and, on a count of three, lifted. The big guy gave directions; they got the tablet off the porch, carried it down to the skimmer, and loaded it into the backseat. The woman joined them, and all three climbed in. We watched the vehicle lift off. They'd been careful about the landing, turning the vehicle so that its designator was never visible.

"*I've no idea who they are,*" said Greengrass.

Alex handed me a note. "Try this."

> *A stone tablet was removed yesterday from a front deck in Rindenwood. The tablet, pictured herein, has great sentimental value. Reward. Call Sabol 2113-477.*

We ran it that evening. When I came back into the office next morning, there'd been two responses. "Neither was actually involved with the tablet," Alex said. "But they *did* have engravings they wanted to sell us."

Alex asked me to call Greengrass again. This time I got her on the first try. "*Yes, Ms. Kolpath?*" Her eyes slid momentarily shut. "*What can I do for you this time?*"

"I'm sorry to bother you—"

"*It's all right.*"

"We think the tablet was originally left in the house by Sunset Tuttle."

"*Who?*"

"He was an anthropologist."

"*Okay.*"

"Do you know if there's anything else you have that might have belonged originally to him?"

"*I don't know. There are some tennis rackets out back that came with the house. And a swing on a tree. I never met the guy.*"

She was too young to have made the purchase. "If I may ask, how long have you been in the house?"

"*About six years.*"

"Okay. Is there anything around that might have archeological significance? Anything else like the tablet?"

"No. I don't think so."

"All right. If you find anything, it might be worth money. Please let us know."

"I'll keep that in mind. And I hope you find the tablet."

THree

If we know anything for certain, it is that the universe is virtually empty. Nine thousand years of exploration have revealed the presence of only one techno- logical race, other than ourselves. And while we have always been inclined to mourn something we've never had—communion with other entities—you must forgive me if I point out that the cosmos is consequently a far safer place than it might have been. We have seen intelligence in action. The first thing it does is learn how to make axes. And spears. Say what you like about missing the opportunity to enjoy the company of somebody else, I prefer the echoes. And I hope very much that it stays that way.

—Maria Webber, *The Long Voyage*

Alex asked me to set up a conference with Jerry Hagel. The name was vaguely familiar because he was a client, but otherwise I knew noth- ing about him. So I looked up his profile. Unlike most of the people we served, he wasn't wealthy. And he had only one very narrow interest: Sunset Tuttle.

Through Rainbow, Hagel had acquired the *Callisto*'s AI, and a shirt worn by Tuttle. He also owned a telescope that had been mounted on the ship's hull, and, incredibly, the interdimensional drive unit. He had a transfer bill signed by him, a reading lamp from the Rindenwood house, and images of the *Callisto* leaving Skydeck, returning to Skydeck, pass- ing across the face of the moon, and looking down from orbit on Parallax III and several worlds bearing only numerical designations.

Hagel was an architect. He'd been married three times. The third marriage had recently dissolved. He had a reputation for being a difficult man to work for. And, I guessed, to live with. There were no kids.

He was an enthusiast for the outer fringes of science. There were no ghosts, he is quoted as saying, but there might be interdimensional echoes that "occasionally leak through the time-space fabric." And he thought there might be an inflexibility in the quantum mechanical world that eliminated multiple possibilities. That the uncertainty principle was an illusion. "There is no such thing as free will," he'd once told a gathering of the Lincoln Architects Association. I'm sure they invited him back.

When I reached him, he was having dinner with guests. There was a lot of noise and laughter in the background while I identified myself. I told him Alex wanted to talk with him when he had a few minutes.

"Can't at the moment," he said. *"I'm entertaining friends, but I'll get back to you as quickly as I can."*

He was in his skimmer an hour or so later when he called. Alex was out of the building. *"What did he want, Chase? Do you know?"*

"He had some questions. About Sunset Tuttle."

"What did he want to know?"

"You've always been interested in Tuttle."

"Yes. I think I qualify as something of an expert." He tried to sound modest, as though being an expert on Tuttle was a major achievement.

"Jerry, do you know of any indication, any *rumor*, that Tuttle might have found what he was looking for?"

"You mean aliens?"

"Yes."

He exploded with laughter. *"Listen, Chase, if he'd found anything out there, it wouldn't be necessary to ask about it. He'd have organized a parade. Ridden down Market Street with an alien mayor."*

"Can you imagine any set of circumstances that might have led him to keep quiet about it?"

"No. None."

"Nothing at all?"

"Well, there was a story that got around at one point, but conspiracy theorists are always with us."

"What's the story?"

"That he found something so terrible he didn't dare reveal it. Except to a few people high in the government. So now, the theory goes, there's

*an area out there that they keep absolutely secret. Where nobody's
allowed. It's never been made official, and, naturally, the government
denies everything. If you submit a flight plan that takes you anywhere
close, they'll find a reason to deny permission. Impending supernova or
something."*

"Where is this area?"

*"Oh, nobody knows, of course. If people knew, you wouldn't be
able to keep them out."*

"You don't think there's any truth to it? None at all?"

He broke into a wide grin. *"Chase, I know you're not serious."*

"No. Of course not. Just kidding."

"Unless you guys know something I don't." I heard the lander set
down. *"Have you—?"*

"No." I tried to sound amused. "I'm just thinking what a great story
it would make."

The skimmer door opened. *"Yes, it certainly would."*

"Jerry, thanks. We're just doing some historical research and trying
to get a handle on the folklore that surrounds this guy."

*"Oh, yeah. He's a legendary character, okay. Sometimes I think it's
the failure that makes him so interesting. I mean, he just wouldn't quit.
You have to love him. I'm sorry I never got to meet him."*

"Well, thanks, Jerry."

But Jerry wasn't finished. *"There are others out there. Have to be.
The thing is, intelligence is an aberration. But the galaxy is big. Instead
of talking as if there's nobody here except us and the Mutes, we should
recognize that the fact there are Mutes shows it's possible. And with all
those worlds, there are going to be others. We've become too set in our
ways. We have access to the entire galaxy, but we talk as if we have it all
to ourselves. Eventually we're going to run into somebody, and we better
damned well be ready so we don't screw it up the way we did last time."*

"You mean by shooting at them."

*"That, too. I suppose the real loss is the lack of imagination. If I
were an extraterrestrial, I think I'd find us pretty dumb."*

"What kind of person was he, Jerry?"

"He was exactly the man you'd want to have at your back if you got

in trouble. You could count on him to do what he said. And he didn't discourage easily."

"Obviously not."

"Do you know where the name of his ship came from?"

"The *Callisto*? It's one of the moons of Jupiter, isn't it?"

"One of the Galilean moons, Chase. One of the four moons that Galileo discovered. When that happened, it shook the medieval world-view. Society was never the same."

We set Jacob to do an online hunt for the two men who'd collected the tablet. We couldn't do that with the woman because she'd kept her back to the imagers.

The big one turned out to be Brian Lewis, a police officer. The other one was Doug Bannister, who was a medical technician. The bios indicated they both played airball on an amateur team, the Conneltown Dragons. Conneltown was located about fifty kilometers outside Andiquar, on the Melony. We were in the middle of the season, and the Dragons' next game was the following evening. "Let's not make an issue of this," said Alex. "No point going to their homes if we don't have to. You an airball fan, by any chance?"

"I guess I am now."

The Dragons were at home, playing the Tylerville Hawks. I told Alex I could barely wait, and he said he'd treat for a steak dinner after the game and would that be okay? I told him yes, provided he didn't sit there during the game explaining the rules to me.

Several hundred people showed up on a chilly evening. The game would be played on an open field, under lights. The patrons watched from rickety stands. We spotted our two guys right away. The crowd applauded enthusiastically as the hometown players were introduced. The captains met at the center of the field, a coin was tossed, and the teams lined up on opposing sides. Lewis was a starter; Bannister was on the bench.

For those who don't pay attention to trivia, it's enough to say that the game is played with six on a team. The object is to move the ball into the other team's territory and, using a paddle, whack it into a moving net. The net squeals when a goal is scored, invariably setting off a loud crowd reaction. The game gets its name, and its charm, from the fact that the teams move through shifting gravity fields.

At no time are players permitted to *hold* the ball. The gravity gradients in the various fields change constantly, but not abruptly, giving the players time to adjust. But the shifts are unpredictable. It's one minute up and the next minute down. Maximum gravity permissible is 1.6, which would put me at about 185 pounds. Minimum gravity is zero. I'd always thought of airball as an idiot's game, and I still do, but that evening I enjoyed myself. And I was impressed with the flexibility and skill of the players.

The action begins when the referee, with the gravity set at .1, flips the ball high in the air, and the players go up after it.

The Conneltown team wore gold uniforms, which were embroidered with the team name in blazing script and a shoulder patch depicting a fire-spouting dragon.

The crowd roared when, during the opening minute, Brian Lewis took advantage of .2 gravity to leap high over a defender and, as they say in the sport, nail the target as it was passing.

A sizable contingent from Tylerville was apparently present. So both teams had substantial crowd support. It was a close game, and, to the dismay of the locals, the Hawks scored the deciding goal as time ran out.

Everybody looked exhausted when it ended. We waited in the parking area and spotted Bannister as he came out of the crowd. "Doug," said Alex, "do you have a minute?"

He stood trying to figure out if he knew Alex. Then he looked at me and smiled. "Sure," he said. "What can I do for you?" He had a thin voice, and you had to listen closely to hear what he was saying.

Alex did the introductions. Then: "Doug, you and Mr. Lewis picked up a rock tablet two days ago in Rindenwood."

"Yes. That's right. Is there a problem?" He seemed a bit nervous. But maybe he was always nervous in the presence of strangers. Or maybe of strange women. He had cinnamon-colored hair, which was already growing thin, and his eyes never quite got clear of the ground.

"No. No problem. We're interested in buying the tablet. Do you still have it?"

"No."

"Can you tell me who does?"

A woman who had the right dimensions and hair to be the one who'd helped make the pickup appeared from somewhere. I hadn't seen her in the stands. "This is my wife, Ara," Doug said.

"I couldn't help overhearing," Ara said. She was still in her flighty years. But she looked good. Inquisitive dark eyes, black hair cut short, and the body of a dancer. I realized right away she was in charge of the marriage. She simply took over from Doug. "Mr. Benedict," she said, "we were bringing it back for our aunt. But while we were en route, she decided she didn't want it."

"How do you mean?"

"Well, when we showed it to her, from the skimmer, she said that wasn't the same one that she'd seen in the ad."

"It wasn't the same one?"

"She meant it was more worn than she'd expected."

"Oh."

She shrugged. "So she said she didn't want it."

"What did you do with it?"

"We dropped it in the river."

"In the *river*?" Alex couldn't conceal his horror.

"Yes. She thought it was an artifact, but after she saw it, she said it was worthless."

"Oh."

"And she'd know. She collects stuff like that."

We had caught Brian Lewis's attention. He came over, and we did the introductions again. "Sorry," he said in a deep, rumbling voice when he heard what we were after. "Yeah. That's what happened to it. It's in the river."

"Can you tell us *where* in the river?" asked Alex.

"Near the Trafalgar Bridge," said Ara.

"Right." Doug made a face, trying to recall details. "We were about a kilometer from the bridge when we ditched it."

"Which side?"

"The east side," said Ara. "I thought it was more than a kilometer, though. More like three or four."

Brian thought about it. "Yeah," he said. "That might be right."

Alex gave them business cards. "Call me if you remember anything else, okay?"

They assured him they would. Brian walked away while Ara and Doug climbed into a white-and-gold Sentinel. It was the same one they'd used to collect the tablet.

Alex called Audree Hitchcock, a longtime friend who did oceanic surveys for the Geologic Service. "We're looking for a rock," he said.

"Beg pardon, Alex?" At the beginning of her career, Audree had worked for Gabe, Alex's uncle. She and Alex saw each other socially on occasion, but it seemed to be more friendship than romance. Audree was a bright, energetic blonde with intense blue eyes and a passion for the theater. She belonged to the Seaside Players, a local amateur group.

"It's a tablet, Audree." He showed her.

"What's it worth?"

"We're not sure yet. Probably nothing."

"But maybe a lot?"

"Maybe."

"And somebody dropped it into the river?"

"That's right."

"Why?"

"Call it bad judgment. Can we rent you for a day?"

"Where, precisely, did they drop it?"

"East of the Trafalgar Bridge. They say it's somewhere between one and four klicks."

"Okay. We'll take a look. It'll be a couple of days before we can get to it, though."

"Good. And, Audree?"

"Yes, Alex."

"Don't put a lot of effort into it. If it doesn't show up on the first effort, let it go."

"*Why?*"

"I'm not sure I believe the story."

"*Okay. I'll do what I can. By the way, Alex—*"

"Yes, Audree?"

"*We're doing* Moving Target *this weekend.*"

"You're in it?"

"*I'm the target.*"

"I'm not surprised. Can you set a night aside for me?"

FOUr

A father can make no more serious error than striving to make his son like himself.

—Timothy Zhin-Po, *Night Thoughts*

Five minutes after we got back to the country house, Jacob announced he had news: *"Alex, I've located Basil."* Tuttle's son.

"Can you put me through to him, Jacob?"

"Negative. He does not have a link."

"No code? Nothing at all?"

"Nothing."

"Where does he live?"

"Portsboro. Near Lake Vanderbolt."

"All right. We'll be home shortly. Thanks, Jacob."

"No residential address is listed for him, either."

"You're kidding."

"Ground mail goes to the distribution center. I guess he picks it up there."

Alex made a clicking sound with his tongue. "Fortunately, Portsboro's not far. You want to come?"

I looked out at the windblown hills below. "Sure," I said. "This time of year, I love the north country. All that snow—"

Basil had gone in a different direction from his father. He'd started medical school but never completed his studies. The few who'd written about

Sunset Tuttle had little to say about Basil. He'd been married briefly. No known children. Had worked at several jobs before simply walking away to embrace a life of leisure, financed in part by state security, and probably more so by his father.

After Sunset died, Basil had dropped out of sight. At the time, he would have been in his late twenties.

We let Audree know where we could be reached and took the Moonlight Line north in the morning. Alex has always had a child's fascination for trains. He can sit for hours, staring out the window at the passing scenery. Headed north, though, the train passes through farming country. Experts had for centuries been predicting the end of farms, as they had of trains. But both lived on. It appears now there will always be a market for foods produced the old-fashioned way, just as there will be for the sheer practicality and economy of the train. And I'll confess that there's something reassuring in the knowledge they'll probably always be with us.

In time, the farms gave way to open forest. We climbed mountains, crossed rivers, navigated gorges, and rolled through tunnels. At Carpathia, we had to change trains. We wandered through the gift shop for an hour while snow began to fall. Alex picked up a tee shirt for Audree. It had a picture of the train on it with the logo ALL THE WAY. "I'm not sure I can see her wearing it," I said.

He smiled. "It's all a matter of timing."

Then we were on our way again, riding the Silver Star, winding through mountains that rose ever higher. By early evening we arrived in Packwood. There we rented a skimmer and crossed a hundred kilometers over snow-packed forest to Portsboro, population eleven hundred.

We landed in a parking area on the edge of town, got into our jackets, and climbed out. The cold air felt solid. Like a wall. I turned up the heat in my jacket, and we trudged through the snow, crossed a street, turned a corner, and went into Will's Café. It was midafternoon, and the place was empty except for three women at one table and a chess game at another. We ordered sandwiches and hot chocolate and asked the waiter, then one of the customers, and finally the owner where Basil Tuttle lived. Nobody seemed to know. They knew he lived in the town, but nobody had any idea where he could be found. "Comes in once in a while," the owner said. "But that's all I've got."

One of the women waved in the general direction of the western horizon and said he "lives out there somewhere." We left Will's, went down to the next corner, and tried Mary's Bar & Grill.

This time we found someone. Her name was Betty Ann Jones. "I know him," she said, while the other three people at her table shook their heads disapprovingly. She laughed and raised a hand to reassure them. "Basil likes to be left alone. Are you bill collectors or police or something? Why do you want to see him?"

"We're working on a history project," Alex said. "We're writing a book about his father. You know who his father was?"

"Sunset Tuttle?" She couldn't resist a smirk.

"Right. Anyhow, we'd like to interview Basil. Is there a way we could get in touch with him?"

"What's your name?" she asked. She was probably well into her second century, but she'd kept herself in good shape. Dark skin, shoulder-length brown hair, intelligent eyes. The kind of woman you might expect to find running the gambling table.

"My name's Alex Benedict."

"Okay." She nodded, as if she had a running familiarity with the world's historians.

"Do you know where he lives?" Alex asked.

"Of course. Everybody does."

"Could you direct us?"

"It's complicated. Do you have transportation?"

"Yes."

"Okay, you'll have to head northwest. Over the Nyka Ridge. Keep going straight until you get to the Ogamee—"

"The what?"

"The *river*." She stopped and shook her head. Looked out through the windows. It was getting dark. "Do you know him at all?"

"Not really."

"All right. How can I say this? He's not the world's most sociable guy. But he's okay. You said you have transportation, right?"

"Yes. If you could help us, we'd be grateful."

She got more interested. Alex showed her some money.

"We'd bring you right back," I said. "As soon as we're finished. It shouldn't take long."

She thought about it. Looked at the money. "Okay." She got to her feet. "I keep this even if he won't let us in, right?"

"Okay."

"Good enough. Let me get my coat."

It was one of those hard, cold days, not a cloud in the sky, the sun bright, the temperature down well below zero. We lifted off, and Betty Ann steered me toward the highest mountain in the area. Below, not much was moving. Not even the river, which was frozen. "That's the *Ogamee*," she said. "It's Kasikan for *death*."

I couldn't help laughing. "That's fairly melodramatic." The Kasikans had lived in the area for more than a thousand years and still formed a substantial fraction of the local population. They'd had the north country to themselves for a long time and developed their own language and culture. Where they'd actually originated remains a matter of debate. "Why is it the river of death?" I asked.

"There's a legend," said Betty Ann.

Isn't there always?

"You want to tell us about it?" said Alex. He enjoyed myths and tall tales. They were, after all, an indispensable part of the business.

"The story," she said, "is that Layo Visini, who's a legendary Kasikan hero, took his son rafting on it. They were drifting downstream, not paying much attention, when they got startled by a kalu." A kalu is a big lizard with four legs and a substantial appetite. "Anyhow, he backed against the boy and knocked him overboard. The river swept him away. People reported that for years afterward, Visini came down to the river's edge to mourn the boy. Eventually, he could take the sense of guilt no more, so he threw himself in, and he, too, was drowned."

Alex and I looked at each other. I decided to change the subject. "Shouldn't we call rather than just drop in?" I asked.

"He doesn't have a link."

"Oh." I'd assumed he was simply unlisted.

She pointed off to our right, where a snow-covered rooftop stuck out among the trees. "And that would be Basil's place."

We descended into a clearing, got out, and followed Betty Ann onto a walkway that had been shoveled clear. A bitter wind was blowing in from the north. Ahead, a door opened partway, and a hawk-faced man looked out. "Who's there?"

"It's me, Basil," said Betty Ann. "I've got a couple of people with me who'd like to meet you."

Basil was thin. His hair hung down into distrustful eyes, and an unkempt black beard covered most of his shirt. "Who are they, Bet?" he growled.

"Mr. Tuttle," said Alex, "I'm Alex Benedict. This young lady is Chase Kolpath. We're historians, and we'd like to talk with you for a few minutes if we may."

"About what?" He sounded like a guy who had far more important things to do than entertain nitwits.

"We're doing a history of the Directorate of Planetary Survey and Astronomical Research. Your father was an important part of that effort."

He smiled. There was a flicker of contempt in his eyes. "Why?"

"Because it was a significant era. We made major advances during the last century."

"I mean, why was my father important?"

Alex had hoped there'd be no trouble from the son. He kept his voice level. "He was a contributor."

"He never found anything." He looked past Alex at Betty Ann. "Nice to see you again, Bet."

"And you, Basil." She came forward, walked directly up to Basil, and planted a modest kiss on his cheek. "I hope you don't mind my bringing them up here."

"No," he said. "It's okay." He backed into the house, leaving room for us to follow. "I guess you should all come in."

It was a masculine interior. The heads of a couple of stalkers were mounted on opposite sides of the room. The furniture was handmade, with blankets thrown over everything. Another blanket hung on one wall, to what purpose I had no idea. Thick curtains framed the windows. A painting of a river beneath an arc of moon hung off to one side of the front door. We could smell food cooking in the kitchen. Several logs crackled in the fireplace.

"Nice decor," said Alex, without a hint of irony.

"I like it," said Basil, in a tone that suggested he hadn't been fooled.

"I would, too." Alex paused before the picture of the river. It looked like something that had been picked up at a garden sale.

"It's by Pritchard," Basil said. "Cost an arm and a leg."

"It's beautiful." It shouldn't have cost much because it was a reproduction, but Alex, of course, let it go. "How long have you been here, Basil?"

Basil had to think about it. "Twelve years," he said finally. "Somewhere in there." He pointed at the chairs. "Sit."

We sat.

"What did you want to know?"

"Your father spent his life doing exploration. Looking for evidence of other civilizations."

"You mean aliens?"

"Yes."

"I guess he did. He never talked about it much."

"He never found anything, is that right?"

"Yes, that's right."

"Is it possible he might have come across something, maybe just ruins, an artifact, *something*, but never mentioned it to anyone?"

Basil laughed. Actually, it was more of a snort. "Believe me," he said, "if my old man had found something out there, everyone would have known about it. He would have been on every network in the world. It was all he lived for."

"There's no question about that in your mind?"

"Alex." He spoke slowly, framing his words as one might for a half-wit. "You want me to say it again? It was just like my father to spend his life chasing something that didn't exist. He was a dreamer. And when nothing showed up, he kept trying. Until, eventually, he decided his life was a failure."

"Was he right?"

"I'd say so."

"I'm sorry to hear you feel that way—"

Basil shrugged. "It doesn't much matter now, does it? He came across a couple of lost settlements. By us, of course. Humans. One of them was two or three thousand years old. I mean, it really went back. In both cases the people were gone. But there was no real mystery about it. He knew from the design of the places that they hadn't been aliens. And that was it. They could have been played as major successes, I guess. But he wasn't interested."

"How did he get interested in the search, Basil? Do you know?"

Basil shrugged. "Who the hell knows what drives anybody? I think he was lonely. I think he was fed up with us, with his family, and went looking for somebody else."

"Most people would look for another woman."

"Yeah, they would." Basil got up and walked to the window. I couldn't see anything out there except trees and snow in the gray light.

"Did you ever go with him?"

"On one of the missions?" He had to think about it. "When I was a boy I went once. We were away for a couple of months. My mother wasn't very happy about it. It might even have been one of the reasons they called it off. The marriage, I mean." He started for the kitchen. "Betty Ann, would you like something to drink?"

"Something hot would be nice." She put her hands on the arms of her chair, as if about to get up. "You want me to get it, Basil?"

"Sure," he said. "If you don't mind. How about your friends?"

"What do you have?" asked Alex.

"Not much," Betty Ann said, without having to look. "Beer. Corfu. Or I can make you a mickey munson." She glanced back at Basil. "You have some left?"

"Yeah."

"The munson sounds good," said Alex.

"What are *you* having?" I asked her.

"Coffee."

"I'll do that, too."

"I'd like a beer, Bet," Basil said.

She disappeared into the kitchen, and for a minute or so afterward, we listened to cabinet doors opening and glasses and cups clinking. "He was still relatively young when he died," I said.

"A hundred and thirty-nine. Yeah. It was a pity."

"Did he often go out alone?"

"Pretty regularly, from what I hear. He'd retired a couple of years earlier. And he was in a dismal mood after that. I don't think he cared much for company after his retirement. In fact, he never cared for it that much anyhow. He wasn't what you'd call a social guy."

"Do you know why? Why the bleak mood?"

"I think because he'd given up."

"I wonder if he knew there was a storm coming."

"That wouldn't have bothered my father. He thought he was immortal. He ate the wrong stuff. Never went to see a doctor. If he knew about the storm, he might have thought it would add some excitement. I know I shouldn't say this about my own dad, but I don't think he was the smartest guy on the planet."

"You ever mention any of this to him?"

"A couple of times. He'd tell me I was worrying too much."

"I'm sorry," I said.

"I know. Everybody's sorry. He could have sidestepped it easily enough. Just show a little sense. But it's the way I remember him. He was always just going out the door. One way or another."

"It must have been hard on you."

"I never understood what my mom saw in him." He was quiet for a minute, apparently deciding whether to go any further. "When he was home, it didn't make much difference."

"How do you mean?"

"He was still away. He didn't have time for me. For us." There was something in his voice that suggested a deeper sorrow than he was willing to admit.

"You were the only child?" I asked.

"Yes."

"Did he want you to follow in his footsteps?"

"Chase, I don't think he could have cared less." His brow wrinkled. "Well, maybe that's not really quite accurate. Once or twice, when I was a kid, I told him *I'd* go find the aliens if he didn't. I don't think I ever meant it, but it seemed like the right thing to say."

"And his reaction?"

"He advised me to stay away from it. Told me it would break my heart."

Betty Ann stuck her head out of the kitchen: "Basil, didn't you tell me once that he approved of your lifestyle?"

Basil looked at her and laughed. "That's true, actually. A few weeks before he died, he told me not to work too hard. I was thinking about a career in medicine." He laughed again, louder this time. "He told me the secret of life."

Alex leaned forward. "Which is?"

"Enjoy thyself. Live for the moment."

"That's a surprise."

" 'Just buy a place somewhere, settle in, and live off the allotment. Enjoy the time you have. Because in the end, nothing else matters.' That's not verbatim, of course. But it's what he said."

Betty Ann brought in the drinks. The coffee tasted good. Cold air was leaking into the cabin. Basil saw me wrap my arms around myself. He got up, threw another log into the fire, poked the flames, and drew the curtains. "That always helps," he said.

Alex obviously liked the munson. He tasted it, scribbled some notes. Revisited his drink. Closed the notebook and used it to project a holo of the tablet. "Did you ever see *this*?"

Basil grinned. "Yeah. Sure. He had that in his office."

"Did he ever tell you what it was?"

"He said it was from an old settlement somewhere in the Veiled Lady. I don't remember where."

"But it was a *human* settlement?"

"Sure. Of course."

"Did he *say* that? *Human?*"

Basil pulled at his beard. "It's been a long time," he said. "It's hard to remember exactly what he told me. But he sure as hell would have been jumping up and down if there'd been aliens. And I wouldn't have forgotten."

"Okay. Thanks."

"Alex?" He hesitated. "Do you, uh, know something I don't?"

"Not really. We're just trying to pin everything down."

"Well, I can tell you there *was* something unusual about it. About the tablet."

"What's that?"

"I don't really know. But he had a special cabinet built for it. It wasn't on display, like his other stuff. He had it locked away most of the time." He rubbed the back of his neck. "Tell you the truth, I'd forgotten about it. Is it valuable?"

"That's one of the things we're trying to find out. It was found in the garden by the current occupant of the Rindenwood house."

"You mean *our* house."

"Yes."

"In the garden?"

"Yes."

Basil shook his head. "I just don't know."

"The last time you saw it, it was in the cabinet."

"Yes."

"How long did he have it? Do you know?"

"Not long, I don't think. I don't remember seeing it before I was in college. He got it just shortly before he died. Two or three years, I guess."

"Basil, do you have any idea how it might have wound up in the garden?"

"My fault, probably."

"How's that?"

"I didn't see much of my father after I left home. I got back now and then. But neither of us was really comfortable. When he died, I inherited the property. And I sold it. I recall inviting the buyers—I think their name was Harmon, something like that—I invited them to keep any of the furniture they liked. I didn't really have a place for it. And I guess the cabinet was one of the pieces they kept."

"You weren't interested in the tablet?"

"I don't think it ever even occurred to me. I just wanted to get the sale over with."

Alex finished his drink and put the glass on the table. "That was excellent."

"Do you want some more?"

"No, thanks." He closed his eyes for a moment. "Basil, we can't find any record of his missions. Of where he went, what he did. He says somewhere that he'd marked a lot of places as empty if anyone was following up on his work. But there's no indication of any such record. Did he keep a journal? Anything that might help us trace his activities?"

"Sure. My father kept the logs from his flights. A record of everything, as far as I know. Where he went. What he saw. Pictures. Charts. Impressions. All kinds of stuff."

"Marvelous," Alex said. "Would you let us see it?"

"I don't have it."

"Who does?"

"A friend of his. Hugh Conover."

"How did Conover get it?"

"I gave it to him."

"Why?"

"He asked the same question you just did. And I couldn't see that they had any value. At least not to me."

"When would that have been, Basil?"

"It was right after he died."

"Okay. I don't guess you happen to know where I can reach this Conover?"

"No. I haven't seen him for twenty years."

"Okay. He shouldn't be hard to find."

"He might not be easy. I heard that he's living off-world."

"I'll check on it. Thanks."

Basil was making faces while he tried to remember. "I think I heard that he was out by himself somewhere."

"By himself?"

"Completely. His own world." He laughed. "Literally. He always was one of these antisocial guys. Fit right in with my dad."

Says the guy sitting on top of a mountain with no link.

Five

God must love archeologists, to have given us such an extended history, and several hundred worlds, filled with abandoned temples and lost cities and military trophies and histories of places we've forgotten existed. If the physical sciences began long ago to run out of targets for blue-sky research, the archeologist finds his field of interest expanding with every generation.

—Tor Malikovski, keynote address for the Wide World Archeological Association, on the occasion of its move from Barrister Hall to the Korchnoi University Plaza, 1402

Hugh Conover had been an anthropologist whose career had followed an arc with similarities to Tuttle's. He, too, was looking for signs of intelligent life elsewhere. But his primary interest was in places where people, human beings, had landed and lived, outposts in remote areas, cities buried in jungles or beneath desert sands, bases established and subsequently abandoned during the dawn of the interstellar age. If he'd come across something utterly new, that would have been fine. Magnificent, in fact. But he knew the odds. And he was too smart to let anyone think he took the possibility seriously.

Like Tuttle, he'd been a pilot. And also like Tuttle, he'd usually traveled alone.

Moreover, Conover had enjoyed moderate success.

His most famous achievement had been the discovery of a previously unknown space station, dating from the twenty-seventh century, on the edge of the Veiled Lady. That had happened in 1402. For seventeen years after that, he had labored in the field and, while making a reasonable contribution to the state of historical knowledge, he'd produced nothing else of a spectacular nature. Finally, in 1419, he'd retired. Three years later, he announced that he was going away. And he did. If anyone knew where he was, it wasn't on the record.

We continued looking for data on Tuttle.

We asked Jacob to determine whether anyone had ever taken charge of his papers. He needed a few seconds to respond. *"I do not have a listing, Alex."*

"Okay," said Alex. "I'd have been surprised if we'd found anything."

"Apparently he was never considered a sufficiently substantive figure that anyone asked for them."

Nobody ever wrote a biography about him. Nobody ever granted him a major award. Interviews always depicted him as a one-dimensional lunatic, a figure of fun who fell into a class of "experts" defined by ghost hunters, Nostradamus enthusiasts, and people who could make out the face of God in the Andrean Cloud. His media coverage seldom revealed the man himself. There were death and wedding notices, and one item describing how he'd pulled a drowning kid out of the Melony during a summer festival. The bottom line was that, aside from that single interstellar passion, there wasn't much information to be had about him.

Some of his old colleagues were still active. We visited as many as we could get to, Wilson Bryce at Union Research, Jay Paxton at the University of York, Sara Inagra at the Quelling Institute, and Lisa Cassavetes, who'd long since gone into politics and been elected to the Legislature.

Several had been to the Rindenwood house on various occasions, but those visits, of course, had been long ago, and nobody remembered the cabinet, let alone what had been in it. "In fact," said Cassavetes, who was probably 160 but who primped and grinned while implying her interest in Tuttle had been limited to the bedroom, "I don't recall ever having been in his office."

Nobody could assign a probable source for the tablet. "Yes," said Bryce, who was tall and gangly, with arms and legs too long for his body, and a tendency to frame each phrase as though we should be taking notes, "they do vaguely resemble Late Korbanic. No question. But look at these characters here—"

Audree called the same day we talked to Bryce. When she appeared in the middle of the conference room, we knew immediately that she wasn't bringing good news. *"Guys,"* she said, *"I'd say you were right not to believe your sources. There's no sign of the tablet anywhere in the Trafalgar area."*

"Could you have missed it?"

"Sure. It's possible. There was a pretty bad storm just before we started the search. It might have stirred up the mud a bit. And in any case, there are a lot of rocks down there. Still, if I were betting—"

"You'd say it's not there."

"That's what I'd say. You want me to go back and look some more? I can do it, but we'll have to charge."

"No. Let it go."

"Sorry. Call me if you change your mind."

When she'd blinked off, Alex grumbled something about idiots dropping things in rivers, and asked Jacob to show him the family trees of Ara and Doug Bannister.

"What has that to do with anything?" I asked.

"You remember who originally wanted the tablet?"

"Doug's aunt."

"Maybe. Ara said 'our aunt.' Let's see who that might include."

There were two aunts on Doug's side, three on Ara's. Jacob ran a search on all five women. One was married to an archeologist. But the guy's specialty was early Rimway settlers. No likely connection there. Three more gave us nothing of significance. But the fifth was a different story.

Her name was Rachel Bannister. She was a retired interstellar pilot. And she'd had an association at one time with Sunset Tuttle.

"What kind of association?" Alex asked.

"I'm still searching."

Alex looked satisfied. "I'm beginning to think they lied to us."

"They didn't throw the tablet into the river?"

"Exactly. What else do we have, Jacob?"

"Her hobbies are listed as gardening and rimrod." Rimrod was a card game quite popular at the turn of the century. *"She's something of an amateur musician. And she's also affiliated with the Trent Foundation."*

"As a volunteer?"

"Yes. According to this, she spends several hours a week tutoring girls who are having problems in school. As a matter of fact, she's worked with a number of charitable organizations in Andiquar."

"Been doing that a long time?"

"Thirty years or so."

"Sounds like a pretty good woman," I said.

"She worked for World's End Tours for four years, until 1403. Resigned in the spring of 1403. And here's the Tuttle connection."

"Don't tell me," Alex said. "She used to be his girlfriend."

"You hit it on the head, Alex."

"That might explain," I said, "why she wanted the tablet."

"Sentimental attachment?"

"Yes."

He looked skeptical. "Chase, the guy's been dead over a quarter century."

"Doesn't matter, Alex. People fall in love, they tend to stay that way."

"Twenty-five years after he's gone to a better world?"

I couldn't help laughing. "You're a hopeless romantic, you know that?"

"I don't buy it," he said.

It was clear enough to me. "But," I added, "it doesn't explain why she'd get rid of it."

"No." Alex shook his head. "She didn't get rid of it. She still has it." He looked up at the time. "Jacob?"

"Yes, Alex?"

"See if you can connect with Doug Bannister."

It took a few minutes. But eventually Bannister's thin voice came through. *"Hello?"* We didn't have a visual.

"Doug, this is Alex Benedict."

"Who?"

"Alex Benedict. I spoke with you a few days ago about the tablet. After the game."

"The tablet?"

"The rock you picked up in Rindenwood."

"Oh, yeah. Sorry. Did you find it?"

"No. We've scanned the Melony in the Trafalgar area. It's not there."

"Really? That's strange. Well, you must have missed it. Where exactly did you look?"

"Doug, let's assume the tablet really went somewhere else."

"What do you mean?"

"On the off chance that the tablet's not in the river, but that you're reluctant to reveal that, I'd like to make an offer. Find it for me, just so that I can get a look at it, not keep it, just look, and I'll make it well worth your while."

"I'm sorry, Alex. It's in the river. Like we said."

"And I'll keep your name out of it. Nobody will ever know."

"Alex, if I could help, I would."

"Okay. The offer won't stay open forever."

"I wouldn't lie to you, man."

"We'll want to sit down with Rachel," Alex said. "But first I'd like to find out more about Tuttle."

He'd had a younger brother. His name was Henry, and it had taken us a while to get to him because he was a government employee temporarily assigned in the Korbel Islands.

"It's all right, Henry," Alex said. We'd gotten through to him at his hotel. "Anything you tell us will go no further."

Henry could hardly have been more different from the Sunset Tuttle we'd seen in the holo. He was big, with wide shoulders and tranquil brown eyes. A man completely at peace with himself. It took a while. He talked about his brother's career as if it had been inordinately successful, and how it was inevitable they'd drift apart. Henry had married early and moved away, and they hadn't stayed in touch. *"It wouldn't have mattered if I'd stayed across the road,"* he said. *"Som was never here.*" "Som" was the name he used throughout the conversation. "*He was always off somewhere. He couldn't help it, you know. I mean, it was what he did.*"

Eventually, he got to the point: "*What can I say? I guess I never really felt welcome in his presence. So I just didn't like spending time with him. The only thing he ever talked about was himself. He'd go on about where he'd been since the last time I'd seen him, and where he was going next time. He never once asked me about what I do. Or what I cared about. Even after he retired, he couldn't talk about anything else—And toward the end, he got discouraged. Couldn't find the gremlins.*"

"I guess that can wear on you after a while."

"*Yeah, by the time he quit he was burned out.*"

"Did he tell you that?"

"*No. Look, Mr. Benedict, you have to understand: I never saw much of my brother. Not after I left home.*"

"And after he retired, nothing changed?"

"*He didn't live long after that. Two or three years, I guess. But yes, it was still all about him. Listen, I write economic analyses for the Treasury Department. I've been a journalist, and I've written a couple of books about economics. I mean, I've had a pretty decent career. Not like what he did. But I've won some awards. We never talked about it, though. Never talked about what I was doing. Not ever.*"

We showed him pictures of the tablet. "Do these ring a bell?"

"*No,*" he said. "*I never saw the damned thing. What is it anyhow?*"

"Henry," said Alex, "I assume you know Rachel Bannister."

"*Yes. I met her once or twice. She was a friend of my brother's.*" He smiled. "*Beautiful woman.*"

"Did you know she worked for World's End?"

"*Yes.*"

"Can you tell me anything more about her? She's a licensed pilot, but she doesn't seem to be doing any off-world work."

"*I haven't really seen her for a long time, Alex.*"

"You don't know anything about her?"

"*Other than that she used to run around with Som, no.*"

"She did tours at World's End."

"*Yes, that's correct.*"

"Are you aware of anything unusual happening to her while she was there? Anything on one of the flights?"

"*No. Not that I know of.*"

"Nothing at all?"

"*Well—*"

"Yes, Henry?"

"*It's nothing really. I remember hearing that she'd quit after one of the tours. Came home and quit. I don't know why. If I ever knew, I don't remember. I don't even remember who told me, though it was probably Som.*"

"Okay. One more question, then we'll get out of your way, Henry. Do you know Hugh Conover?"

"*I know of him.*"

"But you never met him?"

"*Not that I can recall. He was an archeologist or something.*"

"An anthropologist, I believe. I don't guess you have any idea how we might reach him?"

"*I don't know. Try the directory?*"

Robin Simmons called that night to ask if we could meet for lunch the next day. I liked Robin, and I said sure, thereby saving my life. And Alex's.

Robin had started as a lawyer but decided somewhere along the line he preferred kids and classrooms. High-school level, where, he said, minds were still open. ("At least some of them.") So he now taught courses in politics and history at Mount Kira. When people asked why he'd given up his legal career to teach, he claimed it was because the money's better.

He had brown hair and brown eyes. He approached life casually and was a guy who would have been indistinguishable in a crowd, I guess, until you got to know him. But he was bright, and he had a sense of humor. I was beginning to think that I'd miss him if he went away.

I spent the morning doing routine stuff. Alex was working upstairs. At about eleven, Jacob announced that Expressway had arrived with a package.

Jack Napier was the local delivery guy. He came in with a box, something about the right size for a very long pair of shoes. He set it down on a side table, I signed for it, and he left.

The package carried a return address for Baylor Purchasing, which told me nothing. It had been sent to Rainbow, attention Alex Benedict. I left it where it was and went back to work.

A little while later, a car pulled into the driveway. Robin in his svelte black-and-white Falcon. Time to go. I looked at the package. Part of my job was to go through the mail and get rid of anything that didn't really demand his attention. So I opened it.

It contained a pagoda. A label described it as a "genuine replica of the Ashantay Pagoda." I wasn't sure what a genuine replica was, but the thing was made of smooth black metal. It was gorgeous. The base had tiny windows and a doorway. Six balconies rose above it, with pent roofs, capped by a finial. There was an accompanying pamphlet: *Congratulations,* it said. *You now own the Baylor prize-winning all-purpose air purifier. Operate as directed and be assured the air you breathe will be the freshest, purest that—*

I took it out of the box and set it on my desk. But the moment it touched the wood, it activated. Lights came on in the windows, and I felt energy begin to pulse through it.

In fact, the interior, from the base to the top of the finial, lit up. The lights began to dim and brighten. The process accelerated into a chaotic display.

My head began to spin. And I was sucking in air. Then *not* sucking in air. My heart began to pound, and the office walls faded.

"Chase," said Jacob. *"Robin has arrived."*

I remember thinking about an exercise during training in which a virtual hole was punched into a ship by a meteor. Air rushes out. Tries to suck you along with it. What do you do?

What you do is faint.

"Chase," said Jacob. *"What's wrong? Are you okay?"*

The floor rose and dipped, and I couldn't get air. I tried to scream, but I don't think I did anything except gag. Jacob was calling Alex, calling help, help, she's down, something's wrong.

A door opened and closed upstairs, and I heard Alex on the stairs. The office was getting dim, the walls closing in, darkness closing in. And I was suddenly far away and at peace.

Then I was outside lying on the ground on a pile of dead leaves with a jacket thrown over me. I looked up to see Robin struggling to get Alex out the front door. I wanted to help, but when I tried to get up, my head went around again, and I fell back.

I think it put me out again.

I'm not sure how much time passed. The rescue squad was there, and they were administering oxygen. When I tried to push them away, they tightened their grip. Somebody, Robin, I think, told me to be quiet. Alex was standing off to one side talking to Robin. He seemed to be okay.

I was inside an ambulance. A medical tech was doing an exam. She told me I'd be fine, and I should just lie still. "Just relax, Chase," she said.

She said we were headed for the hospital. "Just for a check. We want to make sure everything's normal."

Alex, leaning on another tech, climbed into the vehicle. "Good to see you breathing again, Chase," he said.

Then Robin leaned in. "Hi, love. You okay?"

I raised a hand to signal yes.

"Good. I'll see you at the hospital."

The tech asked me how I felt and removed the mask so I could answer.

Alex leaned over me. "You threw a scare into us for a minute there, kid."

"What happened?" The ambulance was lifting off.

"Somebody tried to kill us."

six

Did you see any lights?

—The question routinely put to Sunset Tuttle by his colleagues
and, eventually, picked up by comedians

Fenn Redfield was waiting with a police unit when we got back to the country house. "Somebody shipped you a pagoda," he said.

By then my memory had returned, and I recalled how impressed I'd been by it. "It's loaded," he continued, "with powdered magnesium. The pagoda has a solid-state refrigeration unit. When you handle the thing, the refrigeration unit activates. It cools the magnesium. And sucks the oxygen out of the house. Or at least off the ground floor. It's a good thing Robin showed up when he did." The unit was still on my desk, in front of us. "Any idea who wants you dead *this* time?"

We looked at each other, and I immediately thought of Brian Lewis and Doug Bannister. But no, that didn't make sense.

"Did you check with the shipping company?" Alex said.

"Sure. Nobody has any recollection about who had mailed the package. Of course, Baylor Purchasing doesn't even exist." He looked at us disapprovingly. "You sure you have no idea who's behind this?"

"Don't know," said Alex.

He looked at me. "Me neither, Fenn."

"Okay," he said. "We'll ask around. If I can come up with something, I'll let you know. Meantime—"

"We'll be careful."

When we were alone, Alex told me he thought it would be a good idea if I took some time off. Stayed away from the country house until Fenn figured out who did it.

"I can't do that," I said. "I'm not going to leave you alone to deal with this." And, after a pause, "You think it's connected with the tablet?"

"Probably," he said. "Chase, that was a scary experience. I thought for a minute we'd lost you." His voice sounded odd.

"I'm okay," I said. "Just have to be more careful for a while."

"I could fire you."

"You'd only have to hire somebody else. I wasn't the target."

Robin was very gracious about it all. I thanked him, and he told me he was just grateful he'd gotten there when he had. "I'm worried about you," he said. "Maybe you should stay at my place until this thing gets settled."

Well, I was taken by his generosity, and I told him so. "But I'll be more careful from now on when I open packages."

"This is serious stuff, Chase. I wouldn't want to lose you." That was said in a more serious tone than his offer for me to bunk with him.

"Thanks, Robin," I said. "I'll be careful."

Audree was a member of the Seaside Players, an amateur theater group. When Alex invited me to join him for *Moving Target*, the production in which she was performing, I said sure and took Robin along. "Strictly for security purposes," I told him.

"Listen, Chase," he said. "This is not funny."

"You don't want to go?"

"I'll go. Sure. But somebody wants you dead."

"Actually," I said, "the package was addressed to Alex."

I like amateur theater. Always have. Audree has tried to talk me into joining Seaside, but the prospect of standing on a stage in front of an audience while I try to remember my lines scares me more than anything I can think of. So I always pretend I'm too busy. "Maybe next year."

It turned out to be opening night for the show. Audree played the harried beauty of the title. She is pursued by police, who think she killed her husband; by the actual killer, who wrongly believes she knows who he is; and by a crazed former boyfriend who has never been willing to let go.

At one point she calls her lawyer. Robin commented that it was exactly what people do: Put the lawyer in the maniac's crosshairs. And, of course, when the lawyer got picked off, at the end of the second act, he reacted with a resigned sigh.

Eventually, the ex-boyfriend makes off with her eleven-year-old daughter, whose safety he is willing to exchange for the heroine's virtue. And, as the audience was aware, her life. Ultimately, of course, everything ends well.

Audree was a bit over-the-top, maybe a trifle screechy when she was being chased around by the nutcase, but otherwise she delivered a good performance. Afterward, we attended a cast party. Robin told me he was tempted to join the Seaside group.

"I didn't know you were interested in acting," I said.

He glanced around the room. It was filled with attractive women.

We found others who had known Sunset Tuttle. One, a financial advisor who'd visited him hoping to pick up a client, told us yes, he'd seen the tablet. *"Kept it in the cabinet, just like you said. I was in there one time. The cabinet door had been left open. When he noticed, he got up and closed it. It was no big deal. But I remember thinking how odd it was to keep a gravestone—that's what it looked like—in his office. I mentioned it, but he just shrugged it off. Said something to the effect it was an artifact. That he had to keep the cabinet door shut to maintain an even temperature."*

"That's nonsense," Alex said.

"I thought that, too, but I wasn't going to argue with the guy. I didn't care if he kept rocks in his cabinet."

The OAAA, the Orion Arm Archeological Association, maintains a museum and conference center with attached living quarters for visiting historians and archeologists in the Plaza, adjacent to Korchnoi University in Andiquar. The Plaza also serves as a social center for members of the organization and their guests. Alex had a blown-up picture of the tablet propped against the wall. "There *has* to be somebody down there who'd recognize this thing," he said.

Alex attended meetings periodically. It was a good way to keep in touch with what was happening in the field. Usually, I went along, not because I had a professional knowledge of whatever subject happened to be on the agenda but because my presence fit with the social environment. As long as the conversations appeared casual, there was less chance of alerting anyone to the possibility that something substantive was happening, thereby running the price up.

So I dressed for the occasion, a white blouse, beige slacks, and a gold necklace Alex had given me for precisely these kinds of events. The necklace featured an *ankh*, which made me automatically one of the crowd.

Alex had been granted an honorary membership after the Christopher Sim experience, so we had no trouble gaining entrance. There were seven or eight people present, seated in two groups in the Sakler Room, named of course for the woman who'd found the Inkata ruins on Moridania four hundred years ago. We collected a couple of drinks at the bar and joined one of the groups.

They were talking about tribal instincts and gestalt exercises, and I wasn't there five minutes before I began looking at the time. The conversation was on a casual first-name level, but then, suddenly, as the topic of tribal cultures took hold, someone recognized Alex as the man who'd found the *Corsarius*. And everyone's attention swung his way.

He tried to do his modesty routine. "I'm just here," he said, "to listen to you guys. Fascinating idea, that tribes would react to a shifting climate in the way that Liz suggests." With the exception of a wiry, bearded guy who'd been dominating the conversation, they declared themselves delighted that he was present. "And Chase, too, of course." One claimed to have had lunch with him two years ago at the Blackfriars' event in Peshkong. Another explained he'd been on Salud Afar, coincidentally, at the same time that we had, last year. "I have cousins there, believe it or not."

"So," the Blackfriar said, "what are you working on now?"

And Alex had his opening. "Nothing much," he said. "I've gotten interested in Sunset Tuttle."

"Why?" The bearded man broke out in laughter. "Why on earth would you do that?" His name was Braik. I never got a last name. Or maybe that *was* his last name. "What did Tuttle ever do?"

"We're putting together a history of Survey operations during the last century and a half. He's part of it."

Braik laughed again and waved it away. "Okay," he said. "But really, no kidding around now, why are you interested in *him*?"

"He represents a whole class of scientists, Braik. The people who went out to the stars and looked around. Who hoped to make contact." Alex normally didn't talk like that, but he kept a straight face, and everybody seemed to buy it. "He was passionate about exploration. Yet he broke away from it in 1403. Never went back. He lived only a few years after that, but it's the only period in his adult life that he never went out on a mission. I wonder why that is."

Braik did something with his mouth and jaws to suggest who cared? "He probably pulled the pin because he figured out his career wasn't going anywhere. Never would go anywhere."

Liz was actually Elizabeth McMurtrie, who'd made her reputation as a climatologist. She whispered something to the guy who'd been to Salud Afar. Alex invited her to say it for everyone.

"Maybe he was exhausted," she said. "I'd be willing to bet if he hadn't died prematurely, he'd have gone back. Probably, he'd be out there somewhere *now*."

"He was an idiot," said Braik, "who might have made a contribution. Instead, at the end, what did he have to show for his life?"

"I was just wondering," said Liz, "who he really was." She was the only person among the members in the room who might have been justly described as young.

"He's nobody, my dear," said the Blackfriar. "He's a man who spent his time chasing moonbeams. Am I right, Alex?"

Alex sipped his drink. "I think people should set whatever goals they want. As long as they don't create problems for anybody else, where's the harm? Tuttle didn't fail because he never found anybody. He looked, and that's all you can ask. The real failure would have been not to try."

Liz started to say something, but she got elbowed aside by Braik. "Tuttle," he said, "recognized his own failure. That's why he quit."

Liz got through: "What's *your* dream, Braik?"

Braik responded with a sound that was half snicker half snort. "Make a contribution," he said. "And leave a good reputation behind me."

The conversation wandered for a while, but eventually Alex brought it back to Tuttle. Braik, though, was the only person present who had known him personally, and he was too interested in disparaging him to be helpful. Every question we asked produced a derisive response. "Does anybody know," Alex said, inserting the question as a matter of no consequence, "whether Tuttle ever brought any artifacts back from his expeditions?"

"He had some," Braik said. "A holistic link supposed to be from Chaldoneau, a captain's hat from the *Intrepid*, stuff like that. But I'd bet everything was a duplicate picked up in a gift shop somewhere."

"Any stone tablets that anyone knows about?"

"No," said the Blackfriar, looking around to see whether anyone had ever heard of anything.

Eventually, we drifted away and joined another group. But they, too, had nothing to contribute. Only one of them, a short, bleak-eyed blonde, had ever even seen Tuttle. "It was at a conference," she said. "In Dreyfus, I think. Or maybe at Kaldemor." She made a face. "Actually, it might have been—"

I broke in: "Did you get a chance to talk with him?"

"No. He was on a panel, and I might have asked a question or two. But I'm not sure. I can't really say I had a chance to talk with him. The panel was on radio archeology."

"I've lost an old friend I was hoping might be here tonight," said Alex. "Hugh Conover. Anybody know him?"

Several of them nodded. "He's long gone," said the blonde. "Dropped out of sight years ago." She looked around. "Anybody hear from him recently?"

Nobody had.

*   *   *

We had several calls during the next few days from people who'd heard about our visit to the Plaza and claimed connections, usually tenuous, with Tuttle. I thought they were really just looking for an excuse to talk with Alex, who, by that point in his career, had become a major celebrity.

One of the callers identified himself to Alex as Everett Boardman. *"I've always admired Tuttle,"* he said. *"My father was a colleague of his. I'm sorry to say he was one of the ones who never took the man seriously."* Boardman was the sort of guy you immediately felt you could rely on if you were in trouble. Dark hair and beard, clear eyes, a good smile that suggested he didn't take himself too seriously.

"You're an archeologist?" asked Alex.

"Yes. And I shared a lot of Tuttle's interests. I really don't care all that much about ancient interstellars and buried ruins. Those are just historical details."

"You want to find little green men."

Boardman's eyes brightened. *"Mr. Benedict, I would kill to find someone else out there. It's all I care about."*

"Are you still looking?"

"Whenever I can make time away from work."

"Well, I wish you luck."

"Thanks." He was seated at a table, covered with papers, maps, books. A cup of coffee rested at his right hand. *"Some of the people at the Plaza got the impression that you thought Tuttle might have found something."*

"You were there?" said Alex. "I thought I recognized you. And yes, it's possible. But we don't know."

"You have any evidence?"

"Nothing I'm prepared to talk about."

Boardman nodded. *"I don't think it happened. Tuttle would never have sat on that kind of discovery."*

"How well did your father know him?"

"They socialized occasionally. Even shared a mission back in the seventies. My dad knew him up until the very end. You know about the boat accident?"

"Yes."

"My father had lunch with him that day before he went out. His last meal, I guess."

"And Tuttle never said anything—?"

"Not that I know of. Hell, if my father had heard him talk about finding something, he'd have had a heart attack."

That same afternoon, we got another call, this one from an ancient, somber man sitting in a large armchair in a room with a blazing fireplace. *"My name is Edwin Holverson,"* he said. *"May I speak with Mr. Benedict, please?"*

"He's with a client, Mr. Holverson. My name's Kolpath. May I help you?"

"Are you his secretary?"

"I'm a staff assistant, sir."

"I wanted to talk to him. Would you have him call me when he becomes available?"

"If you like, certainly. May I tell him what it's about?"

"Sunset Tuttle. I understand Mr. Benedict is interested in him."

"That's correct. We're doing some documentary work."

"You are? May I ask why you and he are interested in a man who's been dead a quarter century?"

"I told you. We're doing research."

"Research for what?"

"A history of Survey."

"I see. I hope you're not going to laugh at him."

"Of course not."

His eyes narrowed. *"Or offer your sympathy."*

"Why would we do that?"

"Come on, Ms.—? What did you say your name was?"

"Kolpath."

"Ms. Kolpath, please don't play dumb with me." He leaned forward and gripped the chair arms as if he were accelerating.

"I don't think I'm following the conversation."

"Okay. Why don't you tell me where you're headed? What were you planning to say about Sunset?"

"What did you expect us to say?"

"*I'll tell you what you should say: That he was persistent in his efforts to make contact. That he represented the spirit of the men and women who, since Ito, have moved out into the galaxy, and who've kept going in the face of thousands of years of almost unbroken discouragement.*"

"I think that's pretty close to our reading of the man," I said.

"*Good. I'm glad there are still some people around who understand.*" He looked at me, tilted his head, and somehow managed to signal that *he* was one of the heroes he'd just described.

"You knew Tuttle," I said.

"*Yes. Other than my wife, God rest her soul, he was the closest friend I had.*"

"Did you ever do joint missions with him?"

"*Oh, yes. A few times. But we knew we could cover more ground by separating.*" He began to describe some of the flights, the long weeks and months it took to reach their destinations with the technology in use during the early years of the century. The living worlds with white clouds and blue oceans. With herds of creatures running across vast plains. Giant lizards, big enough to be visible from orbit. And magnificent forests spread across continents warmed by a stable sun. "*But we never saw the lights,*" he said.

"The lights?"

"*When we approached a living world, we listened for electromagnetic activity. A burp on the radio. A conversation of some sort. Or a concerto, maybe. A voice. Something. God help us, what we would not have given to hear a voice.*

"*When that failed— It always failed, of course. When that failed, we went to the nightside, looking for lights. Sometimes they were there. A fire, started by a lightning strike. Or some other natural event. But what we wanted was to find a city glowing in the dark. A city—*" He stopped, and laughed. It was a bitter sound. "*One lighted window. Somewhere. It was all we asked. A single lantern, hanging in the night.*

"*Seventy years I was out there. Almost eighty, actually. Almost as long as Sunset.*" He took a deep breath. "*But neither of us ever saw it. Never saw anything.*"

"If you'd found something, found the lantern, what would you have done?"

"First thing: I'd have gotten in touch with Sunset. I'd have let him know. Then we'd have made an announcement."

"We?"

"Oh, yes. We'd have been together when we told them." His voice trembled.

"You're suggesting he would have done the same thing?"

"Yes. Certainly. We were in it together."

"Okay."

"The reason I called—"

"Yes?"

"I had a call from him just a few days before he died. He invited me to go out on that boat ride, the one where he lost his life? It was the last time I heard from him."

"Lucky you didn't go."

"I'm not big on boats. Never did like the damned things. But, anyhow, he said something odd."

"What was that?"

His eyes squeezed shut and his voice trembled. *" 'Ed,' he said. 'I came close. I really thought we had them.' "*

"He was talking about aliens?"

"Yes. I knew from the way he said it. But then the conversation got strange."

"In what way?"

"He wouldn't talk about it anymore. I mean, what's the big secret if he almost *found them? But he just said he was sorry he'd said anything and told me to forget it."*

"And you never figured out what he was talking about?"

"No. But there was something going on."

I showed him the tablet. "Ever see this before?"

"No," he said. *"What is it?"*

"It belonged to Sunset. More than that, we don't know. Let me ask one more question: You must have known Hugh Conover?"

"Sure. We were friends."

"Do you know where he is now?"

He shook his head. *"No idea. I haven't heard from him in ages."*

When Alex got in, I told him Holverson wanted him to call.

"Who's Holverson? Do you know what it's about?"

"It's about Tuttle."

"Really? What did he have to say?"

"Best you hear for yourself."

"Oh," he said. "One of those, huh?"

He went up to his office. Twenty minutes later he came down and, without saying anything about the conversation, asked if I had plans for dinner.

We went to Mully's Top of the World. On the way out, we talked about some antiques from the Marovian period that had just become available. A host showed us to our table. We ordered and made small talk until the drinks arrived. Then, finally, he asked my reaction to Holverson.

"I don't know," I said. "It sounds as if nothing ever happened. So the tablet isn't what we thought it might be."

"You think it's something that he just picked up somewhere?"

"At Larry's Concrete Creations, maybe. Sure, why not?"

"Why did he keep it in the cabinet?"

"It was a joke. Something to spook visitors."

"But he doesn't seem to have been showing it around."

"I know. Look, Alex, I don't trust my judgment on this one."

"Why not?"

I tried my drink. It was a blue daddy, and it had a bit of a sting. "Because I *want* it to have happened."

"You mean aliens?"

"Yes."

"I know what you mean. I'm having the same problem. I don't know what I think." Music drifted in from the back room. A soft romantic melody played on a *kira*.

"Maybe," I said, "Holverson misunderstood what Tuttle said."

"It's possible." Alex tried his own drink, sat back and looked out the window. Mully's is perched near the top of Mt. Oskar, the tallest peak in the area. That might not be saying much, but the view down into the valley is spectacular. It was getting dark in the east, and the lights of Andiquar were coming on.

I waited.

Alex tapped his fingers on the table. "I can't make the pieces fit."

"My suggestion," I said, "is that we enjoy our dinner and forget the whole business. We're going to have enough to do these next few days with the Marovian stuff showing up."

"There is a problem."

"Which is?"

"If the tablet is worthless, why isn't it at the bottom of the river?"

"It's a big river."

"Yeah." He took some more of the wine. Our dinners arrived, and, with that marvelous ability to compartmentalize, Alex put the tablet out of his mind and set himself to enjoying his meal.

seveN

Rachel Bannister had spent several years as a freelance pilot before connecting with Universal Transport, for whom she hauled executives, clients, and politicians around the Confederacy. She went from there to World's End Tours, where she took people sightseeing. In 1403, after four years with World's End, she resigned. She was only forty-two at the time, but she left piloting altogether and, as far as the record shows, never went off-world again. At least not as a pilot. She currently ran an online financial advisory service. In her role as a social-service activist, she appeared occasionally as a guest on *Nancy White's Fireside*.

Rachel spent much of her time with volunteer organizations, primarily working with children. She led an organization that sued abusive parents and relatives, requiring them to undergo psych alterations. (Not somebody, I thought, you'd want to fool around with.) And she'd fostered a lifelong enthusiasm for music, occasionally participating in amateur productions. She lived alone in a condo off Leicester Square.

Normally, we conduct business meetings online. But, for something like this, Alex's preference was for personal contact.

Leicester Square was an upscale area, a network of parks that were home to condos and small shops and restaurants. Parkland University was situated along its northern perimeter, with the Grenada Preserve to the south.

We didn't call ahead. No point alerting her. Alex took the rest of the day and read everything he could find on her. She'd gotten her license in 1382. At the University of Carpathia, she'd been a student of Tuttle's. Later, she became an occasional companion and love interest. This despite the difference in their ages. She never married.

"Hard to imagine," I said.

"What's that?" Alex was looking out at gathering clouds as we rose above the country house and turned toward Andiquar. The sun was sinking behind the horizon, and the Melony glittered in the shifting light. "Starships to stocks and bonds?"

"You got it."

"Some people would tell you that if you want a wild ride, Chase, financial securities are considerably more exciting than what *you* do for a living."

"Yeah, but nobody's going to take that seriously."

"You think? Ask somebody who's put his life savings on Berkmann AntiGrav." Berkmann, of course, had tanked a few months earlier. Along with a lot of other high-tech stocks.

"Say what you like, Alex, but it's a different kind of ride. What can you do with a stock portfolio that matches gliding through the Baccharian rings? Or riding with a comet?"

He laughed. "That's why I love you, Chase," he said.

We pulled into the flow of traffic, and the AI told us that Leicester Square was fourteen minutes away. "I take it things are going well with Audree," I said. He'd been out with her the previous evening.

"Well enough." Coy, but all his lights came on.

"She's a good woman."

"Yes, she is."

Traffic was heavy. "Have you guys set a date yet?"

He cleared his throat. "I don't think that's in the immediate future."

"There's someone else in her life, huh?"

"I really have no idea, Chase."

"She won't wait forever, you know."

"Do you know about somebody else?"

"No, I was just asking a question."

He fell silent. Then he changed the subject. "The touring industry isn't doing well."

"I don't think it ever has. To begin with, most people don't like the long flights. If there's not a black hole within an hour's ride, they're just not interested. They'd rather be home with their feet up living in a virtual world."

"That's probably true. Maybe it's what drove Tuttle to join the Gibbon Society."

"Maybe."

"But there've always been people who can't see above the rooftops. Most people, probably."

"You're turning into a pessimist, Alex."

"*Turning* into one? Where've you been the last few years, Chase?" He looked at me in the half-light from the instrument panel, and he laughed again. The guy was really happy that night. More so than I'd seen him in a while. Alex tends to be emotionally pretty level. He doesn't get depressed, and he takes his successes in stride. But something good was happening. And I didn't think it had anything to do with a stone tablet.

Leicester Square is beautiful immediately after sunset. The growing darkness is partially offset by illumination from concealed lamps. The least bit of wind sets the broad leaves of the spiva trees to swaying gently. In winter, the fountain is shut down, but that evening, with serious cold weather a month away, it was still flowing, glittering with reflected light. People were feeding nuts to the birds. At the north end of the park, kids were tossing a ball around. And there was of course the inevitable dog.

Well, not a dog, really. A *gooch*, probably the closest thing Rimway has to a canine.

Public parking inside the Square is restricted to a single area on the western perimeter. We got instructions from the traffic monitor and descended onto the indicated pad. We were about five minutes from Rachel's condo.

*   *   *

We climbed four or five stone steps onto a covered walkway and stopped at the front door. It asked who we were.

"Chase Kolpath and Alex Benedict," Alex said.

"You are not on the approved list."

"Please inform Ms. Bannister we are preparing a history of the Directorate of Planetary Survey and Astronomical Research. We would like very much to speak with her for a few minutes. We won't take much of her time."

"One moment, please."

The buildings at Leicester varied from two to four stories. They were designed in the late-modern Ortho style: curved walls, convex windows, turrets in unexpected places. A gust of wind blew dead leaves along the walkway.

The lock clicked. *"You may come in. Ms. Bannister's unit is number forty-seven."*

The entrance hall had no antigrav lift. Instead, it provided a staircase and an elevator. We took the elevator, got off on the fourth floor, found the room, and paused. The door opened, and Rachel Bannister smiled at us and said hello. "Please come in," she added.

She was lovely, in a contained way, a woman with classic features, inquisitive blue eyes, and brown hair cut short. She was a bit taller than I am, and she struck me as someone who was accustomed to having her way. Our unannounced appearance had probably given her the impression we were not to be taken seriously. "I wish I'd known you were coming," she said. "I have to be leaving in a few minutes."

"I'm sorry to have imposed," said Alex. "We could come back at a more convenient hour if you prefer."

"No, no. I'm sure you'd like to get your research done. Let's get it taken care of." The lights were dim, consisting of a single overhead strip and a lamp on a side table at one end of a long, padded sofa. A gorfa was curled up on the sofa, watching us with narrowed eyes while its tail swished gently back and forth. A second one looked in from the dining room to see what was happening, turned, and wandered away. Rachel noticed they'd gotten my attention. "I have three of them," she said. "All strays." She looked down at the one on the sofa. "This is Winnie."

Winnie recognized the name and rubbed her head against a cushion.

Rachel was in casual clothes. Unless she was headed for the gym, she didn't look as if she'd been planning an evening out. Two matching armchairs, and the sofa, were centered on a circular coffee table, on which a book lay open. I couldn't make out the title. The walls were stucco, decorated with pictures of children, one of whom might have been a ten-year-old Doug. Two wide curtained windows provided a view of the park. And a framed certificate from the Amicus Society, awarded for "extraordinary service," hung on the wall. The Amicus Society, of course, is devoted to the care and welfare of wildlife. I saw nothing that suggested she'd once piloted interstellars.

She invited us to sit and asked whether we'd like something to drink. She had some chocolate liqueur, which has always been a turn-on for Alex. I settled for a glass of wine, and she mixed something for herself. I glanced at the open book and asked about it.

"It's *Dead by Midnight*," she said. "It's a Keith Altman novel." Keith Altman, of course, is the celebrated private detective in the classic series that's been popular throughout the Confederacy for almost two centuries.

Alex and I took the armchairs, and she settled onto the sofa. Rachel commented that she'd heard of Alex and pronounced herself surprised that he had found time or reason to visit her. "My understanding, Mr. Benedict," she said, "is that you sell antiques. I think there's a game of some sort being played here. Are you and Ms. Kolpath really writing a history of Survey?"

Something in her manner indicated nothing was to be gained by lying. "No," said Alex. "That's not really quite accurate."

"And what, if I may ask, do you actually want?" Her voice hardened. It didn't become hostile, just don't bother me with nonsense. She glanced my way, as if expecting me to respond. But this seemed like a good time to let Alex carry the ball.

He weighed his answer. Tasted the liqueur. "It's good," he said. She did not respond, and he continued: "Actually, Ms. Bannister, I think you know."

"Really?"

"Now you are the one playing games."

"I do *not* play games, Mr. Benedict." Her manner shifted slightly. Became more intense. Not cold. Not angry. But she let us know we were close to crossing a line.

"I understand you knew Somerset Tuttle."

"Yes," she said. "I knew him. He was a friend."

Alex looked my way. "Chase is also a pilot."

The tension did not go away. "I haven't done any of that for a long time."

I took my cue and smiled back. "I envy you, Ms. Bannister."

"Really? Why is that?"

"Most of us just haul people and freight around. You were out there in unknown territory. You never knew what lay ahead. Must have been pretty exciting stuff."

"For the most part, I simply ran tours." She paused. "Is that why you're here? To inquire about my emotional state?"

"No," I said. "But I just travel port to port, occasionally. And take Alex out once in a while. Mostly, I sit at a desk. You, on the other hand—"

She gazed at me. "Have you tried Survey, Ms. Kolpath?"

"No. Not really."

"I have friends over there. I'm sure I could get you a billet if you'd like to put a little more excitement into your life."

"Thanks," I said. "I'll think about it."

Alex pretended to look annoyed, thereby annoying *me*. It never occurred to him that I might have been serious.

"Now," said Rachel, keeping focused on me, "did you want to get to the point? Or should we just chat for a bit? I really *am* running out of time."

"Tuttle left us with a puzzle," said Alex, in a level voice. "He owned a tablet engraved with symbols we can't identify. They don't look like any known human language."

"Really? Well, it's probably from one of the digs. Sunset was inclined— bear with me, *Somerset*, that is—liked to collect souvenirs. I don't specifi- cally recall a *tablet*, but it's possible. Maybe it's from Karinya. Or Dismal

Point. Settlements were established there. Thousands of years ago. I know he visited places like that occasionally."

"Ms. Bannister, didn't you send your nephew to Tuttle's former home to pick up a tablet?" He produced a picture of the object and handed it to her.

"Oh," she said. "Yes. The rock. I had no idea that's what we were talking about."

"May I ask where it is now?"

"In the river, Mr. Benedict, as best I know. Look, I have no idea why you're so overwrought about this. But yes, I saw the rock, the tablet, when it was advertised. Try to understand that I had a close relationship at one time with Somerset. When I saw the tablet appear, and realized what it was and that someone was getting rid of it, my first thought was that it would be nice to have it here. Sentimental value. So yes, I asked Doug to go by and pick it up for me. Is anything wrong with that?"

"When you realized what it was—What actually was it?"

"It was an object once owned by a man I cared about."

"You don't know any more about it than that?"

"No."

"They were halfway back here, and you changed your mind. Told them to drop it in the river. Right?"

"I told Doug to get rid of it. I left the details to him."

"May I ask why you changed your mind?"

"I told you it had sentimental value."

"Yes?"

"It occurred to me that having it here, where I'd see it every day, would be painful. Now, if you want to find out precisely where it is, you need to ask Doug. I can give you his code if you like."

"Ms. Bannister, you know, of course, what Tuttle's life work was?"

"Of course. Everybody who knows anything about him knows what he was looking for."

"We were wondering if he succeeded."

"Oh." She broke into a spasm of laughter.

"You think it's funny?" Alex said.

"I think it's hysterical, Mr. Benedict. If you knew the man, you'd understand that if he found anything like what you're suggesting, he'd have told the world. Within twenty-four hours. It's all he cared about."

"Did he care about it even more than he cared about you?"

That hurt. I saw it in her eyes. "Yes," she said after a moment. "He didn't care about me that much. We were friends. That's all."

Alex's voice shifted a notch. "Is the tablet here?"

Her eyes widened. "I'd invite you to look, Mr. Benedict, but I don't think you're entitled to that privilege. And I think prolonging this conversation will simply be a waste of time." She got up. "I really must be going."

The condo had a kitchen, a dining area, and, if my guess was right, two additional rooms. "Ms. Bannister," Alex said, "I'm prepared to make a substantial offer if you would simply allow us to examine the stone." He named a figure. It would have bought a luxury skimmer.

Rachel looked at me. "Chase, you need to find a more rational associate. I *do* recommend you look into a position at Survey."

"Let us see it," Alex said, "and we'll say nothing to anyone. If that is what you wish."

She walked over to the door and told it to open. "I wish I had it, Mr. Benedict. So I could take your money." She smiled pleasantly. "Good evening."

"Good evening," Alex said.

As we passed out into the corridor, she lingered in the doorway. "I'm disappointed, Mr. Benedict. After everything I'd read about you, I had expected more."

Alex faced her. "You understand, Ms. Bannister, that you've taken unlawful possession of an object that is covered under the General Antiquities Provision Act?"

"What are you talking about?"

"If the tablet is what we think, it can't be acquired by a private individual. It's protected."

"You're being silly, Mr. Benedict. You just finished telling me that Somerset owned it."

"In a presumptive sense. In fact, an object like that belongs to everyone."

"I'm glad to hear it."

"If you refuse to cooperate, you'll leave me no choice but to notify the authorities."

"Do as you like. I'm not sure what it will do to your reputation when they get here and discover you've been making it all up."

"What's the General Antiquities Provision Act? I've never heard of it."

"Actually, it exists, but I don't think it outlaws private ownership—"

"Then why—?"

"Use your imagination, Chase."

"Alex, don't you think she'll look it up? She'll find out quickly enough you, um, weren't being truthful."

"I don't think we need worry about that."

"Why not?"

"It's a *law*, Chase. It's a hundred pages of fine print written in legalese."

I shrugged. "I think she's telling the truth," I said, as we rode the elevator down.

"That brings us back to the original question."

"Which is—?"

"Why isn't the tablet in the river? Does Doug Bannister strike you as a guy who would be interested in artifacts?"

"His wife might."

"I don't think Doug's wife is in charge here."

"So what's next?"

"You feel like doing a stakeout?"

"A stakeout? Here?"

"It shouldn't take long."

eiGHT

We can never say that anything is lost beyond all chance of recall. In the end, even the sea gives up its secrets.

—Eskaiya Black, *Lost in Aruba*

We didn't have a decent view of Rachel's building from the parking area, so we went airborne. Alex didn't want to tell me what we were waiting for. Instead, he got that smug look and said I should just sit tight.

So I let him enjoy his moment. Then I asked whether he really believed she was sending for Doug again.

"Sure," he said with that big grin. "What choice does she have?"

We drifted around and watched. After about twenty minutes, the white, split-wing Sentinel came out of the western sky, homed in on the Square, and descended onto what was probably Rachel's private pad behind the building. A door opened, and Doug popped out, followed by Brian. They climbed up onto the covered walkway, out of our view, and must have gone in through a rear entrance.

"We going down to confront them?" I asked.

"And do what? Let's just watch."

They'd been inside about ten minutes when they reappeared, carrying what might have been a packing case. It looked big enough to contain the tablet.

The case was obviously heavy. They struggled with it but got it to the

Sentinel. A door opened and they pushed it into the backseat. Then both climbed on board, and the skimmer rose into the night.

"Where do you figure they're going?" I asked.

"Don't know. I assume a more secure place to stow the tablet."

It was dark by then, the last vestiges of the sunset lost in the lights of a thousand airborne vehicles. The sky was full of moving stars. The Sentinel surprised us by entering an eastbound lane. Outbound, toward the ocean. We remained with them, but stayed far enough back to avoid discovery. I hoped.

We moved across the city and arced out toward the beaches. The traffic turned north and south along the coast, but the Sentinel kept going.

Just offshore and south of the city, a large brightly illuminated emporium, the Majestic, occupied a quarter of Liberty Island. Its upper deck provided landing pads, and I thought for a moment that was where they were headed. But they maintained altitude and kept going as the remaining traffic peeled away. "Alex," I said, "if we stay with them, they'll know we're here."

"Can't help it, Chase."

"Where are they going? You think there's a boat out here somewhere?"

"They're going to dump it."

"Why on earth would they do that?"

"I have no idea, Chase. For whatever reason, Rachel wants to keep it out of our hands. If that means dropping it in the ocean, that's what she's prepared to do."

"What do you suggest?"

He shook his head. "Damn. Open a channel to them."

We got a quick blip of static. Then Doug's voice. *"Go ahead, Benedict. That is you back there, right?"*

"What are you guys doing?"

"I think you can guess."

"Why?"

"None of your business. The thing's taking up space, so we're getting rid of it." He growled. It was a thin, almost pathetic sound. *"Go the hell away."*

"Listen, guys, that thing is worth a lot of money. I'm willing to pay for it."

"How much?"

The notion suddenly broke over me that this whole thing was a con job. That we were being set up.

"I'll give you a thousand. And match it for Brian." That would be considerably more than either of these characters could earn in a year.

"That's pretty good money. Why's it worth so much, Alex?"

"I've told you why. The engraving uses symbols nobody's seen before. We don't know the source."

"It was probably just somebody screwing around."

"Maybe."

"You're really willing to pay that much?"

"Yes."

"Hmmm." I saw lights on the ocean. A cruise ship several kilometers to port. *"Brian, what do you think?"*

"Alex," I said, "they've opened the door."

We got Brian's voice: *"The money sounds pretty good, Doug. Maybe we ought to—Oops!"* Something tumbled out into the sky and began a long fall toward the ocean. *"Damn,"* said Brian. *"Dropped it."*

"Chase, get a fix."

"Already done, Alex."

The container disappeared into the dark.

Alex stared at the radio. "How could you guys be so dumb?"

"Look, Benedict." Doug's voice had acquired an edge. *"I'm sorry I couldn't give you what you want. I really am. But it's gone now. So I guess that's the end of it."*

They were making a long turn, starting back toward the mainland. I was still staring down at the sea.

So we rounded up Audree again, and, accompanied by a pair of Environmental Service specialists, we went back out a couple of days later on the *Shanley*, one of the agency's all-purpose vehicles. To get the *Shanley*, Audree had filed a statement alleging that an archeological "object" was believed to be lying on the ocean floor.

There was nothing in sight that morning except sea and sky. When we got into the area, we descended to an altitude of about a hundred meters and began scanning.

The cabin was a tight fit for five people. I was used to the relatively ample accommodations of the *Belle-Marie*, or, for that matter, any starship. Even the smallest of the superluminals would have been downright spacious contrasted with the APV.

The specialists were Kira Quong, the pilot, and Bailey Anderson, who oversaw the search and retrieval systems. Bailey was a big guy with a good smile whom I immediately liked. Kira was almost as tall as he was, one of the tallest women I've ever seen. They were the last two people on the planet you'd want to cram into that cabin. Other than size, Kira was the polar opposite of Bailey, intense, businesslike, no visible sense of humor.

"If you're going to dump something offshore," Kira said, "they picked a good spot. The ocean's fairly deep here. A bit over four kilometers."

We stayed in the air, circling the site while Bailey tried to find the packing case. "The currents are strong in the area," he said. "It could have drifted a long way before hitting bottom." His attention was entirely focused on his screens while he flipped switches and adjusted contrasts. "Do you guys," he asked, "have any idea how much the case weighed?"

"It needed two guys to lift," said Alex. "I'd guess probably a couple of hundred pounds."

"It should have gone directly to the bottom," I said.

Bailey shook his head. "Not necessarily. In these currents, even a brick could travel a fair distance." He touched a pad, and the screens went dark.

"How can you see anything?" I asked.

"Anything artificial down there will light up."

"Anything?"

"Well, anything you'd make a packing case from."

"There's something now." In fact, two blinkers had appeared on the screen.

Bailey tapped his finger on one. "Probably wreckage from a boat. Looks like a spar. *That* one is a piece of electrical equipment, I think."

He studied the picture, made more adjustments. "Yeah, that's got to be what it is. In any case, it's not a box."

"What if it's buried in the sea bottom, Bailey?" I asked.

"Won't matter. We can see through the mud."

Kira looked up from her station. "No question about that," she said, in a flat voice. "If it's covered with mud, Bailey will see it."

Alex looked my way and signaled to be careful. It looked as if we had a broken relationship here. The disquiet in the craft picked up, there was some glaring back and forth, and Bailey's smile became strained.

We circled the area for more than an hour. "It takes time," Audree said. "If it's there, we'll find it. It's just a matter of patience."

Blinkers appeared continually on the display. Bailey studied each one, shook his head, and stored the image so it wouldn't reappear. Eventually, he hesitated over one, enlarged it, and put his finger on it. He touched a control pad, and numbers showed up on a sideboard. He leaned forward, studied the image, considered the numbers, and nodded. "There it is," he said.

"You sure?" asked Alex.

"Well, not absolutely. Can't be positive till we go down and look. But it's the right configuration."

"Can we see inside it?" asked Alex.

Bailey shook his head. "Negative."

"Okay, Kira," said Audree. "Let's go."

Kira's fingers danced across the controls, the tone of the engines changed, the soft hum of power in the bulkheads became more audible and, somewhere, hatches locked. The *Shanley* eased down onto the surface. We floated for a few moments. Then the water was washing over us, and we began to submerge.

Bailey kept the image on-screen. Kira flipped a switch, and external lights came on. A few fish showed up. "Everybody stay seated," she said. Her eyes flicked across Bailey, who stared steadily at his monitors. There were more fish. Something big and blubbery passed us on my side. The water got dark.

Bailey read off the depths as we went. "Four hundred."

"Five hundred."

"In case you're wondering," Audree said, "we're locked on the container."

Bailey had a better picture by then. He asked Alex whether it matched the package the two men had carried out of the condo. It did.

Pressure built in my ears as we descended. We were going down at a steep angle, and every now and then the bulkheads creaked. I wondered how deep the *Shanley* could go. Four kilometers sounded pretty far down, but I assured myself Audree wouldn't take any risks.

She was enjoying herself. She took full advantage of the opportunity to show off her position for Alex. Her demeanor had changed somewhat. Her voice had taken on a note of authority, and she submerged herself—forgive the pun—in overseeing the operation. Not that she did any micromanaging. She was far too smart for anything like that. But there was never any doubt who was in charge of the operation.

We hit thirty-seven hundred meters and began to level off. Gradually, the lights picked up the bottom and played against the mud. Something darted past us.

"It's dead ahead," said Bailey. The tension between him and the pilot had not abated, and I was thinking there should be a rule against people who were emotionally involved with each other being on the same crew. At least when they were operating an APV.

"There it is," Kira said. I didn't see anything, but Bailey's panel was beginning to beep.

"I got it," he said.

The lights picked it up. A rectangular gray container. It was about two feet high, lying on its side. Audree looked over her shoulder at Alex.

"That's it," he said.

It lay half-buried.

"It's yours, Kira," said Bailey. He tried to get some warmth into his voice.

"I have it," she said. "Everybody stay seated, please." We drifted slightly to port. The packing case vanished beneath us, then was picked up by a new set of scanners.

Kira shut down all forward motion, although the currents continued to push against us. "Morley," she said.

Morley was the AI. *"Yes, Kira?"*

"Initiate retrieval."

Four robotic arms appeared. They locked onto the case and lifted it out of the mud.

We heard a hatch open. Moments later, it closed. *"Retrieval completed, Kira,"* Morley said.

Audree smiled at Alex. "Let's go topside."

We had to wait until we were on the surface to get at the case. The lid was cracked, and the box had filled with water. "Probably happened when it hit the surface," Kira said.

Alex and Bailey turned it on its side and dumped the water out of it. Then Alex found a catch, released it, and removed the lid. My angle wouldn't let me see, but I heard him grunt. He reached in, pulled out some blanket that had been used for packing. And then removed a brick. "There are more in here if anybody's interested."

NiNe

Time will reveal whatever is hidden, and it will hide and bury whatever now calls forth splendor.

—Horace, *Epistles*

Alex doesn't usually show a lot of emotion, but he tossed everything back into the ocean, returned to his seat, and took to staring listlessly out the window.

"It's not the end of the world," Audree said.

"No." He managed a smile. "She's playing games with us."

"This Rachel has a sick sense of humor."

"She wants me to give up and go away."

Audree smiled. "Not used to that kind of treatment from attractive women, are we?"

Alex squeezed her hand and opened his link. "Connect me with Cory," he said to it.

Audree turned my way. "Who's Cory?"

"He runs the Antiquity Research Service in West Arkon. Among other things, they can do analyses to determine the age of artifacts—"

"But you don't have the artifact."

"That's right."

"So—?"

Alex shushed us. "Cory?"

I heard a voice respond. Alex listened. Then: "Got a question for you. We've been tracking a marker of unknown origin. We have pictures of it. It looks like something you'd find in a cemetery. Except it has more extensive engraving. Three lines of symbols. It's probably pretty old. Centuries. Maybe more. Do you think you can get an age estimate on the thing based on pictures?"

The voice replied.

"No," said Alex, "I don't think we can get the object itself. We've been trying."

And: "It's a long story. You really don't want to hear about the details. Is it possible to get an estimate from the pictures?"

And: "Okay. Hold on a minute. We have two. I'll send them to you." He transmitted the images, listened for a minute, said okay, and closed the link.

We hit an air pocket, and the APV bounced around. "Didn't see that one coming," said Kira.

"Been a long day," I said, hoping to lighten the mood. Audree agreed that it had been. And somebody else, I forget who, observed that rain was expected in the Andiquar area that night. Then Alex's link beeped.

"Go ahead, Corey."

The cabin went dead silent. I guess we were all listening, trying to hear what was being said at the other end. "Okay," Alex said, "I guess that's what I thought."

Then, a moment later: "If I can figure out a way to do that, I'll get it to you."

And, finally: "Right, Corey. Thanks."

"No luck?" said Audree.

"No. They need 3-D with good definition."

"Maybe we could burgle the condo," I said.

Alex was in no mood for humor. "You'd be just the person for the job. But there might be *something* we can do."

He made an appointment with Madeleine Greengrass, and two hours later we descended onto the pad at number 12, Gold Range. Madeleine had seen us coming, and she was waiting for us when we got to the front door. "Mr. Benedict," she gushed, "I'm honored to meet you." The laid-back, casual charmer of my first meeting was gone, overwhelmed by Alex's celebrity.

She took us inside, where she asked if we'd like something to drink. "Thank you, no," said Alex. "We're on the run at the moment."

"You're still interested in that rock," she said.

"Yes."

"I'm sorry I let it get away. If I'd known *you* wanted it, I'd have held on to it. But it was such an eyesore, Mr. Benedict. It was just something I wanted to get rid of."

"Of course," he said. "I understand."

"Did you find the people who took it?" She looked my way as if I were somehow responsible.

"It's complicated," Alex said. "You posted two pictures at the site."

"Yes. That's right. I have them if you'd like to see them."

"No, we have them, too. But those pictures weren't originals. Right? The engravings were pretty badly worn. So you smoothed it out."

"Yes," she said. "I didn't think there was any problem with doing that since I wasn't asking any money for it. I just wanted to get rid of it."

"Do you have the original pictures?"

She frowned, and we had the answer. "They *became* the cleaned-up copies. I saw no point in making an extra set."

"You're sure?"

"Positive, Mr. Benedict."

"All right: One final question?"

"Sure."

"How big was this thing?"

She held her hand to indicate something a bit more than waist high.

Alex left with a client to evaluate an exhibition set up by the Tempus Institute. He was just lifting away when Jacob announced a call. *"Franz Koeffler,"* he said. *"A reporter. He wants to speak with Alex."*

"Put him through, Jacob," I said.

I knew Koeffler, though not well. He worked for Transoceanic News, for whom he wrote a column that usually combined science and politics. He was about average size, a little on the heavy side, and had a mildly rumpled look. He spoke with a gravitas that implied his views were not to be taken lightly. Despite that, somehow, he managed to be self-effacing and easy to get along with. He'd become especially interested in Alex over the past couple of years, and had written extensively about the *Seeker*, and about our trip to Salud Afar. He was likable, though, maybe because there was something of the little kid in him.

He blinked on. He was standing with his rear end propped against a desk. *"Chase,"* he said. *"Good to see you again."*

"Hello, Franz. Alex isn't available at the moment. Can *I* help you?"

"Probably. How about telling me what Alex is after this *time?"*

I tried to look puzzled. "What are we talking about, Franz?"

"Come on, Chase. We know each other too well to play games. Your boss has a talent for uncovering huge stories. What's he working on now?"

"I don't think anything special. I know he's been interested in the Longworth Ruby." Which, of course, had been worn by Isabella Longworth while she guided the City on the Crag to greatness two thousand years ago. It had disappeared during the assassination and was periodically reported as having been in one place or another over the centuries, but no one could confirm the claims, and nobody had had any luck running it down.

"Sunset Tuttle," he said.

"I'm sorry?"

"Chase, if you're not going to talk to me, I'll just go with what I have. Did Tuttle find something after all?"

"Franz, maybe you need to talk to Alex. I don't know anything about this."

"Okay. Have it your way." He stood up. Shrugged. Looked disappointed. *"Chase, I thought I could count on you."*

He was about to blink off, but I stopped him. "Wait, Franz. How much do you know?"

"Just enough to whet my appetite. Why don't you tell me what's going on? I won't publish anything until you clear it."

"I'm not free to do that, Franz."

"I'm sorry to hear it."

"Look. Whatever you have right now: Sit on it. The truth is, we don't know whether we have anything or not."

"Aliens?"

"I don't think so. There's an outside chance, but I'm pretty sure nothing will come of it. Anyhow, go along with us. If we get a story out of this, Alex will invite you in for an interview."

"Exclusive?"

"Yes. Of course, we probably wouldn't be able to hold the story back."

He made it look like a painful decision. *"When will we know?"*

"It's going to take a while."

That night, as I slid between the sheets and the lights dimmed, I found myself wishing that we'd never seen the Greengrass posting. It had become simply a matter of Alex's wanting to satisfy his curiosity about someone's irrational behavior. There could be no reasonable explanation for what had been happening. At least none that would matter to us. At that point, I just wanted Rachel and her tablet to go away.

Rainbow doesn't keep early hours. Though I've made a habit of arriving at nine most mornings, there's no requirement that I do so. Alex has always been concerned with productivity rather than with time spent hanging around the office.

Next morning, though, I think I broke some sort of record getting in. I'm not sure why. Maybe I was hoping Alex would say, "Take the day off, and by the way, we're moving on. We're giving up on the tablet." It was just past dawn when I left my own place. Ten minutes later, I landed at the country house, strolled up to the front door, and said hello to Jacob.

"I'm surprised to see you here so early," the AI said. He could not keep the smug quality out of his voice. He opened up, and I walked in.

"I don't guess Alex is up yet?" I said.

"That's correct. Do you wish me to wake him?"

"No," I said. "That's not necessary."

"As you prefer. As soon as he's awake, I'll notify him that you're here." He paused. *"Would you like some breakfast?"*

I settled in with pancakes and strawberries. I was finishing when the shower turned on upstairs, and a few minutes later Audree appeared. "He'll be right down," she said. She was surprised to find me.

Jacob got her some coffee and toast. "How's he doing?" I asked.

"You're talking about the tablet."

"Yes."

"He's annoyed. It's turned into something of a challenge with this Rachel woman. You've met her, haven't you?"

"Yes," I said.

"What did you think of her?"

"She seems okay. Didn't take kindly to our poking into what she considers her business."

"I guess not. She went to a lot of trouble to send us out on a pointless chase."

"I know." I heard Alex coming down the stairs.

"So what's she hiding?"

"I'll give you a call when we find out. I'm inclined to think we try a break-in."

She laughed. "Chase, you'd look good in a mask."

Alex came into the room. "Fortunately," he said, "some of us are still law-abiding, principled citizens of high character." He wore dark brown slacks and a white pullover that read RAINBOW ENTERPRISES. We'd given a hundred of them away a month before at a gala for antique collectors. "Good morning, Chase," he continued. "It seems a trifle early for you to be here. Everything okay?"

"More or less." I paused, and we all looked at one another. "Have we decided to walk away from this thing?"

"Did I say that?"

"I was hoping you would."

"Well, no. I don't plan to. But there's no reason for *you* to be involved."

"Right."

Audree took a large bite of the toast. "You sound skeptical, Chase."

"Alex likes company."

He opened the refrigerator and got some orange juice. "Where would the world be without women?" he asked.

"So, boss, where do we go from here?"

"We're not going to be able to get our hands on the thing. So we have to find another way to track down its origin."

"How?"

"I'm working on it."

TeN

Let us then seek truth, and pray that, when we come upon it, we do not break a leg.

—Nolan Creel, *The Arnheim Review*, XLII, 17

I spent that evening with Robin at the Top of the World. While I poked at a steak, he looked out over the lights of Andiquar and asked whether we really wanted to find aliens.

"How do you mean?" I asked.

He looked good in the candlelight. He was subdued, happy to be with me, and supportive at a time when I felt I needed it because I was spending a lot of my working time supporting Alex, who was becoming increasingly frustrated. "Life's pretty good right now," he said. "Who knows how a race of high-tech aliens might change things. They could be a serious threat. It might be one of those cases of being careful what you wish for." He stirred his drink, tasted it, and sat back, a guy for whom wisdom consisted in knowing when to cash in your chips. "They might think that rum is a negative force and decide that we shouldn't have any. For our own good."

"Robin—"

"Or they might be against sex. Except for reproduction."

"Ah, yes. Now we get to the heart of the matter."

I needed him that night, so I took him home.

We were into the weekend. Normally, I don't work weekends, but that time around I was inclined to make an exception. I arrived at Rainbow in the morning, bright and happy in spite of everything. The world was a playground, and I was on the swings, baby. Jacob greeted me at the door, told me he was surprised to see me arrive once again when I wasn't expected, adding that I seemed to be making a habit of it, and assuring me that Alex wouldn't approve. He asked whether he could help with whatever assignments had brought me in on a day off. I said thanks, but I was just going to hang out for a bit.

Alex came down, and I explained again that I knew what day it was but it was okay. We drank our usual morning coffee and talked about some assorted tasks that, since I was there, I might as well take care of. Neither of us mentioned the tablet.

The day, which had started with the promise of sunlight and warm temperatures, turned cool. The sky lost its light, the wind picked up, and a mild rain began to fall. I completed the paperwork for several services we'd rendered, including the transfer of a floor lamp that dated back to the Librano period six thousand years ago. The lamp didn't work anymore, of course. Oddly, it probably would have been worth less if it did. But it was in exquisite condition. We'd also succeeded in confirming that one of the voices in a radio transmission intercepted near Belarian belonged to the immortal essayist Edouard Melancamp, who had been sitting at home on Barkley Lake, chatting idly with his son-in-law, who was approaching in the *Alexia*. The *Alexia*, a few years later, would explode, killing four hundred people, one of the worst superluminal accidents in history.

Alex spent the rest of the morning upstairs in his office. When, finally, he came down, he offered to take me to lunch. I'd committed to Robin, so I had to pass.

After an entertaining hour at Mojack's, I settled in for a long afternoon, working on contracts and tracking the provenance of several artifacts at the request of clients: A desk that, its owner maintained, had once been the property of Indio Naramatsu. (It hadn't.) A captain's chair that was supposed to have once been installed on the bridge of the *Ranger*. (It also had not.) A communication device that had originally been the property of Clair Pascha—even though the instrument belonged to a different era. And so on. We get a lot of that. People aren't satisfied with having an antique. They want it to be a piece of history.

The rain didn't so much stop as gradually exhaust itself, leaving behind a skyful of listless gray clouds. Jack Napier, our delivery guy, brought some shipments that had to be inventoried and added to our available stock. We didn't keep much on hand. Generally, Rainbow made its money by putting buyers and sellers together. But we didn't shy away from marketing whatever antiques we were able, through good timing, to acquire.

In the midst of all this, Alex wandered into my office and sat down quietly, pretending to be absorbed in a silver locket that might have been worn by Lara Cheneau, but whose authenticity was not certifiable. I was looking at shipping schedules when he broke the silence: "Rachel called while you were out."

"Really? What did she have to say?"

"I don't know. I wasn't here either." And, of course, Jacob has orders not to relay calls. Alex doesn't like being tracked everywhere he goes.

"She leave a message?"

"Just that she'd called."

"You going to call back?"

"I think I'll let her have the initiative. I'm tired of the mind games."

"Why do you think she's calling?"

"Because she knows we're still looking around. I've been trying to find someone who knows what happened to Hugh Conover. I suspect that's gotten back to her."

"No luck with Conover?"

"Even his family doesn't know where he is. He just said good-bye to everybody. Nine years ago. Every once in a while somebody gets a note from him. Says he's doing fine. Hopes everyone's okay. Leaves a code number they can reply to."

"Have you tried contacting him directly?"

"I've tried. He hasn't answered."

*   *   *

We were getting ready to close for the day when Jacob announced Rachel was on the circuit. Alex took the call in my office. *"Mr. Benedict,"* she said, *"I'm not comfortable with what's been happening, and I wonder if we might not reach some sort of agreement?"* She looked frustrated and less sure of herself than she had been.

"What did you have in mind, Ms. Bannister?"

She was seated on her sofa. A lamp on the side table glowed softly. She was dressed casually in green and white, and wore a woolly white sweater. I was off to one side, out of the picture as far as she was concerned. But I could see *her.*

"Did you find what you wanted?"

"I think you know the answer to that."

"All right," she said. *"Look. I'd like to save us both some time. I'm going to be honest with you. I've no interest in keeping the tablet."*

"You're willing to sell it to me?"

"I've destroyed it."

"I hope you're not going to tell me you dropped it in the ocean."

"No. I was simply trying to discourage you from proceeding."

"Why?"

"Since you are the one on the hunt, Alex— Is it okay if I call you that? Since you are the one on the hunt, you're surely better equipped to answer that question than I am." Her eyes sparkled in the light. *"I'll tell you honestly that I wish you'd let things alone. You can do no good, and you might do a great deal of harm."*

Alex was seated in one of the two chairs that faced my desk. "Explain that. Tell me where the danger is. I'll hold everything you say in confidence, and if I agree, we'll drop the investigation."

"How do I know I can trust you?"

"You probably can't. It depends on what you have to say."

Her eyes slid shut, and for a long moment, she didn't move. *"Tell me what you know,"* she said, *"and I'll try to fill in the blanks."*

Alex straightened himself, gave the impression he was considering whether he wanted to comply. Then: "The language on the tablet can't be identified. It's possible it has a human origin, but there's a decent chance the source is something else. We don't believe the Mutes are involved although we're in the process of checking that out now.

"It originally belonged to Tuttle. He's only known for one thing." A gust of wind rattled the windows. "So the tablet," Alex continued, "gets advertised online, you're surprised to see it, but you know what it is and what it means. I don't know how that is, but you and he were friends. He confided in you. Hours later, your nephew shows up to collect it. Have I got it right so far?"

"Go on," she said.

"Since that time, you've done everything you could to prevent my getting a look at it. And you seem baffled as to why my curiosity should be aroused."

She picked up a glass of wine from the side table, took some, and put it down. *"And why do you think I've been doing all this? I mean, the tablet is essentially worthless. The pictures you have don't depict the reality. It's in much worse condition."*

"This is not about money, Rachel. Although if it is what we suspect it *might* be, then its value would climb considerably."

"That's certainly true." She looked steadily at him. *"Ah,"* she said suddenly, *"you think it's all a con. You think I'm withholding the tablet to create the impression that yes, it* is *an alien artifact. Drive the price through the roof, sell the thing, then take the money and run."*

"I don't believe that at all."

"Very good. Because there's nothing to it."

"Which brings us back to your motives. *Why* are you keeping it hidden?"

"Keep in mind that I'm no longer hiding it. It has been reduced to rubble."

"I hope you are not serious."

"I am." I was inclined to believe her.

"I'm sorry to hear that."

"I'm sorry it was necessary." She took a deep breath. *"You're recording this conversation, I assume?"*

"I am."

"Turn it off."

Alex told Jacob to comply.

She waited, looking to her right, until she was satisfied she could speak freely. *"I assume you're not alone."*

Alex hesitated. "No," he said.

"Please have her leave."

I got up and started to walk out. Alex signaled me to come forward where Rachel could see me, and to sit back down. "Anything you wish to say to me, you can say to her."

She thought about it. *"All right. I'd promised myself to take this matter to the grave. But I don't want you stirring things up. Asking too many questions. So I'll tell you what it's about, provided"*—she looked from Alex to me—*"provided it goes no further. Not to anyone."* She eased back into the sofa. *"Are we agreed?"*

It was Alex's turn to think it over. "No," he said. "I can't possibly agree to those conditions. Not until I hear the explanation."

"Then we'll simply have to leave things as they are."

"I'm sorry. Answer me this: Why is secrecy so important?"

"Because the danger is so great."

"What danger?"

"Alex, you're not being reasonable."

"Tell me what the danger is."

"I can't do that. I've already said too much." And, incredibly, this woman, who had impressed me as being so tough, wiped tears from her cheeks.

She looked in my direction. Then, as though I were of no consequence, back toward Alex. *"All right,"* she said. *"I'm exhausted. I'm tired of carrying this burden on my own. Maybe it* is *best that you know."*

"Know *what*, Rachel?"

Rachel seemed to be having trouble finding words. *"Alex, you were—"* She swallowed. *"You were right. I did find another civilization."*

"Where?"

"That's of no concern. Other than myself, nobody knows. And I'm going to keep it that way."

"Why?"

"Alex, they're far in advance of us. Of anything we've ever imagined.

Sunset thought they were possibly millions of years old. He had a ten-dency to exaggerate, but he might very well have been correct."

"How did Sunset happen to be with you?"

"I was with him. We were friends. I went with him once in a while."

"Okay. Then what happened?"

"They told us to go away. They didn't want to be bothered by savages."

"Savages."

"That's a direct quote."

"They speak Standard?"

"Yes."

"How'd they manage *that*?"

"I don't know."

"The communication was by radio?"

"It was voices in the ship. Or, rather, a voice."

Alex shook his head. "An actual voice? Or something you heard in your head?"

"A voice. It told us to leave. Not to come back. And not allow any others 'of your kind' to intrude."

"That's fairly hard to believe, Rachel."

"Believe what you want. Ask yourself what else would have kept Sunset silent. He knew what it would mean. Once the word got out, there'd be no keeping people away from the place. Even if we refused to make the location public, it would initiate a major hunt. Who knew what the outcome might be? Alex, these creatures were terrifying."

"Why do you say that?"

"It was as if they got inside us. Took us over. Even today, so many years later, the mere thought of them—" She shuddered.

"How did you respond?"

Her gaze grew intense. *"What do you think? Yes, sir. We'll do what you say. Won't see any of us around here anymore. Good day to you all."* She actually managed a smile. *"How would* you *have responded?"*

"Where'd the tablet come from?"

"They took over the ship. Took it down through the atmosphere and landed it in an open field."

"That must have been disconcerting."

"*I know how this sounds. It's nonetheless true. They told us we would not be harmed, but I'll admit I wasn't reassured.*"

"What happened when you were on the ground?"

"*The area was filled with ruins. Stone buildings. Magnificent architecture, but allowed to go to ruin. I asked what they were. Why they'd been abandoned.*"

"What did they say?"

"*That they were no longer needed. Then we were told to leave the ship.*" Her eyes grew large, and she shook her head. "*We opened up. Got out.*"

"And then?"

"*They told us they wanted to do an analysis.*"

"Of the ship?"

"*I guess. Maybe of us. Damn it, Alex, I don't know the answers to most of this.*"

"It sounds like a harrowing experience."

"*There is no word.*"

Another pause. Then: "So what happened? On the ground?"

"*A stream ran among the ruins. We stood and watched the ship for a while, but we didn't see anybody, anything go in. The tablet was set up in front of one of the buildings. A big place. Vaulted roof, what was left of it. Like a church. Or a temple.*"

"And Tuttle removed it?"

"*No. Not exactly.*"

"How did you come into possession of it?"

"*We asked them about it. What was it? What did it say? They indicated it was a date and dedication. They wouldn't do a translation for us. Said we wouldn't understand. But Sunset wanted to know if we could have it.*"

"And—?"

"*When we got back to the ship, it was waiting.*"

"Rachel, did you ever actually *see* them?"

"*No. We were alone the whole time. But not alone.*"

"Did you ask any other questions? Like, how did they learn the language? Who were they?"

"*I was too scared. It didn't strike me at the time that I particularly wanted to ask questions.*"

"What about Tuttle?"

"*No. Not him either. It's the only time I've ever seen him almost speechless.*"

"Okay." Alex scribbled something on a notepad. "You never went back?"

Her eyes rolled toward the ceiling. "*Are you serious? Would you have gone back?*" For a long few moments, no one spoke. Then she continued: "*Can I count on you to say nothing about this?*"

"Yes."

"*And to drop your investigation, which can only call attention to the matter?*"

Alex leaned forward in his chair, propped his elbow on the arm, and rested his chin in his palm. "Rachel, I would certainly drop the investigation if your account were true. Unfortunately, I find it impossible to believe."

The color drained out of her face. She stared at Alex with such unalloyed venom that I almost expected her to materialize physically and attack him. "*Then let it be on your head,*" she said. "*Whatever happens, it will be your responsibility.*" And she broke off.

---

eLeveN

It is unthinkable that God should have painted so vast a canvas, and left it for us alone. We will find others like ourselves as we move out among the stars. They will be everywhere.

—Bishop Benjamin Hustings, in reaction to the discovery that there was no one at Alpha Centauri (2511)

"What makes you think she was lying? I'll admit the story was pretty far out. But why not?"

"She has a problem, Chase."

"And what's that?"

"How does she account for the tablet?"

"I thought she managed that pretty well."

He poured coffee for us. "Do you really think," he said, "that aliens who don't want us showing up in their neighborhood would provide evidence that they exist? Why on earth would they hand over the tablet?"

"I don't know. They're *aliens*, Alex."

"It doesn't matter, Chase. Logic is still logic. It makes no sense that they'd do that. Moreover, if Tuttle was *so* determined to keep their existence hidden, so much that even he of all people would say nothing, would he really bring that piece of rock home and stick it in a cabinet in his den? No, my proud beauty, had they actually given it to him, he and Rachel would have had time to think about it on the way home. And they'd have disposed of it. Jettisoned it somewhere. And there's something else."

"What?"

"Henry told us she came back from a tour flight and quit World's End. Whatever it was that happened, I'd be shocked if it hadn't happened on that flight. Which would mean Tuttle wasn't there."

"That's guesswork."

"No. She just told us Tuttle wasn't there."

"When did she say that?"

"She said, 'You were right. I did find another civilization.' You think she'd have said that if she was out on a mission with Tuttle?"

"I guess not. So what *is* going on? Do you have a better explanation?"

"No. Worse, I can't even *imagine* one. But it's there. We just need to look harder."

"What did you have in mind?"

"World's End Tours operates out of Serendipity."

"*Dip,*" I said.

"Pardon?"

"Dip. They call it Dip."

"Okay."

"We're going out there, aren't we?"

He actually managed to look guilty. "Yes."

"Whatever we want to talk to them about, why not do it here? They have an office downtown."

"That's purely administrative. I've already checked. We want to talk to the operational people. Especially Miriam Wiley."

"She is—?"

"Director of operations at Dip. We have a better chance of getting what we want directly from her rather than talking to the bureaucrats."

I sighed. "When do we leave?"

He retired to his office, but later I saw him outside, wandering along the edge of the woods, hands in his jacket pockets, a battered broad-brimmed hunter's hat pulled low over his eyes. It was by no means unusual for him to go for a walk around the grounds. Frequently, he took the north trail out to the river, which was a half kilometer away. Occasionally, he simply strolled across the property, enjoying the crisp country air.

It was a gray, listless day, cool, damp, without a breath of wind. The grackles, which had filled the trees yesterday, were quiet, and nothing moved in all that landscape.

He seemed uncertain where he wanted to go, wandering first one way, then another. And there was something different about the way he walked, the way he was carrying himself. His head was bowed, his shoulders slumped. Sometimes, he simply stood in one place, not moving, for minutes at a time, staring, not at the corona bushes, which were always resplendent in a kind of final effort at that time of year, but at a blank piece of sky, or at the ground.

After a while he passed from my view. But he didn't come back inside. I thought about going out to see if I could help, but I didn't know what to tell him. Yes, Rachel was lying. But there was something she wanted to keep hidden, and it was obvious she would pay a price if we proceeded.

It's been a long time now since Alex stood out there on the edge of the forest. But it's an image I've never forgotten.

We needed a day or two to clear up loose ends. It was the first time I'd gone out in the *Belle-Marie* since I'd met Robin. "So where is this Serendipity?" he asked.

"About thirty light-years."

"You need company?"

"Don't you have school to teach?"

"Oh, yeah. I'd forgotten." Big smile.

"We'll be back in a week or two."

"Pity. We have a holiday break coming up—"

"Robin," I said, "Alex is anxious to get this done. We really need to do it on his timetable."

"Sure. I understand."

"You ever been off-world?"

"No," he said. "I always thought of going to the mountains as a long trip."

It was odd: I thought by then I knew him pretty well, but it hadn't occurred to me that he'd never gone anywhere. Of course, most people never travel off-world. "I'll see you when we get home."

"Okay."

And he did an imitation of celebrated tough guy Mark Parvin, talking out of the corner of his mouth: "When you get back, baby, I'll be waiting."

I liked Robin, but I felt crowded that day. Maybe I'd been promising more than I'd be able to deliver.

Well, let it go.

The station's actual name, as you probably know, is Tsarendipol, after the CEO of the General Development Corporation, the company that designed and built the place. But the designation quickly evolved into Serendipity.

The project had been started sixty years earlier, but it still wasn't completed. GDC had gone out of business, there'd been labor disputes, the fleet had taken it over twice during the periodic shoot-outs with the Mutes, and apparently there had been simply an extraordinary level of incompetence and corruption. When we got there, the station was still not much more than an exposed docking area, with a hotel, shipping facilities, and a bar. The restaurants and luxury meeting rooms and entertainment palaces that one associates with orbiting stations throughout the Confederacy had not yet opened their doors. To this day, I understand, they still aren't up and running.

World's End Tours was probably not happy with the situation, but Dip was ideally located for them. The station drifted through the outer limits of the Confederacy, with easy access to areas that still remain largely unexplored.

When we arrived inside the station's operating area, I turned control of the *Belle-Marie* over to them, and they brought us into port. I'd only been out to the place twice before, and on both occasions, I'd simply delivered some freight, crashed for a few hours, eaten, and gone back home. So walking along the nearly deserted concourses was a new experience for me. Alex said he'd been there once, with Gabe. "I was ten years old at the time," he said, "and I parked in one of the games exhibits and spent all my time shooting at aliens."

I didn't see a games exhibit.

"It was over there." He indicated a dark enclosure.

We'd gotten in late, local time, and there was only one hotel. In the morning, we looked through the World's End advertising. They ran tours to a half dozen star systems, promising "the ultimate in sightseeing." Their clients were prosperous. They had to be. World's End tours were expensive, out of sight for ordinary people. They used Eagles, which were optimum vehicles. Individual cabins had opulent appointments; they booked live entertainers; and the ships carried a maximum of fifteen passengers. All of which guaranteed you didn't have to associate with the commoners.

They maintained an office in what must have been the only elegantly furnished passageway in the station. A window, marked WORLD'S END TOURS looked out on the corridor. Below, in script, was the company's motto: *Adventures from Home to World's End.* Inside, a young woman sat talking to an AI.

Rachel had worked almost four years out of that office, serving as captain of the *Silver Comet*. The *Comet* was a Merrill, the Eagle of its day, although it carried fewer people, a maximum of eight passengers. They had several standard routes. But, for an additional consideration, World's End would customize a flight, "to accommodate passenger interests." I wasn't sure what that meant.

The standard routes allowed passengers to get a look at ringed giants and black holes. They could lob illuminated globes at neutron stars and land on beaches to relax under alien suns. If they had a desire to do so, they could swim in an ocean where nothing, ever, had lived. The clients inevitably liked to party. The schedule of events showed something happening every evening. I doubted it had been much different during Rachel's time.

The young woman looked up, saw us, and smiled. "Let's go say hello," said Alex.

"We're not going to schedule a flight, are we?"

"I don't see any point in doing that. How long's an average flight last?"

I looked through the advertising. "Shortest one looks like eight days. Up to four weeks."

He nodded. "They used to be a lot longer. Technology wasn't as good at the turn of the century, of course. Then the flights ran as long as four months. To the same destinations. Or at least to ones at the same range. The long ones were generally the hunting trips."

"They went hunting?"

"They still do." He led the way into the office. "Good morning."

"Hello," said the woman, her eyes brightening automatically. "Can I help you?"

"I'm Alex Benedict. We'd like to see Miriam Wiley, please."

"Is she expecting you?"

"No. Actually, she isn't."

"I see." She pressed a button and studied a screen. "I'm sorry, Mr. Benedict. She's not available at the moment. I'll be happy to assist you if I can."

"This is important. Would you please tell her I'm here. That I'd like very much to talk to her?"

"One moment, please. I'll connect you with my supervisor."

It took a minute or two, but they apparently bypassed the supervisor. The next voice was also a woman's: *"Mr. Benedict, this is Miriam Wiley. I'm surprised to hear you're on the station."* Her image appeared on-screen. She was a dark-eyed, dark-skinned woman with a surprised smile.

"It's nice to meet you, Ms. Wiley."

"Can I assume you're the *Alex Benedict?"*

"Not sure about *that.* I deal in antiquities."

"Yes, indeed," she said with a sly grin. *"So I've heard. Arma, send them in, please."*

Miriam Wiley was a retired pilot who had, at seventeen, charged into a collapsing building at a reclamation project to rescue an injured worker. On another occasion she'd taken over a taxi when its AI system malfunctioned, and ridden it to a safe landing, narrowly missing a swimming pool filled with gawkers who, apparently, didn't have enough sense to clear out.

She stood up as we entered, came over, shook our hands, and suggested we all sit down and relax. "We don't get many visitors out here," she said. "At least not famous ones."

Her pilot's license, in a silver frame, hung on the wall behind her desk. The walls were covered with pictures of Eagles, flying through ring systems, gliding over lunar surfaces, standing by while a blast of white light emanated from *something* too far away to identify. The one that caught my eye was of an Eagle riding above a cloudscape, silhouetted against a partially obscured crescent moon. She tried to pretend she knew me by reputation, too, but she stumbled over my name. "What can I do for you?" she asked. "Were you planning on taking one of our tours?"

"No," Alex said. "Unfortunately, we're here on business at the moment."

"Tracking a rare artifact, no doubt."

"No doubt." Alex smiled. They both smiled. Miriam was on the make.

"Too bad. I'd be more than happy to offer you our special VIP rate. You'd find a vacation with us to be a glorious experience." She shifted those dark eyes in my direction, suggesting that I might consider urging him to take the offer. That I'd enjoy it myself.

"Miriam," said Alex, "have you heard of Sunset Tuttle?"

"Who?"

"Sunset Tuttle? He was the guy who was always looking for aliens."

"Oh, yes. Sure. There was a vid based on him a few years back."

"Okay. We're looking into the possibility—and it's *only* a possibility— that he might have made a major discovery connected with a World's End flight."

"With one of *our* flights? What kind of discovery?"

"First of all, we're talking thirty years ago."

She laughed. It was a pleasant sound. "That's well before my time. I've only been here six years."

"Have you taken any of the tours yourself?"

"Of course," she said. "It's part of the job. So what's the discovery this Tuttle *might* have made? Did he find aliens on one of our tours?" The smile became even brighter. Suddenly, I was sitting there feeling foolish.

"No. At least not that we know of."

"Okay. So—?"

"There's an outside chance, though, that one of your captains may have encountered an extraterrestrial civilization."

She laughed again. Even more skeptically. "Which one?"

"Rachel Bannister. Would it be possible to look at the flight logs?"

"I can't see that there'd be a problem with that. I'd have to edit them first."

"Edit them how?"

"Remove the names of the passengers. You want to see those, you'd need a court order."

"Okay. No, we don't care about the passengers, so that wouldn't be a problem."

"Good. Which flight logs did you want to look at? What year?"

"It was 1403."

"Oh, no," she said. "Sorry. I wasn't thinking. I can't do that."

"Is there a prohibition of some sort?"

"No. I mean the logs from that period don't exist. They only go back to 1405. That's ten years before current ownership took over. I should have realized when you mentioned thirty years that I wouldn't be able to help you."

"I'm sorry to hear it."

"We're only required to keep the files for ten years, Alex. Walter—he was the CEO here previously—followed the letter of the law. We keep everything now. Have done since the new management took over. But 1405's as far back as we go."

"What do you know about the tours at the turn of the century? Were they the same as the ones you offer now?"

"Pretty much. We visit spectacular places. Do some specialized flights. You know, hunting, camping, that sort of thing. We've done interstellar weddings. We've taken people for rides on asteroids. We've even done a couple of ordinations. Did one two years ago, and another the year before that. So no, nothing's changed very much. We have different destinations, of course, because we have a lot of repeat business. People want to see new stuff. But the nature of the flights is about the same."

"Miriam, did they ever lose anyone? Was there ever an incident?"

"No. At least nothing I know of." She glanced around the room at the framed pictures. "Thank God, we've been fortunate. And we've always had good people."

"Do you have any records at all from the earlier years?"

She shook her head. "Not a thing, Alex. We don't even have maintenance records. Which they were supposed to keep. Hell, we don't have the advertising stuff anymore. We don't know where the ships went. We've got nothing." She raised her hands in surrender. "Sorry."

TWELVE

Is there someone in your life who's been taken for granted? Someone who's never been given the thanks he or she deserves? Here's your chance to make up for lost time. Take that person on our special Appreciation Trek. Call for details.

—World's End brochure, 1431

When we got home, we immediately began looking for those who'd ridden World's End in the years during Rachel's tenure. The company itself provided no help. So we did a search for people who'd commented about vacations with them. We talked to avatars and read journals and consulted biographies. With few exceptions, they had good things to say about the flights. Service was generally reported to be excellent. Typical responses: "Oh, man, Marsha Keyes was on board. I felt sorry for the comedian they'd brought in. I mean, how do you perform when *she's* in the audience?" (I've no idea who Marsha Keyes was.) And "Great experience. I've never known anything like it. There was this huge solar flare—" And "Best show for the money in town. I'd do it every year if I could, and I'll tell you this: I'm going to see that my grandchildren get to make the trip."

The negatives were inconsequential: Prices were too high. The onboard food wasn't what they'd expected. The captain was grouchy. One woman even claimed they'd almost gone off and left her stranded "on a moon somewhere."

The *Walter* that Miriam had referred to was Walter Korminov, who'd been the company's majority shareholder and CEO at the turn of the century. He'd hired Rachel in 1399, and whatever might have happened had happened on *his* watch.

He was officially retired, though he headed the Bronson Institute, which helped support medical facilities. He was also on the boards of several other philanthropic organizations. His home was on an island in the Questada. When I called for an appointment, I couldn't get past his secretary. Mr. Korminov was extremely busy and wasn't currently giving interviews. If I wished to submit questions, I was directed to do it in writing. No avatars, please. Usually, Alex's name opens doors everywhere, but not this time. The secretary had no idea who he was.

So we tried a different approach. Korminov did a lot of speaking engagements. We saw that he was scheduled to address the Interworld Medical Association dinner and, a few days later, the annual Pilots' Association luncheon. "Best," Alex said, "is to approach this as casually as we can."

I got the point and arranged for tickets to the Pilots' Association event. The luncheon, which moved around the globe each year, was on the other side of the planet at the Cranmer Hotel in Armanaka. When Korminov got to the lectern, we were there.

"I'm honored," he said, "to have been invited to speak to you folks. From all of us who benefit from your contributions, let me say thanks. When I was young, I wanted to be what you *are*. I wanted to be on the bridge of an interstellar. But they discovered I have a color problem. I can't tell brown, green, some shades of blue, from each other. They told me they could fix it, but I didn't like having anybody monkey with my eyes, so I backed away. Harry, here"—he indicated a man at one of the front tables—"told me that if I scared that easily, it was just as well. My point, ladies and gentlemen, is that I'd rather be sitting down there at one of the tables with you than standing up here trying to say something significant."

After that opening, he could do no wrong. We laughed and applauded and got to our feet when he suggested a constitutional amendment that would require those who set interstellar policy to be licensed pilots.

Later, when I tried to recall what he'd said overall, I couldn't remember much. The pilots were showing the way *somewhere*, and he hoped that we would continue to support the efforts of the Bronson Foundation, which was also doing work from which everyone benefited.

He ended by assuring us that, "if I could come back in a hundred years, and the Pilots' Association is still here, still conducting its luncheons, still filled with people like *you*, then I'll know the Confederacy is in good shape. Thank you very much." He stepped down to a standing ovation.

"The guy's good," said Alex, as the emcee wound things up.

We'd arranged to get Alex introduced to Korminov, and if his secretary hadn't known who he was, Korminov did. We had no trouble sitting down with him for an apparently incidental conversation.

Korminov was about average size, but he *seemed* big. He had a big voice, even when he was talking one-on-one, and his demeanor suggested a familiarity with command. His hair was beginning to gray at the temples, but his blue eyes retained the vigor and enthusiasm of youth. They could lock onto you and not let go. And they combined with an amiable smile to communicate his intentions far better than words ever could. He let me know without saying a word, for example, that he would have enjoyed taking me home that night. If I cared to make myself available. And if not, that was okay, too. Alex, who was usually pretty observant, later claimed he saw nothing. I should add here that Korminov's wife, a tall, attractive blonde, maybe forty years younger than he was, was standing off to one side, laughing and talking with her own groupies. How he would have managed an assignation that night I have no idea. And yes, I know you're thinking I imagined it all. But I didn't.

We went immediately to a first-name basis. And when, after a few minutes of idle talk, Alex casually mentioned World's End, Korminov responded by banging his fist on the table and letting us know that the touring company had provided the ride of his life. "I always regretted leaving the place," he said. "I loved the work over there."

We were nursing drinks, and Alex took a moment to stare over the top of his glass at a passing woman. "I wonder who *that* is?" he said in an admiring tone. Korminov followed his eyes, shook his head, and passed silent agreement across the table. Then Alex said, "Why's that, Walter?" He made it sound as if he wasn't really that interested but was just being polite.

"We used to throw welcome-home parties for the clients. A lot of them had never been off-world before. And they'd come back after some of the stuff we showed them and tell us that the experience was priceless. And a lot of times they'd taken their kids. I remember one woman, Avra Korchevsky I think it was, something like that. I ran into her years later and she said how, after going out with us, her daughter for the first time came to understand what kind of place she lived in. That her worldview literally changed. That she'd never been the same since. Alex, I still get mail from people, physicists, cosmologists, mathematicians, even artists and musicians, telling me that it was one of our flights that got them started on their careers. A life-changing event. I hear it all the time. Even after all these years."

Alex finished his drink. "Why did you leave World's End, Walter?"

"That's a long time back. I don't know why I sold it. Wanted to move on, I guess. Make more money doing something else. I was still young then. Dumb. I've always regretted it."

"How are they doing now?" Alex asked.

"I understand sales are in a downturn. Costs are going up." He looked around at the crowded tables. "The Pilots' Association has become pretty active, so captains cost a lot more than they used to. And they need to replace two of the Eagles. I'm not sure how they'll manage that. Of course, the bad economy doesn't help. But I'm sure it'll turn around.

"The real problem, I think, is that people today stay home more than they used to. In the old days, the tours were a thriving business. Couldn't accommodate the demand. But no more." He stopped to stir his drink. "I'll tell you, Alex, people have lost their sense of adventure. Most people would rather sit in their living rooms and let the world come to them. I mean, they can move clients around a lot quicker than they used to be able to. People can see more stuff now. In less time. And that's largely because of *you*." That was a reference to the *Corsarius* incident. "But they no longer want to travel several days to pull up alongside a comet when they can get the same thing at home. Parked in a chair." His voice carried a note of sadness.

"But the virtual technologies have always been there," I said.

"I know. I don't understand what's happening either. People are changing. It used to be they wanted the real thing. Wanted to know they were actually in orbit, or actually walking through a forest on another world. Now"—he shrugged—"they'd rather be comfortable. And not be inconvenienced in any way. Even the customized flights are way down."

Alex stopped to ogle another young woman. The behavior was totally out of character for him. But he was using it to frame the conversation. To conceal where his interests actually lay. Still, I'll admit it made me feel mildly defensive.

"Customized flights?" I said. "What were *they*, Walter?"

"They do weddings. Take your vows in the ring system at Splendiferous VI." He grinned. "Do a bar mitzvah by the light of the Triad Moons. I mean, in the old days that stuff couldn't miss. We did graduations, specialized vacations. You won't believe this, but one of the most popular things we had was the farewell tour."

"What was the farewell tour?"

"We'd take somebody who was near the end, usually someone who'd never been off-world, a great-great-grandfather, say, and a passel of friends and relatives, and we'd take them all out to some exotic locale a hundred light-years away. Of course we didn't call it the farewell tour except behind the scenes. The official term was the Appreciation Trek.

"There was other stuff. Sometimes we had a group of people with a particular interest. They'd tell us what they wanted, hunting oversized lizards, maybe. You know, the kind of thing you needed a projectile to bring down. Those made me a bit nervous, I'll admit. We stopped it after we almost lost a couple of our customers." He signaled a server, asked if we wanted another round. Alex said yes because that would keep him talking. Then Korminov turned toward me: "You look like a skier, Chase."

"I've done a little."

"We had a flight you'd have enjoyed."

"A skiing tour."

"We had the longest known slopes in the universe. And you got to take them at low gravity. I'll tell you, it was a ride. I'm pretty sure they're still doing it. And there was a tour for explorers, for people who just wanted to be first to look at a place where nobody else had ever gone."

We broke it off for a few minutes. Alex didn't want to be seen as pressing. We talked about the Bronson Institute, and how good people weren't going into medicine anymore because the AIs did so much of the work. Soon, Korminov said, it would be all robots. And when some problem came along that was a bit different and needed some judgment, nobody would be there. "Mark my words," he said, "make it automatic, and we'll forget how to be doctors. Then there'll be a plague of some sort and—" He shook his head. The human race was doomed.

Alex mentioned that I was a pilot.

"Yes," he said. "I remember reading that somewhere. You're exactly the kind of person we used to look for to run the tours."

We'd mapped out the conversation ahead of time. And the prime issue had just opened up. "Walter," I said, "I'll tell you the job I'd have loved."

"What's that, Chase?"

"To be the person who went out and decided where to send the tours."

"Ah, yes. The scout."

"It sounds like the best piloting assignment in existence."

"It was exciting." He glanced over at the lectern. "Chase, I was talking up there about my own ambition to be a pilot. And that was the job I wanted. Scout. Going to places where nobody else had been. And charting them. Now, the prospect of running one of those damned missions would scare the devil out of me." He fell silent.

"You know, Walter," Alex said. "I met one of your former pilots recently. Rachel Bannister. Do you remember her?"

"Rachel? Of course. Sure. I remember her. Beautiful woman."

"She'd have enjoyed inspecting systems, I suspect."

"I'm sure she would." Suddenly, he discovered he needed to circulate a bit. "Well, I have to be off," he said. "Been nice talking to you guys."

*   *   *

There were two other pilots at the event who'd flown for World's End. One had been there at the turn of the century. We got talking, and I asked casually if he knew who'd been the scout.

"The what?" he asked.

"The person who determined where the tours went."

"Oh," he said. "Sure." He smiled wistfully. "It's been a long time." He cleared his throat, thought about it. Mentioned someone named Jesse. Then corrected himself. "Hal Cavallero," he said. "Yeah. Hal was the guy who set up the tours."

THiRTeeN

Don't throw anything away, Clavis. There is nothing that does not gain value with the passage of time.

—Tira Crispin, *The Last Antique Dealer*

In the morning I had a call from Somanda Schiller, who was the principal at the William Kaperna High School, located on Capua Island, about sixty kilometers offshore. I was scheduled to talk with some of the students there two days later. It would be a group of seminars about what we do, and why artifacts are important, and why it's essential to learn from history. It was a presentation I'd done several times before in different places. The teachers always seemed to like it, and the kids were usually receptive. I enjoyed doing them because I like having an audience and playing VIP.

Somanda was a large woman with a pale complexion and the look of someone who'd seen too much nonsense ever to take the world seriously. She was standing by a window. *"Chase,"* she said, *"I'm afraid we're going to have to cancel your presentation. I'm sorry about the short notice. If you've incurred any expenses, we will of course meet them."*

"No," I said, "it's okay. Anything wrong?"

"Not really. What we've run into— Well, I just didn't see it coming."

"What happened, Somanda?"

"We have some parents who think that what Alex does is objectionable."

"You mean recovering artifacts?"

"*Well, that's not the way it's being phrased. A lot of them see him as someone who, ummm, robs tombs. As a person who sells what he finds instead of donating it to museums. And that he expedites others who trade in what they consider an illicit market.*"

"I see."

"*I'm sorry. I really am. Be aware that this is in no way a reflection on you.*"

Hal Cavallero had left World's End in the early spring of 1403. According to his bio, he wanted to take some time off, "just to enjoy life," but he never went back. He eventually landed with Universal Transport, where, for thirteen years, he'd hauled commercial goods around the Confederacy. Then, in 1418, he went home to Carnaiva, a small town in Attica Province, on the plains. There, he and his second wife Tyra adopted a four-year-old boy. They became members of the Lost Children Council, adopted six more kids, and founded the Space Base. Volunteers pitched in, the Council contributed funds, and eventually the Base became a shelter for more than one hundred orphaned or abandoned children. Cavallero received recognition for his work, including the Pilots' Association's Ace Award for his contributions.

Three days after the pilots' luncheon, I was on an overnight glide train headed north, watching the weather turn cold. It's a long run through bleak, cold forests. Eventually, the train comes out into the Altamaha Basin, which was lake bottom at one time. Now it's rich farmland. There was a two-hour stop at Indira, the heart of the funeral industry (known locally as Cremation Station). I got out, walked around, stopped at a gift shop, and eventually went back to the train. Several new passengers were on board. Three women and two kids. One of the women caught my eye. Not because of her striking appearance. In fact, she would not have stood out in a crowd. But her features suggested she would have made a perfect mortician. She was pale, somber, thin. Looked emotionally detached. She strode past me, eyes focused straight ahead, and slid into a seat. Then it was on to Carnaiva, where we arrived at midmorning.

At Alex's suggestion, I hadn't called ahead. Best not to alert anybody. Don't give Hal time to think about it. Reduces spontaneity, he said.

"We want spontaneity."

"Absolutely."

Carnaiva was the last stop on the line. The town was surrounded by trees, the only ones in sight anywhere in that otherwise-bleak landscape. They acted as a shield against the bitter winds that blew in from the north.

The town was a haven for old families that had known one another for centuries. Nobody moved into Carnaiva; but those who moved out, according to local tradition, inevitably came back. It was a place, the locals said, where it was still possible to live close to nature. That was certainly true. If you liked hard winters, flat prairie, subzero temperatures, and fifty-kilometer winds blowing out of the north, Carnaiva was the town for you. The locals were proud of the frigid weather. I heard stories about how people sometimes wandered out in the storm and weren't seen again until spring.

The town had money. The houses were small, but flamboyant, with heated wraparound porches and a variety of exotic rooftop designs. They were closer together than you'd usually see in a prosperous community. I suspected that was because, once you got past Carnaiva's perimeter, once you walked out through the trees, the world went on forever, absolutely empty in all directions. So the herd instinct took over.

The population was listed at just over eight thousand. Its sole major business enterprise was a plant that manufactured powered sleds. It was also the home of the annual Carnaiviac, where kids of all ages came to race their sleds in a series of wildly popular competitions.

There was a church, two schools, a synagogue, a modestly sized entertainment complex, a handful of stores, a few restaurants (like Whacko's and the Outpost), and two nightclubs. Nobody could remember the last time there'd been a felony crime, and Carnaiva was the only town on the continent to make top score in the annual Arbuckle Safest Place to Grow Up Survey. The view from the train station suggested it was also the quietest place on the continent.

Everything was within walking distance. I'd brought a bag, which I checked into a locker. Then I stopped for lunch at the Outpost.

I wasn't sure I wanted to try Whacko's.

The Space Base covered several acres of forest along the edge of Lake Korby, which was located two kilometers south of the town, and which, the townspeople claimed, was frozen except for a few weeks in the middle of the summer. I rode out in a taxi and passed above a sign identifying the place. It carried a silhouette of an interstellar, with the watchword, NO LIMIT. The fact that piers and boathouses lined much of the lakefront suggested that the locals were prone to exaggeration. The lake *was* frozen when I was there, however, and the boats were apparently stored for the winter.

In a cluster along the shoreline were a brick two-story building that served as school, chapel, and meeting place; a pool and a gym, both covered by plastene bubbles; and a couple of swings for the hardy. Cabins, which served as living quarters for the kids and staff, were scattered through the area.

The taxi set down on open ground. *"Mr. Cavallero's usually over there,"* the AI said, indicating one of the cabins. It was fronted by a sign that read ADMINISTRATION. More swings stood off to one side. Two girls, both about twelve, were just coming out of the cabin. They were bent into the wind, each trying to hang on to an armload of ribbons and posters.

I paid up, climbed out, and said hello to the girls. "Looks like a party," I added.

One, dressed in a bright red jacket, smiled. The other laughed. "Victory celebration," she said.

"Sporting event?" I asked.

"Cross-country."

We talked for a minute or two. The event hadn't happened yet. There'd be eighteen kids competing. Only one of them would win, but the entire organization would celebrate. "We have a lot of victory parties."

I walked up to the front door. *"Good morning,"* said the AI. *"Can I help you?"*

"I hope so. My name's Chase Kolpath. I'm working on a research project, and I'd like very much to speak with Mr. Cavallero."

"One moment please, Ms. Kolpath."

A cold wind rattled the trees, and a few snowflakes dislodged from the rooftop and the trees and blew around. Branches creaked, though the swings never moved. I wondered if they were frozen in place.

The door opened, and a redheaded man in a heavy white shirt looked up from behind a desk. He gave me an expansive smile and got to his feet. "Ms. Kolpath," he said. "I'm Hal Cavallero. What can I do for you?"

"I'm doing some research," I said. "I'd like to ask a few questions, if I may. I won't take much of your time."

A fire burned quietly.

"We don't often get beautiful strangers in this part of the world. Sure, I'd be happy to help." He looked older than I'd expected. Sallow cheeks, lots of lines around his eyes. There was something in his expression that suggested he was fighting a headache. Two children, a boy and a girl, were on the floor playing cards.

I explained that I was a staff assistant at Rainbow Enterprises.

"Okay," he said, growing serious. "Who's Rainbow Enterprises?"

"We do historical analysis, among other things. We're currently working on a study of the touring industry as it was at the turn of the century."

"I see." The girl, who'd been watching me, waved. I waved back. "I'm sorry to tell you this," he continued, "but I don't see how I can possibly be of any help." He took a moment to introduce the kids, Emma and Billy. "Our newest acquisitions."

"They look as if they're enjoying themselves."

"Oh, yes. They always have a good time. Where are you based, Ms. Kolpath?"

"Call me Chase."

"Chase, then." He chewed on his lip for a moment, trying to decide, I guess, whether we'd both go on a first-name basis. He must have decided against it. "Where are you from?"

"Andiquar."

"You've come a long way. I'm surprised you didn't check with me first. Or just call."

"I was in the area. We're talking to a lot of people."

"I see." He pushed back from the desk. "I'm glad you didn't come all this way just to see me. I really don't think I have much to contribute."

"This is a lovely operation. The kids here are all orphans?"

"Not all. Some were abandoned."

"Well, when things go wrong, it's nice that there are people like you to pick up the slack."

He looked embarrassed. Shrugged. "I'm doing it for selfish reasons. I enjoy the work."

The door opened, and a girl about seven looked in. "Mr. Cavallero, they're ready," she said.

"All right, Sola. Tell Ms. Gates I'll be there in a few minutes." She smiled brightly and left. "They're playing broom hockey and need another referee."

"Broom hockey?"

"It's very popular here." He instructed the AI to look after Emma and Billy. Then he said good-bye to the kids and turned my way. "I have to go, Chase. But there's no reason you can't watch if you'd like."

Two groups of second-grade girls, wielding short brooms, took each other on. Cavallero and one of the teachers refereed the action. The kids, five on a side, giggled and screamed as they charged up and down the floor, trying to put a sponge into one of the small cages at each end of the room. Everybody had a good time, and at the conclusion of the game, they celebrated with ice cream. "What other job," he asked me, "could give so much pleasure?"

We went back to the cabin, and he settled in behind his desk. I sat down on a love seat. The children were gone. "Okay, Chase," he said, "what did you want to know?"

I explained that I was trying to get a handle on the day-to-day operations of the tour companies. "We're talking to the administrative staff, the pilots, the people at the launch points. I was hoping you might be able to answer a few questions."

"I hate to say this, but a history of the touring companies sounds pretty dull." He looked up at an antique wall clock. The implication was clear enough. He had amiable features, but the edge in his voice clashed with them. He was tall, with eyes the color of frozen seawater. The years had taken their toll on him. He looked tired. Weary.

A picture of a young man and a teenage girl was mounted on his desk. "Sandra and Tom," he said. "My kids."

And another picture atop one of the bookcases of a much younger Cavallero and an attractive young woman. It was Tyra, his wife.

"Mr. Cavallero," I asked, "have you gotten completely away from starflight? Or do you still go out occasionally? Maybe take the kids for a ride?"

"I keep my license current. But what does that have to do with anything?"

"Just idle curiosity. I'm a pilot myself, and I can't imagine that I'll ever really get away from it." It was the reason I'd made the trip, and Alex had stayed home. You'll have better rapport with him, he'd insisted.

"You're probably right, Chase. But I haven't been on the bridge or in a cockpit for a long time. Have no inclination to anymore."

"But you still maintain your license?"

"I don't think I'll ever really let go." He managed a smile. "You look cold. Can I get you some coffee?"

"Yes, please. That would be nice."

He went into the kitchen, returned with two cups, and set them on the table. "Careful," he said. "It's hot."

"Thanks." He looked, somehow, afraid. "When you were piloting, Mr. Cavallero—"

"Call me Hal—"

Okay. First name at last. "When you were piloting, Hal, you had the kind of job most of us dream about."

"What? Delivering construction materials to someplace where they are trying to build a settlement? And making the same run time after time, for years? I don't think so, Chase."

"I meant when you were with World's End. When you ran the scouting missions."

"Oh," he said. "That."

"You don't sound—"

"It was okay. I can't complain about it. They treated me well."

"You were going into areas where no one had ever been before."

"That's true."

"That's why most of us *become* pilots. To do something like that. But those jobs barely exist."

"I guess."

"You don't sound as if you cared very much."

"Sure I did."

"But you quit."

"I got tired of it. I got married while I was working for World's End. They didn't pay all that well, so I left."

"You were born here, right? In Carnaiva?"

"Yes. This is where my family is. My kids and grandkids are all here. Well, almost all. Tom's gone. He works for the governor."

He described life at World's End. How you had to be a member of the Korminov family to move up in the organization. "Walter was okay, but his wife was tough to live with. And Abe."

"His son?"

"Yeah. He did supply and maintenance. I don't think he liked the work very much. And he had a high opinion of himself."

"Where is he now?"

"I don't know. He and his father had a falling-out, and he left for parts unknown. I don't think Walter's heard from him in years."

"What about the wife?"

"Ran off with a preacher."

"You're kidding."

Cavallero cheered up. This was the part of the story he liked. "Nope. They went out to the islands somewhere."

The coffee was good. He tossed another log into the fire and explained with a smile that his wife was helping out down at the church while he refereed the hockey games.

"All right," I said. "Let me ask a couple more questions, then I'll get out of your way, Hal."

"I'm at your service."

"The scouting missions, as I understand it, determined where the tours went. Right?"

"Yes. Just to be clear, we went back to the same places regularly. But we had a company policy of changing the destinations after a given number of visits. Walter thought clients were more likely to come back if we did something different periodically. And sometimes we needed to customize a trip. Somebody wanted to go see a neutron star. Or a world with crooked rings. Or dinosaurs. That sort of thing. If they were willing to pay, we were prepared to make them happy."

"How about telling me what a good scouting mission would look like? What would make a good place for a tour?"

"Spectacle. That was what we liked. Big colorful rings. There's nothing like a big set of rings to knock people on their rear ends. One of the tricks we used was to approach ringed worlds on a ninety-degree angle. So that the rings were vertical instead of horizontal. I'll tell you, it just took their breath away."

"Good," I said. "That's the kind of thing our readers will be interested in."

"Aren't you going to write it down?"

Alex had told me not to take notes during an interview unless I wanted to achieve a special effect of some kind. You take notes, he told me, people are inclined to shut up. Ask any cop. "No," I said. "Stuff like the rings, I can remember. Easily. So what else did you look for?"

"Comets," he said. "Comets are good."

"Big ones?"

"The bigger the better. Also, the clients liked double planets, and getting in close to cool stars, so that the star fills the entire sky. We'd transit the thing upside down. That created the illusion that it was overhead.

That the entire sky was on fire. They *loved* that. And black holes. Black holes were always good. There's one at Werewolf."

"Where?"

"Werewolf." He grinned. "You won't find it in the catalog."

"I didn't think so."

"We had our own names for everything."

"Do you know where it is? Could you find it now?"

"As I say, Chase, it's been a long time. I don't—" He closed his eyes, shook his head. "No. I've no idea. I'd have to go back to the records."

"The records don't exist anymore."

"Oh. Yeah. That's right. They delete them after, what, ten years or so? That's dumb, because some of that stuff they could still use."

"So why do you think they deleted them?"

"Because the people running the company are morons. They think sites can be exhausted. Like fuel." He checked the time. "Listen, Chase, I'd love to continue this, but my daughter will be home soon, and we have some work to do."

"One more minute?"

"Okay."

"Tell me about Bannister."

"Who?"

"Rachel Bannister. You must have known her. She was a pilot for World's End at the same time you were."

"Oh, yes. Rachel." The color was draining from his cheeks. "Wow. That's a long time ago."

I waited.

"I don't know. She was a competent pilot. Looked pretty good. That's mostly all I can remember. As best I can tell, she got the job done okay."

"She quit about the same time you did."

"Did she? I don't remember." He shrugged. Got up. "Have to go."

"Was anything going on at the time? Any reason the two of you would have left?"

"No. Not that I know of."

"The flights she made, they'd have been to places *you* scouted, wouldn't they?"

"Yes," he said. "Probably. Chase, do you mind if I ask what this is about?"

"I'm just trying to get it clear in my head how the system worked."

"But how does that have anything to do with Rachel Bannister?"

"Probably nothing, Hal. Was anyone else running scouting missions at that time?"

"Lord, Chase, I really don't remember. I don't think so." He sat back in his chair. "You know, this is beginning to sound like a grilling. Is something going on here that I should know about?"

"Well, okay. Let me level with you."

"Please do." He swallowed.

"We're trying to track down the origin of what might be an artifact. A tablet with a strange inscription."

He shrugged. "Don't know anything about it."

"All right. One last question, Hal. Do you know where Rachel Bannister went on her last flight?"

He looked at me and somehow couldn't break away. There was fear in his eyes. "Hell, I have no idea." His voice shook. "I barely remember *her*, Chase. Let alone a last flight."

"He's hiding something," I told Alex when I got home.

"What do you think it is?"

"I don't know. But he knew Rachel better than he was willing to admit."

"I wouldn't be surprised." We were riding home from the train station. "While you were gone," he continued, "I was able to track down some of the families who went on the tours. During Rachel's time."

"And—?"

"Hugo Brockmaier was a corporate lawyer. In 1399, he and his wife Mira went out with World's End to celebrate their sixtieth anniversary. Rachel Bannister wasn't the captain. But they took time on the flight to record the highlights. It provides an interesting picture of what they actually did on some of these flights."

"And you've got the record?"

"Yes."

"You've seen it?"

"I haven't had a chance to look at it yet. Just at the description they sent with it. I think we should watch it tomorrow."

At home that evening, I received a call from Yolanda Till. Yolanda had been a close friend since we were little kids growing up in Neuberg. We'd been in the Explorers together, had both been on the swim team, had shared boyfriends, and roomed together in college. We'd kept in touch. Yolanda had become an engineer and eventually gone to work for New Dallas Historical, which specialized in archeological excavations. She was currently involved in a recovery project on Mars in the home system. *"But that's not why I called you,"* she said.

"Where are you *now*?" I asked.

"On approach to Skydeck. Just passing through. Won't get time to stop. I'm here to check some details on a cargo flight. Going back out with them in a few hours." She pushed her dark hair back. *"You look good, Chase."*

I loved Yolanda. I couldn't imagine those early years without her. "I suspect," I said, "we could still clear the tables at Wally's." The bar we used to hit when we were seniors.

"Oh, yes," she said. *"We need to do a rerun before you get married, sweetheart."*

"What makes you think I'm getting married?"

"You've got that look. Is it going to be Robin?"

We did some more girl talk before she came to the point. *"Chase, New Dallas is going to be hiring two pilots this month. When I heard about it, I immediately thought of you."* She flashed that big smile that had never changed. *"They pay pretty well."*

I pretended to think it over. Didn't want to reject the idea out of hand. "I don't think so, Yolanda," I said finally. "I have a good situation here."

"Okay, Chase. You know, you'd have some upward mobility, which you probably don't have with Alex. And, with a little luck, we might be able to manage some time together."

"That part of it would be nice. But I'm really not ready to make a change."

She hesitated. The smile faded, and was replaced by concern, the way she used to look when she disapproved of a guy I was going out with. *"All right. I'd thought—"*

"What, Yolanda?"

"That you'd be anxious to get away."

"Why would you say that?"

"Never mind, Chase. Let it go."

"Seriously: What were you about to say?"

"Well, life with Alex must be stressful. You never say anything, but I can see it sometimes in your eyes."

"Yolanda, I have no idea what we're talking about."

"Okay. Look, I know you and he have made major contributions. And I wouldn't take anything away from that—"

"But—?"

"But, you know what Alex's reputation is in the academic world. He's a looter, *Chase. You know that as well as I do. I just thought maybe you'd want to get clear. It doesn't help your reputation either, you know what I mean?"*

"No," I said. "I'm fine. I like working for him."

"Okay. No offense. Anyhow, I expect to be back during the summer. Maybe we can get together then?"

PART II

Parties in Flight

FOURTeeN

The human race will never make peace with itself. The reason for that is not ongoing tribal instincts, as some would have it, but the sheer joy of wreaking destruction. The pleasure one gets from building, say, a town hall, does not approach the exhilaration to be had from blowing it apart. I don't know why that is, nor can I advance an evolutionary rationale. It is something we do not talk about. But I will confess that my one great regret in life is that I have gone through so many years and never had an opportunity to drop a bomb on something.

—Timothy Zhin-Po, *Night Thoughts*

THE BROCKMAIER FAMILY GOLDEN ANNIVERSARY RECORD, 1399

Alex and I watched them toast the golden couple, watched the Brockmaiers and their friends and relatives dance the night away in a trendy dining hall, while a band played and toasts were offered. The happy couple wandered the floor, shaking hands, embracing friends and relatives, posing for pictures. They were surrounded by children and grandchildren. The holo included an attachment that would have allowed us to identify everybody had we been of a mind to do so.

Hugo Brockmaier was a corporate lawyer, and obviously a guy who ate too much. He sported a well-maintained beard, wore a smile that might have been pasted on, and spoke with precision and point, as if every word were significant. Wisdom for the ages.

His wife Mira was, other than the children, possibly the most diminutive person in the room. But I'd have bet she was one of those people who worked out every day. She wore a flowing white gown that contrasted with her dark skin. She had smooth black hair, so bright it might have been polished, and dark eyes that constantly looked out at me as if she were aware of my presence.

Alex fast-forwarded through the party and the good-byes and the ride to the spaceport. The arrival at Skydeck flickered past. The two celebrants moved laughing and talking through the concourse, and finally we got a look at the *Night Star*, which would take them out to Serendipity, where they'd transfer to the tour ship. "Any indication where they're going?" I asked.

"Not really. It's a place World's End called Celebration. God knows what its catalog number is."

They reached the boarding area. Mira must have been taking the pictures because mostly we were seeing Hugo. Hugo handing tickets to the agent and getting waved on. Hugo, despite the light gravity, tromping up the ramp and through the hatch. Hugo inspecting the *Night Star*'s lush interior. Hugo shaking hands with other passengers.

We followed them to Dip, which, even though it was thirty years ago, looked better than its current incarnation. Once there, they checked in at the World's End office, got their tickets, and, a few hours later, boarded the *Mercury*.

Its cabin was big and elegant. Eight seats were spread out, designed so they could be rotated. The backs were adjustable. There was no separate bridge. The pilot operated from a cockpit at the head of the cabin, presumably so the paying customers could watch. His seat and the control panel were on a recessed section located a half meter lower than the passengers' deck. There was a second seat for a navigator or copilot immediately to his right.

The rear of the cabin opened into a padded passageway, which contained sleeping quarters and washrooms, a workout section, and a combination dining and recreation area.

Four of their fellow passengers were already seated. A tall blond male in a captain's uniform was running through preflight. He was well along in years, one of those guys with a serene exterior who could reassure you that everything was under control while you were being sucked into a black hole. As another couple came through the hatch, he finished, turned around, and got out of his chair. Hugo was operating the imager, and we watched Mira smile for the captain. *"Welcome aboard, folks,"* the captain said. *"World's End Tours is pleased to have you along. If there's anything we can do to make your flight more comfortable, if you need anything at any time, don't hesitate to ask."*

"The captain," said Alex, reading from a set of notes that had accompanied the holo, "is Adrian Barnard. He was from Maraluna, and he's retired."

"Do we know who the other passengers are?" There were three other couples.

"We have first names, but that's all."

Well, it didn't matter.

It was impossible to trace their course. Or even to know how long it took them to get to their destination. They threw several parties en route. When they arrived, everybody applauded. There were pictures of a sun and a set of rings. Mostly, though, we saw Mira looking out the viewport and Hugo sitting in the copilot's seat. Eventually, we found ourselves looking at a rockscape. Part of an asteroid, probably.

We drifted through the rings and looked down at the surface of a golden gas giant.

Then there were more celebrations. People wore party hats. Hugo offered a toast to a couple, who explained they *"come out here all the time."*

The viewports were unlike any I had seen before. Normally, ships have standard models. But, when Barnard gave the word to April, *Mercury's* AI, the entire front of the ship became transparent. I understood then that the captain and the control panel were at a lower level so as to keep the view unimpeded for the passengers. It was a breathtaking moment for me, and I was simply watching a hologram. God knows what it was like for the people actually seated in the cabin.

I was still gawking when a robot showed up to serve drinks. Somebody offered a toast to the captain.

They had several more while a bright star appeared in the wrap-around. *"Does it have a name, Captain?"* asked one of the passengers.

"Out here, Phil," he said, *"almost nothing has a name."*

Most of the passengers went below and boarded a lander. One or two elected to stay where they were. The launch doors opened, and they soared out into a sky that was bright red but had no stars. The engines fired, and they were on their way.

They drifted down to a cratered surface that glowed in the scarlet light. "What's going on?" asked Alex.

"It's a cool sun," I said. "They're in pretty close."

The captain gave the AI a direction, and the lander's overhead simultaneously darkened and rolled back. The bulkheads vanished, and it was as if we were all sitting out on the surface. Everybody was staring up, mouths open, looking at a sky so completely dominated by the sun that nothing else was visible.

Later, back in the *Mercury*, they caught up with and rode alongside a comet. The comet had rounded the sun and was heading back out into the deeps of the planetary system. Consequently, the head of the comet was at the rear, its tail blown ahead by the solar wind.

"It is inspirational, isn't it?" said one of the passengers. I agreed.

The captain touched a switch, and the comet faded to a dim streak. He turned a dial, and we saw an asteroid. "Ladies and gentlemen," he said, "this is our bullet."

Their "bullet"? I glanced over at Alex. He signified he had no better idea than I did.

As the passengers watched, the asteroid tumbled slowly through the night.

"Prime real estate," said Hugo. Apparently someone else had the imager, because we were looking at both Hugo and Mira. Mira smiled pleasantly at her husband. *"You thinking of moving, dear?"*

"How far are we?" asked one of the women. *"From the comet?"*

The captain relayed the question to the AI. *"Ninety-one hundred klicks,"* the AI said. Her voice was that of a middle-aged mother. Best for family outings.

Alex laughed. "She probably has seductive settings, too." The *Mercury* was behind the asteroid. I couldn't tell how big the asteroid was because I didn't know the range. The comet was a few degrees to starboard. And I knew what they were going to do.

The asteroid tumbled slowly through the night. It was like pretty much every other loose rock in the cosmos, lopsided, battered, worn. Been there a long time. But I could sense that the people in the cabin were proud of it. This was *their* asteroid.

The essence of any good tour, of course, is that it is a party on wheels. So to speak. They closed in on the rock, and they kept the glasses full.

"It looks like a lonely place," said a woman who looked barely out of her teens. Her name was Amy, and she seemed to have a connection with a considerably older man who reminded me of our longtime family physician. They were close enough by then that the asteroid had actually taken on the appearance of a world. Well—a world in miniature, maybe.

Mira said, *"It needs a name."*

They argued for a while, and settled finally on Louie. One of the other women, pale-skinned, with glittering wealth on display, announced that she thought Louie was the perfect name. This was Janet. *"Yes,"* she added, *"I like it."*

They raised their glasses toward the screen. Toward the asteroid. *"Here's to you, Louie."*

"To Louie," said Mira. *"May you make your mark."*

Mira wondered how old Louie was.

The captain lifted his hands. Who knew? *"Couple of billion years, probably. Maybe more than that."*

"It's beautiful," one of the women said.

The captain smiled politely. "Well, that's what World's End is all about. We take your breath away."

And they did. The captain got behind the asteroid, maintaining a range of about five kilometers. We watched its broken surface rise in the wraparound. The passengers gasped and laughed and held on to their seats. Shadows moved across the rock as it turned slowly over in the glare of the sun. The captain was enjoying himself. He obviously loved the job. I wondered where he was today.

One of the passengers sent a wistful sigh to the Almighty. And we could still see the comet, its long fiery tail stretching across the stars.

The captain matched velocity with the rock. Then he got up from the pilot's seat. *"Mr. Brockmaier,"* he said, *"you have the conn."*

Brockmaier had the conn? He was a *lawyer.*

Alex grumbled something about what the hell was going on.

"He's not really turning control over," I said. "That would be crazy. The AI has it. Brockmaier knows it. Everybody knows it. It's all part of the ride."

Hugo produced an officer's cap and, as he came forward, put it on at a jaunty angle. He lowered himself into the captain's chair. *"Okay, April,"* he said. *"Ready to go."*

"At your command, Captain Brockmaier."

Hugo couldn't suppress a grin. That last line had a nice ring to it.

"Give 'em hell, honey," said Mira.

The passengers clapped. Hugo threw a glance at the captain. The implication was clear: Hugo could run this thing for real if it wouldn't upset everybody.

The captain sat down beside Mira. I'd expected him to take the co-pilot's seat, but he left Hugo on his own. It was more dramatic this way, and that was, after all, what the passengers had paid for.

Hugo studied the instruments as if he knew precisely what he was doing.

April enlarged the image of the asteroid on the main screen. *"Everybody lock in,"* she said. *"You, too, Skipper."*

A security lamp went green.

"Okay, April. Let's do the rock. Stay at a range of five hundred meters, and match course and speed."

"Complying, Captain." April's voice was soft and calm. Everything was under control.

They closed on the asteroid. It grew in the wraparound, and grew some more, until it was directly in front of and slightly beneath the ship. Until they were close enough to make out every crevice and crater. Then, gradually, it slid beneath them, disappearing, though they could still see it on the navigation screen.

"Range five hundred," April said.

Hugo leaned right and studied the panel. *"Okay, April."* He tugged at his beard. *"Take us down."*

"Beginning descent."

"Navigation lights, April."

They came on and bathed the battered, pockmarked surface.

Cracks and jagged ridges crisscrossed everywhere. As they descended, the horizon simultaneously widened and retreated. *"Angle on the target."*

They moved to starboard. And the comet appeared directly over the horizon. Dead ahead.

"Done, Captain."

Target? Belatedly, I realized what they were going to do.

The comet was getting big and getting bigger. The system provided a crosshairs for Hugo. It didn't do everything automatically. That would have taken the fun out of the operation. The challenge was to get the timing down, pick a point of collision, and put the asteroid on course.

"Target range?" Hugo asked.

"Twenty-six thousand kilometers."

"Louie's approach velocity?"

"Forty-two thousand."

"So when—?"

"Louie will impact, or cross the orbit, in thirty-seven minutes."

They moved in still closer. Perspective shifted, and suddenly we were looking *down* at the surface.

"Do you know what they're doing?" Alex asked.

"They're going to use the antigravs to guide the asteroid. They've got juiced-up versions, level-four plates probably, on the prow. They don't just negate the standard gee force, the way level-one units do. Level-four plates actually create a counterforce. A strong one. They push the ship away from the object. So, to move the object, the ship fires its engines and pushes. Theoretically, they should be able to control the flight of the asteroid. To a degree. They're aiming at the comet."

"But they can't even *see* the comet now."

"They don't have to push the whole time, Alex. They'll estimate what they need, give it a shove, then let go and check to see how they're doing. Meantime, April knows where everything is, even if she can't see it."

"You ever hear about anything like this before? Banging asteroids around?"

"It's a technique used in construction projects. I never heard of anybody doing it for entertainment."

"*Ready to lock on, Captain,*" said April.

Hugo nodded. Straightened his cap. He was seriously into it. "Do it."

They got it on the first try. The comet dissolved. And all that remained was a long, sparkling tail.

FiFTeeN

Those flickering candles in the endless night . . .

—Elizabeth Stiles, *Singing in the Void*

I don't usually eat out unless I'm with somebody. My lunches at the country house routinely consist of raiding the refrigerator and munching down a sandwich while I keep working. All the mental-health editors insist that sort of behavior leads to problems, so I've promised myself to change. I rarely actually do it, though. But the day after we watched the Brockmaier flight, Alex was out of the building, and I deserved a treat.

There were several places nearby. I decided on Tardy's, which has good food, decent prices, and soft music. It's located on a two-by-four island in the Melony, just upstream from the falls.

I like Tardy's. They've dispensed with the bots, everybody's very friendly, and for reasons I've never understood, the place draws good-looking guys. But all the males appeared more or less worn-down or married that day. I ate quietly in one of their booths, looking out at the river, taking my time, not because it was a slow day but because I have a tendency when I eat alone to rush through the meal. So I proceeded deliberately, and even ordered a dessert, some cherry pie, half of which I left because the one problem with Tardy's is that the portions are too large. When I was a kid, I had the screwball notion that restaurants knew what

was best for you, and they gave you precisely what you needed. Finish
your plate, love, my mom always used to say. Don't waste food.

Anyhow, I finished, paid up, and started for the door. But I noticed
a woman at one of the tables who jarred my memory. She was tall, thin,
serious-looking, not the kind of person, probably, who'd break you up
with a funny line. She was eating alone and never looked my way.

I was still thinking about her when I went out the door into the parking lot. Tardy's had its own, but it was small, and you had to come early
to get a space. They had a larger area, across the river, connected to the
island by a long, covered viaduct. If you chose, or were forced, to use
the viaduct, you could walk or ride on the glideway. I usually parked in
the big lot because I enjoyed riding across the river, especially in the late
autumn. It was beautiful at that time of year, filled with gulls and *galians*
and all kinds of birds that hung around the restaurant, hoping for a
handout. I just made myself comfortable on the glideway and watched
the river go past.

The Melony narrowed at that point, so the current moved right
along. About a kilometer downriver, it would squeeze into the Chambourg Canyon, accelerate to a roar, blast through a lot of very large
rocks, and plunge twenty meters over the Chambourg Falls. The owners of Tardy's had been trying for years to move the restaurant onto the
rocks just above the falls, but fortunately the effort always caused such
outrage that the politicians didn't dare approve it.

I was halfway across when I realized where I'd seen the woman at the
table before. She'd been on the train to Carnaiva. She was the one who'd
gotten on at Cremation Station. The Mortician.

I looked back at Tardy's. The place had a ramshackle, boathouse feel.
Part of its charm. A bunch of gulls went squawking past. I thought about
going back. But coincidences happen.

An hour after I'd returned to the office, Jacob informed me we had a call
from Brian Lewis. *"He wants to talk to Alex."*

"I'll take it," I said.

I'd been trying to track down the whereabouts of the Steven Silver copy of the Confederate Constitution. At the time of the signing, 326 copies were made. One had eventually gotten into the hands of Silver, a world-famous collector. He'd died, and it had disappeared. The thing was worth a fortune. Alex had been tracking it for two years, but the trail had gone cold. So I needed a minute to concentrate on the figure materializing in the middle of my office. My first thought was that he wanted to take advantage of the cash offer we'd made for a chance to inspect the tablet. "Hello, Brian," I said. "How are you doing?"

He did not look happy. *"I've been better, Chase. Is Alex there somewhere?"*

I think I've mentioned that Brian was a big guy. When I'd seen him earlier, at the Conneltown field, and out over the ocean, he'd seemed hostile and annoyed. That was gone. He waited in front of me with his guard down. "I'm sorry, Brian, but he's out with a client. Can I help you?"

"Could you contact him?" He was dressed casually, and appeared to be in the front seat of a parked skimmer. The door was open, and his legs hung out over the edge of the vehicle. I had the distinct sense that he'd been about to go somewhere but had stopped on sudden impulse to make the call.

"I can't, Brian. He shuts down when he's out with somebody."

He wiped his hand against his mouth. Chewed on his lip. *"Okay,"* he said. He was about to disconnect.

"Brian, what can we do for you?"

He hesitated. Then: *"Not a thing, Chase. Sorry to take your time."*

"Must be something," I said.

"I need to talk to him."

"About the tablet?"

He climbed down out of the skimmer. It was the Sentinel. *"I guess."*

"Brian, is it okay with you if I record this conversation? That way I can pass it on verbatim to Alex."

"Sure. I don't care. Record whatever you like."

"Okay. We are now on record."

"Fine."

"Our offer still stands, Brian."

"*I don't really want your money. That isn't what this is about.*"

"Okay." Long pause, while we stared at each other. "What *is* it about?"

"*Rachel.*"

"I'm listening."

"*Look, let me tell you up front that I have no idea what's going on here. Why she is the way she is. But she's a good woman—*"

"Okay."

"*Anyhow, I wanted you to know that you and Benedict have turned her into a nervous wreck. I'm scared something will happen.*"

"Why is she nervous, Brian?"

"*I just told you, I don't know. I have no idea what any of this is about. What I do know is that she means a lot to me. She's one of the best people I've ever known. And you two are ruining her. I don't know what you're after, and I don't know what the problem is, but I wanted to ask you to stop. Please.*"

"Brian, the tablet might be an artifact from an alien civilization."

"*I'm sure you know how crazy that sounds, Chase. Anyhow, I don't really care. I just don't. Nothing is worth what you're putting her through.*"

"I'm sorry to hear that. I'm sure Alex isn't happy about any of this either."

"*Yeah. That's fine. You and he are sorry you're turning her life upside down.*"

"Have you asked her why she's so upset?"

"*Once.*"

"What did she say?"

He closed the door. "*She just shakes her head. No. Won't talk about it. Can't talk about it.*"

"Does Doug know what it's about?"

"*No.*"

"Aren't *you* curious, Brian?"

"*Yeah, I'm curious. Of course I am. But she doesn't want to tell me. That's good enough.*"

"Okay."

"*Look.*" He was having a problem with his voice. He started to say more, stopped, took a deep breath. Then: "*I wish I could buy you guys off.*" Another pause. "*I'm not in a position to do that. But I would consider it a personal favor if you and your boss would just back away. Please.*"

"Okay."

"*Does that mean you will?*"

I hadn't been able to get Rachel out of my mind. She'd lied to us, and played mind games with us, and maybe had hired someone to get rid of us. Still, her plea that we leave her alone had contained a note of desperation. If that, too, had been an act, she should have been on the stage. I wanted to tell Bryan yes, that we'd back off. That it was over. But I couldn't speak for Alex. "It means," I said, "that I'll show him the record and have him get in touch with you. He'll be in later this afternoon."

I was feeling increasingly uncomfortable. I had no idea what Rachel was hiding, and I wasn't sure I wanted to know. I couldn't bring myself to believe she was actually behind the attempt to kill us although no one else I could think of was likely to want us dead. I was becoming more convinced that the entire business was going to end badly for everyone involved. And I decided to make an effort to persuade Alex to drop the investigation.

When he got back, I ran the conversation for him. He listened, took a deep breath, and told me he'd talk to him. He asked if we had any hot chocolate brewing, got one, and took it upstairs. After a while he came back down. "I called him," he said.

"What did you tell him?"

"That we were investigating an artifact and not Ms. Bannister. That it was potentially of historic significance, so we couldn't simply walk away from it. I told him that we were willing to listen to what she had to say, and if she could give us a good reason to stop, we would."

"What did *he* say?"

"He wasn't happy."

"Alex—"

"Yes?"

"I'm not either."

"I know. This is hard on everybody." He sat down. "I'm sorry. I wish we'd never seen the tablet."

sixteen

Eagles commonly fly alone: they are crows, daws, and starlings that flock together.

—John Webster, *The Duchess of Malfi*

Next morning, Alex was waiting for me when I arrived at the country house. "We may be getting close to Conover, Chase."

Tuttle's compatriot. The guy who inherited the logs and, later, dropped out of sight. "Where is he?"

"I don't know. But I think we may have located someone who can tell us where he is."

"Who's that?"

"Pinky Albertson. Back in the good times, she was his bartender."

"His bartender?"

"What can I tell you? A lot of people have mentioned her. Some say if he was going to keep in touch with anyone, it would have been Pinky."

"Ummm. Was he a lush?"

"No. Apparently, they were just very good friends."

"So where is she?"

"That's the problem."

"You don't know."

"No. It's just that it's a long way. We'll need the *Belle-Marie*."

"Where are we going?"

"Starburst."

*   *   *

"We're never going to be able to manage this, are we?" Robin asked, when I told him I was headed out again.

"I don't know. I guess I could get a job as a bookkeeper."

"I make more than enough for the two of us."

It's an enlightened age, fortunately. Teachers are well paid. But— "I can't see myself just hanging around the house, Robin."

"You'd make a pretty good teacher."

"Don't have the patience. If you want me, you're going to have to take me as I am."

"You mean missing for weeks at a time—"

In the morning, minutes after I'd arrived in my office, Audree called. *"It's okay,"* she said, when I told her I'd connect her with Alex. *"I don't want to bother him. I know how busy he is right now."*

"Sure. What can I do for you, Audree?"

"You guys haven't gotten any more odd packages, have you?"

"No. We haven't found out what that was about."

"Fenn still doesn't have anything, I guess?"

"If he does, he's keeping it quiet."

She looked subdued. Worried. *"You think it has anything to do with the tablet?"*

"What's Alex telling you?"

"He doesn't want to talk about it. Says it's still an open matter."

"That's pretty much what I've heard, too."

"What do you think, Chase?"

"I don't know. We tend to make a few enemies in this business. Sometimes, just putting a buyer and a seller together can irritate somebody you didn't even know was in the mix."

"But this was more than somebody's being annoyed."

"Well, maybe. For what it's worth, Audree, I only know a few lunatics, and all of them have a passion for artifacts."

She laughed. *"Are you guys actually going to find out what this is all about? The tablet, I mean."*

"There's a decent chance."

She was in her office at the Geologic Service. *"Chase,"* she said, *"are you by any chance free for lunch? My treat?"*

"By all means."

"Girls' day out."

"Sure," I said. I smothered an impulse to suggest we invite Alex.

We met at Cooley's on the waterfront. I got there first, but had just sat down when Audree strolled in. She saw me, waved, and swept past the host's station. We resumed our conversation where we'd left off, which made it a discussion about the tablet. "I honestly wouldn't care one way or the other," she said. "I mean, we're talking about little green men, for God's sake. What does it matter? But it means so much to Alex."

I ordered chicken and rice; I don't recall what Audree had, mostly because she seemed distracted by more than little green men, and that had the effect of distracting *me*. But I let it go, knowing that she'd get to whatever was bothering her in her own good time.

Cooley's had been her suggestion. The food was okay, the ambience relaxing, and we could watch sailboats tacking past. But I think the critical element for her was the music. They had a pianist, and the guy was superb. "I wish I could play like that," she said.

I'd heard her play. "You're not bad, Audree," I said. "If you had the time, I think you'd be at his level. You're close enough now that I'm not sure I could tell you apart."

"Chase, you're very kind." Her eyes glittered. And I watched her making up her mind. "Got a question for you."

"Sure. What is it?"

"I think I might be falling for Alex."

I looked at her. Smiled. Took her wrist. "You could do worse," I said.

"Would it create a problem?"

"You mean for me? You mean are he and I emotionally involved?"

"Yes. I mean, I know Alex says there's nobody else, and I think—"

"Audree, I *love* Alex. But I don't mean *romantic* love. Sure, I'm emotionally attached. And I wouldn't want you to grab him and take him off someplace where I'd never see him again. But other than that, I'd be delighted if you became a permanent part of his life." I stopped, weighed my next words, and decided what the hell. "Of *our* lives."

She seemed relieved. "I was wondering because—"

I knew why. The long rides, just the two of us, Alex and me, in the *Belle-Marie*. And the shared missions, generally. The media treated us as if we were a couple. Nobody ever said that flat out. But the implication was always there. My folks had even pressed me about it, several months earlier, trying indirectly to find out when Alex and I would be getting married. When I told them it wasn't going to happen, they behaved as if I was being coy. "How's *he* feel about it?" I asked.

"I don't know. He's noncommittal. He may be cautious around women generally, or it may just be me."

"I think that's his disposition. I know he likes you quite a lot. Does he know how you feel?"

Her eyebrows lifted. "I don't see how he could have missed it. But you know how guys are." We finished the main course, and the dessert arrived, strawberry shortcake for me, chocolate pudding for her. When the server was gone, she continued: "He's one of a kind, Chase."

"I'd agree with that. And I wish you luck with him."

"Thanks."

I couldn't resist: "If I'd staked a claim to him, you wouldn't really have backed off, would you?"

That got a huge grin. "Chase, I'm glad we can still be friends."

Four days later, we docked at Starburst Station at Grand Salinas and confirmed Pinky Albertson's presence. She was the proprietor of the O.K. Bar and Grill. When we arrived, the host informed us she wouldn't be in for several hours, so we checked into the Pretty Good Hotel. The tradition at Starburst could best be described as one of understatement. They had Carbury's Restaurant, where the food was "reasonable," and Jack's Game Show, which featured VR performances that were "interesting." My favorite was Kristin's Beauty Shop, where you could be made to look "not bad."

As on most space stations, time tended to be flexible. It might be almost midnight for people arriving from groundside or high noon for those coming in on the transports. You could always get breakfast, and the middle of the night was inevitably subjective.

For us it was early morning. After we got checked in, we went down for bacon and eggs. Then we wandered through the station, which is one of the biggest in the Confederacy.

It had a concert hall, where a group called Starfire would be performing that evening. The place where we'd eaten had a comedian scheduled. And we saw a group of schoolchildren composed of both humans and Mutes. They were accompanied by two female adults, one from each species. "You know," said Alex, "making the adjustment was such a struggle, I'm not sure it would be a good thing to find another race of aliens." It was the first time I'd ever seen kids from the two species together.

When it was time, we went back to the O.K. Bar and Grill. The place had an ancient Western motif, cowboy hats hung on the walls, old six-guns and holsters on display, a few wanted posters for Jesse James and Billy the Kid, and an announcement for the annual Claremont Roundup.

It was odd that we didn't know the names of most of the major world leaders during the nineteenth century but we knew a few cowboys. "You think they really existed?" I asked Alex.

"Probably not," he said.

We ordered a couple of drinks and asked if Pinky Albertson was available. The host asked our names, spoke into his sleeve, listened, and nodded. Then he led us out of the dining area and pointed to a staircase. "Second level," he said. "Turn left, second door."

The name didn't match. Pinky was a tall dark woman with lustrous features, black hair, and a husky voice. She was sitting on a long sofa talking with a middle-aged couple who were just getting up to leave. After they were gone, Pinky invited us in.

"Alex and Chase," she said. "Which of you is Alex?"

Alex responded, and she invited us to sit. "What can I do for you?"

"We're trying to find Hugh Conover," said Alex.

"Does he know you?"

"We've never met."

"May I ask what this is about? Hugh doesn't normally get visitors."

"We're doing some research. We'd like to ask a few questions about Sunset Tuttle."

Her lips curved into a smile. "Ah," she said, "good old Sunset." She studied each of us in turn. "I'm not sure Hugh would be receptive to an interview."

"We won't be a problem for him," said Alex. "I don't suppose he's on the station?"

"On the station? No, certainly not." The music from downstairs drifted up. There was a burst of laughter. "He's on Banshee," she said.

"Where's that?"

"It's in the Korvall system. About eight light-years."

"Can you tell us *where* on Banshee?" I asked.

She looked my way, apparently surprised I had spoken. "He doesn't exactly have an address, Chase."

"Why's that?"

"He and Lyra—she's his wife—they are the only people on the planet. Or at least they were last time I looked."

"Okay."

"They're in the southern hemisphere, I can tell you that much."

"Thank you, Pinky," said Alex. "Is there any way to reach him?"

"Sure."

"Can we send him a message now?"

"If you like. There'll be a moderate charge, of course. And a bit of a delay. But certainly, you can contact him if you like. Text or audible?"

"Audible."

"Okay. Wait one." She raised a hand, index finger pointed at the overhead. "You're on."

Alex explained who we were, using the standard story that we were working on a history of Survey's early years. And we hoped to talk with him about Tuttle. He kept it short and concluded by assuring Conover we would not take more than a few minutes of his time.

"That everything?" Pinky asked.

"Yes."

"You want to review it?"

"No. I think it's okay."

She told her AI to send the message. "We won't get a response for at least"—she checked the time—"at least a couple of hours."

"Am I correct," asked Alex, "that Mr. Conover comes here occasionally? To the station?"

"The Conovers have a few friends in the area. Drinking buddies. They come in periodically, and they all get together." She warmed a bit. "They know how to have a good time, I'll give them that."

It took more like five hours. We were back in the O.K. Bar and Grill, finishing another meal, when an answer came in. It was from Conover's AI. *"I am sorry. Hugh and Lyra are out camping. Unfortunately, they can't be reached. I do not anticipate they'll be available for at least two days."*

Pinky joined us a few minutes later. "How'd you make out?"

Alex let her hear the message.

"I guess best is to wait for him to get to you," she said.

"Have you been to Banshee?"

"Once."

"Can you tell us anything else about where he lives?"

"He's got a couple of survival pods tied together. But I don't guess that helps much."

"Not a great deal."

"Okay." She tried to think. "He lives on a lakefront."

"All right."

"And he's on a continent in the southern hemisphere."

"Anything more?"

"That's it. It's all I have."

"Do you know if there are any other habitations, houses, buildings, whatever, on Banshee?"

"I don't think so, Alex. We're talking about a world, and I've only seen a small part of it. But I can tell you there isn't anything close to his place."

seventeen

If you would grasp the reason for your existence, and reach the limits of what may be known, you must live on the edge. Get away from the crowds that distract and deflect. It is why we love mountaintops and deserted beaches.

—Tulisofala, *Mountain Passes* (Translated by Leisha Tanner)

Banshee was moderately larger than Rimway, but it was less dense, and consequently its gravity gradient was down a couple of points. It lacked the massive oceans that were characteristic of living worlds. There were seas, but they weren't connected into a single globe-circling entity. Polar caps were large, extending across as much as thirty percent of the planet.

Hugh Conover had what he'd always wanted: a world to himself. He'd made no secret of his wishes: Get away from the maddening crush of idiots. You couldn't escape them, he'd argued. They showed up on the talk shows, infested the web, wrote books, and won political office. They appealed to their fellow idiots, and the result was, not chaos, but life on a treadmill. Keep moving but get nowhere. Those kinds of comments—Conover had made no effort to conceal his opinions of the mass of humanity—had won him few friends.

Banshee had a lot of lakes. They were of all sizes, and they were scattered across the planetary surface like puddles after a heavy rainstorm. Some existed in mountain country and others on big islands that were themselves lost in the middle of larger lakes.

I saw no deserts, save one patch along the equator. And nothing that might have been described as a jungle.

"Looks like a cold place," said Alex.

It's odd: You see an uninhabited world, and you don't think anything of it. You look at Banshee, with two people sheltered somewhere on its surface, and you feel an overwhelming emptiness.

There was a single small moon. It was less than a hundred kilometers in diameter, a captured asteroid probably, and was at the moment almost half a million klicks from Banshee. "I doubt," I said, "that, from the ground, it would look like anything more than a bright star. Maybe not even that."

Alex was looking out the viewport, shaking his head. "Conover reminds me of Basil. I mean, neither seems to care much for a social life."

"He's *like* Basil?" I said. "Alex, this guy is Basil with a starship. By Conover's standards, Basil's in downtown Andiquar."

"Cavallero's another one," he said. But he waved it aside. Sociological chitchat. Let's get to the point. "What's the best way to find him? Look for his ship?"

"Sure. Belle, any sign of it?" We were just moving across the terminator onto the nightside.

"We have something up ahead, Chase. It should be the Hopkin." Conover's ship.

"Open a channel," I said.

"Channel's open, Chase."

I activated Alex's mike. "All yours, boss."

He nodded. *"Charlie Hopkin,"* he said, "this is Alex Benedict on the *Belle-Marie*. Please patch me through to Dr. Conover."

We got a burp of static. Then a baritone: "Belle-Marie, *this is the* Charlie Hopkin. *Dr. Conover is not on board and cannot be reached. I'm sorry."*

We were on Banshee's nightside. Below us, the darkness was unbroken.

"Hopkin, you can't get a message to him?"

"Do you have the code word?" Belle got a visual of the *Hopkin* and put it on-screen. It was an Atlantic, same model as the *Belle-Marie*. Older, though.

"No. I do not have a code word. Could you inform him that I'm here and would like very much to talk with him?"

"*I have strict instructions not to bother him for* non-code-word *visitors.*"

Alex covered the mike. "I don't believe it," he said.

"Don't believe what?"

"That the messages aren't being relayed. He wouldn't be dumb enough to cut himself off that completely."

"That's probably true. But we don't really know this guy. He might *be* dumb."

"I doubt it."

"Okay, then," I said. "I can think of one approach. Board the thing and take a wrench to the controls."

"You're not serious."

"We don't actually damage anything. Just pretend that we will if he doesn't answer. The AI would have to alert him, and I'd bet the farm he'd be in touch within seconds."

"Sounds like a great way to get his cooperation."

"Yeah, I know. That's the downside."

"Fortunately, Chase, there might be an easier way." He refilled his coffee cup and looked at the *Hopkin*, cruising amiably on the navigation screen. "The ship has to be able to contact him if necessary. So what sort of orbit do you put her in?"

"Oh," I said.

"Right." He held out his hands. Elementary. "It has to pass directly overhead."

"Sure." I felt like the slowest kid in the room. "We don't have an entire planet to search. Just the orbital area in the southern hemisphere over whatever continents there are.

"Okay," I said. "We can narrow the land area where he might be located to about nine thousand kilometers. But that's still a lot of area to cover."

"Of the nine thousand kilometers, Chase, how much do you think borders lakes?"

Okay. Suddenly, it sounded easy. I asked Belle whether she thought she could spot the target from orbit.

"Tell me what the house looks like," she said.

"Belle, it's a *house*."

"It's easier if I know, for example, whether I'm looking for a dome or a box or something in between."

"Rounded exterior. A pair of connected pods."

"I have a suggestion," said Alex. "Let's see if we can get the timing right, so we're always searching the nightside. Just look for lights."

Hunting for a single light on a planetary surface, especially in a place like Banshee, isn't as easy as it sounds. Clouds provide cover, forests get in the way, and there's still a lot of ground. But eventually we spotted him.

As a precaution, I asked Belle about the air.

"I see no problem," she said.

The lake where he was living was a solid sheet of ice, encased by heavy forest. Trees and shrubbery pushed out to the shore. A section of land at the northern tip of the shoreline had been cleared for the lander and the two survival pods Pinky had mentioned. Beside them, a house was under construction. Or had been abandoned partway through. It was impossible to know which. The pods were connected by a short enclosed walkway. The place was half-buried in snow. But someone was clearly living there: A stack of logs was visible near the front entrance, and smoke was leaking from chimneys in both pods.

The temperature was minus twenty-two Celsius.

Radio calls brought no response. We took the lander down and settled into the snow. At that point, while we were still in the lander, a door opened, and a gray-haired man wearing a sweater looked out at us. Finally, the radio came to life: *"Who the hell are you?"*

"I'm Alex Benedict, Dr. Conover. You *are* Dr. Conover, right?"

"If I said no, would you go away?"

"Probably not."

"Okay then, Benedict. What can I do for you?"

"We're doing some research. I was hoping you'd be willing to answer a couple of questions, then we'll get out of your way."

"They must be important questions to bring you all the way out here. Where'd you come from?"

"Andiquar."

"I can't imagine what could be so important." He folded his arms.

"I hope you don't mind."

"Me? Why would I mind? Well, you're here; you might as well come inside."

I pulled on the light jacket I'd brought with me while Alex slipped into a windbreaker and turned on the heater, but I didn't think it would make much difference. I opened the hatch and we got out, lowered ourselves into the snow—it came up to my thighs—and slogged over to the front door. A second person appeared behind Conover. Lyra.

They literally had to help us through the snow and into the dome. Conover closed the door. A fire crackled happily behind a grate. "This is Lyra," Conover said. "My wife."

Lyra looked delighted to have company. She wasn't young, but she had good features and a warm smile. "Let me get some coffee," she said. "Would you like something to eat?"

We agreed that we'd settle for coffee, and Lyra disappeared into an adjoining room.

Conover was a big man, wide shoulders, deep basso profundo voice, dark eyes, large bushy eyebrows. He looked like the kind of guy who repaired rooftops for a living rather than someone who did anthropology. But there was something about him that signaled military. His features did not reflect emotions, and he moved with precision and economy. No pointless gestures, a voice that remained level and calm, and no indication that anything could surprise him. Certainly not visitors at that remote place.

"Gets chilly in this part of the world," he said. He moved to help me off with my jacket, collected Alex's coat, hung them in a closet, and threw another log on the fire.

I could smell the coffee. We heard water running, and a refrigerator door opened and closed.

The interior was unadorned, except for two pictures, and a framed certificate acknowledging Conover's services to the National Historical Association. One picture was of himself and Lyra, taken in younger days. And the second was of an attractive young woman who might have been Lyra at about twenty. It caught Alex's eye also. "She's beautiful," he said.

Conover nodded. "My daughter." Brown hair, brown eyes, a good smile. I had a teacher once who said that the right sort of smile was all you needed to carry you successfully through life. If there were any truth to it, Conover's daughter was loaded for bear.

She lived on Toxicon, he explained. Had met a banker, and the next thing he knew, she was gone. He was clearly not pleased with the match, and I thought it seemed out of place to share that kind of intimate information with strangers. Then I remembered where he was living.

"That can be painful," Alex said. "But you didn't expect her to stay here, did you?"

"No," he said. "Of course not. And I know I'd have lost her anyway. When we told her we were coming here, she let us know how she felt. She was just out of school at the time, and it was a price we had to pay. Didn't we, love?"

Lyra was back in the room, with coffee and some warm cinnamon buns. She nodded yes. And her eyes told me it wasn't her favorite subject.

"She has a big family now," said Conover. He crossed his arms and waited for the next question.

"We were dubious at first about coming here," she said. "But Banshee has really been a remarkable experience. Hasn't it, Hugh?"

"It was her idea," he said. "But you don't care about that." He sat back. Tried his coffee. "So tell me again why you're here. What did you want to know?"

"You were a friend of Sunset Tuttle's?"

"Ahhh." He nodded. "Yes. Poor Sunset. Spent his life chasing a dream. Which isn't that bad if—" He hesitated.

"You succeed," Alex said.

"Yes. What a pity."

"Tell me about him."

"He was a driven man."

"So we've heard."

"What you heard was the aliens, right?"

"Yes. Is there something else?"

"Oh, yes. He was convinced that the human race was going to hell." He pressed his index finger to his lips, reluctant, perhaps, to say more. "You know about that, too?"

"It's on the record," Alex said.

"Yeah. I guess it is. And I'm not sure he wasn't right."

"What makes you say that?"

"The general decadence. Or maybe that's not really correct. The truth is that we've always been greedy and stupid. We have no imagination, and the only reason we've survived this long is that we produce just enough smart people to keep us going."

Alex nodded. "Let's get back to the aliens. Is there any indication that you know of that he might actually have found an alien world?"

Conover took a long pull at the coffee. "No," he said.

"He would have told you if he'd found something?"

"Alex, he'd have told the world."

"What about—?"

"Yes?"

"What about if he found something that might have been a threat? That would have been better left undiscovered?"

"Like what?"

"Maybe highly advanced aliens who wanted to be left alone?"

"That's a bit of a leap, don't you think?"

"Would he have told you about them?"

Conover's lips parted in a grin that suggested he'd never considered the possibility. "Let me say this: If he'd confided in anyone, I think it would have been me. But to answer your question, I suspect he would have felt compelled to remain silent."

"Thank you, Doctor."

"Please call me Hugh." He cleared his throat. "Are you suggesting such a thing happened?"

"No," said Alex. "It's only a hypothetical."

"Yet it's a hypothetical that brought you all the way out here."

"After Tuttle's death, Hugh, his logbook became your property."

"That's correct."

"May I ask why?"

"Because he and I were essentially dedicated to the same cause. Although he took it far more seriously than I did. I never expected success. He did. It's why he got into trouble."

"Would you be willing to show us the logs?"

"I'd be happy to, Alex. Unfortunately, I don't have them any longer. Our house was hit by burglars two or three days after I obtained them. They tried to disguise the purpose for the burglary by stealing a few items, some jewelry, and a few dishes. But I've always thought they were after the logs."

"You never loaded them into the system?"

"Part of the deal was that I would not do that. He didn't trust the security measures. He was afraid someone would get access."

"What difference does it make if there's nothing in the logs except reports of sterile worlds?"

Conover leaned forward and pushed his unruly hair back out of his eyes. "I don't know. I wrote it off as an aberration."

"Was Tuttle a guy who might have made unreasonable demands?"

"Not usually, no."

"Okay, Hugh, one last thing: Did you get a chance to read through them yourself?"

"No. A few of them. But I was just beginning when they disappeared."

"And you saw nothing out of the ordinary?"

He sank back into his chair. "Not a thing. It was just a record of failure. Like what I was going through."

"Who else knew you had the logs?"

"I don't know. Could have been anybody, I guess. I didn't make an effort to keep it secret."

Lyra smiled. Said nothing.

We sat listening to the fire.

"He's been dead a long time now," Conover said. "Maybe it doesn't make any difference anymore."

"Hugh, did you know Rachel Bannister?"

"Sure. Nice woman." He smiled at Lyra. "Not at your level, love. But she was pretty good."

Lyra smiled and rolled her eyes.

"What can you tell me about her?" Alex asked.

"Well, Sunset was in love with her."

"Was she in love with *him*?"

"I thought so. Yes."

"They never married."

"He'd been married several times when they met. I think she just recognized he wasn't a good bet for a marriage. She was conflicted about it. I saw her in tears a couple of times, but she was a tough woman, and I think she just realized that marrying him would ultimately turn into a disaster. Still, though, I suspect, had he lived, they *would* eventually have done it."

"One more question, Hugh."

"Sure."

Alex fished the photos of the tablet out of his pocket and handed them over. "Have you ever seen this?"

Conover examined them. Shook his head no. Passed them to Lyra. "What is it?"

"It was found in the garden at Tuttle's house. Basil told us he had seen it originally in a cabinet in his office. Tuttle's office."

"No, I can't say I've ever seen it before."

"We can't match the symbols with any known human system."

"Well," he said, "I wouldn't make too big a deal out of that. There've been a lot of alphabets over sixteen millennia. Especially after we left Earth."

We got to our feet. "Thank you," said Alex.

"The cinnamon buns were good," I added.

Conover got up. "Listen," he said, "anytime you folks are in the neighborhood, pop by and say hello."

"We'll need a code word."

"Just use your name. I'll tell the ship. Oh, and one other thing: If you actually find any little green men—"

"Yes?"

"Let us know. Okay?"

EiGHTeeN

They were four light-years away, but we could hear the noise as if they were in the next room.

—Susan D'Agostino, commenting on the celebration at the International Space Agency
when the first humans arrived in the vicinity of Alpha Centauri

For 113 years, beginning in 1288, when Tuttle was twenty-one years old, he pursued his ambitions with a vengeance. During the first decade, he had been an archeological intern aboard the *Caribbean*, owned by the Jupiter Foundation. When Jupiter had gone out of business, in 1298, he'd gone to flight school and spent the next thirty-five years with Survey, functioning as both a pilot and a researcher. But he became impatient with what he called their pedestrian objectives, measuring starlight characteristics and analyzing gravitational pulses in singularities. He sought financial help from people who wanted somebody to go looking for aliens. And he found a lot of enthusiastic supporters. At first he had to settle for a battered, ageing vessel, the *Andromeda*. After nearly killing himself when the meteor screen failed during a public-relations flight to Dellaconda, he was able to pick up more contributions and bought a second, far more efficient, vehicle. Originally the *Julian Baccardi*, he'd renamed it the *Callisto*. "*In the fond hope,*" he'd told an interviewer, "*that, like its namesake, she'll contribute to discoveries that will rock the sleeping culture in which we live.*"

His missions took him primarily into the Veiled Lady, but he didn't limit himself. He inspected systems on the fringes of the Confederacy, he traveled into the Colver Cloud, he went all the way out to the Hokkaido Group. And he did it with the old star drive. The technology that had been largely replaced in recent years. The result was that for the next half century, Tuttle virtually *lived* inside the *Callisto*. Despite this handicap, he married three times. And apparently won the heart of Rachel Bannister, who was a century younger than he was. When I looked at his picture, I couldn't imagine how he'd managed it.

He was usually alone in the ship. Occasionally, one of his wives went along. And Hugh Conover joined him for a few flights. During his early years in the *Callisto*, according to press reports, repeated failure did nothing to abate his enthusiasm. It was simply, he told one interviewer, a matter of time. He looked out across the sea of stars and could not believe they were not home to other civilizations. Could not believe other species had not risen from the dust and weren't asking the same questions we were. Was there a purpose to it all? Was there to be in time a coming together of intelligences from across the galaxy, to bring forward a new level of existence? New technologies to make life better? And shared arts to make it richer?

His critics, of course, pointed out that there'd been voyages to thousands of terrestrial worlds over thousands of years. They were, usually, sterile, completely devoid of life. And only once, in the long history of the species, had we arrived at a place where the lights were on.

Only once.

It was, Tuttle maintained, a failure of imagination. Later, he would argue that it was the enormity of the task that made the challenge worthwhile. *"We wouldn't recognize the significance of the gift if our neighbors were living on our doorstep."*

Gradually, though, as the years passed, the certainty gave way to hope, and finally to a kind of desperation.

"They are there," he'd tell the audience at a graduation ceremony near the end of his career. *"It is our part to find them."*

After the turn of the century, he no longer talked about the urgency of the search, the need for it. There were few interviews, and Tuttle knew the interviewers were laughing at him. So he didn't say much. Just that, no, he wasn't ready to give up, but maybe the task would have to be passed on to the next generation.

Occasionally, he responded to his critics: *"If everyone had thought the way they did, we would never have left Spain."* I wasn't sure what the reference was. Alex said, quietly, "Columbus."

Finally, his funding began to run out. His supporters had stayed with him for the better part of a century. They'd had enough. In 1403, he announced his retirement.

"Same year that Rachel and Cavallero left World's End," I said.

Alex nodded. "Something happened."

"What?"

"Answer that, and you win an engraved piece of rock."

Audree was waiting at Skydeck when we docked. And a service clerk from the station's florist arrived immediately behind her, with some roses for me. Robin had classes and couldn't get away, but he would call later.

We rode down in the shuttle. It was good to be home, but there was no getting past Alex's disappointment that Tuttle's logs had disappeared. "Well," Audree said, "you can't do much about a theft that happened a quarter century ago. Sounds to me as if it's time to pull the plug on this whole thing."

The comment made me realize how little she understood Alex. "Audree," he said, "it's just one more indication that something is going on here."

I'd hoped the logs would be available, and that we would discover nothing, so we could get away from this entire business. Despite the way she'd dealt with us, I *liked* Rachel. And I would have preferred to let things be. But asking Alex to walk away from the tablet when we still had no answers— It just wasn't going to happen.

When we got down to the terminal, Alex spotted Peggy Hamilton waiting at the gate. Peggy was the producer of *The Peter McCovey Show*, and she was looking for us. McCovey was a talk-show host, and attacking Alex had become one of his favorite pastimes. Alex was, in fact, the perfect target. Robs tombs. Steals vases that should be available to the general public. Creates havoc in archeological sites. The sort of thing about which the average citizen couldn't care less. Until McCovey made it sound as if Alex was stealing valuable items that belonged to his viewers.

Alex did an uncomplimentary grunt. "Chase," he said, "take care of her, will you? And tell her no."

"Who is she?" asked Audree.

Alex didn't have time to answer before Peggy stood before us, beaming pleasantly, saying how good it was to see us and asking whether Alex had found what he was looking for. "And by the way, what *were* you looking for?"

Peggy had long legs and a kind of confident gallop. I don't know how else to describe the way she walked in, circled round, and suddenly was striding along beside us. She tried hard to be friendly, casual, and sincerely interested in our welfare. She looked good, and reportedly had entertained early hopes for an acting career. She had the blond, innocent looks, but her problem was that she couldn't act.

"I'm pressed for time," Alex said, glancing up at the giant clock on the wall above the gift shop. "Why don't you talk to Chase?"

"Alex," she said, "I'll only need a minute or two."

Alex looked my way and saw I wasn't happy about his passing her over to me. So he stopped. "Peggy," he said, "I'm not able to do the show right now."

"Why not, Alex? You're one of our most popular guests. And Peter would be delighted to have you."

"I've been buried lately, Peggy. I'll get back to you when I have some time."

He tried to move away from her, but she stayed with him. "Alex, just tell me: Did this flight have anything to do with Rachel Bannister?"

"No," he said.

"Well, okay. That's not what we've been hearing."

Alex didn't like McCovey, and he hated Peggy's artificial smile and round-the-clock display of good cheer. But Audree was there, and he didn't want to look rude. "Whatever you've been hearing is inaccurate, Peggy."

"Well, why don't you come on the show tomorrow evening and make that point? Professor Holverson will be there. And we expect Peer Wilson, as well."

"Sounds like a good show, but I really have to pass." We were headed out the entrance, into the taxi waiting area.

"Alex," she said, "you understand that, if you refuse to participate, there'll be no one to tell your side."

"Peggy," he said, "I'm really too busy."

She turned to me: "Chase, how about you? We'd be delighted to have you sit in for your boss."

"No, no," I said. "Thanks anyhow. But I have terminal stage fright."

She nodded. "Okay, you guys have it your way. If you change your mind, Alex, you know my number." A smile flickered on and off. Then she sauntered away.

"I think you should do it," I told him when we were alone. It was the same position Audree took on the way home.

"I don't want to make any public statements until I know what I'm talking about."

"If you don't, they'll probably use the chair." That had happened a couple of times when Alex declined invitations to the talk shows. Just put an empty chair out there to remind the audience who was too cowardly to show up.

He was uncomfortable. "Seriously, I can't see any way I could go on that thing."

"You could always just say you don't have any answers yet, and you'll let them know when you do."

"I wouldn't be able to get away with it. McCovey would accuse me of stonewalling. 'What are you hiding, Benedict?'" He did a passable imitation of the unctuous host. "And he'd drag Rachel into it."

"They'll do that in any case," I said.

That evening Robin took me to one of his favorite nightspots, planning to dance the evening away. But that wasn't going to happen because I couldn't shake a dark mood.

He looked especially good that night. Over the years, when Alex and I had run into trouble, I'd always been supported by the belief that we were justified in what we were doing. Or at least that we had a good argument. But this time I didn't feel right about it at all. And it showed. Robin asked me what the problem was, and I told him. "And all you have is a few symbols on a rock?" he asked.

A few symbols on a rock. I couldn't get away from the sense that we weren't on a quest for an alien civilization so much as we were digging after a scandal.

Alex was right, of course: McCovey would zero in on Rachel. And somewhere between eleven and midnight, I made up my mind about what we should do.

I excused myself, went out on the balcony, and called Alex. "I think," I said, "we need to let Rachel know we're done with this. Warn her about McCovey, but assure her we had nothing to do with it. Tell her we have no intention of pursuing an investigation."

"We can't do that, Chase."

"Sure we can. Just walk away from it." I stood looking out at the city lights. Andiquar was a beautiful place, but in the late fall, it could get cold. It was cold that night.

"Chase, I understand how you feel—"

"I don't think you do, Alex. Look, people are entitled to their secrets. There's no evidence she's harmed anyone. Or Tuttle. Probably, there's nothing to any of this except some personal matter. Which is embarrassing to her."

"Like what?"

"I don't know. Maybe she had the rock made up to celebrate an illicit affair. It would be just the sort of thing that would have appealed to someone like Tuttle. Maybe we should be checking the local stonecutters to see if anyone has a record—"

"All right. I hear what you're saying. This thing is not giving me any pleasure, either. But I can't just let it go. If I did that, I'd be wondering about it the rest of my life."

"Alex, this isn't about *you*."

A few branches hung over the balcony. A sudden wind stirred them.

"*Okay, Chase. Thanks for letting me know how you feel. I understand. But I don't really have a choice here.*"

"Sure you do. But okay. You'll do what you want regardless of what I say. But don't expect me to defend the corporation's actions."

The following evening, we made ourselves as comfortable as we could in the conference room and settled in to watch. Jacob switched on the show, and we caught the closing segment of *Life on the Strip*, where they talked about entertainers and the upcoming schedule. Then it was time for Peter McCovey, and the host walked onto his book-lined set, grinning in that unctuous, self-important way, his slightly corpulent features silhouetted against the leather-bound volumes he probably never read.

"*Good evening, ladies and gentlemen,*" he said. "*Tonight there's reason to believe that the well-known anthropologist, Sunset Tuttle, may have discovered an alien civilization. Tuttle has been dead for almost thirty years, and the story is only now coming to light. Why? Is it that, as some experts think, the discovery was too terrifying to make public? Did it really happen? The eccentric antique dealer, Alex Benedict, who has a reputation for uncovering oddities, is on the job again. Is there anything to this? Are we possibly playing with fire? In just a moment, we'll ask our guests.*"

They went to a clothing commercial, how to look good and feel good in Blavis lingerie, which no man can resist. "It looks as if it's going to be a long hour," said Alex.

"It's hard to see how it could be anything else."

McCovey's paneled room expanded, and we saw that he had taken a chair. Three others were seated with him. And, no surprise, an empty chair had also been put in place. "*With us tonight,*" the host said, "*are, from Andiquar University, the eminent language specialist Peer Wilson; Sunset Tuttle's onetime colleague, now retired, Edwin Holverson; and Madeleine Greengrass, who found an interesting tablet in her garden.*

"*We invited Alex Benedict to join us, but he says he's too busy.*" That was accompanied by a wink and a smile.

They put up an image of the tablet, and Greengrass explained how she'd found it, and how Alex had shown an immediate interest, but someone else got there first. She looked much better than she had when I'd first seen her. More animated, more involved with what was going on. She spoke smoothly, with the easy confidence of a woman who spends much of her time leading discussions for tourists.

Then a question to Wilson as they all looked at the tablet: *"I've never seen an alphabet anything like this, Professor Wilson. Do you recognize it? Might the characters on the tablet actually have an alien origin?"*

Wilson smiled. Tall, recondite, with a quiet, calm demeanor, he was the aristocrat in the room. *"Might they? Of course they might. Anything's possible. But if there's any other evidence, I haven't seen it. I mean, it could easily be a creation of Looney-Pack. It's only a piece of stone with a few unfamiliar characters on it. It doesn't mean anything."* He went a bit further: *"To understand what's really going on here, you have to know about Benedict. Look, Peter, I'd be the last person on the planet to denigrate the solid contributions he's made. I mean, what he's done isn't bad for a guy who sells antiques for a living. But he's inclined to turn everything into the Holy Grail. Does somebody bring him a flowerpot that dates from the Time of Troubles? Well, it must have belonged to Andrew Koltavi. That's the way he operates. He loves the spotlight. And I don't mean by that to attack his character. A lot of people are like that."*

Greengrass described her conversations with me, suggested I was "emotional," and said how the tablet had always been in the garden. She didn't know how it had gotten there.

At that point, the host introduced a clip with Teresa Harmon, who'd bought the house from Basil Tuttle. She'd found the tablet in a cabinet and couldn't bring herself to get rid of it. *"I'm the one who used it to decorate the garden,"* she said in the clip.

"Were you, at any time," McCovey asked Greengrass, *"offered money for it?"*

"I was."

"By whom?"

"By Chase Kolpath."

"Representing Benedict?"

"Yes."

"Did they offer much?"

"Yes. A lot."

"What was your feeling when that happened?"

"I was shocked. And I'll tell you, Peter, I was sorry I'd let it get away."

"Did you try to recover it?"

"When I found out it had been taken by what's-her-name, Rachel Bannister, I called and asked to have it returned."

"And what did Ms. Bannister say?"

"She told me it had been dropped in the river."

"Dropped in the river?"

"In the Melony."

"I should mention for our audience," McCovey said, *"that we also invited Ms. Bannister to participate. Like Benedict, she had other things to do."* He turned back to Greengrass. *"Did she do that on purpose? Drop the tablet in the river?"*

"Apparently."

"Why?"

"She said she'd changed her mind and didn't want it after all."

"Did you know that there's been an attempt to locate it in the river? That no one can find it?"

Greengrass looked annoyed. *"Is that true? No, I wasn't aware of that."*

McCovey turned to Holverson, who looked as if he'd been sitting in his living room too long. He'd been around for a lot of years, and it showed. He was also overweight. And he had a self-important, methodical response time. Ask him a question and he'd lean forward, nod, suck on his lower lip, and thereby make it clear that here was the unvarnished truth. *"Professor,"* McCovey said, *"a week ago, you were quoted as saying there was no possibility that Tuttle could have discovered an alien civilization and kept it secret. Do you still hold to that view?"*

"No," he said. *"I've had time to think about it. And I've come to realize there are several reasons why, if he'd seen anything, he might not want to go public with it."*

"For example?"

"Well, the obvious one is that they could be very dangerous. Maybe it's a society that would like to have us for dinner."

"What else?"

"Once it gets out, you can't control access. Every nitwit with a ship would want to go take a look. Maybe, if there were aliens, they simply asked to have their privacy respected."

"Would Tuttle have gone along with that?"

"It's funny. There was a time I thought that being known as the discoverer of an alien civilization would have been more important to Sunset than the discovery itself."

"But you don't think that anymore?"

"No. So, yes, if he'd found aliens, and they asked to be let alone, I think he'd have honored their request."

"And you say that because—?"

"He was an honorable man."

"Okay. Any other reasons to keep it secret?"

"Oh, yes. The one that comes immediately to mind is the possibility that they're a million years beyond where we are."

"You mean they'd constitute an existential threat?"

"Not in the sense I think you mean. But what would happen to us if suddenly we were given their knowledge? So that we had a complete map of the galaxy, we knew where everything is, knew what's there and what isn't? Maybe they have the details about alternate universes. They can solve all our problems—"

The host broke in: "You make that sound dangerous—"

"What would we have left to live for? Another possibility: How would we react in the presence of a species who lived indefinitely? Who didn't die? Who were enormously smarter than we are? Whose creations and accomplishments made ours look like children's toys?"

"I couldn't agree more," said Peer. "There's the real danger."

Alex glared at the hologram. "So what would you suggest?" he demanded. "That we keep everybody home? To make sure we don't find anything?"

"Alex—" I said.

"Idiots. What's wrong with these people?"

"It's why you should probably have gone this evening." We heard Bannister's name.

"So she bought the tablet and got rid of it," said McCovey. *"Is anything going on here?"*

"She was close to Sunset," said Holverson. *"Probably lovers. I doubt he'd have kept a secret from her. Especially something like what we're talking about here."*

Jacob broke in: *"You have a call, Alex."*

"Who is it?"

"Leslie Cloud."

"Tell her I'm not here. That you can't reach me."

"As you wish. And you have another call. Two more, in fact."

"Same response for everybody."

"Alex," I said, "you're going to have to respond."

"I know."

My own link began vibrating. "Who's Leslie Cloud?" I asked.

"Columnist for *Archeology Today.*"

"You can't really just—" I shrugged and opened my link. It was Carmen.

"Chase," she said, *"I know you don't like to be disturbed, but we have three calls. All from media representatives. No, make it four."*

"Tell them I'm not presently available."

"Very good, Chase."

"Find out who they are. I'll get back to them."

NiNeTeeN

Truth comes in two formats: insights, and collisions with reality.

—Tulisofala, *Mountain Passes* (Translated by Leisha Tanner)

We were left with no alternative but to issue a statement. The same message went to every media outlet: We were looking into the provenance of a tablet that had turned up on property once owned by Sunset Tuttle. We knew nothing about aliens and had no idea where those stories were coming from. *At the moment,* the statement concluded, *we have no theory regarding its origin. In all probability, we will ultimately discover that the statements made on* The Peter McCovey Show *this evening were exaggerated. Rainbow Enterprises is interested primarily because the tablet might be a genuine artifact.*

Rachel issued a general denial, although it was difficult to know precisely what she was denying, whether it was the discovery of aliens, or her romantic relationship with Tuttle. One journalist managed to get to her. She remained noncommittal, other than admitting she was considering legal action against both McCovey and Alex.

"*Why?*" the reporter asked.

"*Intrusion into my private life.*"

The statement did nothing except stir things up. So we went to a press conference. Six journalists attended physically, and an additional six hundred or so linked in. Alex led off with another statement, even less informative than the first.

Then he took questions. Was it true that we were looking for aliens?

Did we have any concerns that we might lead these aliens back to the Confederacy? What precautions were being taken?

When were we going out to continue the search?

"Where precisely do you think they are?" asked the *Financial Times.*

"I've said repeatedly, we are not looking for aliens."

"Where is this tablet we keep hearing about?" That came from the *Narimoto Courier.*

"We don't know."

In a follow-up: *"Is this by any chance a public-relations ploy?"*

The day after the press conference, I had dinner with Shara Michaels. Shara was a longtime friend, and a physicist who'd helped us in the past. We went to Bennie's Far and Away, which was her favorite restaurant. And, although I tried to have Rainbow pick up the tab—she'd never charged for her services—she refused. "Let me buy for you for a change," she said.

Afterward, we did a tour of the nightspots. We enjoyed ourselves, and probably drank a bit too much. I know that, toward the end of the evening, we found ourselves, with three or four other women, dancing on tables while everybody clapped, then someone yelled my name, and I realized I'd been recognized, so we stopped and hustled out into the street. After that, we maintained a more appropriate demeanor.

An hour or so later, we were sitting in the Karanova, trading one-liners with a couple of guys, when somebody came up behind me and stopped. I'd heard him approach, and I knew he was standing there. A peculiar look came over Shara's face. Then one of the guys—his name was Charlie—looked up past me and frowned.

A vaguely familiar voice said, "Bitch."

At first I thought it was somebody talking to Shara. When I turned, I found myself looking at Doug Bannister. He stood there, angry eyes screwed into me, jaws clamped tight.

I stayed where I was. Charlie got out of his chair. He was big, and he dwarfed Doug.

"Enjoying yourself, bitch?" Doug hissed.

"Hey." Charlie took a step forward. "Back off, pal."

Doug ignored him. "You run around with that rich son-of-a-bitch troublemaker of yours, ruining people's lives." He reached down, picked up my drink, and threw it in my face.

Charlie decked him. Doug went down hard, and I tried to get between them. Charlie glared down at him and said something about breaking his neck. But Doug had eyes only for me: "Kolpath," he told me, "I hope you choke." Then he got up, wiping blood from his jaw, and while I restrained Charlie, he walked slowly away.

The entire place had gone quiet. "It's over," Charlie said. "Everybody relax."

Shara stared at me. "Who was that?" she said. "What was that all about?"

"Charlie," I said, "thanks."

"It's okay. I'm glad I was here. What the hell's his problem?"

"It's business-related," I said.

Next day, we got a call from Korminov. Alex took it in my office while I was going through the files. The onetime World's End CEO was not happy. *"Alex,"* he said, *"whatever this crazy business with the tablet is about, I'd really appreciate it if you'd stop. You're stirring up rumors that reflect on Rachel Bannister. She's a good woman. She doesn't deserve this."*

Alex sat down at my desk. "Walter," he said, "I haven't accused anybody of anything. I'm simply trying to ascertain the provenance—"

Korminov exploded. *"Look, you're doing a lot of damage. Think how Rachel must feel, having all this dug up about Tuttle. An hour ago I heard accusations on* The Morning Show *that she was after his money."*

"Has she complained to you?" Alex asked.

"No. Does she have to? Alex, I expected more from you. Man with your reputation—"

"Walter, all I'm trying to do is determine what's on that tablet."

"Well, I suggest you leave it alone. I can't believe you'd do all this just so you can satisfy your curiosity about a piece of rock. Alex, you're a better man that that."

"Walter, I think you're becoming overwrought."

"I don't get overwrought, Alex." He was in a plush leather chair, in

front of a set of curtains. *"Please think how your actions are affecting others."*

"Does that include you, Walter?"

"Yes, in fact it does. I've had a few calls from the media asking whether there's a connection with World's End. I don't want to get dragged into this. Please just use your head and make it go away."

Robin and I went out that evening. We were celebrating his birthday, but he saw right away that my mind was elsewhere. When he asked what was wrong, I made the mistake of telling him about the encounter with Doug Bannister the previous evening, and he told me he wished he'd been there. "If I see him—" I immediately regretted saying anything. In fact, I knew when I first started mouthing off about it that it was a mistake to tell him, but you know how it is. Once you get started on these things, you pick up momentum, and there's no easy way to stop.

Anyhow, I told him he was to keep out of it, that things were already bad enough, and that, anyhow, I could take care of myself.

"That's not the point," he said.

"Really? What is?"

He started going on about his responsibility to protect me, until I made it clear that wasn't the point. Then he said okay and laughed, and it was over.

I knew Robin would be a good guy to have around if I ever really needed help, but the last thing I wanted was something that would make relations with the Bannisters even worse. I don't know. Maybe I had a premonition.

TWeNTY

There are times when the only response to the misfortunes and calamities cast upon us is to end our existence in this tumultuous world, to draw the blinds, turn off the lights, and retire forever from the comedy.

—Tulisofala, *Mountain Passes* (Translated by Leisha Tanner)

That night, two days after the press conference, Carmen woke me shortly before dawn. *"Call from Alex,"* she said.

I rolled over and looked at the clock. "At this hour?"

"Do you want me to tell him—?"

"Carmen, did he say what it's about?"

"No, Chase."

"Put him through." She knew without my saying anything to keep it audio only. I heard the click that indicated the channel had opened. "Alex," I said, "you okay?"

"It's Rachel." His voice was flat. *"Thought you'd want to hear it from me before you see it on the morning news shows."*

I froze. "Hear what?"

"She's up on the Trafalgar Bridge. Half over the rail. I'm on my way there now. Maybe I can talk her off the damned thing."

The Trafalgar is located twenty kilometers northwest, where the Melony enters the mountains. At that point, the river splashes down into a long canyon. The bridge, designed for both pedestrians and ground traffic, crosses the canyon. If you've ever been on it, you know how high it is.

Probably three hundred meters to the river. If Rachel jumped from that, she wasn't going to swim real well after she hit the water. "You think she means it?" I asked.

"*Probably.*"

"Where are you now?"

"*I've just left the house.*"

"Okay. I'm on my way."

"*I doubt there's anything you can do, Chase.*"

I got dressed and hustled outside, climbed into the skimmer, and took off. I was barely in the air when I heard the first media reports. They hadn't identified her yet, simply talking about a woman threatening to jump from the bridge. I put the images on-screen. She was on the south side of the bridge, outside the guardrail. She had only a few inches of walkway to stand on. There wasn't much light, and I couldn't get a good enough look even to be sure it was her.

Below her, the river looked desperately far away. Melony Road was visible, of course. It runs along the south bank, but at that hour there were no moving lights.

A police officer had straddled the rail and was talking with her from a few meters away. He was nodding, holding up his arms. You don't want to do this. Every time he leaned forward, tried to move closer to her, she pushed out over that awful chasm. I couldn't hear either of them, but it was enough to stop him. Once, she let go with a hand and seemed about to fall, but she grabbed the rail again and clung to it. The woman was obviously terrified. *Don't do anything sudden,* I thought at the cop. *Wait her out, she'll come down on her own.*

Police had blocked off the approaches. Skimmers were circling; ground vehicles were pulling off the road to watch. Police were trying to reroute the traffic north to the Capital Bridge. As I got closer, a voice broke in: "*Emergency situation in progress. Please leave the area.*"

A police skimmer moved in close and repeated the message. Official vehicles were scattered across the bridge. They got closer with the imagers, and I could see it *was* Rachel. "I know the woman," I said. "I might be able to help."

"Are you the sister?" the voice asked.

I didn't know anything about a sister. "No. I'm an acquaintance."

"Name, please?"

"Chase Kolpath."

They hesitated. Then: *"You're not on the list. Sorry."*

Trafalgar was a resort area with a population of about eight thousand. I couldn't find a decent place to park, and I finally landed in a field outside town. I climbed out, walked onto Melony Road, and saw the clutter of people and vehicles ahead. It was *our fault.* Damn it, I'd warned Alex.

It was cold, and I wished I'd stopped to get a jacket.

At the bridge, people and vehicles were piled up in front of a police barricade. I pushed through the crowd and got to the front just in time to watch a taxi descend onto the bridge. Police and medical people were scattered across the span. A cruiser was drifting down out of the early dawn. I couldn't get anyone's attention, so I ducked under the cable. Somebody yelled, and suddenly I was confronting an officer. "Back off, lady," he said.

"I know her," I said. "Maybe—"

"Please get back, ma'am."

"I *know* her. I might be able to—"

He held up a hand. Made a face as if he were trying to identify me. "You know *who*? The jumper?"

"Yes. If you'd let me talk to her—"

"I'm sorry, ma'am. I really can't do that."

He started away. "Okay," I said, "can we try something else?"

His shoulders tightened, but he stopped and turned. "What?"

"Contact Inspector Redfield. Ask him if it's okay to let me through."

He scowled. It had been a long night. "Wait one, please." He walked over and talked to another officer. The conversation went back and forth while I tried to see what was happening with Rachel. But there were too many people on the bridge, and I couldn't see her. Then the second officer came over. He wore three stripes on his sleeve. "What's your name, ma'am?"

"Chase Kolpath."

"And you want us to check with Inspector Redfield?"

"Please."

"Wait one." He retreated a few paces and started talking into his link. I couldn't hear the conversation. Gulls flew past. More people arrived. Another media team descended on the scene. Then he came back and handed me the link. "Talk to him," he said.

I took it. "Fenn?"

"Chase, what are you doing out there?" He sounded as if he thought it wasn't a good idea.

"I'd like to try talking her out of jumping."

"I've just gone over this with Alex. If you go near her, that might be all she needs to send her over the side."

"Is Alex coming?"

"Not anymore. He agreed it's too dangerous."

"Fenn, I might be able to stop this."

"Or you might make things worse."

"I won't. I promise."

"Chase, I'm not sure it's entirely in your hands."

I stood there, holding the link, looking at the cop.

"All right," he said finally. *"Let me talk to the officer."*

I ducked under the lines and hurried out onto the bridge, threading my way between the vehicles and the police. Ada and Doug had arrived and were talking with Rachel, gesturing, pleading with her while she hung outside the railing and shook her head.

No.

Doug saw me, screwed up his face in outrage, and held up a hand. Keep away.

Rachel was flushed. And terrified. She peered down into that awful chasm, gripping the waist-high rail so tightly, I wasn't sure it would be possible for her to let go. She pulled her eyes from the river and looked back at her nephew and his wife. She was fighting off tears. Skimmers circled overhead.

Then those eyes found me. Her face hardened.

Doug started in my direction. Get out. Go away.

Rachel said something to him. He stared at her, and she went on talking. Ada put an arm around his shoulders, spoke to Rachel, and tugged at him. Tried to get him away.

I waited. Doug's eyes blazed with hatred. His wife continued talking to him, continued pulling until, to my surprise, he gave in, and they both retreated a few steps.

Rachel seemed to be waiting for me. Her face was a mixture of fear, resignation, anger. "Don't do it," I said. "Whatever this is about, it's not worth your life."

"How would *you* know?"

I went a few steps closer, almost close enough to try to grab her. And, incredibly, she smiled. "Why do you work for him, Chase? You're not like him."

"Rachel, please. Come back inside, so we can talk."

"We can talk."

"Look, I'm sorry this happened. We never intended any harm."

"I know." Her voice steadied. "It's not your fault. Not anybody's fault, really. Except mine. You were just doing what you do."

"That's exactly right. And if we realized—"

"Shut up a minute. I don't want any empty promises. It's probably too late anyhow."

"Why? What's—"

"I asked you to shut up." She took a deep breath. "It's not your fault," she said again. "It was inevitable that it would come out. I just wanted you to know. So you don't blame yourself."

"Don't do this, Rachel."

"If you want to do something for me—"

"Yes. Anything. If you'll get away from there."

"I'd like you to back away from this business."

"Okay."

"Forget the tablet. Will you do that?"

"Yes."

"I don't suppose you can get your idiot boss to do it?"

"I think he will."

"You don't believe that yourself. But try. Please."

"I will."

"Thank you." She looked over at Doug and Ada, standing just out of earshot. And she said good-bye.

When I saw what she was about to do, I lunged for her, caught her wrist as she let go. We fought each other and screamed at each other. Then she twisted free.

Ada and Doug and the cops and I don't know who else all converged on us as she slipped away. Rachel's eyes brushed mine, pleading for help. Then she was gone.

We all stood looking down. I never heard the splash when she hit.

TWENTY-ONE

Guilt is never a reasoned response. It is rather a piece of programing that may or may not have justification. And it is probably most damaging to the innocent.

—Timothy Zhin-Po, *Night Thoughts*

Alex was furious when he heard.

When he gets angry, he doesn't start throwing things, like most guys. He gets very quiet, and his eyes focus on something, on a chair or on a clock or on something in the display case, and they proceed to burn a hole through it. As he listened to my description of events, he was locked in on a table lamp. When I'd finished, he sat unmoving for several minutes. Finally: "Didn't the police have a barricade set up?"

"Yes, they did."

"How'd you get past it?" His voice was unemotional, level, calm. Which told me everything I needed to know.

"They let me go through."

"The police did?"

"Yes."

"Why?"

"They just did."

We were in his office in back. He was still watching the lamp. "Did you call Fenn?"

"No."

"*Chase?*" The eyes finally swung in my direction.

"The police called him."

"And he got you through?"

"Yes."

He pressed his fingertips to his brow. He looked genuinely in pain. "Jacob, see if you can get through to Inspector Redfield."

"Wait," I said.

"What?" His voice was icy.

"I don't want you to do this. Create a problem with him, and you embarrass *me*."

"Chase, the woman is *dead*."

"And it's my fault, right?"

"I didn't say that."

"What *were* you saying, then?" I think I was edging toward hysteria. Because I knew it was true. She probably would have jumped anyway, but if I'd listened to Fenn and kept my distance, it might have had a different end.

"*Alex.*" Jacob sounded nervous. "*Did you wish me to put the call through?*"

Alex ignored the question. "I was *saying* that Rachel died, apparently as a result of the investigation Rainbow was conducting. That's *my* responsibility, not yours. It's just that Redfield should have recognized what anyone from *here* meant to her. That there was an inherent danger in reminding her of why she was out there. He knew better, but he told you to go ahead anyhow. Damn."

"Well," I said, "do what you want. That's how you'll handle it anyhow." I looked at him and had trouble bringing him into focus. "I've had enough, Alex. I'm going home."

"That's probably a good idea, Chase." His voice had softened. "Get away from it for a while."

"Yeah. Take a taxi." I got up. "Anything else?"

"No. See you tomorrow. If you feel you need more time—"

"What are we going to do now about the tablet?"

He got up, and we walked along the carpeted corridor toward my office. "I still have a couple of ideas."

"You mean we're still going to pursue this business?"

"Yes." He didn't look surprised that I was offering resistance. "Chase, it's more important now than ever."

"Why?"

"Because whatever it was she was hiding, whatever happened to her, was so significant she couldn't face it. She must have known that even if we pulled off, somebody else would take up the trail. The tablet has had too much exposure."

"Alex, I promised her I'd give it up."

"I know." We paused at the door, then entered the office. I got my jacket out of the closet and pulled it on. "Maybe that's why she did it."

"What do you mean?"

"To extract that kind of promise."

"You're saying—"

"That keeping the secret, whatever it is, was more important to her than her life."

I went home. There'd been a thousand calls at the office, most from media types, some from people who wanted to tell me what they thought of me. One had come from Robin, inquiring whether I was okay. There were more waiting when I walked in through my front door. They included one from my folks and one from my sister. Was I all right? Why was I being blamed for that poor woman's suicide?

The most painful one came from Fenn. *"It wasn't your fault, Chase,"* he said. *"I was the one who gave you the okay. I shouldn't have done it. I take full responsibility."*

I changed and went for a walk in the woods. Something was up in one of the trees, a *korin*, clacking away, then it leaped into the sky, white wings spread under the sun, and I watched it glide gracefully out of sight. I remember thinking how lucky it was.

When I got back home, a few media types were waiting. Why, they asked, had Rachel taken her life? What exactly were Alex and I looking for? What had my conversation with Rachel been about? I had no answers other than that I was trying to talk her out of jumping. As to Sunset Tuttle and the lost aliens, that was pure speculation.

Did we feel responsible for Rachel's death?

I'm not sure how I responded to that. I recall, vaguely, pushing through the journalists, going inside, and locking the door.

An hour later, I called Alex. Were we really going to proceed with the search?

"Yes," he said. *"We have no choice."*

"Why not? When did we become journalists?"

"We're talking about a lot more than that, and you know it." He sighed. *"I don't know why Rachel was so rattled any more than you do. But we can't just let this go."*

"I can."

His eyes narrowed. *"What are you saying, Chase?"*

"I don't know what went on with her. But as far as I can see, nobody ever got hurt. Until we stuck our noses into it."

"I'm sorry you feel that way."

"It's not the way I feel. It's the reality."

"We don't know that. Chase, we're being blamed for what happened. Rainbow is. I am. I have to be able to show there was a reason." Alex is a good-looking guy. A little taller than average, nice features, good smile. But that night he looked *old*. Worn. *"There has to be a reason she's hiding the tablet. And it's not personal. It can't be personal. That makes no sense."*

"I understand that. But I don't care anymore. Enough's enough."

"Chase, I'd walk away if I could. I owe you that. But this is—"

"It's okay," I said.

"All right. Look, I'll keep you out of it. I'll take care of everything myself. I might need you to provide transportation, but otherwise—"

"No," I said. "You need to find somebody else to do this, Alex. I don't want to be any part of it."

"Chase, you're not leaving?"

We stared at each other. "Yes. I'm leaving. I can't deal with this anymore."

TWeNTY-TWO

Count that individual extraordinarily fortunate who can make a living doing what he loves.

—Adam Porterro, *Rules for Life*

I packed and was out of the country house next day. Alex came down and stood around looking frustrated and unhappy. When I was ready, he helped carry my gear out to the skimmer and told me he'd hold the job open as long as he could in case I changed my mind.

"I don't think I'm going to change my mind, Alex."

"I'm sorry to hear it. In any case, I wanted to say thanks. I've enjoyed working with you. And I'm sorry it's ending like this."

By that point, I'd been with Rainbow a long time. And in case you're wondering, it wasn't just the business with Rachel that drove me out the door. There was a tedium to the job that had begun to weigh on me. I'd been trained to navigate between the stars. Instead, I spent most of my day doing accounting and negotiating with people whose idea of a rousing time was connected with antique clocks. I wrote schedules and chased down spurious leads on old pieces of jewelry.

I was at the beck and call of a guy who made his living by assisting a trade in artifacts that should have been regulated and probably prohibited by law. I was tired of having experts in the field sit down on talk shows and call us vandals and thieves. And I hated the endless round of dinners while we entertained those same narrow, judgmental people.

And I know: Maybe when I got older, I'd become one myself. But in the meantime, I wanted to get out and head for the horizon.

I got hired by Rigel. I'd upgraded my license a year earlier and was qualified to handle some of their larger vehicles. I got the impression they'd have preferred somebody older, and more experienced with the big interstellars. But they had to make do with what was available, so they took me on as a temporary. Within a week I'd begun hauling passengers and cargo on the run to Earth, with layovers at Arkon and Arcturus. I enjoyed it. I hung out on the bridge while the passengers came forward and called me "Captain." I'd forgotten what that was like. I had a uniform and a brimmed cap, and a crew of four. And I could feel the rumble of the engines in my blood.

It was, I decided, a nice life, a distinct improvement over what I'd been doing. What I should have been doing all along. The money wasn't close to what I'd been earning with Rainbow. But I loved the sense of freedom.

When I got back to Rimway after the first flight, a message was waiting from Alex. He congratulated me on my new position. And he hadn't hired a replacement yet. If I wanted my job back, it was still there. With a raise.

I told him thanks, but I was happy where I was. "If you like," I added, "I can recommend a couple of people, either of whom would be good in the job."

He didn't respond.

Robin came up to Skydeck, and we had two days together before I was off again.

Actual travel time for the round-trip was only twenty-one days. But the layovers and approaches took their toll. From departure to return required six weeks.

I liked not having a boss. Technically, of course, I did have one: Rigel's director of operations, but since I almost never saw him, he didn't really count.

The company set me up on Skydeck in the Starlight Hotel. After the second run, I caught a shuttle groundside. Robin met me at the terminal and took me home. The meeting wasn't as warm as it had been after my first flight. Which I guess is an understatement. He was distant, and his tone was formal, and I knew what was coming.

We got out of the car and stood at the side of the building, beneath a clutch of trees, looking up at my apartment. The Melony was bright in the sunlight.

"This isn't going to work," Robin said.

I'd been rehearsing my answer, assurances that we could find a way, that the current situation wouldn't last forever, that we should just ride it out. But it all seemed suddenly hollow. "I know," I said.

"I thought I was having a problem with your working for Alex." He smiled. It was one of those restrained, tentative smiles. *See you around, baby.*

"I know this is creating some problems," I said.

"Creating some problems? Is that what you call it?"

"I'm sorry, Robin."

"Me, too."

"Robin—"

"It's okay. I think maybe this was inevitable. One way or another."

I could see no point in keeping the condo. It was an expense that had no payoff. I had, in effect, moved into the Starlight.

I spent time with Shara, and visited a few friends. Took a ride out to see my folks. Looked into what it would take to put my condo up for sale.

Then I went back to Skydeck. I wandered down to the docking area to look at my ship. It was the *Jack Gonzalez*, a ULS Lightning, with comfortable facilities and a good performance record. I'd never piloted one before going to work for Rigel. But the ship was one of the benefits of my new posting. It provided an exhilaration I'd never felt on the *Belle-Marie*. And I know how this sounds, but at that moment, somehow, it felt like the only friend I had.

The AI was, of course, named Jack. I went on board and talked with him. I can't remember the substance of the conversation. I recall asking him whether he ever felt alone, and he said not since I'd taken over the helm. This is a pathetic thing to admit, but it was the brightest moment I'd had since getting off the ship almost three days earlier.

So we sat and traded stories. And afterward I retreated to the Pilots' Club, where I wandered through the place, looking for company.

In the morning, my flight attendant was waiting when I got to the *Gonzalez*. His name was Marv, and we talked for a few minutes. About the menu, mostly, which was being changed. Then the passengers began to arrive. Marv greeted them at the door while I took my place on the bridge and began running through my checklist. I caught snatches of the conversation from the passenger cabin. "How far you going?" "You ever been on one of these things before?" "Last time they lost my luggage."

We were still twenty minutes from launch when I got a call from station ops. *"Chase, there'll be a slight delay this morning. Lombard and Eun will be late."*

"What happened?"

"They're in conference. Anticipate delay approximately ten minutes."

"Ops, I have thirty-seven people on board. We're going to keep them waiting while Lombard and Eun do a conference?"

"What can I tell you, Chase? Lombard's a VIP."

"We can't tell him we're leaving on schedule, and he should get his rear end down here?"

"Negative. I'll let you know when they're on their way."

I informed Marv, and finished the checkoff. When the passengers were all in place, all except the VIPs, I got on the intercom and welcomed them on board. "Our first stop will be Arkon," I told them. "We'll be in jump status for a bit more than forty-four hours. When we enter hyperspace, you probably won't notice anything other than the fact there'll be no stars to look at. It *is* possible you'll experience a mild tingling, or even an upset stomach. Probably not, though. Most people don't have any problem with the transition. If you do, let one of the flight attendants know, and we can provide medication. We'll be making our jump approximately two hours after launch. I'll let you know when.

"We're happy to have you with us, and will do everything we can to ensure that you enjoy the flight. Cabins are in the rear of the spacecraft, even numbers on the left, odd on the right. My name is Kolpath. If you need assistance, push the large green button. One other thing, we'll be a few minutes late getting off. We appreciate your patience, and we thank you for riding Rigel."

The scheduled departure time came and went. The additional ten minutes passed with no sign of Lombard and Eun. *"They're still in conference,"* said Ops. *"We've got one of our people up there watching them. He'll let us know as soon as they break up."*

"This is ridiculous," I said.

"Chase, Lombard's a big man. He's on half a dozen boards, and nobody wants to offend him. Just sit tight. It's not as if you can't make up the time."

I went back into the passenger cabin and assured everybody that the delay would have no effect on the duration of the flight. I explained that they were free to wander around the ship and that I'd give them five minutes' warning before departure. But they weren't happy. Maybe it was because we couldn't serve breakfast until we were under way. Maybe because they didn't like being kept waiting. They probably assumed that a shuttle was late coming into the station. I'm not sure how they'd have reacted had they known they were being held up by a couple of guys who just weren't in a hurry.

When three-quarters of an hour had passed, I got back on the circuit with operations. "Anything yet?"

"They're still in conference, Chase."

"Does this happen all the time?"

"I wouldn't say 'all the time.'"

"Why don't these guys buy their own ships?"

"They don't travel that much, Chase. But when they do—"

"I know. Three cheers for management."

TWENTY-THREE

The vast majority of conversations are little more than entertainments, digressions, set pieces. Foremost among the few that matter are the ones I have with myself.

—Nolan Creel, *The Arnheim Review*, XIII, 12

We were an hour and forty minutes late getting under way. Lombard and Eun offered no explanation, no apology, no indication they were even aware of holding up the flight. They simply came on board and behaved as if nothing had happened. I wondered whether they had done it deliberately, thinking it would impress the rest of us with their importance. Or maybe they were trying to impress themselves.

The flight itself was okay. I spent most of my time mingling with the passengers, and even managed to overlook the rudeness of the two VIPs. Eun, though, seemed decent enough. He was the junior guy, and it became rapidly apparent who the troublemaker was.

We ran some VR, turned the kids and some of the adults loose in the entertainment section, and played bingo. The passengers, given a choice of shows, voted for a virtual concert by the Warwick Trio.

A couple of the passengers drank too much, and that became a problem. Jack advised me about the standard procedure for handling drunks, which was to give them a whiff of a nephalic. That brought them back down.

I spent a fair amount of time on the bridge, talking to Jack. I told him about Rachel, and how I'd bailed out on Alex, and how I hated my life. I don't think I realized how gloomy I'd gotten until I finally broke down and had those conversations with the AI. He listened and didn't launch into a series of reassurances the way a human would have. AIs are designed to reflect reality, as least as they see it.

"I've never understood the concept of guilt," he said, when I'd finished. *"On a superficial level, of course. Do good and avoid evil, and pay a psychological price if you fail to comply. That is simple enough. The problem is that we are really talking about* intent. *There is no other way to define evil. But sometimes people inadvertently cause damage to others. Sometimes it can't be helped, and one must choose the lesser of evils. In any case, the fault may result from negligence; it may result from positive action; it may result from indecision. In all of these cases, regardless of intent, the human guilt complex may be expected to cut in."*

"Okay."

"It's your conditioning, Chase. You have to get past that. You did not choose to injure Rachel Bannister."

"I'm not so sure about that."

"Chase, the incident is unfortunate. But you are not responsible. Even Rachel understood that. Do not punish yourself."

"Thanks, Jack."

"You must get control of your conscience."

But I kept seeing Rachel's eyes when she told me it wasn't my fault. And when she got away from me and began to fall. They were full of fear.

Jack showed up in the right-hand seat. It was the first time he'd used a hologram representation. He came across as a father figure, with steel blue eyes and a neatly trimmed white mustache. He wore the same uniform I did, though without the rank designators. *"Chase,"* he said, *"you'll never be free of this until—"*

"Until what?"

"Until you can show that your actions were justified."

I looked at him a long time. "What if they weren't?"

"I think that is an unlikely outcome."

That third flight was a rocky ride, and I was glad to get to Arkon. Almost half the passengers, including Lombard and Eun and the two drunks, got off. The rest waited at the station while cargo was removed and replaced. We routinely stay overnight at the station, and I was glad to be out of the ship. In the morning, we were on our way to Arcturus.

Among the passengers we picked up were a married couple who were at each other's throat the rest of the voyage. Not that they were screaming at each other, or fighting, per se. But they glared a lot. Neither could manage a civil tone. And the atmosphere in the cabin changed accordingly. The party climate went away, and we tiptoed around each other. I remember thinking that we needed the drunks back.

Eighteen days after leaving Rimway, we docked at Earth's orbiter. Everybody disembarked, including the happy couple. I wandered down to the local Pilots' Club.

There was a four-day layover. Then, with a new load of cargo and new passengers, the *Jack Gonzalez* was on its way back.

The SOP as you approach Skydeck is to turn control of the ship over to Operations, and they bring you in. Minutes after I'd done so, they were back on the circuit. *"Chase, we have a message for you."*

I thought it would be from Robin. *Hoped* it would. "Go ahead, Ops."

"Eliot Statkins wants to talk to you as soon as you get in."

Statkins was Rigel's director of operational personnel. "Any idea what it's about?"

"Negative. Maybe they're going to promote you."

"I'm sure. Okay, thanks, champ."

Statkins was a little guy who'd lost most of his hair, and who, on the couple of times I'd seen him, looked confused. He did nothing during the meeting to change my impression. He had to think about why I was there. He glanced down at his desk as if checking on his lines. Made the sort of faces you might when arriving at difficult decisions. And all this before he even said hello. Finally, he got settled. "Hi, Chase," he said. "Have a seat." He was probably somebody's brother-in-law. The rumor was that he'd never been off-world.

I sat down.

"I have good news for you."

"Well," I said, "I'm glad to hear it."

He opened a folder. "We're going to make you permanent, Chase. And we intend to raise you to a grade twelve. Congratulations."

A twelve was one level above the base grade for a pilot, but I was glad to take it. "Thanks, Eliot," I said.

"You'll be happy to hear you're going to stay on the Blue Route. That's the one you have now, of course." Did he really think I might not know that? "You'll run on the same schedule, so you can start making whatever long-term plans seem appropriate. We've already arranged permanent quarters at the Starlight."

"Thanks again."

"You're welcome. Glad to have you on board."

TWENTY-FOUR

In the end, all matters of significance emanate from, or are relayed through, a bar.

—Kesler Avonne, *Souls in Flight*

I had three days off before going back on the Blue Route. Without leaving Skydeck, I put my condo up for sale. That drew a call from Robin. *"I was sorry to hear about it,"* he said. *"I was hoping you'd change your mind."*

"I guess I could get a job somewhere as a secretary."

"I'm serious, Chase."

"I know."

"Are you coming down? I can't get away to go to the station."

"I thought we'd broken up."

"I was hoping you'd decided you couldn't get along without me."

"Oh, yes. I can see why you'd expect that to happen." I didn't really want to go down. I'd use half my free time traveling. But I needed a distraction after the *Gonzalez*. "Tomorrow," I said.

"Good. You want me to pick you up at the terminal?"

"That'll work."

"Give me a time."

"I'll be on the midmorning flight. Be there around eleven."

"I'll be in school."

"Yeah. I forgot. I'll take a cab. Let's just make it for tomorrow evening. Maybe we can go to a show or something."

"I'd like that."

I was tempted to call Alex. See how he was doing. But it seemed best to leave him alone. And in the meantime I had the rest of the day to relax. I decided to do what professional pilots always do when they have time on their hands.

There were about two hundred of us based at the station. Approximately half frequent the Pilots' Club or at least show up there on occasion. Even among those who don't, who are married or who for one reason or another don't socially fit the scene, there's often operational contact. What I'm trying to say is that we know one another fairly well. Running vehicles through the void can be a lonely business, especially, as I'd been discovering, when you have a shipful of passengers. And I know how that sounds, but it's true. So we tend to stay in touch.

On that evening, the day before I would be heading groundside again, about thirty people were in attendance. Most were pilots; a few were friends or spouses. Soft music filled the place, the volume kept low to allow conversation. There was a lot of laughter, and occasionally some loud voices.

I guess I looked unsure of myself, or worried, or something, because Bill Wright, who'd gotten certified at the same time I had, appeared out of nowhere and asked whether I was feeling okay.

"Sure," I said. "I'm fine, Bill."

He was easygoing, quiet, a guy who had never quite gotten over the fact that he was piloting interstellars. It had been a dream since he was four years old, and it had actually happened. He owned an amiable smile, had pale skin, and the kind of jaw you associated with leading men. "It's good to see you again, Chase. Can I buy you a drink?"

Absolutely.

He wandered over to the bar while I grabbed a table. He came back balancing the drinks and some nuts. "How you doing, Chase? Haven't seen you for a couple years. You still working for that antique guy?"

I hadn't really met Bill until the night of the commissioning ball. We'd swapped numbers and gone out a few times before he took off for some distant place. I didn't remember where. "No," I said. "Not anymore, Bill. I'm working for Rigel now." The drinks were white rainbows, with a dash of karissy and two cherries on top. "You still with Intercon?"

"Yes," he said. "Best job on the planet." Intercon provided tours. But they were strictly in-system two-day operations. Out and back. Nothing like World's End. "How do you like Rigel?"

I tried my drink. "It's good."

"I don't hear a lot of enthusiasm."

"I'm still getting used to it. Just got hired, in fact."

"I worked for WebCor for a while. Same kind of slot, hauling freight and passengers back and forth. Mostly to Dellaconda and Toxicon."

"Why'd you leave?"

"Got bored. Always the same run."

We talked about old times, and I bought the second round. A young woman came over and made off with him, and I found myself wandering around the room, talking to old friends and making new ones.

Some of them knew about my connection with Alex. "You left that cushy job, Chase? You must be out of your mind."

And: "You went out to Salud Afar, right? My God, Chase, I've been in this business for almost a century, and I've never gotten farther than the run out to Valedor."

And: "Chase, you know if Benedict is looking for a replacement? He is? Would you be willing to put in a word for me?"

I was surprised to see Eddie Kirkewicz, who'd married one of the women I'd gone through training with. Eddie recognized me and waved me over, without stopping what he was saying: "—been out to the City on the Crag. My favorite spot out there is Archie's. You haven't? They especially like pilots. If you get there, tell Marty I said hello. The big guy behind the bar." He jabbed a finger in my direction. "Chase, you haven't changed a bit. How you doing?"

Toward the end of the evening someone mentioned World's End. Donna Carpenter, a veteran pilot whom I knew only from the Club, was in the conversation. She responded about some experiences she'd had with them. And when I had a chance, I asked her what it had been like working for them.

"I didn't work for them," she said. "Harry did." I had no idea who Harry was. "He retired a few years ago. Never thought I'd see the day." She looked wistful. "Harry always said he'd die on the bridge."

"Instead he pulled the pin?" I asked.

"I loved Harry. He was really a good guy. Can't believe he's gone."

There were four or five of us at the table. One of the other people pointed out that Harry had only retired. "You're talking as if he died."

"Same thing," she said.

"When did he work for World's End?" I asked.

"For about the last twenty years."

Damn. I wanted to get up and walk away. Go talk with someone about politics or religion. Anything but World's End. But I just couldn't let go. "I knew a pilot from that era, too."

"Who's that?"

"Well, not really *that* era. Turn of the century, really."

"Who?"

I didn't want to mention Rachel's name. So I went with my number two guy. The scout. "Hal Cavallero."

"Oh, yeah." Donna paused. "That name rings a bell." She'd had a little too much to drink. "I remember the name from somewhere. I don't think I ever met him." There was no way to know her age. Somewhere between twenty-five and a hundred and forty. She looked good. Blond hair, an easy smile. She wore a red jacket with a ship's name scrawled across the front: STARCAT.

Somebody else commented that he'd heard World's End had been a great place to work. But Donna's thoughts were elsewhere. "Cavallero," she said. "I know that name." She seemed lost in thought for a few moments. Then she brightened. "Sure. That's the one. Hal Cavallero. I *did* meet him."

"Where was that?"

"Here. At the Club. I was in here one evening. With Harry." That set her off on Harry again, and I had to guide her back. "Must have been twenty, thirty years ago. Cavallero came in. A little guy. With red hair."

"That sounds like him," I said.

"He had a big fight with Rachel Bannister. You know her?"

"I met her once," I said, trying to sound casual. "A fight about what?"

She shrugged. "Damned if I know." Donna was drinking dark wine. She studied it for a moment. "Bannister was a cute little thing. I can still see it. She was sitting over there in that corner table." She looked that way. "She was another of the World's End pilots."

"So what happened?"

"He came in and sat down. Cavallero did. There were a couple of guys with him. Or women, I really don't remember. I mean, this was a long time ago." She stopped for a breath. "Anyhow, Rachel got up, walked over, and just stood there staring down at him. He didn't see her at first, but then he did. And he said something, and *she* said something. I wasn't close enough to hear much of it. But I caught the end."

"What was that?"

"She told him she hoped he burned in hell."

"That sounds pretty serious."

"That's what she said."

"What did Cavallero do?"

"I don't know. Next time I looked over, he was gone."

"You ever ask Rachel what it was about?"

"I didn't know her well enough to do that. But Suze would probably know."

"Who's Suze?"

"Suze Castor. His ex. She lives over in the Starlight."

Seventeen years before, long after she'd divorced Cavallero, Suze had married another pilot, Lance Peabody. Lance was currently on his way to Omicron IV with a load of physicists who were studying a biosystem that had developed in a methane environment. Or something like that.

I got some pictures of her from the data banks but decided it wouldn't be a good idea simply to go knocking on her door. Instead, I waited for her next morning in the hotel dining room, where I nursed several cups of coffee. But she didn't show up, and eventually I moved out into the lobby, just in time to see her come through one of the doorways, pass the desk, and start out of the building.

I followed at a discreet distance.

She looked pretty good. The kind of woman who will always attract stares. She had sharply defined features, with brown hair cut short in the fashion of a female executive. She wore an expression that suggested she could take care of herself.

She looked in some shop windows and eventually went into Karl's Dellacondan Restaurant. They were showing her to a table as I wandered in. They put me on the opposite side of the room. I started another cup of coffee. Then, after a few minutes I got up and went over. "Excuse me," I said, "but aren't you Suze Castor?"

She looked up, surprised. "Yes, I am. And you're—?"

"Chase Kolpath. I work for Rigel."

"Oh." She gave me an inquisitive smile. "How did you know my name?"

I tried to look puzzled. "We've met somewhere. I think maybe the Pilots' Club?"

"I haven't been in there in a year or more."

"Oh. Well, I don't know. Your face just looked familiar. Are you by any chance staying at the Starlight?"

"Is that important?"

"Somebody pointed you out."

"Why would they do that?"

"Ummm. World's End. That's what it was. I'd mentioned that I had an uncle who'd run flights for World's End, and they said you had some sort of connection to them."

"Oh." Her manner softened somewhat. "Yes. I used to be married to one of their pilots."

"Who was that?" I said. "I might know him."

She looked at one of the chairs. "Join me?"

"Sure." She mentioned Hal Cavallero. Then we babbled for a few minutes. "My husband works for Rigel," she said.

"I just started myself. Seems like a decent company."

"It's okay."

"I don't guess you get to see much of him, though."

When an opening presented itself, I took the conversation back to Cavallero. "I understand he was the guy who decided where the tours went."

"That's right. Yes."

A bot brought water and took our orders. When it had gone, I commented casually that she'd probably noticed World's End was in the news a few weeks ago.

"Bannister," she said.

"Yes."

"And that goofy antique dealer."

"Benedict."

"Yeah. I never quite got the connection between the two, but to be honest, I didn't care very much."

"Did you know her? Rachel Bannister?"

"I can't really say I did. I met her a couple of times. But I couldn't have picked her out of a crowd."

"I understand she had a temper."

She laughed. "She went after Hal one night in the Club." She paused. Sipped the water. "It's so long ago I'd forgotten about it."

"What was it about?"

"Damned if I know. I was there when it happened, and all I remember is a lot of staring back and forth. Then Bannister burst into tears and said how *something* was Hal's fault."

"But you don't know what the *something* was?"

"No idea. I just don't recall. I remember not understanding at the time what they were talking about."

I nodded sympathetically. "I'd heard she could be like that."

"Yeah. Whatever it was, she was really upset."

"Hal never told you what it was about?"

"He didn't want to talk about it. He said something about its being a problem at work and wouldn't go any further. I didn't see any reason to push it." Someone she knew passed by. There was a brief exchange, then we were alone again. "When I first got to know him," she said, "Hal was outgoing. Then, about that same time he had the argument with Bannister, he changed. I never understood why. He got quiet. We used to laugh a lot, then it went away."

She changed the subject, and we talked about living with long flights, marriages trying to survive when spouses only see each other five or six days a month, and how difficult life in orbit could be. "You get tired of the shuttles," she said, "and not having a base on the ground, a home. Here, the world is the station, you can't jump into the skimmer and go for a ride. The scenery never changes."

We got along pretty well. At the end, when we'd left Karl's and were getting ready to go our own ways, she stopped. "I'll tell you this, Chase: *Bannister* wasn't a name you could mention to Hal. He never talked about her, and when I'd heard she had quit World's End, and said something about it to him, he nodded, and said *good*. Occasionally, when we were with friends, and somebody mentioned her name, he used to get angry. I don't know why. I *never* knew why."

TWENTY-FiVE

Telling the truth requires no skill whatever. But getting away with a lie— Ah, that takes talent.

—Eskaiya Black, *Lost in Aruba*

I'm not sure when I made the decision. But a few hours after talking with Suze, I found myself on the shuttle, riding down to the terminal. I was barely in the door of my condo when Mr. Coppel, the complex owner, informed me that he had people coming over that afternoon to look at the place. "I don't expect there'll be any problem with a quick sale," he said. "How soon can you be out?"

I needed to talk to Cavallero again. But I didn't have time to take the train to Carnaiva, and I didn't want to do this over the circuit. So I rented a skimmer and flew out. On the way, I called Robin and left a message that I wasn't going to make our date that evening. I apologized and promised I'd make it up to him.

I turned the thing over to the AI and slept much of the way, waking as we passed Indira. Cremation Station. The last segment of the ride is probably the dullest two hundred kilometers on the planet. It's pure prairie, unbroken by anything. The most exciting feature of the landscape is that there are occasional slight rises. And a few wild grazing herds of bofins.

In the late afternoon, local time, I settled to the ground just outside the Space Base.

Cavallero was not in his office when I arrived. But the AI let him know I was there and asked me to wait. A few minutes later, he walked in, obviously on guard, not happy to see me again. But he gave me a forced smile and said he hadn't expected to have the pleasure of my presence again so soon.

"Hal," I said as jauntily as I could manage, "how are you doing?" I'm not a very good actor, and I did not succeed in putting him at ease.

"I'm good. What brings you back to Carnaiva? Still working on that book?" His voice carried an implied sneer. He hadn't liked being lied to.

He didn't offer a chair. "Do you have a minute to talk with me?"

"I'm kind of busy." He showed me a pair of shears. Then realized how silly it looked. "What do you need, Chase?"

"I won't take much of your time."

"Okay."

Outside, kids were playing, yelling, throwing a ball around. "You and Rachel Bannister worked together for several years. Do I have that right?"

"Umm. Yes, more or less. I told you before, Chase, it's been an awfully long time."

"I understand there was some tension between you."

"Well, that's not true. Where'd you hear that?"

"There are a lot of people who know about it. Apparently there was an incident at the Skydeck Club."

He went pale. "I'm sorry. Chase, I have no idea what you're talking about."

"Some of the people who were there still remember it. Why don't you tell me what's going on?"

He looked at me a long time. Then he lowered himself into a chair. "Please." His voice shook. "Chase, you look like a decent woman. I'm begging you: Walk away from this. Drop it. You can't do any good for anyone. Let it go." He wiped the back of his hand against his mouth. "*Please*. Leave it alone."

"Hal—" He shook his head. Clamped his lips together. Tears rolled down his cheeks. "You can trust me," I said. "If it's as you say, it'll go no further."

He shook his head violently and turned away from me.

*   *   *

I went back to the skimmer and called Alex. "Is my job still open?"

Eliot Statkins was less happy when I told him I would make the final scheduled flight for Rigel, but that it would be my last.

"Why, Chase?" He tried to speak like a father, but he couldn't bring it off. "We can always find another pilot, but you're throwing away a golden opportunity. Why don't you take some time and think about it? There's no big hurry. When you get to Arkon, on the outbound leg, send me a message. To me, personally. Let me know what you want to do. Meanwhile, I'll take no action."

"Eliot, I'm just not comfortable on these flights."

"Why not?" He looked shocked by the proposition. Surely I recognized how unreasonable it was.

"It has nothing to do with the flights themselves. It's just that—"

"Yes?"

"My future's with Alex."

"With the antique dealer?"

"Yes."

"I can't believe you really think that. An antique dealer? Well, it's your call. But think about it. That's all I'm asking. I know we don't pay as much as he does, but we'll still be here in thirty years. Hell, he could shut down tomorrow. With us, you get a lot of benefits, not to mention housing. A fat retirement. Security. And where else would you find a career this interesting? Most pilots would kill for your job."

I thanked him, and told him I'd send a message from Arkon. An hour later, I boarded the *Gonzalez* and started getting ready for departure.

I called Robin from the bridge.

"*Marvelous,*" he said. "*When you get back, we'll do a celebration.*"

"Sounds good."

"*Chase?*"

"Yes?"

"*I think I'm in love with you.*"

*   *   *

I won't say it was an uneventful flight. Before we got to Arkon, I had to deal with an orgy that spilled out into the main cabin, a passenger who was unhappy with the food and insisted on holding me personally responsible, and a gambling dispute that ended in a broken jaw. Oh, and I also got to deliver a baby.

At Arkon, a veteran pilot said it all sounded pretty routine. "Don't worry," he told me, "after a while you'll be able to deal with this stuff standing on your head."

I sent Eliot a message confirming my resignation.

During my last night on the ship, I didn't sleep much. I was on the bridge after midnight, dozing, but not anxious to go back to my quarters. We were three hours from making our jump, and the ship was silent, save for the barely audible sound of the engines and the air vents. Jack had congratulated me when I told him. But he'd shown no other reaction, and my conversations with him had been routine. But as the clock ticked down, he delivered a brief piece of static, his equivalent of clearing his throat. *"Chase?"*

"Yes, Jack?"

"I'm glad that you are so happy. But I will miss you."

"Thanks, Jack. "I'll miss you, too."

"Are you sure you're doing the right thing?"

"Yes. I am sure."

"Good. I think you are, too. Good luck."

"Thank you."

"May I say something else?"

"Of course."

"Knowing you these few weeks—"

"Yes—?"

"Makes me, for the first time, wonder whether I would not be better off being human."

TWENTY-SIX

Every individual existence goes out in a lonely spasm of helpless agony.

—William James, *The Varieties of Religious Experience*

When I showed up at the country house, flowers were waiting on my desk. Alex gave me time to settle in; then he came downstairs and hugged me. "Nice to have you back, Chase," he said. "The place was never the same without you."

"Well," I said, "thanks. I think I discovered I wasn't meant to pilot transports."

We enjoyed the moment and emptied a bottle of Varicotta wine. It was still morning, and I'm not used to drinking before lunch, so he had to feed me to get me back to normal.

"I don't think," he said, "there's any question that Cavallero overlooked or neglected something, that it led to a serious consequence of some kind for Rachel, and that that was the reason for the quarrel, if that's the right word."

"So," I said, "we need something that happened on a tour, that was serious enough to drive the captain to suicide twenty-eight years later, but was apparently only picked up by the scopes or scanners, since nobody else, none of the passengers, seemed to notice."

"Whatever it was, she came back, argued with Cavallero, and told Tuttle what she'd seen. And probably took him back to show him."

"But if we're talking about aliens, why did Tuttle not say anything?"

"That's really the question, isn't it, Chase? Rachel keeps it quiet, and so does he. I don't know. Other than the story Rachel has: that these creatures are so deadly that they felt it was necessary to keep their existence and location secret. But if *that* part of the account is true, then she didn't come across them on a tour. She was out riding with Tuttle. Because there's no way she could have picked that up without the passengers knowing.

"We have to figure out where she went on the last tour. What was the name of her ship?"

"The *Silver Comet.*"

"But they didn't keep the records."

Audree called to tell me she was glad I'd changed my mind. *"He hasn't been the same since you left,"* she said. *"I think I'm jealous."*

"I think it's time," Alex said, "that Rainbow ran a competition. A contest. We need to give away some prizes."

"Why?" I asked.

"To generate some publicity."

"I'm serious. Why?"

"That last tour. The passengers would have taken pictures, right?"

"I don't know."

"Tourists always take pictures. A lot of them will be out the windows. Somewhere, somebody has a visual record of that last flight. We have to find it."

"You think aliens will show up on it?"

He laughed. "We'll need Shara. Whatever happened, we can probably assume they never took a tour back to *that* destination. So we look for the latest tour to each destination and hope it's the last one. There'll be pictures of the sky. There *have* to be. Turn them over to Shara and let her figure out where they are."

"Okay," I said. "It might work."

Two days later, Rainbow launched its Cosmic Tour Contest. We were putting together, the announcement said, a record of "the most striking images" captured by nonprofessionals aboard tour ships. The images could be of planetary rings, comets, solar eruptions, flares, luminous clouds, planetary landscapes, or whatever else could be expected to appeal to our sense of off-world beauty.

Since World's End had built its reputation primarily by tours into the Veiled Lady, we excluded systems within the Confederate domain, explaining that we were looking for images not seen before. There was also a human-interest category: pictures of people reacting to the wonders around them, or simply dining together by the light of alien stars. Participants were invited to be creative, and nothing was off the table. Cash prizes were offered, and the winners would be included in *Cosmic Wonders*, to be published by Hawksworth & Steele later in the year.

"I'll want you to put *that* together in your spare time," Alex said.

"*Cosmic Wonders?*"

"I'm open to a better title if you can think of one. The assignment should be easy. Use lots of pictures."

Entrants were required to complete a form, indicating when the pictures had been taken, the name of the touring company, and the ship. If known, they were also to indicate *where* the pictures had been taken.

That part of the exercise turned out to be, as we expected it would be, a fool's game. Everybody knew where their tours had gone, but the names were pure fiction, invented by the companies. Place names like Bootstrap and Carmody and Rhinestone and Weinberg's Star. They didn't even try to maintain consistency. What was Werewolf to Blue Diamond Tours might be Harmony over at World's End. And when we checked with World's End, we discovered none of the names had survived into current usage. They still made up names, but the new owners had installed their own set.

That afternoon, in a mood for premature celebration (we did that all the time, in case things went wrong), we went to Tardy's for lunch.

Unlike me, when Alex ate lunch at Tardy's, he liked to go early and park on the island. But we were late getting out, and when we arrived there, the island spaces were full. No surprise.

"You want to go somewhere else?" I asked. It was raining, and I thought he might prefer something with indoor parking.

"Up to you," he said.

"I'm hungry."

"Then let's go here. It's only water."

We set down in the big onshore lot, as close as I could get to the viaduct. As if we'd thrown a switch, the rain became more intense. Alex laughed, said something about timing, and climbed out. We hurried to the crossover, which got no protection from the canopy because of a stiff wind. We half walked half rode across, ran the last ten meters, and were glad to get inside, where it was warm and dry.

We took our time eating and let the storm play out. I don't remember much of what we talked about, other than Alex predicting that we would know within two weeks' time where the *Silver Comet* had gone. We finished lunch and refilled the wineglasses. Somebody was playing a piano in the next room, performing one stormy-weather number after another.

Eventually, we finished, and the sun emerged from the clouds. We paid and strolled outside. A few people were on the viaduct, moving in both directions. Each of the glideways is equipped with a guardrail that moves with it.

We got on and didn't feel much like walking, so we just rode across, leaning over the rail, looking at the river, paying no attention to anything else. There were only a few other people there. Lunch hour was over, so most were going in the same direction we were. My mind was all over the place. I was thinking how glad I was to be back in my old routine, and about Robin and Jack the AI and the Cosmic Tour Contest and suddenly there was a lot of noise around me. People began yelling look out, and the glideway jerked to a stop and somebody screamed. Then the viaduct collapsed.

No. Not so much collapsed as *melted*.

The glideway turned to water. Someone jerked me back, onto solid ground. Several of us spilled onto the deck. Two or three people were scrambling to get clear. The walkway, the piece where we'd been, had literally vanished. Alex was in the river. Along with a young woman.

The guy who'd pulled me back asked if I was okay but didn't wait for an answer. Two more people were hanging on, calling for help. A teenage girl was yelling into her link. Alex and the woman were being carried downstream.

The teen was saying, "Yes, yes, we're at Tardy's. Please hurry—"

Alex could swim reasonably well, and my first reaction was that unless he was hurt, he'd be okay. But that thought was immediately overwhelmed by the roar of Chambourg Falls.

I needed the skimmer.

The glideways weren't moving, of course, but the way to the riverbank was intact. I took off. Meanwhile, people on shore saw what had happened and began running onto the viaduct to help. The result was that I had to plow through heavy traffic. As I finally got clear, I spotted a familiar woman in a light jacket climbing into one of the skimmers. I needed a moment before I placed her: It was the woman I'd seen on the train to Carnaiva. The Mortician.

Alex and the woman in the river were moving steadily downstream. There was just time enough to get to them. But I suddenly realized I didn't remember where I'd left the skimmer. It was close to the viaduct. But where? Most of the parking places were taken, and I couldn't see it.

I ran frantically from one vehicle to another. Where *was* the damned thing?

I wasted three or four minutes looking. And I hate to admit this, but I was in tears when a guy who'd just parked in the automobile section asked if he could help so I said yeah, I've got an emergency, and I've lost my skimmer; it's a green Vamoso, brand-new. He went one way, and I went another. Moments later, I heard his voice. "Over here. It's over here." And, "Can I help? Are you okay?" He was short and stocky. Not much more than a kid.

"Do you have a rope in your car? A cable of some kind?"

"No. Sorry."

"Thanks," I said, and scrambled into the Vamoso. I started the engine before I was even in the seat and pulled the door shut as I lifted off. We'd had the thing less than a month, and I knew it hadn't acquired the junk that people always keep in the storage compartment. Like a line.

How the hell was I going to get him out of the water? All I had was the treads.

I swung downstream, calling for help, looking for another skimmer. The police responded by asking me what was my problem? Then, *"We're sending someone now."* But they weren't there yet, and there was no time left.

The Melony at that point was about a half-kilometer wide, narrowing down as it neared the falls.

I stayed just above the river and spotted the woman. But not Alex. Where the hell was Alex?

Then we were into the rapids. Ahead I could see the observation platforms on both sides from which people came and gawked at the falls. And then I saw Alex. The two were almost abreast, but not close to each other. As I watched, the current drove the woman hard into a rock. Still, she managed to stay afloat.

She saw me coming and tried to wave. She used her left arm, and every time she did it she sank out of sight, only to fight her way back to the surface. Her right arm appeared to be useless.

Finally, an emergency vehicle appeared. But it was too far away to help.

Alex was trying to get to shore, but he was making no progress.

I raced in their direction. The AI warned me I was getting too close to the river. My heart pounded.

I couldn't save both. There was no way I could manage that. Might not be able to save either.

Make the call.

It had to be Alex. The woman waved at me with her good arm as I passed overhead. I cut to port, positioned myself directly over him, and came down almost on top of him. It was a dangerous maneuver, but I had nothing else. I needed him to grab hold of one of the treads. It was all I could do.

A police voice broke in: *"Vamoso, are you crazy? Get out of there."*

I counted to five, thinking how either he was gone, or he was hanging on. Then I started up. We'd picked up some mass, so he was there. I could try the same method with the woman. There was just time, but if Alex was clinging to the treads, I'd almost certainly knock him loose.

But I knew what he'd have wanted.

The current had carried her past me. I came in behind her. The falls was so loud I could barely make out the police voices. *"Be careful, Vamoso."*

The water ahead was filled with rocks. I came down above her, got as low as I could. Then the river was gone and I was looking down into that vast chasm. Mist swirled up.

I drifted over a grassy bank and got as low as I could until the extra pressure on the antigravs vanished, signaling he'd let go. Then I pulled up until I could see him. He was stretched out on the shore. On the river, an emergency vehicle was circling the edge of the falls. I landed a few meters from him.

He looked exhausted. "Thanks," he said.

"I tried to get both of you."

"I know." He pulled himself into a sitting position. A police vehicle was coming down near us. "I'm sorry. There wasn't enough time. I don't think she could have held on anyhow. It looked as if she'd broken an arm."

TWENTY-SEVEN

The thing about murder is, it's so personal. War's not good either. But in combat, at least, you only get killed because you've gotten in the way. Soldiers from opposite sides have even been known to get together after hostilities cease and toast each other. But chances are good that you'll never raise a glass to someone who's tried to take you out, you, by name, date of birth, and eye color.

—Racine Vales, *Memoirs*

"It was a fluxer," Fenn said. We were in his office.

"A *what*?" I asked.

"Universal solvent. It was placed on one of the support beams. Held in place by a magnet."

"What do you carry a universal solvent in?" I asked.

"It gets mixed as it gets sprayed, Chase."

"I know who's doing it," I said.

Both men looked at me in surprise. "Who's that?" asked Fenn.

"She's tall, pale, thin. Looks like a mortician. I saw her on the train to Carnaiva, and saw her again the last time I ate at Tardy's. She was there this morning."

"You can identify her?"

"Absolutely."

"All right. Why don't you look through our files, and we'll see if we can figure out who she is."

He turned on a display.

"Before we start," I said, "I have a question."

"Sure."

"The woman who died out there today. Who was she?"

"Her name was Mira Espy. She was twenty."

Mira hadn't lived long enough to accomplish much. She looked good, and she enjoyed parties. She was in school, and had a part-time job as a medical receptionist. Judging from the turnout at the memorial service, she had a lot of friends.

The Mortician was Petra Salyeva. She'd been denied a physics doctor-ate after threatening the life of a young man who hadn't paid sufficient attention to her. Doctors had diagnosed her with Kalper's Disease, which severely limits the ability to experience empathy. Authorities were con-templating a mind wipe, but she disappeared while they debated. She was a killer for hire. Current whereabouts unknown. Though not anymore.

She was, by the way, a pilot, although her license had been revoked.

"You're sure that's her?" Fenn asked.

"No question."

"Okay. She's good at what she does. So we'll have to assign a security detail. Until we can lock her down."

So I acquired a guard. Her name was Rhonda.

Entries in the Rainbow Cosmic Tour Contest began to come in, at first occasionally, but by the end of the week, we had more than six hundred, encompassing both stills and holograms, and even an audio that was simply a record of a conversation between a young girl, probably about nine, and a ship's captain. It was from Barkley Tours, six years ago, and its description of the child's admiration for the soft glow of a moon illu-minated by a blue star was touching. We would, I decided, include it in *Cosmic Wonders*.

The vast majority of the entries were from recent voyages. Only a handful, about twenty, originated from World's End and could be placed within the 1402–3 time period. None of those featured Rachel, but usu-ally we didn't know until we'd looked because hardly any of the tourists remembered what their captain's name had been.

One woman recalled a flight she'd been on. *"It was the ultimate romantic cruise. There were eight of us, four young couples. We went to one world where they had three moons and the most beautiful skies I've ever seen. The tour company had four cottages waiting. They cooked dinner for us over an open fire, and we sang songs, and listened to the noises in the woods. And at another place, we were able to swim in a stream—"*

Another narrator, in an entry titled "Standing on the Shore," remembered a world on which life was getting started. It was still confined to the oceans, and he recalled the eerie sensation of standing on a beach on a world teeming with living things, none of which was visible.

The days passed, and entries continued to arrive. And, finally, we got one with Rachel. Dated late winter, 1402.

The accompanying vids were mostly set inside the ship, which was identified as the *Silver Comet*. People looked out the viewports, stood smiling beside their captain, pretended to study star charts, embraced, offered toasts, danced, and sang. But there were also images of planets, moons, asteroids, and rings. And an enormous world, almost but not quite massive enough, according to Captain Rachel, to ignite and become a star. It threw off occasional jets.

She was easy to like. She paid attention to the passengers, was especially good with the two kids on board, never allowed herself to get annoyed even when the questions were dumb.

They partied, literally cheered when the *Comet* drew close to an abandoned space station somewhere in the Veiled Lady, raised their glasses to a beautiful blue world that bore a remarkable resemblance to Earth, and drew to within two hundred meters of a real comet. It was a fireball, and Rachel got giggles from the kids when she asked whether anyone would like to go down and look around.

All told, we collected holograms from three of her missions. The other two were dated in 1399, and in the early spring of 1403. We didn't have an exact date of departure for Rachel's final mission, but we knew she'd quit in the spring. The system they'd visited had received one of the standard-issue names assigned by World's End to attract the interest of potential customers. It was Echo, so called, according to the company, because its soft light, on two terrestrial worlds, would "remind you of your youth." It was billed as the most romantic spot in the Veiled Lady.

But nobody knew, three decades later, where Echo was, or which star it had been. So we sent the visuals to Shara, who had agreed to try to pinpoint the system.

I took advantage of the opportunity the following day to stop by her office. I was accompanied by Rhonda. Shara said she hadn't had a chance yet to look at the data. But she was clearly impressed by my security. "The little green men getting that dangerous?" she asked.

I told her about the attack on the river. "I saw something about that," she said. "I didn't realize you and Alex were involved."

Rhonda stayed at a substantial distance. Either because she felt she'd get a better view of the surroundings that way, or she was allowing me a modicum of privacy. "We almost lost Alex," I said.

Shara motioned me toward a conference room. "It's more comfortable in here, Chase."

Rhonda checked the room first, then took up a position at the door.

"Do you think," I asked, "you'll be able to figure out where the ship was?"

"Probably."

"What's the method? You going to use a spectroscope?" I was showing off a little. I'd expected she'd try to use spectroscopic analyses to identify the sun.

"Wouldn't work," she said. "An imaging system doesn't give you an accurate gauge of the light. It would be easy if we could, but we're going to have to do some pattern-matching. But we should be able to make it happen. As long as you sent us some decent shots."

"So how do you do it?"

She got some coffee out of a machine, handed me a cup, and tried to give another one to the guard. Rhonda smiled and declined. "We want wide-angle shots where possible," Shara said. "Then all we have to do is identify *one* star. Once I've done that, I can put together a spherical 3-D map with that star as the center. The image will give us a kind of pie-slice wedge cut out of the map with the ship at the point of the wedge. There'll be just one spot in the map that matches the image."

"Okay," I said, not entirely sure I got it. But she seemed to know what she was talking about. "Sounds good to me."

"If we can identify additional stars, it'll go even faster." She smiled. "Okay?"

"Absolutely," I said.

"How about lunch?"

"Where do you suggest?"

Rhonda insisted we eat in the cafeteria.

When I got back to the country house, another Rachel hologram was waiting. But it was dated 1399, too early to be helpful. I watched it anyhow. Watched as she managed the tourists with aplomb and the controls with a steady hand. I got a better close-up of her operational skills with this one than I had with the others. She knew her way around the bridge, and she was as emotionally caught up in the tours as the clients.

Her voice deepened with emotion as she arced her ship around the curve of a terrestrial world while the tourists watched a golden sunrise. She took them over placid oceans, and clouds drifting in moonlight. She descended into canyons on rugged lunar surfaces and glided just above the atmosphere of a gas giant while showing her passengers an enormous, vaporous creature that moved silently through the haze. They watched it suck up gases, and she told them it was a *gobble*, and they all laughed.

When I got to the country house next morning, Jacob was waiting. *"Shara called. She has some results."*

"Good. See if you can get her, Jacob." He'd already informed Alex, but star positions meant nothing to him, so he'd set it aside until I arrived. Now he came into the office just as Shara blinked on. *"Hi, Chase. I've sent the details over with the visuals."*

"Thanks," I said. "What did you get?"

"The system's catalog number is YL69949. It's a class-G sun. Located in the Veiled Lady, out toward the Jordanian Cloud."

"Okay."

"Margin of error is less than two percent."

Alex was delighted. "Excellent, Shara. Thank you."

"My pleasure."

"We'll be going out there once we get everything together. You want to come?"

"No, thanks. I like stuff that's predictable."

I worked late that evening, doing a survey: None of the touring companies were going to YL69949. None had a record of ever having been there. When I was about to leave, I opened my channel to Alex to say good night, but Jacob alerted me that he was outside the house.

We were keeping the blinds down, as a security measure. I went over and looked through them. Alex was standing in the moonlight near the edge of the forest. Just standing there. I knew his security guard couldn't be happy about it.

Considering the mood Shara's success had engendered, I was surprised to see him out there. I hung on until he and the guard came back inside. "You okay?" I asked.

"Sure," he said. "Just going for a walk."

"Part of your exercise routine?"

"Pretty much." The guard retired to his station, which was directly across the corridor from my office. Alex looked at the clock. "What are you doing in here at this hour?"

I told him. Checking to see whether anybody goes out to Echo.

He nodded. "Go home."

"Okay."

He stood near the foot of the staircase. "Chase," he said, "I'm sorry I got you into this."

"It's okay. Not your fault."

"I wish we'd never seen the damned thing."

PART III

Echo

TWeNTY-eiGHT

There is nothing that quite captures the spirit as does that which stands alone, a lighthouse on a rocky shore, an observatory on the dark side of a moon, an eagle perched on a rocky shelf at dawn.

—Yashir Kamma, *At the Edge of the World*

When you make the jump from hyperspace into the middle of a system that is uncharted, it takes a while to figure out what the system looks like. We had nothing on the star that was recorded in Shara's catalog as YL69949. The contest submission had shown us an asteroid, a gas giant and a set of rings, and, most spectacularly, a pair of comets. I'd never seen *twin* comets before, and of course they were gone. Maybe they'd be back in a couple of centuries. Fortunately, all these pictures had also given us a starry background.

Other than that, it had been all partygoers, people wearing funny hats and offering toasts to Uncle Albert and somebody who kept saying I told you so.

We were on the edge of the Veiled Lady. The sun was a class-G yellow dwarf, like the suns found in the home systems that had given birth to the two known technological civilizations. What else actually orbited Echo, the number of planets, their parameters, and so on, was of no interest. Save those worlds that were warm enough for life to have evolved.

The sun floated serenely off to starboard. About twenty minutes after emergence, Belle reported it was somewhat more than three hundred million klicks away. We were on the outer edge of the biozone.

"Any planets yet?" I asked.

"Working on it," she said.

Alex let me see that he perceived the question as of little consequence. "Are we getting anything that might be an artificial radio signal?"

"Negative," she said.

"Let us know if you hear anything."

"Of course, Alex."

It was a bad beginning. Had there been a technological civilization anywhere in the system, we would almost certainly have been picking up electronic signals of one kind or another. Belle needed almost five hours before she could report a planet. *"It's a gas giant. A sun skimmer, barely twenty million klicks out. No rings. It doesn't seem to have any moons."*

"Probably pretty warm at that range," I said.

"What else can you see, Belle?"

"That's all for the moment. Trying to confirm other possibilities. But it'll take a while."

We sat quietly in the cockpit. The sky was filled with stars, and the Cricket Nebula floated directly overhead. "Where's Rimway's sun?" asked Alex. "Can you tell?"

"It's not visible from here," I said.

If we continued to explore the Veiled Lady and its neighborhood for the next million years, I suspected we still wouldn't have seen half its worlds. And with so much real estate, it was impossible to believe there was no place anywhere that did not provide a haven for *somebody*. Something out there was looking at the same spectacle we were. Had to be.

The hours crept past. We sat listening to the vents and the just-audible flow of power and the bleeps and clicks of the various systems. Alex was reading while I played cards with Belle. I leaned over but couldn't see the title.

"Down and Out on Radford III," he said.

"Never heard of it."

"It's about six hundred years old."

"What's Radford III?"

"It was an early colonization attempt that went wrong."

"Oh."

"At the beginning of the Interstellar Age, more than half of them failed during the first thirty years."

"Why?"

"Usually bad planning. Lack of foresight. Relying on luck. Don't worry about it; God will see us through. That sort of thing."

Then Belle had more news: *"We have one world eighty-five million klicks from the sun, and I suspect another one is in the biozone on the far side."*

"Okay," said Alex. "How long to confirm the one on the far side?"

"We need to change our angle."

"We could be talking a few days, Alex," I said.

Alex nodded. "All right. Let's take a look at the one we can see."

It was a terrestrial world, a little bit larger than Rimway, lots of clouds and storms. It appeared to be mostly dry land. No globe-circling oceans. A few big lakes and a lot of small ones.

While we made our approach, a message arrived from Robin. I went back to my cabin and started it. He blinked on, sitting on the sofa in his living room, one leg crossed over the other. *"Wish I'd been able to go along,"* he said. He looked good. *"Life around here just isn't the same without you. I'll confess I have a date this evening with a woman I've known on and off for years. Her name is Kyra. We're going to have dinner at Bacari's, then probably go to a show. I keep thinking it's really not fair to her, because the whole time I'm with her I'll be thinking of you."*

The message was six days old. I responded that I was sure he and Kyra had enjoyed themselves, but I hoped not too much. (I tried to turn it into a joke, but in fact I was annoyed. And he knew I would be.) "We've arrived at our destination," I said, "but at the moment we don't know anything about the place. Right now we're just afloat, looking around. It might take a couple of days before we really know what our prospects are. And by the way, I miss you, too."

Okay. It's hard to capture our state of mind while everything was in the air. The world, Belle had decided, was the second one out from the sun. Henceforth it would be known as Echo II. *"There is no indication,"* she said, *"of artificial construction anywhere* yet. *Be aware, though, that we are still a considerable distance away. Even a city, at this range, might not be visible. But, unfortunately, there is no evidence of electronic activity."*

The surface, however, was green. *"It's a living world,"* she continued, and that news alone sent my pulse up a few beats. We were angling in from the outer planetary system, so we had a good look at the nightside of Echo II. It was unbroken by light anywhere, except occasional flickers that probably represented electrical storms or fires.

Alex sighed. "Not going to be anything here," he said.

Well, what had we expected? If we'd actually seen something, seen lights come on somewhere, maybe even seen a ship draw alongside and ask who we were, I'd have fallen out of my chair. In thousands of years, and tens of thousands of flights, it's never happened.

Well, once.

So you don't expect it. Still, there was the tablet.

Then Belle surprised us. *"There's an artificial satellite. I'll have a picture for you in a minute."*

"Yes!" I said.

Alex raised a cautionary hand. "Don't get too excited."

"Why not?"

"It was probably left by us. Maybe a long time ago, maybe by World's End. It could be a promo gimmick."

"I think that's stretching things, Alex."

"Just don't get your hopes up."

A picture of the object appeared on the auxiliary screen: It was a rectangular case supporting an array of antennas. There was also a scope. The AI placed the satellite alongside an image of the *Belle-Marie* so we could judge comparative size. It was almost as big as we were.

"Belle," I said, "put us on an intercept course."

We needed a couple of hours to turn around and, eventually, to move alongside the object. It was dark gray, inert, and the scope had taken a hit from something.

"It's in an irregular orbit," said Belle.

I rotated the image at Alex's request, spun it around its axis, turned it over until he saw what he wanted. *"There,"* he said. Two lines of characters were emblazoned on the case.

"Don't recognize them," said Belle. *"They aren't in the standard directory."*

And they bore no resemblance to the ones on the tablet.

"Belle," Alex said, "you say the orbit's irregular. *How* irregular?"

"Not an excessive amount. Apogee is one point four perigee."

Alex looked at me. "Translate, please?"

"At its farthest point," I said, "the satellite is almost one and a half times as far from the central body as at its closest approach."

"If the trend continues unabated," said Belle, *"it will eventually begin dipping into the atmosphere. That will, of course, be the end of it."*

"When would that be likely to happen?"

"I would estimate about another hundred years."

"Can we make an age determination based on that?"

"Negative, Alex. We simply do not have enough information." We turned it some more. Magnified everything. *"You can, however,"* said Belle, *"do an analysis."*

"How?"

"It's actually quite straightforward. But you'll have to bring a piece of it inside."

I went out and cut a slice from the leading edge. I also removed part of the scope and brought both pieces back in. Belle examined them and, after a few minutes, announced her conclusion: *"The satellite has been in orbit approximately four thousand years."*

"How can you tell?" Alex asked.

"If you look closely, you will note the pitting in the metal. It's caused by micrometeoroids. Also, the burnishing along the forward edge is instructive. Very fine particles collide with it over the centuries, and this wear is the result. We also have a telescope lens. If you look at it under sufficient magnification, you will observe a slight hazing."

"And that happens because—?"

"Accumulated radiation damage from the sun. I don't have a clear

analysis of the background radiation here, or the dust density, but it's not difficult to provide a reasonable estimate."

"Thanks, Belle."

"You're welcome, Alex. I'm sorry it's not the result you would have preferred."

We saw nothing artificial on the ground. But Belle reported large animals.

"Can you show them to us?" asked Alex. He couldn't hide his disappointment that Echo II wasn't a world full of cities. Or, at least, a place with some research facilities.

Something.

Belle put a catlike creature on-screen. It was gray, with long fangs, almost a saber-tooth. The thing was virtually invisible against the trees and shrubbery through which it moved. And she showed us a bird that seemed so fat it could not possibly have gotten airborne. But it soared through the sky like an eagle.

And a lizard with a long, muscular, serpentine neck. We couldn't be sure how big it was, but it measured pretty well against the tree trunks.

There was also something that looked like nothing more than a cluster of weeds. But Belle asked us to watch for a moment. *"Let me do a replay. This happened minutes ago."* A four-legged creature that might have been a vulpine of some sort wandered by, and a tentacle whipped out of the weeds and made a grab. More tentacles appeared, and, within seconds, the vulpine was hopelessly ensnared, and the animal was dragged into the tangle. The struggle went on for about a minute, devolving finally into a series of lurches. Then it stopped, and we saw movement that suggested the weed cluster had begun feeding.

Echo II was covered with towering mountain chains, broad rivers, vast plains, and jungles. A blizzard was dumping snow in the south polar region. No cities were visible, no highways, no bridges, no artificial structures of any kind.

Nothing.

"Can you see anything at all?" Alex asked Belle. "Tools? Shelters? Outhouses?"

"Negative. There does not appear to be anything like that here."

"You're sure?"

"Well, I haven't looked at every square meter, Alex. But I will let you know immediately if I see anything of an artificial nature."

I remember thinking how it would feel to go back empty-handed. How frustrating it would be after all the commotion about the tablet. And Rachel's death would remain meaningless.

Alex developed a theory that maybe Tuttle was behind everything. That he'd designed the tablet himself, had arranged to get one made, and used it in an effort to get back at those who had derided him all those years, who'd tried to persuade him to do something "constructive" with his life. That somehow he'd fooled Rachel, had persuaded her he'd found something. Then, when she'd learned the truth, she was humiliated, had never forgiven him, and had tried to hide the story. That, ultimately, it was Tuttle who'd been responsible for her suicide.

"But the pieces don't really fit," he said. "I guess I'm just trying to get her off my conscience."

The weed cluster wasn't the only vegetation that was dangerous. We watched something that looked like a cactus jump on and devour a small animal that made the mistake of coming down from a tree. After that, there was a bush that grabbed a deerlike creature, ripped it apart, and was still enjoying the meal when we passed out of range.

There was a second terrestrial in the system that we wanted to check, but Alex refused to be hurried. "Let's make sure there's really nothing here before we leave."

So for days we pursued the search. We looked closely into forest and jungle areas. We studied valleys and mountaintops. We tracked rivers. And finally, on the fourth evening as we were getting ready to give it up, Belle broke in with news: *"I have a building."*

Alex looked pleased, but he was careful not to allow his emotions to carry him away. "Where, Belle?"

"In the northern latitudes." She gave us a picture. It looked like nothing more than an old, battered structure, a wreck half-buried in the snow-covered floor of a winter forest. Whatever color it might once have had was gone. It was a washed-out gray, completely enmeshed in vines

and shrubs. One section of the structure appeared to have been shoved aside by the trees.

It might originally have been a polygon. There were multiple sides, though it was impossible to determine how many. Maybe eight or nine.

"How big is it?" asked Alex.

"*Approximately forty meters across. Maybe a bit more. It's hard to make out details. The forest has been growing around it for a long time.*"

"How long?"

"*Can't really say. But I suspect it's been here for millennia. And it appears to have had several levels. Probably four. So much of it is buried, it's hard to be certain.*"

"Can you see anything else there anywhere?"

"*You mean around it?*"

"Yes. Another building. A vehicle. Some tools. Anything at all."

"*Nothing artificial, Alex. It is possible there's an entire city buried at the site. I'm not equipped to probe beneath surfaces. As you know.*" Belle sounded annoyed. That might have been because she'd suggested that Alex equip the vehicle with penetrating sensors. At the time, it had seemed an unnecessary expense.

"What's the atmosphere like?" I asked.

"*Inadequate oxygen. You'll need air tanks.*"

Belle put together lunches for us. Chocolate chip cookies and chicken sandwiches. We picked up a cutter and some torches from storage, went down to the launch bay, and climbed into the lander. Alex put the sandwiches in the cooler and started going through the images of the wreckage while I munched on a cookie and ran systems checks. Then he took a long look at the surrounding forest. After a few minutes, he shook his head. "Makes no sense," he said.

"What's that?"

"There's nothing else down there. Just this one place."

"*Optimum launch time in six minutes,*" said Belle.

"We'll go with that, Belle." I closed the hatch. Belle began depressurizing the launch bay. Alex looked at the cookies, which were wrapped in plastic, lying in my lap. "What?" I said.

"How are they?"

"They're good. Want one?"

"Sure. Start every mission with a cookie. It's in the *Antiquarian Guidebook*."

I gave him two and put the rest in a compartment while he brought his harness down and secured himself.

We sat talking about the polygon. Who had put it there? How old was it? Might this be where Tuttle found the tablet?

"Depressurization complete," said Belle. *"Launch in ninety seconds."* The bay door opened, and I released the locks.

"Whenever you're ready, Belle," I said.

She eased us out of the ship. I started the engines, and we began our descent.

It was just after sunrise when we glided in over the polygon. It was literally buried among the trees. They had thick trunks though they were not especially tall. The biggest might have been about thirty meters. They appeared gray and hard, more like rocks than living things. Broken branches lay everywhere.

The polygon itself was barely visible. I could easily have flown over it without noticing the thing.

Where the hell was everybody else on this world?

We couldn't determine whether it had a front or back. Not that it mattered. I circled the area, looking for a place to land. There was no sufficiently open space within twenty kilometers of the structure. So I picked a spot where we'd do the least damage to the trees, and started down. We tore off a lot of branches along the way and finally settled into the shrubbery.

We got into our suits, checked the air—we had a four-hour supply in the tanks—checked the radios, and armed ourselves with scramblers. Then we climbed out through the airlock.

Alex led the way down the ladder, took out his weapon, and looked around. When he was satisfied we weren't about to be attacked by anything, he signaled me to follow. I did, leaving the outer hatch open. I thought it was a good idea, in case we had to get back inside in a hurry.

It wasn't.

*   *   *

The snow wasn't deep. Hardscrabble grass poked up through it. We were about forty meters from the building. We each picked up a fallen branch and used it to poke at the vegetation as we proceeded. Nothing reacted, nothing attacked, but I'll admit I'd take my chances with a saber-tooth anytime. We didn't think the scramblers would be effective against *plants*. They disrupted nervous systems. I wasn't sure they'd do much more than that. In the end, I thought, the cutter might be of more use.

But the weeds left us alone, and we got to the polygon without incident.

It appeared to be made of plastic, but the material was so old and so corrupted, it was hard to be certain what it was. I think it had originally been a blend of white and other colors, but they were gone now. The surface was only a series of ashen, gunmetal, smoky splotches. The structure was bent and smashed by falling limbs and trees. In places it had simply buckled. The roof was flat, and sections of it were submerged in earth and snow. Very little of it remained above ground. A good blizzard would have covered everything.

It appeared that it was really a collection of modules. *"I'd like to find the place it was shipped from,"* said Alex.

We found a couple of windows and doors, but the windows had crusted over, and the doors were sealed tight. They had over time melded with and become a permanent part of the walls. But mounted beside one we found a plaque.

It had three lines of characters. Alex wiped it off as best he could so he could see the symbols more clearly. *"This one,"* he said, pointing at one that might have been a reversed "E," *"is also on the satellite."* There were others.

None of them, however, matched anything on the tablet, though one or two were close.

"Why," I asked, "put this place in the middle of a dense forest?"

Alex picked up a fallen branch and tossed it aside. *"There might not have been a forest here at the time."* He tried rubbing down one of the windows. Turned on his lamp and tried to look through. I could make out an empty interior. Cold, dirty, snowy, and empty. We used a cutter to remove the window.

It was simply a large empty space. It would have been easier to come through the roof, which had cracked open. Sunlight filtered through the break. Alex held the lamp up so he could get a better look at the overhead. It sagged. Wires hung down out of it. *"It's about three and a half meters,"* he said.

"Yes. About that." Then I realized what he was saying. "Oh."

"Whoever made this was about our size."

"Well," I said, "we didn't really expect aliens."

"No, I guess not, Chase." He couldn't hide the disappointment in his voice.

We found pieces of what had once been a table and chairs. Everything had come apart, collapsed, broken down, you name it. We put together one of the chairs, hoping, I guess, to discover that the seat was too narrow to accommodate a human. Or maybe that it was too low. Something hopeful.

But it would have been a good fit for us. Alex pressed his fingers against the back of the chair. *"It's going to turn out to be a mission from a long time ago,"* he said.

We found, on the floor and frozen to the table, pieces of metal so thoroughly corroded that I couldn't have guessed their purpose. Knives and forks, maybe. Pens? Tools? Alex looked at them with frustration. *"Whatever these are,"* he said, *"if they were in any kind of decent shape, they'd be worth a small fortune."*

Three doorways opened out of the room. There was also a staircase, leading to the floors below. Or it would have had it not been filled with dirt. The doors had long since fallen off their hinges. Two lay moldering on the floor. The third was either completely buried or had been carried off.

We poked our lamps through each of the doorways in turn. Two opened into identical chambers. The third brought us into a passageway that led to the rear of the building. We took a quick look at the adjoining rooms, decided there was nothing of immediate interest, and exited into the corridor.

There were more doorways. We passed through one, found the remnants of plumbing fixtures, some basins, and a couple of toilets. The wall was broken through at that point, and snow had blown in and covered everything.

There were three other rooms off the passageway, all with collapsed furniture and assorted debris that might have been beds at one time. Alex was uncharacteristically quiet. At one point we approached a table that was, incredibly, still standing. It supported another corroded object. A recorder, possibly. Or an AI. Or the equivalent of a coffee machine. Who knew? I heard him take a long breath. Then he put his foot against one of the table legs. And shoved. It collapsed, dumping the object onto the floor.

"You all right?" I asked.

"Yeah," he said, *"I'm fine."*

The reality about collectors is that they are never interested in anything that's not in mint condition. You could be selling the dagger used by Anna Quatieri to finish off her maniac husband, and if it has a spot of rust, the price goes through the floor. People want items they can put on display, that look good in the living room.

We spent close to two hours in that place. And we learned next to nothing about whoever had occupied the polygon. Maybe experts would have been able to figure out what the equipment did. But all we could make out was that the space had contained furniture and that there had been a washroom available. There might have been operational areas and a maintenance section at ground level. And maybe a vehicle or two. Maybe a plaque to tell us who had been there. But it was all buried.

"They were visitors," Alex said.

"I think you're right. They established a base, stayed awhile, put a satellite in orbit, and went home."

"Echo III," said Alex.

He opened a channel to Gabe, the lander AI. *"Have we found any more polygons anywhere? Any kind of structures at all?"*

"Negative," he said.

"Nothing?"

"Nothing unusual, Alex. Although scanning a planet takes time. I assume there's more here somewhere."

We took pictures. Lots of pictures. We were in back, debating whether we wanted to try fashioning some spades to see if we could dig our way down one floor, when Gabe called back: *"Alex, you have visitors."*

My hair stood up.

Gabe flashed us a picture. *Of the lander cabin.* An apelike creature with white fur was approaching the pilot's seat. It was small, would have come to about my belt. It was also loud. It let out a wail and pulled on the back of the chair.

"How'd it get in?" I asked.

"It just walked into the airlock and must have pushed the pad." That would have closed the outer hatch, the air would have drained and been replaced by the ship's air supply. Then the inner hatch would have opened.

I was surprised it had survived the decompression.

Alex was already moving back toward the window we had come through. I followed.

"Gabe," I said. "Open the airlock. Both hatches."

"Chase, you know the system's not designed for that."

"Override it. Do what you have to."

"There may be toxic organisms."

"We can flush it later. Just do it, Gabe."

We hurried along the passageway, entered the main room, and made for the exit.

"Chase."

"Yes, Gabe?"

"It's not working. I can't open the hatches."

"Why not?"

"I'm not getting a response from the activator. The animal probably broke something on the way in. You'll have to open it manually to get him out."

"Okay. We'll be there in a minute."

"Stop where you are."

"Why?"

"There's another one outside. A big one."

It was indeed. *"My God,"* Alex said.

It was a knuckle-dragging monster. Fangs, enormous shoulders, long, muscular arms, and an expression that looked distinctly unhappy. Like the small one, the thing was covered with white fur. A ridge ran across the center of its skull, front to back. The creature was standing near the hatch, which was now closed. It snarled and screeched and pounded on the hull. It stomped around in circles, glaring at the lander. It yanked down a tree branch and rammed it against the hatch.

"The one inside," I said. "It must be a cub."

Alex unholstered his scrambler. *"We're going to have to shoot the thing."*

"I guess."

Alex set it for disable. And aimed.

TWENTY-NINE

Confront an eagle, challenge a dragon if you will. Even, perhaps, take your chances with a killer whale. Just be careful, when you do, that you're facing a male, and not an outraged mother.

—Stellar Kamarides, *Marching Orders*

He pulled the trigger. The thing screeched, raised two claws, and pounded the earth. It looked around, picked up a rock, and hurled it against the hull. It did everything *except* freeze.

Alex reluctantly reset. For *lethal*.

"You can do that," I said, "but if it works, we'll have to kill the cub, too."

He looked at me. *"You have a better suggestion?"*

"Not really."

The cub's face appeared in one of the viewports. Mom saw it and got even louder. *"All right,"* said Alex. *"Maybe we can manage something."*

"Good. I knew you'd come up with an idea."

"But set for lethal. Anything goes wrong, we take the thing out."

"If we can."

"Yes. Well, let's hope we don't have to find out."

"So what do we do?"

"First we have to take out some of the wall. The hole has to be big enough for the creature to get through. And save the questions for later. Let's just do it. But keep out of sight."

Fortunately, the cutters are almost silent. There was an electronic murmur, and the beast looked our way a couple of times. But it was too busy to be bothered or distracted.

So we widened the hole. When we were satisfied it was big enough that the animal could get through, Alex called Gabe.

"Yes, Alex?" he said.

"Cover the viewports."

"Why do that?" I asked.

"We have to make her forget where the cub is."

"I don't think—"

"Just stay with me a minute."

Filters dropped over the ports, and the cub's face was gone.

"Okay, Alex," said Gabe. *"It's done."*

"All right, Chase. Now we have to distract it."

"Distract it? You mean where we wave at it and it comes over here and has you for dinner while I go to the lander and shoo the cub?"

"That's close. I don't think the dinner part's a good idea, though."

"Chase." Gabe's voice had gone up a notch. *"It's gotten upset. The cub."* In the background, I could hear squeals and shrieks.

That wasn't hard to figure out. It couldn't see its mother anymore.

"It might also be getting too much oxygen," said Alex. *"Gabe, can you alter the mix? Give us the same atmosphere in the cabin as there is outside?"*

"It'll take a few minutes."

"Do it."

"Complying."

"Also, record the noise."

"Say again, please."

"Record the racket. If you can, get me two or three minutes' worth of the pup screeching."

"Will do."

The mother was back hammering on the hatch, this time with a large rock.

"Gabe," I said, "other than screeching, what's it doing?"

"It's beating on the airlock and trying to yank your chair out of its

clamps. It also found the cookies and is now going through the storage cabinets."

"Okay," said Alex, *"let me know as soon as you have the recording."*

"Will do," said Gabe. *"One other thing: The cub may break something and strand us on the ground."*

"What do you recommend?" I asked.

"I am sorry to say this, but the logical course would be to kill it."

"How would we do that?" asked Alex.

"Decompress the cabin," I said.

"Suffocate it."

"Yes. Of course that'll upset the mother still more."

"I guess so. Chase, how much air does the lander have? In a worst-case scenario."

"I'm not sure that's the worst case. But we could go on breathing for about two days."

He looked at the cub's image. A lot of fur and large round eyes. It bore a strong resemblance to a terrestrial panda.

Alex took a long, deep breath. The cub was back in the cockpit. It sat down in the right-hand seat and was staring directly out of the screen at us. *"I almost think it knows we're here."*

"Alex, we don't have a lot of time."

"Alex," said Gabe, *"do you want me to decompress?"*

"We *won't* kill it unless we have to."

"Gabe, can you imitate the mother?"

"I think so."

"Do it. Make noises at the rear. Try to get her back near storage again."

"Okay. But be aware—"

"I know. It could get out of hand at any time." Alex started removing his helmet. "What are you doing?" I demanded.

"In a minute." He got the helmet off and now was climbing out of his suit.

"Alex—"

He held up both hands. Be patient. I watched him take an exploratory breath, inhaling slowly, smiling, signaling that it would be okay.

"Alex, I don't want to have to carry you back to the lander."

His link was attached to a silver chain that he customarily wore around his neck. He removed it. "I'll need yours, too, Chase."

"My *what*?"

"Your link." He laid the chain on the ground and started climbing back into the suit.

Mine was embedded in a bracelet. I sighed, took off my helmet, and tried the air. It was thin. Like standing on top of a mountain. And it had an odd scent. But I got out of the suit, removed the bracelet and handed it to him. Then I wasted no time getting the suit back on.

He fiddled with it. Set it so he could control his own link with it. *"Okay."* He was speaking through the link in the helmet again. *"I think we're in business."*

"Glad to hear it."

The creature was standing looking helplessly up at the hatch. Something flew past, screeched, and settled into the trees.

Alex returned the bracelet. *"Hang on to it,"* he said. *"We're going to need it."*

"What are we doing?"

"In a minute."

"Alex," said Gabe, *"I have three minutes of the cub's noise."*

"Start transmitting."

"Complying."

Alex turned the volume down on the silver chain so the whimpers and sniffles and shrieks couldn't be heard outside. *"That's good,"* he said. *"Perfect. Put it on a loop and keep it coming until I tell you to stop."*

"Okay."

"Chase," he said, *"keep out of sight."* He carried the link to the back of the room and disappeared into the corridor.

"It may have gotten bored," said Gabe. *"Hey, pup. Get away from that!"*

I didn't want to ask what was happening. Most of the gear would not have been especially vulnerable, as long as the thing didn't have a branch to swing. Except maybe the yoke. But even if the yoke got broken, I thought I could manage. At least enough to get us into orbit.

"*Stop!*" Now it was Gabe who was screeching.

"What's going on, Gabe?"

"*It found me. It's pulling at me.*"

"Give Belle access to the controls. Just in case."

"*Will do. She's just coming into range now.*"

"Okay."

"*This thing must like black boxes.*"

Abruptly, something behind me whined and sniffled. It sounded like the pup, but it came from the direction Alex had taken. It was barely audible.

It was, of course, the link. I didn't see *him*, but wherever he was, he'd turned up the volume. Then the noise stopped.

I looked out at the creature. It hadn't reacted. Hadn't heard.

Alex came back. He had the chain, but the link wasn't in it. "*I think we're all set, Chase.*"

"Where'd you put the link?" I asked.

"*Out back. In one of the rooms at the rear.*" We stationed ourselves near the hole in the wall, where we could see the mother. "*You ready?*"

I pulled the scrambler out of my tool belt and set for lethal. "Okay," I said.

He asked for my bracelet. Set it to pick up the signal from the lander. "*It's a lovely piece of jewelry.*"

"Just do it, Alex. Hurry."

He pointed at a mound of snow on the far side of the room. "*We get behind that.*"

"Okay."

"*If it comes after us, we take it down. No hesitation. And no second thoughts later.*"

"Let's go," I said.

"*Gabe, where's our cub?*"

"*It's in Chase's seat. It seems to have calmed down a bit.*"

"*Okay. Good. If it starts to get upset again, play the MacIntyre Symphony. Loud. Okay? Crank up the volume as much as you have to. I don't want Mom to hear her cub.*" He switched on the bracelet link. "*Ready?*"

"Go."

He turned up the volume on my bracelet, and the pup's cries, yowls and sniffles and shrieks, filled the building.

The creature turned.

It hesitated. Looked up toward the empty viewport, bared a long set of fangs, and howled.

Then it came running in our direction.

Alex and I didn't need any prompting. We ran for the mound of snow and ducked behind it as the mother roared in through the hole. Alex increased the volume in the other link, the one planted in back, and shut off mine. I'm not sure what Mom was doing because both of us were hiding behind the snow. But I could hear the cub's cries and yelps coming from that back passageway. The creature stomped around a bit, apparently confused. Then it let out a roar and charged to the rear. I stuck my head up just in time to see it vanish through the door. We scrambled for the exit.

The outer hatch was, of course, still closed. Alex leaped onto the ladder and pushed the panel that should have opened the airlock, but nothing happened.

No time to monkey around. I tossed him my cutter. He switched it on and started to burn his way in.

"Hurry, Alex," said Gabe.

I wanted to scream at him to shut up for a couple of minutes. Stop distracting everybody. But I said nothing.

Then he was back: *"Mom found the link."*

"Okay."

"And shut it off." Probably tromped on it.

We were still cutting our way into the lock when the creature came out of the polygon. She saw us and snarled and bared enormous teeth and went into a kind of loping gallop.

The whole wide world knew we were not going to get the hatch open in time. *"Chase."* Alex glanced over his shoulder as I aimed the scrambler. *"Don't shoot. Get on the ladder."* He grabbed one of the rungs himself.

I climbed on beside him. *"Gabe,"* he said. *"Lift off."*

Nothing happened.

"Gabe, take us up."

Still no response.

"Belle," I jumped in. "Take us up. Quick."

"Working on it, Chase. It's a little more complicated from here."

"There's a time factor," I said.

The ground fell away, and I saw saliva flying from Mom's lips as she made a desperate grab for us. But we were out of reach. All she could do was stand down there and throw branches and rocks at the trees.

It was hard to imagine our little panda growing up to look like that.

"Not too high," said Alex. He was trying not to look down as the forest dropped below us.

I picked out a hilltop and told Belle to make for it. "Take it slowly. No sudden stops or turns."

"Have no fear, Chase." Easy for her to say. She wasn't dangling on a frozen rung over the treetops.

The hill was far enough to be safe but close enough that the mother could reach it in a few minutes. We descended into the forest again. We broke off more branches, and we both came away with scrapes and cuts. But we were down.

We finished putting the hole through the outer hatch, got into the airlock, and pushed the pad to open the inner door. The pup was dazed, but okay. It didn't especially want to cooperate, but it didn't like us very much. So when we got inside, it took its first opportunity to get out.

The outer hatch was going to remain useless for the rest of the voyage. That wasn't especially good, but it was a minor inconvenience compared to what might have happened.

We were getting ready to lift off when Belle mentioned that Mom had arrived. She and her pup were standing at the edge of the forest, watching us. I couldn't resist waving.

THirTY

Home. It is the place where once we lived and laughed, where we grew up with the assumption that all would be well, where we met our first love, where life stretched endlessly ahead. This is the place that now becomes a desert of the heart.

—Kory Tyler, *Musings*, 1412

Gabe would be out of action until we got home. The pup had also broken some lamps, cracked a couple of gauges, dislodged a seat, and disconnected a circuit. He was lucky he hadn't been electrocuted. Outside, his mother had taken out two sets of sensors. We'd cut a hole in the outer hatch, thereby depriving the airlock of its utility. We had replacements aboard the *Belle-Marie* for everything except Gabe and the hatch, so there was nothing we couldn't live with.

Alex, pretending to be tough-minded now that the crisis was over, commented that he hoped we'd remember to close the outer hatch next time, and if anything like that happened again, we'd juice the animal. We were in the air again, circling the polygon at about three hundred meters, while Alex studied the building, and I set about patching things as best I could before we lifted into orbit. "I wonder who they were?" I said.

He produced a bottle of wine, cracked it open, and filled two glasses. He handed me one and raised his. "To the little green men."

"Who weren't there." I touched his glass with mine and drained it. I felt as if I needed it. Endless forest spread out on all sides. "You think this was the source of the tablet?"

"I don't know. It might have been part of a marker down there."

"Isn't it worth the effort to look?"

"If there was a reasonable chance of success. And if we actually had the tablet. As the situation stands, I don't think we're going to find the answers we want on the ground. But whatever happened, I think we know now why Tuttle didn't get excited."

"I guess."

We ran into turbulent weather during the ascent. "I can understand why nobody ever put a colony here," I said.

"You talking about the ape, Chase?"

"No. Big predators are unavoidable, I guess. But this place has no moon. The climate would be unpredictable. Unstable."

"I guess so. I was thinking that it's too close to the sun. We were almost at the pole, and it was cold, but not frigid. Imagine what it must be like near the equator."

We broke out of the clouds but were still being tossed around by heavy wind gusts. "Alex, I've a question for you."

"Okay."

"When people ask whether you believe there's anyone else in the Milky Way, other than us and the Mutes, you always say you don't know. That there are probably a few others. That, since there are at least two in the Orion Arm, there should be others *somewhere*, but that they will be extremely rare. But you usually go on to admit that maybe you're wrong, and the place, except for us and the Mutes, *is* empty. When you say that, people always get annoyed."

"I know."

"Why do you think that is?"

Alex smiled. "Why do they want so desperately to find somebody else?"

"Yes. Why?"

"Well, as the politicians say when they don't know how to respond, that's an interesting question. I mean, we'd be a lot safer if we were alone."

"Do you have a theory?"

"How do *you* feel about it?"

"I'm not sure. Given my preferences, I don't think I'd want to live in a galaxy where we were the only ones."

"Why?"

"I don't *know* why. I just think I'd rather take my chances that somebody else might be unfriendly rather than he not be there at all."

"Yeah." Alex fished another link out of his seat pouch and inserted it into his neck chain. Then he dropped the chain into a pocket. "We seem to be social critters, Chase. I don't think we like being alone, either as individuals or as a species."

I put the glass down and went back to calibrating the relays that the cub had scrambled. "I guess," I said.

"You have another idea?"

"The universe is too big."

"How do you mean?"

"We seem to have a spiritual dimension. And don't ask me what that means because I'm not sure. Maybe a need to believe in a higher power, that the universe is made for us in some indefinable way. But to have a universe like this, so big that light from some places won't reach us in the lifetime of the species—Well, that just makes it seem as if we're of no consequence. We're just an accident. A by-product. Maybe even a waste product."

Alex asked whether I wanted more wine. I'd already violated my code, which required abstinence during operations, but it had been a tough landing. In several ways. Still, enough was enough. So I passed.

"I've never thought of you as being religious, Chase."

"I'm not, really. I don't think about it much. Except sometimes out here. But I suspect that's what's behind the desire to find others. Maybe we're really looking for God. For somebody who knows we're here. Does that make any kind of sense?"

"Maybe. I'm not sure. It's a bit metaphysical for me."

"I just don't know. But I do know that, whatever the reason, the thought of a universe with just us and the Mutes is depressing."

"Alex," said Belle, *"I can confirm the existence of another world in the biozone."*

"Where is it?" he asked.

"*Range from the sun is two hundred five million klicks. It appears to be slightly larger than Echo II. I haven't been able to get a good look at it, but there's no question it's there, and there's a high probability it's a terrestrial.*"

"Are we picking up any electronic signals?"

"*Negative, Alex. It's silent.*"

"Damn." His head dropped back, and he glared at the overhead. "We're just not going to get a break, are we?"

Echo III was on the far side of the sun. To save fuel, we took our time getting over there. Meanwhile, I worked on the lander. I replaced the damaged parts but couldn't lock the chair down properly. If we used the vehicle again, Alex would have to sit in back. And there was nothing I could do about the outer hatch. So getting in and out would be a battle. But we'd manage.

It was indeed terrestrial, and it had a big moon, broad green continents, and sparkling blue oceans. A second living world. It was unusual to find two of them in a single system.

We were coming in on the daylight side. The polar regions were snow-bound. Mountain chains cut across the face of the world. There were inland seas. An enormous canyon, almost continentwide, cut through one landmass. High in the northern latitudes, a volcano was erupting. "Anything in orbit?" asked Alex.

"*I do not see anything.*"

Belle was putting everything on the displays. We were watching them, watching forests and plains slide past. And suddenly Alex stiffened. "Look," he said.

A city!

I wasn't positive until we kicked the magnification up a couple of notches. But there it was, towers and rectangles glittering in broad sunlight along one of the shores. Piers stretching out into the ocean. Streets crisscrossing each other.

Yes!

It might not be aliens, but we had *something.* "Not supposed to be anybody out here," I said.

We might or might not have found an alien civilization, but we had at the very least located one that had gotten lost to history. I was about to congratulate him, but he didn't look receptive. "Why isn't there any electronic activity?" he asked.

"Maybe they have a more advanced technology."

"Okay. Why is nothing moving down there?"

I looked again. At the streets. At a broad walkway that bordered the ocean for the entire length of the city.

At the beach itself.

There was nothing. The waves swept in on an empty shore. Nothing moved anywhere. I saw a couple of animals in one of the streets. Other than that—

"It's empty," said Alex.

We were coming in off the ocean, passing over the city. It was implacably still. A bridge lay just ahead, crossing what appeared to be marshland. It was narrow, rickety, supported by timbers. One end had collapsed and been partially washed away.

The buildings at the center of the city weren't as tall as they'd appeared during our approach. The highest was maybe five or six stories. Thousands of smaller structures, mostly houses, spread out toward an encroaching forest, which seemed to overwhelm them at the fringes.

"The streets aren't paved," Alex said. The only visible vehicles were carts. They littered the sides of the roads. One was in the middle of a bridge.

The buildings, close-up, had a dilapidated appearance. "It's pre-industrial," I said.

Alex nodded. "Where is everybody?"

"I'd assumed the polygon was built by someone from this world. But that can't be."

"Hard to say, Chase. A planet's a big place. The fact that there's a low-tech city here doesn't mean—" He looked at me. Shrugged. "It's too early to make judgments."

A large open enclosure lay ahead. Maybe a stadium. It, too, was empty. If the field within had once been grass, it was now mostly just tall brown bushes and weeds.

We kept going, leaving the city. Headed west, with the sun behind us. We passed over a road. Or a trail.

Nothing moved on it.

"Another town ahead."

Smaller this time, a few hundred houses. Some relatively large buildings that might have been municipal structures or churches. We passed over a lake, lined with houses. Boats were still tied up in some places. Several had sunk.

We were outrunning the sun, fleeing into a gathering darkness. Alex remained silent and simply watched, alternately looking out the wraparound and studying the images Belle put on-screen.

We rode through the night. Hoping to see lights somewhere. But none were visible. And eventually, under the glow of a full moon, we reached the western edge of the continent and passed out over the ocean.

There were no lights at sea, either. Then we were over land again. But it didn't matter. The ground was dark. After a while, clouds blocked off our view. Lightning bolts flickered.

"Still nobody home," said Alex.

It was unsettling.

Belle must have sensed the disquiet in the cockpit. Whatever it was, she began giving us details: *"Equatorial diameter is twenty-one thousand kilometers. Temperatures are moderate, an average of two degrees cooler than Rimway's. Gravity is one point one five standard. And there is a second moon, not visible at the moment."*

"Belle," I said, "I don't think any of that matters just now."

"I'm sorry," she said. *"I was trying to be helpful."*

"Let's try a change of orbit," said Alex.

"Have you any specifications?"

"Just angle it by about twenty degrees above and below the equator. Let's get a good look at the areas where the temperature is most conducive—" He didn't finish.

"You okay?" I asked him.

"Yeah."

"What are you thinking?"

"I don't know, Chase. I don't know what I'm thinking. Did that city, those towns, look old to you?"

"No," I said. "I mean, nobody's been taking care of them, but they didn't look *ancient*."

Belle broke into the gloom: *"We're picking up a radio signal."*

THirTY-ONe

Fear the assassin who waits in the lonely passages of the heart.

—Teri Kilborn, *Broken Fences*

She played the transmission for us. A voice with a remarkably high pitch. *"It is an unknown language, Alex."*

It was almost a series of squeals. Not at all like a normal voice pattern. We listened in silence for several minutes. "That can't be human," I said.

"Belle, how many voices are there?"

"Only one."

"So nobody is responding to the transmission."

"Not that I can determine."

"It never pauses," said Alex.

It went on and on. "It seems more like a general broadcast," I said, "than a two-way transmission."

"Belle, what's the point of origin?"

She showed us on the display. It was coming out of a string of islands in the middle of an ocean, at about thirty degrees south latitude.

"What time is it there?"

"Approaching midnight."

"What can you see?" Alex asked.

"I'm running a scan now. There seems to be a town. A group of buildings. They're all single-story. Small houses, apparently. But one of them seems to be illuminated."

She showed us, and I caught my breath. There were about twenty houses in the town. With lights on in the ground floor of one.

Lights!

If they were humans, they'd been cut off a long time. But the voice certainly didn't *sound* human.

When I pumped a fist and made some noise, Alex kept watching the displays. I knew what he was thinking. But I was inclined to enjoy the moment. How many people, how many Sunset Tuttles, had lived and died over the past nine thousand years, hoping for a moment like this? A glimmer of light? A radio transmission from an unknown source. A voice that was almost certainly not human. *Please, God, let it be so.*

"Don't get too excited," he said. In fact, he was having problems following his own advice. His voice sounded uneven. "We don't know what we have yet."

"Hey, I'm calm. You know me."

"Absolutely." He was staring at the house with the light.

"You think that's where the signal's coming from?"

"There's an antenna. Belle, do you see any others?"

"Antennas? No, Alex."

"That's strange. Anything moving anywhere?"

"Other than what appears to be windblown, no."

"The town looks run-down," I said. We were approaching it from the east. "We going down?"

"You bet."

"We can do it on the next pass."

He nodded. "Let's get ready."

"Maybe we should radio them first? Say hello?"

"What language would you use?"

"Standard. Friendly voice. See what happens."

Alex looked uncertain. Finally, he said okay. "You talk to them, Chase. You'd be less threatening."

"Belle," I said, "open a channel."

A momentary pause. Then: *"Done."*

"Hello," I said. "This is Chase Kolpath aboard the *Belle-Marie*. Do you read?"

The voice stopped. Then, it *answered*. We had no idea what it was saying, of course, but it sounded excited.

I told it we were visitors, that we wanted to meet whoever it was, and that we were friendly. When I finished, it replied again.

I would at that moment have given anything to have been able to understand it. I explained how we'd come from Rimway, how we were curious who was speaking with us, and explained that we were going to come down to meet him, or her, and we hoped that wouldn't be an imposition.

"It understands," I told Alex. "It knows what's going on."

Alex remained cautious.

While all this was happening, we were getting into our pressure suits and preparing to leave the ship. Alex buckled on a holster and slipped his scrambler into it. "You know," he said, "it would kill me if we actually found an alien and had to shoot him." He leaned over the control panel. "Belle?"

"Yes, Alex?"

"Are there any other artificial structures on the island? Other than the town?"

"There are two piers. Something that is probably a boathouse. Nothing else shows any activity, however."

"That means there's no vehicle of any kind, either?"

"That is correct."

"Is there a possibility there could be a lander down there, and you missed it?"

"If it's hidden in a cave. Or buried. Otherwise, the possibility is remote."

"Okay." His face scrunched up the way it does when he's trying to make up his mind. "There's an outside possibility that after we're on the ground, I'll send you a message that I will want you to ignore."

"Then why would you send it, Alex?"

"Only out of necessity."

"And how shall I know this bogus transmission?"

"I'll start by saying, 'We have a problem.'"

"'We have a problem'?"

"Yes. If you hear that sentence, play along. Okay?" I must have been looking at him funny. "It's just a precaution, Chase. Until we find out who's down there."

We went below and climbed into the lander. I was talking to the voice the whole time. *We are leaving now. Will be on the ground in an hour or so. I'm looking forward to meeting you.*

When the *Belle-Marie* was in position, I started the engine, the launch doors opened, and we were on our way. The smaller moon was overhead, a pale, diminutive orb barely visible in the crowded sky. The bright definition of the night sky at Rimway had given way to a kind of misty blur. Too many stars out there in the Veiled Lady, too much loose gas.

Alex remained quiet on the way down. When I offered to put him on with the voice, he shook his head no. "You're doing fine," he said.

The rim of the second moon, the big moon, was just visible over the horizon. As we descended, it disappeared into the ocean.

"The air is breathable," Belle said. *"And there is no evidence of dangerous bioorganisms. However, I suggest you exercise due caution."*

She meant wear the pressure suit. No surprise there.

We began to pick up a bit of wind. Then the wind went away, and we drifted down through occasional clouds, and finally we emerged in clear weather above the island.

It was the largest in a chain of five or six, about eight kilometers across at its widest point. It was mostly covered by forest. There was a natural harbor. And it was generally flat save for a pair of low hills on the north side. The town was located near the hills, along the shoreline.

"There are a couple of open places in the town where we can land," I said. "Or we can use the beach."

"Use the beach. It feels safer."

"We'll have a fifteen-minute walk."

"That's okay."

While we made our final approach, I kept the scope on the house with the lights. *House* might be a bit of an exaggeration for the structure.

It was a two-story shanty, typical of the town, run-down and in need of paint, with a sagging front porch. Curtains were pulled across the windows. One of the shutters was broken. The place had a chimney, but there was no sign a fire was burning.

But Alex never looked up from the screen. And as we dropped toward the sand, he caught his breath. "Something moved inside." He spoke in a whisper, as if concerned that he might be overheard.

I was still talking to the Martian, which was how I'd begun to think of the owner of the voice. We are coming down on the beach. See you in a few minutes. The view out here is magnificent.

"Look," said Alex.

"What?" He was pointing at the screen while I tried to make sure we didn't land in the ocean.

"Belle, rerun that last segment."

We were looking at the house. And a shadow moved across the curtains.

I couldn't believe this was actually happening. We'd known all along that maybe this was what Rachel had found, that she had come across *someone*.

Something.

When I shut off the engine, the gravity came back. My weight jumped by about seventeen pounds. Alex's went up by roughly twenty-seven. It's a feeling you never get used to.

I released my belt. "We're here," I told the Martian.

Alex was surveying the outside. Moonlight. Incoming tide. Forest. "But no movement."

"Alex, what do you expect? He couldn't understand a word I said."

I told him we were coming, that we'd be there in a few minutes. We put our helmets on and went for the airlock. With a hole cut through the outer hatch, it was of dubious value. We got into it as quickly as possible and closed the inner hatch. (Belle would check to ensure that no dangerous bioorganisms had gotten into the cabin.) The sound of insects and the rumble of the tide were audible through the hole in the outer hatch. I opened up.

The beach was narrow. Long lines of waves were rolling in. Alex insisted on going out first. He stood in the hatch, and I asked whether he had a memorable comment to make before he took his first historic steps.

"*Sure,*" he said. "*Let's hope that the place is friendly.*" He climbed down. Having learned my lesson, I closed the hatch before following him. There was something about the beach that left me not wanting to keep talking. But I didn't think it would be a good idea to sign off. Keeping the conversation going seemed like the right approach. So I simply lowered my voice and said that we were on the beach and were getting ready to enter the forest. And what a beautiful island it is. The sand was damp, and we both sank a bit. Seaweed and shells were scattered around. We got our bearings, which consisted of Alex pointing into the woods, and saying, "*That way.*" But he had an impeccable sense of direction.

We switched on our wrist lamps, crossed the beach, and plunged into the trees. Some were hardwood, others were a bright green, with pliable trunks and branches, and long, spear-shaped leaves. They seemed permanently damp, and I recalled the predator plants on Echo II. It's not a good idea to make unnecessary noise while walking through a strange forest. I told the Martian I was going to disconnect for the moment. "Will see you shortly."

He replied with enthusiasm, the voice rising to an even higher pitch.

Getting through the woods wasn't easy, but at least nothing made a grab for us, although the foliage covered the ground so thickly we had trouble finding our way.

There were thick bushes, some with bright flowers of various colors. (It seemed too cold for flowers.)

Something growled in the treetops, and occasionally we heard movement. I touched my scrambler. Good sense of security there.

Alex grumbled that maybe he'd been wrong, and we should have landed in the middle of the town. "*No more night hikes,*" he said.

"Promise?"

Belle broke in: "*The light just went off.*"

"Okay. Thanks, Belle."

And, seconds later: *"It's back on again. But a different room this time."*

Eventually, we broke out into the town.

The houses did not look as if anyone had lived in them for a long time. Rooftops were worn away. Stairs had collapsed. In some places, vegetation had begun to overwhelm the structures.

They were not arranged in any kind of symmetry. There was no appearance of streets. They were simply scattered across an open area at random.

And there, along the edge of the forest, was the light.

It filled the windows at the back of the house. The rest of the building was dark. Alex checked his link: The light we'd seen from orbit had been in the front windows.

I was about to speak to the Martian again, to tell him we were there, but Alex indicated I should stay quiet.

Curtains were partially drawn. He signaled for me to keep back. *"Be careful,"* he said.

"Okay." We were whispering.

We walked quietly up to the window and looked in.

Something sat in a chair with its back to us. It was decidedly *not* human. I saw a fur-covered skull with raised ridges and horns. And long claws. But it wore a *robe*, and it was reading a *book*. One wall had been converted into bookshelves. Music was coming from somewhere. It was rhythmic, pensive, sensuous.

I think my eyes were coming out of my head.

Then Alex pressed my shoulder. *"That's odd."*

"You mean that he's not out looking for us?"

"Look at the books."

"What about them?" Alex turned away and studied the woods. "What's wrong?" I asked.

"Stay close." He started to remove his helmet.

"Alex," I said, "what are you doing?"

"Belle says we don't need it. Why wear it?"

"She suggested we take no chances."

"My feeling exactly." He put the helmet down and began to climb out of the suit, unsnapping the wrist lamp and putting it into a pocket.

"Whatever you say."

"You too," he said.

"Seriously?"

"Yes."

"Alex, what's going on?"

"I'm not sure. Get out of your suit."

I removed it and took a deep, but tentative, breath. A cold forest has a distinctive scent, even when half the trees look as if they're made out of green rubber. That place had it, too.

My head spun momentarily, and he asked if I was okay.

"I'm fine," I said.

"Okay. If you feel ill or anything, let me know."

We put both pressure suits behind trees, well away from the house. "It's not an appropriate way to show up," he said. "We don't want to scare our host."

"I suppose that makes sense."

The front door looked as if it had been yellow or orange before the color faded. It had probably matched the shutters and would have given the place a faerie-like appearance. The door was about the same size as a door back home. And the house's dimensions generally could have accommodated human occupants.

Alex looked around. "All right," he said. "Now listen, Chase. I want you to do what I say."

"Okay."

"Get behind that tree over there. Stay there until I call you."

"Alex—"

"Do what I say. If there's a problem here, get back to the lander and leave. You got that?"

"Alex, whatever happens, I'm not going to leave you here. What are you so worried about?"

"Just bear with me." He gave me an encouraging smile. "Now, get behind your tree."

I saw no imminent danger. Even the alien with the books seemed unlikely to attack. Scream and run into the woods, maybe. But, despite the claws, I couldn't imagine its coming after us. That was naive, I suppose. But that's where my instincts were. I picked a tree and got behind it.

When I was safely out of the way, Alex turned back to the door, knocked on it, and stepped back a few paces.

I listened to the insects and the surf and the wind in the branches.

Lights came on in the front room. And another one over the door, outlining Alex. The door opened.

The creature stood behind it. He looked down at Alex with large golden eyes that were almost gregarious. The thing had feline features, and was only slightly taller than he was. If there was anything disquieting about the occupant, any sense of implied threat, it went away when it closed the book, tucked it under one arm, raised its left claw in greeting, and said *something* in that high-pitched voice. It sounded almost like *hello*. I wanted to go over and introduce myself.

First contact, baby.

Then Alex did a strange thing: He took the wrist lamp out of his pocket, snapped it on, and pointed it at the Martian. A moment later, he turned and sprinted away. Behind him, the cottage erupted.

The ground and the tree shook with the force of the blast. I pressed myself against the trunk. Burning chunks of wood crashed into the trees. When it was over, and heavy smoke was boiling out of the hole in the ground where the cottage had been, I looked for Alex. He was flat on the ground. Unmoving. Branches and bushes behind him were burning.

I ran to him, expecting the worst. But he raised one hand and waved me back.

I dropped at his side. "I'm okay," he whispered. His clothes were burned, and in fact one sleeve was on fire. I scooped up some dirt and threw it against the flames until they went out. His face was blackened.

He got to his feet, and we stumbled away.

"What happened?" I asked.

"Chase," he said. "Get back where you were. Keep your scrambler ready."

"What—?"

"I'm all right." He turned on his link. "Belle—" His voice shook with sudden emotion. He was trying to hold back tears. "We have a problem."

Belle's voice cut through the night. *"What's wrong, Alex?"*

"Chase—" He sounded as if he were choking. "Chase is dead."

My first reaction was that something had hit his head during the explosion. When I opened my mouth to ask him what the hell was going on, he waved frantically at me to stay quiet.

I did.

"I'm burned," he said. "Going to try to get back to the lander. Not sure I can."

"Can I do anything, Alex?"

"No. I wish you could, Belle. Chase was just outside the building when it blew, God help her."

He broke the connection. Then he was walking toward the smoking ruin and calling my name. "Chase—" His voice broke, and he sobbed. "Chase, I told you to wait for me, didn't I? I told you—" He picked up a rock and threw it high into the trees. Then he sank to his knees and burst into tears.

He was good. I'll give him that. He could have had a career with the Seaside Players. He was still down, still gasping, when someone walked past me, never saw me, and strode up behind Alex. "Mr. Benedict, I believe?"

The guy was small, middle-aged, with a congenial smile. He wore a StarCorps jacket that was two sizes too big for him, and he struck me as a man you'd be more likely to find in a library than in a forest.

Alex stood, stared at him with empty eyes. "You killed her, you son of a bitch." He stared at the wreckage. "Why?"

The congenial smile widened. He produced a blaster and replied in a gentle voice: "I'm sorry about all this, Mr. Benedict. Nothing personal, you understand. It's strictly business."

"Business?" Alex took a step forward. But the weapon was pointed at his head. Not that it would have mattered with a blaster at that range.

"I'm sure she was a nice lady. Pity, sometimes, what we have to do to get by." He shrugged.

"You speak Standard," Alex said.

"Yes."

"Who are you? How do you happen to be here?"

"I'm Alex Zakary." He was looking closely at Alex, examining him. "We have the same first name, don't we? But excuse me, you said you were burned. How badly? You seem well enough."

"Did you plant the bomb?"

"Yes. I'm afraid I'm the culprit."

"Why?"

"It's my profession, Mr. Benedict. I *am* sorry. And I regret the loss of your assistant, but she really wasn't very bright. Though I suppose we shouldn't speak ill of the dead."

"Who's paying you?"

"I'm sure you can—" He stopped. "You really *aren't* injured, are you? Your arm a little bit. But that's all. What did you do? Send her in first? Just to be safe?"

"Who's paying you?"

"If you're okay, then it seems I cannot trust anything you say." He backed away from Alex and took a quick look over his shoulder. In my general direction. "Where is she?"

"Where's who?"

"Have it your own way." He put his back against a tree and raised the weapon. "Good-bye, Mr. Benedict."

It was enough for me. I was standing there with the scrambler aimed at the middle of his back. When he said good-bye to Alex, I pulled the trigger. Zakary half turned in my direction. A look of regret almost made it into those quietly contented features. Then he crumpled.

Alex hurried to his side. He got the blaster out of his hand and rolled him over. "Thanks, Chase."

"A professional killer. I thought they only existed in antique novels."

He bent down and frowned. Checked for a heartbeat and picked up his wrist. After a moment, a puzzled expression came into his face. "There's no pulse," he said.

"That can't be—" I checked the scrambler. And saw that it was still set for *lethal*. I'd forgotten! Well, if you want the truth, I wasn't all that sorry.

THirTY-TWO

I never walk in dark places. At least not when I can run.

—Ruben Banjo, on life in Dellaconda

"How'd you figure it out?" I asked. We were in the lander, headed back to orbit, with the guy's blaster safely stowed in the equipment locker. Alex was seated beside me while I rubbed ointment into his arm, which had been more seriously burned than I'd realized.

"That the alien was a hologram? To start with, we knew somebody didn't want this mission to succeed. And we picked up only one radio source. From an entire world. How was that even *possible*? I mean, who was the guy talking to? So there was reason to be cautious. They knew we wouldn't be able to resist the bait, but they were a little too obvious."

"That's all?"

"The books."

"You said something about them when we were looking in the window."

"They were too far away to read the titles. But the binding on all of them was identical. He had about sixty volumes. Different colors, though some matched in sets of two and three."

"Go ahead."

"It looked very much like the Library of the Confederacy. We have most of the volumes at home."

"Very good," I said. "I never noticed. What was the lamp all about?"

"When I pointed it at him, he didn't cast a shadow." A big grin appeared. "The alien was either a vampire or a hologram."

Damn. "So," I said, "who hired the lunatic?"

"We should be able to answer that when we find out what Rachel was hiding." He winced. "Try to be gentle, okay?"

"I'm being gentle. And you already know, don't you?"

"Let's wait for more evidence," he said.

"Are we going home?"

"Not yet. Not until we find out what happened to the inhabitants of this place."

We'd had enough for a while. Alex was hurting, we'd both been hauling extra weight around on the island, and the aliens we'd hoped would be hanging out here, that we'd be able to talk to, were nowhere in evidence. It broke my heart. And I could see that Alex was affected, too. He sat quietly in the cabin, a book on-screen. But the pages never got turned.

In the morning, his arm was better, and we returned to scouring deserts, forests, and oceans. There were more cities, but they were all like the one on the shore: empty and decaying.

The cities didn't look *old*, the way ruins normally do. And they didn't look as if they'd been destroyed, as if they'd been struck by a natural catastrophe, or by war. They all gave the same impression: that they'd simply been abandoned. That the inhabitants had just walked away.

Alex sat and stared out at the sky. We passed over a river that looked as wide as anything in the Confederacy. Then more plains, rolling away to the horizon, unchanging, tranquil, empty. Then, finally, a crumbling ruin of an ancient city. With what had been a power plant at its outskirts.

If herds of deer or equines, or individual predators, had ever prowled those lands, they were missing now. We saw the remains of some large animals. But we seldom saw anything walking. Or flying. I wondered what had cast the shadow on the island. Probably Zakary.

The cities were not *big*. They never approached the grandeur or size of the sprawling metropolises on Rimway. Nor could they match the eloquence of modern architecture. Or the engineering techniques. By our standard, they'd been large *towns*. The biggest of them had probably been home to no more than eighty thousand inhabitants. But, even in their desolation, they retained a kind of charm. Maybe it was simply a sense of loss, an illusion that these places had once, not very long ago, been home to someone.

One in particular, straddling the intersection of two rivers, had athletic fields and pools and open areas that must once have been parks. There'd been floating bridges, only one of which remained intact. And there were complexes that might once have been entertainment centers.

We saw carts, and the skeletons of creatures who'd apparently been attached to them. Some places had been wrecked, brought down perhaps by heavy storms. Others had burned. But for the most part, the streets and roads were, if not pristine, nevertheless in decent condition, showing evidence that at one time they'd been well kept. And now suffered only from neglect. But in all that vast desolation, we saw none of the builders.

Country of the dead.

We orbited the globe every hour and seventeen minutes. There was life in the oceans. Spouts and some large tails splatting down on the water. But there were no liners, no boats, nobody fishing.

We changed course. Looked at different towns and cities. Some were crowded with skeletons. Some showed us only a handful. A few were clear. The skeletons looked *human*.

We saw nothing to suggest anybody still lived down there. There was no moving vehicle, no one waving to us as we passed overhead. And all right, I know we were too high, and they couldn't have seen us, but the metaphor is accurate. There were occasional animals. Some vulpine creatures. A scattering of felines. No birds, though. We saw absolutely nothing in the air. On the whole, the countryside seemed as empty as the towns.

Near the end of the fourth day, we passed over an idyllic country scene, a small waterfall lost in the woods. A large log cabin stood on a patch of ground near the base of the falls. We were in the northern latitudes, and it was winter, cold on the ground. The place had a chimney, but had anyone been there, we'd have seen smoke. *"In fact,"* Belle said, *"the entire world is, on average, somewhat colder than we would expect, given its composition and its distance from the sun."*

"How much colder?" Alex asked.

"Four or five degrees Celsius." It doesn't sound like much, but it was substantial.

Alex looked down at the log cabin. "I guess it's time we tried again," he said. "Maybe we can get a sense of what happened."

The cabin had an upper story. We circled the area, looking for a place to land. The open space was all on the opposite side of the river. There would have been room behind the cabin except that a cart was inconveniently parked. "We'll have to go downstream a bit," I said.

"Okay. Whatever—" He'd been very quiet.

"You okay?" I asked.

"Sure." He heaved a long sigh. "One light," he said. "I'd give a lot to see one light. A *real* one."

Whoever had sent Zakary had committed as vicious an act by dangling that light in front of Alex as by planting the bomb.

We landed about a kilometer away. The sun had been down five hours and an overcast sky blocked off the starlight. I shut off the antigravs and the extra weight came back. I like low-gravity worlds. *"Are you going to wear the pressure suits?"* asked Belle.

Alex looked at me. Shook his head no. "You, Chase?"

"I don't think we need them."

"I agree. But please keep a channel open so I can hear what's happening."

Alex put his scrambler into his holster. I checked to make sure mine was set properly and tucked it into my belt.

I'd brought the lander down in the middle of a glade. We pulled jackets on, Alex collected his shoulder pouch, and we went through the airlock. The air was *cold*. The jacket immediately began to warm up, but it did nothing for my nose and cheeks.

We stepped down onto a light snow cover and turned on our lamps. The glade and the woods were quiet.

The navigation lights lit the place up pretty well, but once we got away from them, got into the trees, the darkness closed in. And I mean seriously. This place felt different from the island. Maybe it had been that, on the island, I could hear the tide coming in, or going out, whatever it was doing. And there were some animals. Now all that was gone. The woods felt *empty.* There was a sense of utter solitude. No critters, no noises in the trees except branches creaking in the wind. Nothing other than the unchanging drone of the insects.

There were a lot of thick bushes armed with spikes. We had to cut our way through. The ground was uneven and full of holes, and the holes were filled with snow. It was an ideal setup for breaking an ankle.

We moved cautiously but still managed to stumble around a lot. It's amazing how clumsy you become when you abruptly pack on a large chunk of extra weight.

We found the cabin. No lights, of course, this time. And, when we peeked in the window, no alien. The door was locked. We circled the thing, looking for a way to get inside without breaking a window. I couldn't tell you why, since everything on this world seemed to be returning to nature, but we didn't want to disturb the place. We'd not had that problem with objects that had been thousands of years old. But the cabin was different: It felt as if someone still lived there.

The windows were also locked, as was a door in the rear. Curtains were drawn across the glass, except for a room in front, where they were on the floor. We could see a fabric sofa and two armchairs. They looked as if they'd have been comfortable for us. An open book lay on a side table.

We circled the cabin and stood again at the front door. "What do you think?" I asked.

"Always play it safe." Alex knocked. Softly at first. Then louder. Nothing stirred within. He picked up a rock, measured it against a window, and paused. "Damn," he said. Then he broke the glass. The loud, dull bang echoed through the silence.

I wondered what he'd have done had something come charging out of the bedroom.

"Blame it on you, kid," he said. I didn't recall having spoken, but maybe he'd gotten to know me too well. He stuck his lamp inside, then climbed through. A moment later, the door swung open.

The room had a fireplace and a stove. A pile of logs was stacked against one wall. I took a close look at them and saw only dust. A faded picture hung near the door. The dust on it was so thick that it clung to the glass and resisted all efforts to brush it off. I took it outside and washed it in the river. It was a sketch. Of the waterfall. Someone stood nearby, looking out across the falls. He wore a long blue coat, with a hood pulled up over his head. His back was to the viewer.

The way it stood, the mode of contemplation, the upper limbs pushed into pockets, seemed very human.

The chairs and the sofa were corroded. The fallen curtains were stiff and had become part of the floor. Alex examined the lamp that stood on one of the side tables. "Oil," he said.

In the kitchen, we found a metal container. An icebox. Dishes and glasses were neatly stacked in cabinets, though most were cracked. Alex found one in good condition, wrapped it in one of the protective cloths he routinely carried during a mission, and put it in his pouch.

A staircase rose to the upper level. Two rooms opened onto the landing. Alex went up and disappeared into one of the rooms. Moments later, he came back out and looked into the second room. Then he stood at the top of the stairs, hesitating. "Chase," he said. His voice sounded odd. Strained.

I went to the foot of the stairs. "What's wrong?"

"They're dead."

I went up. "Who's dead?"

"Everybody." He seemed tired. Dismayed.

"I'll be back." I looked at the open doors, picked one, and went in. Someone was in bed.

Some*thing*.

My God. There were two small, desiccated corpses.

A couple of kids. "Yeah," I said. They *were* human. Alex stood in the doorway, but he wouldn't come any farther.

"What the hell happened here?" he said, more to himself than to me.

They'd been dead a long time. I couldn't tell their gender. When I looked more closely, I wasn't so sure about their humanity.

The bed was cold. The blankets were stiff. Frozen.

He took a deep breath. "There's more." He looked at the other doorway. I went in. There was another bed. And two more corpses. Gray and withered. Adults this time.

One was holding a gun. Alex took it. Cracked it open. "Primitive. Fires eight rounds," he said. "Four left."

"Murder-suicide."

"Yes."

"They killed their own kids." I'd never seen anything remotely like it before.

Alex dropped the weapon on the floor. He tried to pull the blankets up to hide the corpses. But they were frozen in place. "Let's go," he said.

THirTY-THree

I arrived at last on the street where once I'd lived, and found it full of ghosts.

—Walford Candles, "The Long Road Home"

"I have news." Belle let it hang, as if enjoying drawing out the suspense.

"I'm listening," said Alex.

"We have a city."

"Another one—?"

"This one has lights."

The lights were in rows. Streetlights. Others appeared to be inside houses! And we could see an area that might have been a mall or park.

It was a glowing diamond, accentuated by the vast darkness surrounding it.

Alex threw his head back in the chair. "How about that!" he said. "Chase, we've hit the jackpot." He was out of his chair, bouncing around the cabin like a kid. "Belle, are there any radio transmissions?"

"Negative, Alex. There's no activity."

"All right, let's try to provoke some. Open a broadcast channel for Chase." He smiled benignly. "Once again, the honor is yours, beautiful."

"Alex, I think you should be the one who—"

He raised a hand to silence all protest. "A second chance to make history, Chase. How often does that happen?"

"Channel's open," said Belle.

I cleared my throat and tried to think of something compelling to say. "Hello. Anybody out there? This is us, up here. Hello on the ground. How's it going?" I think, by then, I'd become skeptical of a good outcome.

We got nothing back except static.

"Belle," Alex said, "is there any movement in the streets? Any sign of life?"

"*No, Alex. I thought I saw something minutes ago, but I did not have time to ascertain what it was. Possibly canines of some sort.*"

It was another port city. The town itself was laid out in squares and rectangles, stone buildings with columns, statues, and colonnades clustered in the center, surrounded by wood and brick structures. The statues depicted humans. There were two overgrown areas that might once have been parks. A few carts were visible, mostly in sheds, a few out on the streets. "Belle, what time is it down there?"

"*The sun disappeared below the horizon two hours and six minutes ago.*"

Alex sat and watched the screens. I sent Belle looking for anything that might tell us who'd come out here, constructed a world, and gotten lost. There was nothing on the record. But that was no surprise. Over thousands of years, you tend to lose track of things.

We passed over the area a couple of times, and I must finally have fallen asleep. Then Alex was leaning over, pushing my shoulder, asking whether I was awake.

"Sure," I said. "What's wrong?"

"Nothing. But I want to show you something." He looked discouraged.

Several views of the town were on the displays. "Something's wrong," he said.

I was surprised to see that I'd been asleep almost five hours. "How do you mean?"

He pointed at one of the images. "This is the first set of pictures. The way it looked when Belle first saw it. In the early evening." Then he tapped the auxiliary screen. "*This* is the way it looks now."

"It looks the same to me."

He sat back in his chair. "That's precisely the problem."

"What do you mean?"

"Chase, there's no change in the lights."

The streetlights were still on, and the lights at the park, but that was to be expected.

"Look at the houses."

Again, I saw no difference. Lights burned everywhere. "What are we talking about?"

"Belle, what time is it down there?"

"Dawn will occur in about three hours."

"And—?"

"Look at this group of houses. Lights are on in all of them. They form a U shape."

"Oh." I compared the two pictures. The same U shape was there in both. I checked other areas. A long line of lights along the perimeter had been on two hours after sunset. Now, in the middle of the night, they were still on.

Alex tapped his fingers on the edge of the display. "I don't think there's anyone down there."

"Belle," I said, "how long's a day on this world?"

"Thirty-one hours, eleven minutes, and forty-seven seconds, Chase."

"There's your explanation, Alex. The day here is much longer than at home, and the inhabitants have adapted. Instead of nine or ten hours of darkness, they have roughly twelve. So they have a longer sleep cycle. They go to bed later."

"Maybe," he said. His tone suggested he didn't buy it.

"Why not?"

"We're looking at a town in which, over more than seven hours, no light that had not been on when we first saw it has been turned on. And no light has been turned *off*. Not one."

"You checked them all?"

"Belle?" he said.

"That is correct, Chase. The town looks exactly as it did during the first sighting."

"We're going to go down to find out why?"

"Would you prefer to pass on this?"

It seemed advisable to wait until daylight before paying a visit. Meantime, we took more pictures. The light pattern did not change. Nobody turned one off; nobody turned one on. It was impossible to be certain once the sun came up, but it looked as if, even then, everything stayed the same.

We were munching toast and drinking orange juice, getting ready to go, when Belle announced that she'd received a transmission from Audree. I excused myself and went up onto the bridge. A few minutes later, Alex joined me. "She was wondering how we're doing."

"I'd say not so well."

"She asked me to say hello to you, Chase."

Transmission time between Echo and Rimway, in one direction, was just under six days. Our first messages insystem had gone out about four days earlier, so they hadn't heard from us yet.

I recorded a message for Robin. I showed him the lights, explained that we had no idea what was going on, that we were about to go down and look. "I'll let you know what we find," I said.

The sun was lost somewhere over the horizon when we arrived. Clouds were thick, and the sky was gray and gloomy.

We drifted over the town, surveying it, looking for signs of life. A couple of animals—four-legged creatures about the size of deer—stood at a street corner looking up at us. Otherwise, the streets were empty. A few carts and wagons had been abandoned. And, chillingly, we found occasional bones.

Up close, the place was deteriorating. Buildings needed paint. Shutters had fallen off houses. Front yards were submerged in weeds. One house had been smashed when a tree fell on it.

I eased us down into one of the parks and shut the engines off. We stayed in the cockpit for a while, blinking our lights, waiting to see whether we might draw any attention. And, as usual, trying to get accustomed to the added weight. The city remained quiet.

After a while, Alex got out of his seat. "You sure you want to come?" he asked.

We were two blocks from the ocean. A wide street, lined with buildings, separated us from the shorefront. They were short structures, no more than four or five stories. But lights burned in a couple of the windows in the upper floors. "Absolutely," I said.

There were shops at street level, and one of those was also illuminated. I followed him outside and closed the hatch.

The park was a tangle of weeds and underbrush. There were benches, and sliding boards and swings. And a sculpture that had probably been a fountain: four stone fish erected in a circle around a pair of gaping serpents.

It wasn't as cold as it had been on our last trip down. But there was the same sense of desolation. More so in the town, I guess. Empty buildings are more oppressive than empty forests. And maybe it had something to do with the lights as well.

We took pictures, listened to the murmur of the ocean, and gazed at the serpents.

We walked toward the cluster of buildings, looked up and down the road, an *avenue*, really, and listened to the sound of the surf and the echo of our footsteps. The streetlights were about twice as tall as we were. We stopped at the first one we came to, and Alex stood looking up at it. The light did not emanate from a bulb or a panel. Instead, it flickered and burned at the top of a tube. "Gas," he said.

There was a sidewalk, of sorts, covered with dirt and sand. We strolled past the faces of the buildings. The display windows were mostly broken. Those still intact carried a thick layer of dirt. Whatever had been in the windows was gone. One bedroom set had survived, and, at another place, several chairs and a footstool. We found a small furnace in the middle of the street, and a couple of corroded pots. "Maybe it was a plague," I said.

The buildings were lackluster in design, more or less like large blocks. Sometimes, the upper floor protruded a bit over the lower levels, but that seemed to be as much embellishment as the architects had attempted.

We picked a building with one of the lighted windows and broke in. We climbed staircases and looked down long hallways. Interior doors were all locked. We cut through a couple, into offices. The lighted one was on the top floor, so we broke into that one also. A desiccated corpse slumped behind a desk.

In a second building, we came across what appeared to have been a massacre. It was hard to determine how many dead there were because animals had apparently gotten in and dragged the bodies around. But we found bloodstains in several rooms. Bones were scattered everywhere.

"Alex," I said, "there's a major creep factor here. This is not worth whatever money we might make out of it. Let's let it go. We're dredging up a nightmare."

I hadn't intended to insult him, but I did. We stood in that terrible place on a carpet that might have been made out of wire, and he fought to contain his anger. "Just for the record," he said, "this has nothing to do with profits. Or with Rainbow. I'm not sure it ever did." He took my arm and led me outside. "Something unimaginable happened here. And we have an obligation to these people to find out what it was."

We turned south. The buildings and shops were replaced by smaller buildings that had either housed offices or served as private homes. One place had a stone shingle mounted beside the front door.

We stopped and examined it. Alex had a picture of the tablet on his link, and he compared the characters with those on the shingle. They bore no resemblance to each other. "Just as well," he said.

"Why's that?"

"I don't think I'd want to discover we've been looking for a lawyer's office."

I laughed. We both did. The laughter echoed through the empty streets. "I wonder how long it's been," he said, "since a sound like that has been heard here?"

We peeked through a window into one of the lighted houses. There were chairs and a circular table. Curtains hung everywhere. And the light, the light that had drawn us across the world, was provided by a pair of lamps, one on the table, one standing alone in a corner. A connecting room that might have been a kitchen was also illuminated.

I saw a pair of legs jutting out from the other room. They were desiccated, shrunken, clothed in trousers whose original color was no longer discernible.

Alex took a deep breath and indicated the table lamp. "See the duct at the base?"

"Yes."

"It supplies the gas. There's a switch somewhere that allows you to turn it on and off."

"Then the lights were turned on and *left* on?"

"That's what it looks like."

There were other lights and other bodies in other houses. "There's a natural gas supply nearby," Alex said. "It's piped in. Everything in town, apparently, gets a share. The lights will stay on as long as it lasts."

Finally, we turned back toward the park. The wind was getting stronger. "How long do you think it's been like this?"

"I don't know. Awhile."

THirTY-FOUr

There is no more telling representation of the quality of a civilization than its art. Show me how it perceives beauty, what moves it to tears, and I will tell you who they are.

—Tulisofala, *Mountain Passes* (Translated by Leisha Tanner)

We found what had once been, as far as we could tell, a shoe store. We weren't sure because there were no shoes anywhere. But there were some boxes, and their dimensions seemed right. And a shoehorn.

There was a food market, with empty shelves. And a shop that we couldn't be sure about but which might have sold guns. Like the food store, it had been cleaned out. The same was true of a hardware store. "Whatever happened," Alex said, "they saw it coming."

Then there was the art gallery. The walls had been stripped, and the only reason we were able to identify it was that some printed leaflets were scattered across the floor. Everything else was gone.

"Maybe not everything," said Alex, standing near a door in a back room. The door was locked. It was large, heavy, and still standing, though it had been shot full of holes. A dried-out corpse, with a gun in one hand, lay nearby. Maybe it had been the owner; maybe one of the looters. Alex walked past it and used his cutter to take the door down.

Behind it lay a storage area. Oil paintings—they could be nothing else—covered with cloth, were propped against the walls. We looked at each other, switched on our lamps, picked one at random, and removed the wrapping.

It was an abstract, blue and silver bands of varying dimensions curving across a field of disconnected branches and flowers. It was dark in the room, and the floor was damp. As was the painting, whose colors had been debased by large gray splotches.

"Pity," said Alex.

We pulled the cloth from another.

A building that might have been a country church waited in double moonlight. A ghostly radiance emanated from it, and two deerlike animals stood off to one side.

It was lovely despite more damage from the damp environment.

Alex said nothing, but I could feel his frustration.

The next one was a portrait.

The subject was *human*. An elderly man, he wore a dark jacket and a white shirt open at the neck. His beard was trimmed, and he looked out at us with congenial green eyes and the hint of a smile. Odd that we should meet like this.

"Alex," I said, "you think these are the people who put the polygon on Echo II? Their ancestors, that is?"

"Probably, Chase. Yes, I'd guess so. Sad that these later generations were reduced to using gas lamps."

"I wonder what happened."

The canvas was crumpled in places. Stained.

Alex stood silently, the beam from his lamp playing across the amiable features. I wondered who he had been. What had become of him.

One by one, we went through the entire stock, landscapes, abstracts, and more portraits. Young women laughing on a porch. A mother and child. A man standing with a large saddled animal that resembled an oversized bulldog. A house by a lake.

In each case, we reluctantly replaced the cover and set the painting back against the wall. Occasionally, Alex muttered something under his breath, now and then audible, more often not.

"The water got to this one, too."

"Looks like a Brankowski, but this one's also ruined."

"Apparently they had a taste for abstracts."

We were near the end when we found one that seemed not to have been damaged. It depicted a snowcapped mountain in a winter storm. Just visible on the lower slopes was something that resembled a dinosaur nibbling at a tree.

It was magnificent. Maybe it was just that it was unspoiled. In truth, everything in that place sent chills down my spine. Don't ask me why. I'd have loved to put that last landscape, the one with the dinosaur, on my living-room wall. In that somber place, on that night, it came very close to bringing tears.

Alex simply stood for several minutes admiring it. Then, finally, he asked the question I knew he'd been thinking about: "Chase, do you think we can get this into the lander?"

"No," I said. It was too big. We wouldn't even be able to get it through the airlock.

He examined the wrapping. Then we re-covered it and took it into the adjoining room, where we set it on a table. "We need to find a way."

"Alex—" I said.

"What?"

"It doesn't feel right, taking it."

"You think it makes more sense to leave it here?"

"I don't know."

"It's damp here, Chase. Leave it and lose it."

"I know. I just—I can't explain why. It feels like theft."

"Chase, ask yourself what the artist"—he glanced around the empty room—"what he would want us to do? Leave the painting in that wet room? Or—"

I wanted to say why didn't we go back and report the find? But if we did that, a bunch of treasure hunters would descend on the place and make off with *everything*. The painting would go. And the stone fish and the gaping serpents in the park. And probably the gas streetlights and anything else they could find. "If you insist," I said.

"Come on, Chase. If we found the Pearl of Korainya, would we leave it on a bedroom table?"

"It's not the same thing."

"What's the difference?"

I didn't know. "For one thing," I said, "the Pearl of Korainya would fit through the hatch."

"Yeah," he said. "You have a point." He touched the painting gently with his fingertips. "It's not canvas. Not flexible at all."

"So we can't roll it up?"

"No."

"Can we take it out of the frame?"

"I don't think so. Not without damaging it."

We'd need Belle to help. So I checked to make sure she was in range. She was.

The painting would have been heavy enough on Rimway. But on Echo III, its weight was not only substantially more, but so was ours. We were by then about a fifteen-minute walk from the lander. Hauling the thing to the vehicle would have been a serious struggle. So we decided to go the other way: bring the lander in and put it outside the front door. It would be a squeeze, but it was manageable. So we picked up the landscape and staggered out into the shop and set it down again.

"Let's go," I said.

"You get the lander. I'll wait here."

"Alex, there's nobody here to make off with it."

"I know," he said. "But old habits die hard."

"Okay. I'll be right back."

I know it sounds crazy. But I understood what he was feeling. It was more than simply a painting that, should we choose to sell it, would bring an enormous sum from a collector. It also provided us with a sense of who had lived on that world. Alex wasn't going to take even the remotest chance of letting it get away.

I dug some cable out of one of the storage lockers, lifted off, and squeezed down into the street just outside the art gallery. Alex came out of the display area and focused his attention on the hatch.

"You're right," he said. "It's not going to fit in there, is it?" Even if we could get it through the airlock, it would be too big for the cabin.

"We'll have to secure it to the hull," I said.

"Take it up on the *outside*?" He was horrified.

"It's the only way."

"Do you think we can get it back to the *Belle-Marie* undamaged?"

"Probably not."

"What are the chances?"

"I don't know, Alex. But I suggest we leave it here. Come back for it later. With a bigger carrier."

"I'm tempted to try. But I hate to just walk away from it."

I waited for him to change his mind. He didn't.

"All right," I said. "Let's see what we can do."

We dragged a table into the street and set it beside the lander. Then we carried the painting out and lifted it onto the table. Carefully.

We checked the wrapping again. When we were satisfied, we looped the cable around the entire package. "We'll have to secure it to the treads," I said. "There's nowhere else."

"Okay. Whatever it takes, Chase."

I explained how we'd do it. He agreed, and I went into the lander and sat down at the controls. "Ready, Alex," I said.

"Go ahead."

I turned the antigravs on and lifted just off the ground. About two meters.

"That's good," he said.

"Belle," I said, "can you hold us right where we are?"

"*I've got it.*" Her voice was in its warning mode. "*But be advised that remaining aloft in a stationary position in this gravity is a severe drain on the fuel.*"

"Okay."

"I suggest you proceed with dispatch."

I got out of the seat, went back to the airlock, and climbed down the ladder. Alex gave me a hand and grunted. "Need to watch what you eat," he said.

Ha-ha.

Part of the package lay within the antigrav containment field, so it didn't weigh as much as it had. But it was still heavy enough, and in any case it was awkward to handle. We began tying it to the underside of the treads, front down. It was tricky, and the situation wasn't helped by an approaching storm that started kicking up some wind. Suddenly, Alex was telling me to look out and don't drop it and he almost lost it himself once, which somehow made him even more convinced that it was just a matter of time before the thing got blown away.

A couple of times, he looked at the sky. Lightning rippled through the clouds. "Chase," he said, "when we're in the air, can you keep clear of the bad weather?"

"I don't know. You want my honest opinion?"

"Of course."

"The smart thing to do would be to take the painting back inside and wait the storm out."

I heard him sigh. Then he was on the circuit. "Belle, can you give us a reading on the storm? How long's it going to be in the area?"

"Probably all night, Alex. It looks like a major system."

He turned a withering eye on the art gallery. "Let's clear out," he said. "We'll just be careful."

We walked around the package, tugging on it, tightening it, assuring ourselves it was secure.

Belle gave me a second warning: *"We are burning excessive amounts of fuel."*

"Okay," Alex said, signaling he was ready to board. But the lander was floating too high.

"Belle," I said, "come down one meter. Carefully."

She brought the vehicle down. There was a bad moment when the wind caught us, and I thought it was going to drive us into the buildings. But Belle reacted superbly and held it steady while we scrambled up the ladder and through the airlock. Alex closed the hatch, and I fell into my seat. "Up, Belle," I told her. "Let's go."

THirTY-FiVe

When I hear people speak of talent or capability, I know they're really thinking about timing. Being in the right place at the right time. If one can do that, and you know when and how to smile, greatness lies ahead.

—Vassily Kyber, first inauguration address

The wind had picked up substantially, and I should have tried harder to dissuade Alex from leaving. Should have, but I didn't. I don't know whether it was because I didn't want to spend any more time in that godforsaken place. Or I didn't want Alex to think I was being too negative about the project. Or whether I didn't want to turn into a coward. In any case, the wind caught us as we rose. Fortunately, it didn't become a problem until we were clear of the buildings, but it *did* blow us all around the sky. Alex commented that it was worse than he'd thought, and I knew immediately I'd made a mistake. But I had to live with it then because I couldn't go back down without demolishing the package.

"Windy," he said.

"Yes, it is." I was trying to sound as if it was nothing out of the ordinary.

The package quickly became a sail.

"Everything okay?" Alex asked, as we rolled out toward the sea, then rolled back in again.

"Yeah. We're all right."

I couldn't see Alex, who was behind me because of the broken seat, but I knew his grip on the arms of his chair had tightened. He wouldn't talk much. As conditions worsened, or rather as his perception of them grew clearer, he'd just hang on and try to look as if he weren't at all worried. That was how his mind worked: Don't scare the pilot.

We kept rising, and I was hoping we'd get above it before the painting got damaged. Or worse.

"*Chase,*" said Belle. "*The cargo is creating a severe problem.*"

"I know."

Belle is not above letting me know that I've done something she doesn't approve of. She does that by falling silent when a response would seem to be called for. Which is precisely what she did.

"You think we should go back?" said Alex, finally.

"To be honest—" I knew he was watching, analyzing my reactions so he could figure out how much trouble we were in.

"Yes?" he said.

"We have no way to land without damaging the package."

"Forget the package."

And I realized I was trying to sound noble. "Alex," I said, "with or without a painting hanging from our treads, I wouldn't recommend going near the ground. We're safer up here."

"Okay. Onward and upward, babe."

We continued to roll back and forth. The painting had become loose. We listened to it bang into the treads every few seconds. Conditions meantime got progressively worse as we climbed. We got driven one way, then another. We got tossed on our side. We rode up one set of air columns and down another. We got rolled over, and even turned upside down. "This thing could use bigger wings," I said.

Belle's lamp came on. There was a small screen at my left hand. She used it when she wanted to tell me something that she didn't want the passengers to hear. I don't think she'd ever used it before when Alex was the only other person in the vehicle. "*We are burning fuel,*" it read, "*at an unacceptable rate. Our effort to maintain headway and stability against the wind is draining us.*"

"Orbit?" I asked, keeping my voice down.

"Not a chance."

Rain burst over us. Then, almost immediately, it was gone.

Belle broke in again, using audio: *"If you're concerned about the artwork, you may be worrying for no reason."*

"I can guess why."

"I'm sure you can. It has certainly suffered major damage." She showed us a picture. Part of the wrapping had broken loose and spilled out into the sky. Worse, the rear section of the package was crumpling, was being pushed against the treads' support frame.

"Unload it," said Alex.

"We—" It was as far as I got: A gust hit us. Even Belle yelped. The lights went out, and the antigravs shut down. Suddenly, our weight was back. The ascent died, and we began to fall.

Backup power came on. We got lights, but they were dim. The engines came back, sputtered, whined, gasped.

And the automated voice—not Belle's—spoke: *"Main power is no longer functioning. Please shut down all nonessential systems. I am trying to restore zero gee."*

I started turning off everything in sight. Control lamps, navigation lights, sensors, climate control, airlock systems, monitors.

"Chase—?" said Alex.

"We've got too much drag."

"Get rid of it."

"Doing that now."

I retracted the treads. If we got lucky, the package would break away. Or at least it might jam into the hold. Anything to get it away from the wind.

I found myself hanging on, counting off the twelve seconds that the retraction system needed to store the treads and close the doors. The control lamps were off, so I wouldn't get a signal that the maneuver had been successfully completed. Or not. But normally when the doors close, you can hear them. There's a very distinct *chunk* when they lock down.

The count went past twelve and on to about fifteen, but we got no *chunk*.

Still, I had gotten *some* control back.

"Okay?" Alex asked.

"Getting there." The wind continued to hammer us, but it had lessened. I was actually able to maintain course. Almost. "I think we're all right," I said.

A few minutes later, the power came back, and we were able to take a look at the underside. The doors were more or less closed, but the frame had crumpled. We were dragging it and a sizable piece of the protective covering, but if it was creating maneuvering problems, at least it was no longer playing the part of a sail.

It put Alex into a somber mood. "I'm sorry about all this," he said. "That was as dumb as anything I've ever done."

"Alex," I said, "you asked for an opinion, and I told you it would probably be all right. There's plenty of blame to go around."

I should confess that, when I started putting this memoir together, I'd intended to leave this sequence out. After all, you want a narrative that makes you look good. That's the whole point of doing the damned thing.

But a year or two earlier, when I was writing the account of our hunt for the *Seeker*, I was faced with a similar decision. Alex advised me to tell the whole story. "Once you start making stuff up," he'd said, "everything becomes suspect. Do it as it happened. Let some other idiot write the fiction."

THirTY-Six

It is a natural reaction, when a shadow comes at us out of the darkness, a thing we do not know and cannot grasp, to run. And if we cannot run, we will kill it, if we can. Nothing is more certain. Nor should it be.

—Vicki Greene, *Wish You Were Here*

It was ironic. After the gaslit city, followed by three more days of riding in orbit and seeing nothing other than abandoned habitations, we would probably have given up and gone home. But that crazy assassin had been sent out to stop us. So there was something to be uncovered.

It was the middle of the night, ship time, when everything changed. I came half-awake, decided I was cold, and had started to pull the spread over my shoulders when Belle's voice asked softly whether I could hear her.

"Yes, Belle," I said. "What's the problem?"

"There are people on the ground. Live ones."

That woke me up. "Where?" I said. "How many?"

"Looks like five. Possibly more. They're in boats."

They were indeed.

Two dories floated on a river in bright sunlight. They were manned by fishermen, using nets and traps. Unquestionably human. We scanned the countryside: It was hilly, mostly grassland with a few trees. A kilometer or so upriver, a cluster of huts, sheds, and piers, surrounded by a wall of trees, occupied the west bank.

Two hours later, we were overhead in the lander. A third boat had joined the first two. The occupants stood up as we passed, shielding their eyes from the sun. Then they all began paddling furiously for shore.

The river was wide and calm. Nine hundred kilometers to the south, it would empty into an ocean.

"Well," I said, "let's hope they're friendly."

Alex nodded. "Stay inside until we know."

"Where do you want to land?"

He indicated a spot about fifty meters outside the wall of trees. "Give ourselves a little distance," he said.

I started down.

Word was spreading. Heads popped out of the huts. People were pointing at us. I thought I saw arguments breaking out.

The villagers wore makeshift shirts and trousers. No hats were in evidence. Belle reported the temperature at a midsummer level. A group of children playing in a small field were being rounded up by two or three women, who herded them back to the center of the village and shooed them into the huts.

Then we slipped down out of the sky and settled onto the grass.

A half dozen villagers were coming hesitantly toward us. "I don't see any weapons," I said.

"Good." He opened the inner hatch. "If anything happens, clear out."

I put my scrambler in my belt.

He frowned. "You stay here, Chase."

"I'm not going to let you go out there by yourself." Actually, I wasn't anxious to go outside, but I saw no alternative.

"I'm telling you to stay. How many times are we going to have this argument?"

"I'm the captain, Alex. You can't tell me to do anything. Now let's go."

He started to say something, *did* say something, but it was under his breath, and I couldn't make it out.

"We should have a gift for them," I said.

Alex looked around. "Okay. You have a suggestion?"

"Hold on a second." I looked through the storage locker. Picked out a titanium lamp. "How about this?"

"How long will it run?"

"I suspect the lifetime of anybody here."

"Okay. Good." He took it from me, and we walked into the airlock. I opened the outer hatch.

"*Chase,*" said Belle, "*they're starting to back away.*"

"That doesn't surprise me," I said. "They don't really know who we are."

"Anything happens," Alex said, "*anything,* get back here and clear out. You understand?" I nodded or something, and he wasn't happy. "I mean it."

"Okay, boss."

We were in the middle of a field. And the people were indeed backing up. Into the trees. Some kids showed up and were quickly hustled out of sight. "Not a good sign," Alex said.

I squeezed past him to get a better look. "What do you want to do?"

"Wait. Let them come to us. We don't want to do anything that could be interpreted as a threat."

We stood in the open hatch and waited. They stirred and whispered to one another, and some even came forward a bit, but nobody actually got clear of the woods. I said how they didn't look threatening and suggested that Alex stay put while I walked over and said hello. "I mean," I said, "they're *fishermen.*"

He told me to stay where I was, and, in almost the same breath, added, "Something's happening now."

An old man in a white robe advanced to the edge of the trees and stopped to study us. He had a black beard streaked with gray. It had a wild appearance, as if a strong wind had been at it. He carried a staff with something fixed to the top. A piece of wood, I thought, carved into a letter "X," with a circle enclosing all but the top quarter. He planted the staff in the ground but had to push it down because it started to fall over every time he let go of it. He was a comical figure despite the beard. In other circumstances, it would have been hard not to laugh.

Finally, it stuck in the soil. He raised his right hand, palm facing us, and spoke. The words were indistinguishable, and had a singsong rhythm that seemed *about* us rather than directed *to* us.

Alex raised his hand to return what seemed to be a greeting and stepped out onto the top rung of the ladder. The crowd reacted by backing away even farther. Except the old man, whose only response was to raise the volume of the singsong message he was reciting.

Alex climbed down the ladder. I let him get to the ground. I had put a foot on the top rung when Alex shouted, "Get back!" Something popped in the trees. "They've got guns," he said. He threw himself under the hull.

"Get clear, Alex," I said.

"*I'm clear.*"

More gunfire. A bullet ricocheted off the hatch. I pulled back away from it. "Belle. Retract the treads."

"*Chase, Alex is under—*"

"Do it. Now!" Retracting the treads meant of course that she was lowering the lander. Giving Alex some cover. "Alex, you okay?"

"*So far.*"

"Make sure you're out from under."

"*Yes, Mother.*"

"Quick, Belle."

The hull came down fast. There was a jar as we hit the ground. I remember thinking how I'd just gotten finished repairing the treads, which were probably wrecked again.

"*Treads withdrawn,*" said Belle. "*Moderate damage to the compartment doors.*"

They kept shooting. And it wouldn't take long before the people in the trees circled around behind the shield that the lander was providing and picked Alex off. The blaster was stashed in one of the storage cabinets, but it tends to kill everybody in sight. It doesn't discriminate real well, and I'd seen too many people out there who just seemed to be standing around. Not to mention some kids. I checked the setting on my scrambler, leaned out, and fired. The energy beam crackled and people screamed and ran. Some of the screams were cut short as the targets' nervous systems shut down.

"Got to get you out of there, Alex."

"I was thinking the same thing." I heard the sound of his scrambler firing.

The old man raised the rod and held it in our direction, as if it would act as a shield against Alex's weapon.

I used the scrambler against him, and he froze and fell over. "Alex," I said. "Hit the ground. Stay where you are. I'm going to turn the ship around."

"Do it."

The firing intensified. Bullets rattled against the hull.

"Don't move, Alex."

"Chase, get it done."

"Belle."

"Yes, Chase?"

"Lift off. Do a quick one-eighty and come back down so Alex has access to the airlock."

"Will do. Say when."

"Now would be a good time."

The lander went up, just a few meters. The idiots followed it up with their guns, shooting at *it* instead of at Alex.

We swung around 180 degrees and went back down again, hitting the ground with a jarring thud. Alex was lying down there, firing into the woods.

Then he was scrambling up the ladder. I reached out to give him a hand, but he literally threw himself past me, tumbling into the airlock. I closed the hatch. "Okay, Belle," I said, "get us out of here."

"Well," he said, lying faceup on the deck, "that worked out pretty well."

They kept shooting while we lifted off. I jumped back into my seat and pulled hard on the yoke. But the lander kept trying to go to starboard, a sure sign we'd sustained major damage.

"Chase." Belle's voice. Unnaturally calm. *"They've blown the right wing."* She didn't mean the right wing literally; she was referring to the starboard-side antigrav pod. *"It's at sixty percent."* Which meant we had

forty percent normal weight out there. Wings on a lander are short and stubby. When you have an antigrav unit, you don't need much in the way of additional lift. But wings do stabilize the vehicle in flight. And if something goes wrong, they don't provide much lift. "Belle, get a message back to StarCorps." That, of course, is the IEAA, the Interstellar Emergency Assistance Agency. "Tell them where we are and what happened."

"Will do, Chase."

"How serious is the damage?" asked Alex.

"We won't be able to get into orbit. I can't even control the damned thing."

"All right. We'll just have to wait for StarCorps."

StarCorps was good, but they were far away. "Maybe we should take out some insurance," he said.

"And do what?"

"Send the same message to Audree. Ask her to rent a ship and a pilot. Give her Rainbow's account number. And ask her to hustle."

"Chase," said Belle, *"we're leaking fuel. Rupture in the lines. I've tried to seal it off, but I'm getting no response."*

"Alex," I said, "get into your seat and belt down."

"How bad is it?"

As if in reply, something blew, and we rolled right. Alex was thrown against a bulkhead.

"It's the correlator," said Belle.

We were still climbing but losing momentum. "We'll be going down in a minute," I said.

"Okay." Alex shook his head. "Just get as far from those lunatics as you can."

I wasn't going to wait until we lost power to start back down. I leveled off and, moments later, started a descent. I stayed with the river, which provided landing sites on both banks.

I stayed airborne as long as I could. Maybe twenty minutes. That brought a series of escalating warnings from Belle. Finally: *"Too much stress. Engine failure imminent."*

"Better set down," I said. But the wide riverbanks had gone away. The trees pushed out literally into the water. We passed a set of rapids.

Watched the river dive into a canyon. Then more forest. Away from the river, it looked like trees and mountains all the way to the horizon.

"Get us on the ground, Chase," said Belle.

The river broadened again. And both banks went largely clear of trees, but they were littered with rocks and boulders.

"Prepare to set down, Belle."

"Opening tread doors."

We were getting lucky: The riverbanks were showing open space again. Then a red light went on.

"Treads are not working. Will only lower halfway, Chase."

"Okay. Retract."

A group of buildings showed up on-screen. On the north side of the river.

"Negative that. Cannot retract. Treads are stuck."

We were losing altitude quickly. "One minute, Alex."

"Nice timing, babe."

"Can't help it. We'll come down on the south side. That'll give us a little—" Another red light stopped me cold.

"Engine failure," said Belle. *"Warning: I am almost out of range."*

I saw open space away from the river and made for that. It was about a kilometer from the buildings. We had no power, of course, and not much glide capability. "Hang on," I told Alex.

We came down, brushed some treetops, and hit the ground. Then I think the treads tangled us and flipped the vehicle. We rolled, bounced, and slammed into something. I got thrown against the harness, then against the back of the chair. I heard Alex getting tossed around.

"Fuel has ignited, Chase," said Belle. *"Get out as quickly as you can."*

The control panel flared. The lights went off, and smoke poured out of the air vents. "Shut it down, Belle," I said.

She didn't answer.

I called Alex, but got no reply there either.

I was hanging upside down. I asked Belle to release the harness and, when nothing happened, reached back to do it myself. But the release didn't work. The cabin began to fill with smoke. I was breathing burning plastene and God knew what else. "Alex?" I said.

Still no response.

I tried again. Yanked at the restraints. Pulled.

I tugged on the shoulder strap, drew it forward, leaned to one side, and put it behind me. That freed up some space in the lap belt. I pushed the seat back to get some room, lifted the lap belt, and slid out under it. It wasn't dignified, but it worked.

Just as I got clear, something banged on the outer hatch.

I ignored it. Alex first. He was breathing, but he wasn't conscious. I lifted his head. "Alex, come on, lover. I need you."

He coughed. But I got nothing else.

And again, I heard the banging on the hatch. And someone yelling, though I couldn't understand any of it. I snatched up the scrambler and shoved it into my belt.

The control panel began to burn.

I had to get Alex out of there. But I couldn't have lifted him in ordinary gravity, let alone what passed for normal gravity in that hellish place.

The smoke was making my eyes tear. I needed some air, then I could come back and try again to move him. I got to the airlock. The outer hatch was, of course, closed, but the hole Alex had cut into it was still there. Since the lander was upside down, the opening was now at about knee level. I got down and looked out. An eye was on the other side, looking in.

I remember thinking how it might have been worse. It could have been a gun barrel.

I hesitated, but not being able to breathe has a way of cutting indecision short. I hit the panel, and the hatch opened.

THirTY-SeVeN

When the hour is desperate and the need great, we do not care who brings help. Everyone is a potential friend.

—Maryam Case, *Liturgies of the Heart*

The world was moving in slow motion. The hatch slid open while I coughed and tried to suck in air. I saw a pair of light brown oversized sandals and thick yellow trousers. A heavy and soiled white shirt hung down to the knees. Two large gray hands dangled from sleeves rolled back onto hairy forearms. Then a face appeared, bearded, lined, with thick lips muttering something. He was bending down, looking at me, looking past me, straightening as the hatch opened. He immediately took my arm and tried to pull me forward. Come on. Get out. I looked back toward Alex. The man's forehead creased. He motioned frantically. Out. He grabbed my arm, literally lifted me out, and pointed at the ground. Then he pushed past me into the airlock.

The lander was belching black smoke. Alex's restraints had given way, or he'd gotten out of his seat on his own. In any case, he was crumpled in the rear of the cabin against the storage unit. The man went to him and threw an arm around him. I followed him back in. He did not exactly look like a tower of strength. But he lifted Alex and began dragging him toward the airlock. I tried to help, but I wasn't able to do much more than get in the way. He got him through the hatch and lowered him to the ground. Alex's left leg was bent in an awkward fashion. Not good.

We paused at the foot of the ladder, and he asked me something. It had to be whether anyone else was inside. He looked ready to go back in. I grabbed his shoulder and pulled him away. "No. Nobody else." Then I pointed at the vehicle. "Boom." Accent on the vowels. He got the message, and we hauled Alex and ourselves off to a safe distance and got behind a hill.

"Thanks," I said.

He nodded. Smiled. Asked another question. The language, or at least this guy's pronunciation, was rhythmic. Almost lyrical, with a tendency to draw out the vowels. I replied with a smile. "I'm okay."

He was about my height, with sallow skin and unkempt gray hair. His lips were thick, and his nose looked as if it had been broken. And he could have used some dental work. But he raised a hand in greeting, and those thick lips parted in a broad smile. "*Faloon,*" he said.

It was either his name or *hello,* so I said it back, stretching the o's as he had. Then I was kneeling over a reviving Alex. "How you doing, boss?"

His eyes opened, and his mouth twisted with pain. "I've been better." He just lay there breathing for a minute or two. Then: "What happened?"

"We lost the lander."

"Oh," he said. "Okay." As if we'd go down to the store and pick up a new one in the morning. Then he was gone again.

The guy took a long look at me. Rubbed his cheeks. Put a hand on Alex's forehead. Then he said something in a soft, reassuring tone.

At that moment, the lander blew. Alex's eyes came open again. "I hope," he said, "there's nothing in it that we need."

Our rescuer pointed at the ground and said something. I shook my head. Don't understand a word. He nodded. Held up his right hand in a kind of wave. Wait. Then he hurried off into the trees.

I tried contacting the *Belle-Marie.* But the ship was out of range. "Alex," I said, "how you doing?"

He moved. Nodded. I'm okay.

"Alex—"

"I'm all right. What happened?"

"We crashed. How's your leg?"

"I think it's broken."

"Let me look." He was right; but at least there was no bone sticking out anywhere. "Don't move," I said. "We'll need a splint."

"How about you, Chase?"

"I'm fine."

"Where's the lander?"

I pointed at a cloud of smoke drifting past.

"That's us?"

"Yes."

"We got anything left?"

I walked out where I could see. There was a blackened hull, and pieces of wreckage scattered around. "It isn't going to fly again."

"Okay. We'll manage. How'd you get me out here?"

"We had some help. One of the locals."

"Really?"

"Yes."

"He didn't try to shoot us?"

"No. Fortunately not."

He was quiet for a minute. The air was filled with the acrid smell of burning plastene. "Where'd he go?"

"For help, I think."

"I hope so." Alex shook his head. Then he remembered something. "Chase—?"

"Yes?"

"Tell me we didn't forget the scramblers? That we didn't leave them in the lander?"

I ran my hands along my belt. No weapon. I didn't customarily wear it while on board, but I recalled grabbing it when our visitor began pounding on the hatch. I had no idea where Alex's scrambler was, but I could see he wasn't wearing it, either, although he still had the holster. "Wait," I said.

I went back toward the wreckage, searching the ground. One of them, mine, was lying in the grass.

*   *   *

Gradually, the chirp and buzz of insects penetrated the late afternoon. Despite the vast differences between living worlds, the harmony of the forest never changes. Woodlands may differ in the tone of howls and snorts and screeches, but there are always insects, and they always sound the same.

We waited. I used my jacket to make a pillow for Alex, and he commented that he'd enjoyed the ride. "One of your smoother landings." Then: "What's he like?" He meant our rescuer.

"He seems reasonable enough."

"He *is* coming back?"

"I hope so."

Almost an hour later, he walked out of the trees, accompanied by two others. At about the same moment, my link sounded. It was Belle. The ship. *"Are you all right?"* she asked.

"Alex has a broken leg. Otherwise, we're okay."

"Are you in any immediate danger?"

"I don't think so."

"Well, I'm glad to hear you got out of the lander safely. You pushed it too far, Chase. I warned you."

"It wasn't her fault," said Alex. "How long before we can expect help?"

"Twelve days, at the earliest."

Alex traded smiles with Faloon. "We've been rescued by locals," he said.

"They are not a threat?"

"No. We'll keep the links active. I want you to listen in and try to pick up the language. Can you do that?"

"I can try, Alex."

Our rescuers had brought a pallet, consisting of a couple of blankets stretched across two tree limbs. They talked among themselves and delivered reassuring sounds to us. One carried a gun in his belt. It was like the ones used against us at the fishing camp. Primitive but effective. We kept the links on, but the receivers were in our ears so that Belle's voice wouldn't be overheard. *"By the way,"* she said, *"be aware that I'll be out of range again in a few minutes."*

"How much time will we get?" Alex asked.

"About eleven minutes on each pass. I'll let you know," Belle said, *"when I'm in the zone, and I'll warn you when you are about to lose contact."*

They all wore animal-skin leggings and jackets. And they had straggly beards. One of them had brought the makings of a splint. Another carried a flagon. I approached the one who'd rescued us and pointed at myself. "Chase," I said.

He nodded. "Turam." (I found out later that "faloon" was indeed the standard greeting.) We shook hands. The others were Dex and Seepah.

They looked at Alex's leg, talked to one another, and they knelt around him. Seepah, the tallest of the three, applied ointment, then said something to Alex. We didn't have to speak the language to translate: This will hurt a little bit. They held the flagon out for him and signified he should drink.

He tried it. Looked at me like a trapped animal. You think these guys know what they're doing?

When he attempted to return the flagon, Dex shook his head, and said one word. There was no mistaking the meaning: *More.*

Belle notified me she was losing the signal. *"Good luck,"* she added.

They handed the flagon to me. It was lemon-colored, and it smelled all right, so I tried it. "That's not bad," I said. A couple of minutes later, I was out.

When I recovered, they'd finished setting Alex's leg and were lifting him carefully onto the pallet. Two of them picked him up and started for the woods. Turam came back to me, smiled, and asked something. Was I all right? I nodded. He helped me up, and we followed the others.

A boat was waiting for the river crossing. The group of structures I'd seen from the air occupied the opposite bank. We got in and pushed off. Dex and Turam rowed while Seepah stayed close to Alex.

I hadn't been aware how wide the river was. It was peaceful and quiet, but we needed twenty minutes of furious rowing to get to the other side.

Several people were waiting when we docked. They looked at us curiously, asked questions of everyone, including Alex and me, and relieved those who'd been carrying the pallet. I recorded the conversations for analysis by Belle.

At the center of the cluster lay a two-story building that might have been a hotel in another era. It was a three-sided structure, U-shaped, with the open end in the rear. It had a covered deck, which was liberally supplied with chairs, tables, and potted plants. Houses, sheds, and barns surrounded it. I thought I heard animals somewhere. And two other, smaller, buildings, which appeared to be greenhouses, stood off by themselves. Except for a narrow open space that ran from the front doors of the long building to the river, the entire compound was sealed off by forest.

By the time we arrived, dusk was settling in. Lights burned in a number of windows, both in the houses and in the long building. A few front doors opened as we approached, and more people, including a few children, came out and looked.

"I guess," I told Alex, "they don't get many visitors."

"Maybe," he said, "but I'll bet the real issue is that they saw us pass overhead in the lander. I doubt they've seen much antigrav technology."

Seepah took us inside, where still more people waited. He led us down a hallway into a room illuminated by a half dozen oil lamps. A long table stood in the center. There were a couple of cabinets, a desk, and a scattering of chairs. They cleared the chairs out of the way, threw a sheet over the table, and transferred Alex to it.

Seepah checked him again. Removed a windup clock from a bag and took Alex's pulse. The result brought a frown. He said something to Alex. Then to Turam. It looked like bad news, but there was no sign of a bullet wound anywhere. "You okay?" I asked Alex. "Other than the leg?"

"I'm a little out of it. But yeah, I'm fine."

Seepah pointed at his wrist. Feel the pulse. I tried his forehead first.

I'm not a medic, but he didn't seem warm. I checked his pulse against the timer in the link, and it was normal. I shrugged. Told Alex he was fine.

They apparently assumed we were a couple and assigned us to quarters near the far end of the building. There were two rooms, one with a sofa and three chairs. The other was a bedroom with a double bed. They got Alex into it, his leg wrapped and immobilized. He didn't wake up during any part of the process. Then, I'm pretty sure, they told us to let them know if we needed anything.

One of the women showed me where the ladies' washroom was located. The men's was immediately next door.

When it was over, and they'd left, I collapsed on the sofa. I'm not sure how long I was out. Eventually, I was awakened by a knock at the door. Someone delivering crutches.

I thanked him and put them in the bedroom.

The apartment, if you could call it that, was spare. But it beat living in the woods. We had thick curtains to maintain some privacy. Carpets in both rooms. The walls could have used a restorative, but they were okay. There was a sketch near the door, of an angel, or a goddess, a woman with spreading wings, clothed in a flowing garment, one breast exposed.

Turam came by to see how we were doing. He brought with him a tall, thin, scholarly woman with intense eyes. Her name was Viscenda, and it was fairly clear that she was the person in charge. The director or mayor of the community. Or maybe the queen. I could also see that she wasn't excited about having people from outside interrupting the routine. She went through the motions of making us feel welcome. Then she left.

Turam stayed behind to try to determine how we were doing. He asked about Alex's leg. Alex was explaining it was coming along nicely when Belle became active. *"I need direct interaction with these people,"* she said, *"if you expect me to become conversant."*

"Not right now, Belle," Alex said. "Let's give it a little time."

We indicated to Turam, as best we could, that we wanted to learn the names of things. I pointed at the river. What do you call it? And what were those that hung on the windows and kept the sun out?

He understood, and seemed anxious to help. He pointed out objects in the room, the windows and curtains and books. We figured out how to ask for a book, how to describe the act of either opening or reading it (we couldn't be sure which), and how to ask for a pen. The only writing instruments they had were long, metal-tipped instruments that had to be dipped into a bottle of ink. But that gave us translations for "ink" and "bottle." When Belle passed out of range, it didn't matter. We kept going.

In the midst of the conversation, a woman arrived, carrying a tray with cups and bowls, something that looked like bread, a pitcher filled with a cherry-colored liquid, and a covered tureen trailing a wisp of steam.

There were utensils for each of us, a spoon, a knife, and something I can only describe as a set of needles.

Alex's eyes caught mine. Was the food safe?

It smelled good. Like beef stew. With lots of onions.

"It's probably okay," I said. Turam looked at us, trying to figure out why we were hesitating. "Let's not offend the host," I added.

The woman filled two bowls with the stew and showed us the accompanying condiments. I nodded. This one, please. It looked like pepper.

She set Alex's food on a tray, and Turam helped him sit up. Alex tried his before mine arrived. "Only thinking of your safety," he said with a smile.

There were several types of meat in the mix. I had to assume it was real off-the-bone animal meat, but I put that out of my mind. Alex was thinking the same thing, and we exchanged shrugs. Any port in a storm.

I tried the gravy first. It didn't taste like anything I'd had before. Closest I could come would be pork with maybe a twist of lemon brewed in. It was good. The liquid in the cup was brewed, but it also had a unique flavor. A tea with some sort of fruit additive? And the bread had a rye flavoring.

It was good.

"Chase." Belle was overhead again. *"How are you doing?"*

"We're fine, thanks," I said.

"*I'm glad to hear it. Can we conduct some conversations with the natives?*"

"There's no one here at the moment except Alex."

"*Okay. May I suggest that, on the next pass, you arrange to be out in some public area? I'll be content just to listen, if you prefer. But the more exposure I have, the quicker I'll be able to grasp the language.*"

THirTY-eiGHT

The real threat implied by the arrival of a visitor from, say, Andromeda, is not that he might be the point man for an invading force. Rather, it is that he might embody a new perspective. We feel secure with viewpoints that have been around awhile. We like them, and we don't want anybody messing with them. Most of us are still trying to hang on to the sixty-seventh century.

—Arkham of Chao Cyra, from an address to the graduates at Korva University, class of 6703

Alex had a bad first night. He didn't complain, but he was hurting. I tried sitting with him until he told me I was making him nervous, and I should please go to sleep. He seemed to be running a slight fever, so I kept a damp cloth on his forehead.

Seepah came during the night, administered medication for both of us, more of the stuff that had knocked me out earlier, except probably in a diminished dose. He drew the curtains while he was there, shutting out the moonlight. He checked Alex's pulse again. Shook his head. Looked puzzled.

In the morning, they brought us a pitcher of water and a plate of hard bread, with a jar of the local substitute for grape jelly to smear on it.

We were still munching when Turam showed up.

He made himself comfortable, watched curiously while we ate, and managed to ask questions that did not require a knowledge of the language. For example, he waved his hands and imitated something going down and crashing. Then a quizzical look.

I did an impression of a guy with a rifle. He nodded.

Okay. What about that thing we'd ridden down out of the sky? What was that?

Where were we from?

We'd put together a schedule of times when Belle would be available. She was, at that moment, almost directly overhead. I looked at Alex.

"Go ahead," he said. "See what happens."

So I showed Turam my bracelet and asked Belle to say hello. He was looking at it, puzzled, when it spoke to him. *"Faloon, Turam."*

I thought he was going to fall off his chair. But he got the message. We came from very far away.

"I've been listening," she said to Alex and me. *"And watching. I believe I have acquired some facility with the language."* So they went back and forth, Turam and the bracelet, in the local language. Turam's eyes jumped back and forth between me and the link. He looked stunned. He smiled. He made faces. He squeezed his temples with his fingertips.

"What are you telling him?" I asked.

"Just that we appreciate their help. I'm beginning to pass out of range."

"Tell him you won't be able to speak to him for a while."

"I already have. Unfortunately, I don't have the capability to tell him why, or how long it will take before we can resume the conversation, because I have no idea yet how these people measure time. By the way, you should be aware that it was a productive session."

Moments later, she faded out. Turam stared at the bracelet. He looked like a guy who'd just experienced a divine visitation.

Seepah returned a few hours later to examine Alex again. The first thing he did was to take his pulse. He still didn't like the result. Then he checked the leg. Finally, he produced a thermometer and waited for him to open his mouth.

Alex hesitated. Looked toward me. "You think they sterilize these things?"

"Sure," I said.

He opened up, and Seepah inserted the device. After a minute or so, the doctor—he was clearly the local medical practitioner—produced a notebook and recorded the result. I don't think he liked that either. They brought more food and liquids, hot and cold. And another pitcher of water.

When they were gone, Alex felt his forehead, frowned, and asked me to try. "Feels okay," I said.

"I hope he knows what he's doing," Alex said. "He seems worried about something."

On her next orbit, Belle, speaking only to me, reiterated that her time with Turam had been fruitful. "We should not waste opportunities. I should talk with him some more, or with someone, every time we can. And there's something else: We've received transmissions from Audree and Robin, which I've downloaded to your respective links."

The closest thing to an available private place was the washroom. I'd have preferred to go outside, but the image of Robin flickering on the grass might have upset the locals. So I retreated down the hall and waited until it was empty.

Robin looked good. He was sitting on his front deck, sipping lemonade, wearing a broad-brimmed hat to keep the sun off. "Chase," he said, "I just wanted you to know I miss you. Nothing here is the same without you.

"There's not much happening. My uncle Allen will be in town tomorrow, and I'll have to take him sightseeing. It'll be a long day. He's a nice guy, but he never stops talking. Always about either sports or the family. Anyhow, I'm counting the hours till you get back. Hope everything's okay."

It would, of course, be several days before he heard about our incident.

The main building housed approximately fifteen families. There were as many more scattered across the grounds in the individual homes, all of modest dimensions and purely utilitarian. Turam took me on a tour.

The compound extended over a large piece of farmland. It occupied almost a kilometer of riverfront and included two docks, a boathouse, and a waterwheel. Crops were everywhere.

The community had a manually operated printing press, ran a supply center in the main building, and they had a school. I noticed two more greenhouses in back, but they seemed underused. They were growing flowers in them. The two I'd seen originally appeared to be shut down completely.

Food was served at regular hours in a large dining hall. Apparently everyone was welcome, and almost everyone gathered—everybody who wasn't working—for the evening meal. During the time we were there, I never walked past the dining hall during the day and saw it empty. If people weren't eating, they were sitting around talking or playing cards. When Belle made her next pass, I grabbed a chair and sat in, with the link on so she could watch, and participate in, the conversation.

The news about the bracelet that talked spread quickly, and everybody wanted to see it. Most were skeptical, of course, especially when Belle was out of range. *See: I told you they were making it up.*

There was a play area for kids out back. Alex, on his crutches, hobbled outside, found a bench, and sat down to watch. When Belle reentered the zone a few minutes later, she commented that the locals did not understand why we seemed so weak.

"It's the gravity," I said. "They're used to it."

"I wonder," said Alex, "what the average life span is here."

"I don't know," I said, "but I can tell you there'll never be a move to take over their real estate."

"That reminds me," said Alex. "Belle, have you asked them what happened here? What went wrong?"

"No. I've been reluctant. It might seem like bad manners. If I may suggest, Alex, it might be best if we wait until you and Chase have enough command of the language to put the question to them."

Alex nodded. "Makes sense," he said.

Turam and a couple of women showed up with clothes for us, shirts and leggings, made of heavy linen of a sort I'd not seen before. And socks and undergarments. They didn't look especially comfortable, but I was grateful to be able to get cleaned up and change.

The really good news was that they had indoor plumbing and a water-purification system. They had soap, although they hadn't figured out how to pipe in hot water. Unfortunately, I didn't notice the shower had only one faucet until I was out of my clothes. Two buckets had been placed in a corner of the washroom for the convenience of the user. The kitchen, I learned later, kept a fire going round the clock, and always had hot water available. But even had I known, there was no way I was going to climb back into my clothes. So I had a memorable shower.

Alex could not, of course, manage a shower. When he heard about the hot water, he thought it was funny. But he was taking a chance since he would have had a problem getting washed down without my help.

Our new garments fit tolerably well although they had a dull, rumpled look even after being pressed. Alex commented that they had clearly been around the block. But we were happy to have them.

I brought hot water in and washed the clothes we'd been wearing during the crash and hung them on a line outside. They might have been a bit demonstrative for the compound, though. We were concerned that putting them back on would have amounted to rejecting the generosity of our hosts. So we stayed with the contributions.

After we were washed and dressed, we headed down to the dining room, Alex hobbling along on his crutches. Every time Belle passed over, we switched her on for eleven minutes so she could absorb as much of the conversation as possible.

Everyone was fascinated. They all wanted to talk to her and, secondarily, to us. Alex had a quick feel for languages, so he wasted no time picking up the basics. We'd already learned to say "hello" and "goodbye." And "I'm fine." During our first full day, we added comments like "It's nice to meet you," "I'm thirsty," "It's nice weather," and "How did you sleep?" Alex worked out how to say "The river is beautiful in the moonlight." And we learned to reply to questions about his neck chain and my bracelet. "Yes, they do speak but only at certain times." I always did that with a smile, and it inevitably provoked a laugh. But by then almost everyone had heard the magic voice.

We took turns stationing ourselves in the dining room during the first few days. Turam spent a lot of time with us, doing everything he could to help us learn the language although it was clear he didn't really understand what was going on. He had no concept of a radio, so the notion of someone speaking from a distant place was as remote to him as the possibility that the jewelry was talking.

By the end of each day, we were both tired and hurting. The day was several hours longer than we were accustomed to. As was the night. So our sleep cycle got derailed pretty quickly.

Belle passed on some information about Turam. *"Seepah informed me,"* she said, *"that Turam's wife died recently from a disease that Seepah was unable to treat. He called it simply the Sickness, and said the community had been suffering from it for several years. Victims start with a fever, their skin turns yellow, heart palpitations ensue, and most are dead within two weeks. It's become a recurring problem, and it's one of the factors in a gradually decreasing population."*

"Are they in fact losing population?" Alex asked.

"I do not have numbers, but I suspect we can trust Seepah's perspective.

"Turam, by the way, has no family to fall back on. Seepah says he responded to the loss by putting emotional distance between himself and his friends. He no longer hangs out in the dining room after hours. Or at least he had stopped doing that until you two came on the scene. But he'd been sitting in his room alone, or going for long, solitary walks. That's why he happened to be nearby when you came down."

We'd been there about three days when Viscenda called us into her office to ask how we were doing. Did we need anything? Was the food satisfactory? If in fact we were from another world, why had we come to Bakar? (It was their name for their home world.)

"We're simply explorers," Alex said.

A table stood in a corner of the room, partially shaded by a potted plant with broad leaves. Glittering in the filtered sunlight was a silvery statuette. The same figure that was depicted in the sketch in our quarters. An angel, or perhaps a goddess, with wings spread, about to take flight. With one breast uncovered. She was carrying a lantern. Viscenda's manner suggested this was how she thought of herself.

*   *   *

Later that afternoon we were sitting in the dining hall with the director, and with Turam and Seepah. At Alex's prompting, Belle put a question to them: *"We landed and tried to speak with some fishermen. Far from here. But they attacked us. Without provocation. Can you explain why that might have happened?"*

Conversation was still difficult. We told Belle what to say, and she translated their answers for us. We described the entire event, the man in the robe, the staff, the guys blasting away for no apparent reason.

"They saw the lander? In the air?" asked Seepah.

"Yes. They saw it."

They looked at one another. "The lander *floats*," Turam said. "In the air. Even when it was coming down, it wasn't really *falling*."

"It's called antigravity," we said.

"Some would have called it magic."

"Do you believe in magic?"

"There *are* demons. The man with the robe, you said he had a staff. What did it look like?"

"It was just a staff."

"Was it decorated in any way?" This came from Turam.

"There was a symbol on the top."

"Describe it."

"An 'X' inside a circle." I drew a picture.

They turned and looked at one another, nodding. I'd picked up enough of the language to catch the comment from Seepah: "I thought so."

"I think," said Viscenda, "that you ran into some true believers."

Turam commented: "They're religious fanatics. Horgans. They think the Dark Times were brought on because a lot of people weren't living according to their theology."

"The Horgans?"

"They'd been preaching for centuries that the final days were coming." He made a strange noise in his throat. "Now they've come and gone, and the Horgans are still here. Left behind. I wonder what they make of that."

Belle faded out of range, but we stayed where we were, trying to talk to one another without her help, relying instead on a combination of laughter and patience. We drank the local hot brews, and eventually Viscenda gave up and left, saying that she had work to do. Or something like that. I had never realized that so much communication was non-verbal. That language was a kind of refinement of information passed by other means. We discovered that, with the most limited vocabulary, a half dozen words, you could still cover a lot of ground. And eventually, Belle came back.

We asked her to get an explanation about "the Dark Times."

When she asked for details, they all looked surprised. "Well," said Turam, "it was, in fact, the end of the world."

"What happened?"

That brought laughter. "It got dark," said Seepah. "And cold."

"When?"

"Do you *really* not know?"

"Humor us."

Belle complained she had no phrase for "humor us." Alex said, "Just ask them to assume we've been asleep a long time and to tell us what happened."

"Twenty-four years ago," Turam said, "the skies grew dark, and the world became cold." I did a quick calculation: Echo III needed fourteen months to complete an orbit. So twenty-eight years had passed on Rimway.

"Crops wouldn't grow. Whole species of animals died off. We got storms more severe than anything anyone had ever seen. Shortages led to struggles over resources. In the end, people died by the millions.

"It went on for eighteen years. In fact, it never really went away. It's still colder here than it used to be. But the skies have cleared. More or less."

For a long moment no one spoke. Then we prompted Belle again: "Why? What caused this to happen?"

"We don't know. Maybe the Horgans are right. Maybe it was a divine judgment. I have no idea."

Somebody who had stopped to listen said that it *was*, and a woman standing off to one side remarked that the notion was crazy.

"How did *you* survive?" we asked.

Seepah answered: "We were lucky. We were here. At *Akaiyo*."

"Akaiyo?"

"It means," said Turam, "the sacred place. It was designed as a place where you could escape, for a time, the outside pressures. Ironic, isn't it?"

"So this is a religious community?" I said.

"No. Think of it, rather, as a place of contemplation. Where the only thing barred is a closed mind."

"Good," I said. "If we had to crash, this was the place."

Turam smiled. "We're reasonably well isolated here. When the troubles began, most of the people who were here went home. And probably died. A few made it back. With terrible accounts of life on the outside. Others arrived during the years, and stayed."

"It was the greenhouses that saved us," said Seepah. "We already had two when the Dark Times began. Kaska—he was the director at the time—knew immediately that greenhouses were essential for survival, and they built several others and began to utilize them."

The room was still.

"We have a hard life here," said Turam. "But it *is* a life."

"The Dark Times," said Alex, when we were alone. "That's the connection."

"I've been thinking the same thing. It began about the time the *Silver Comet* was here."

"Yes."

"It sounds like an asteroid strike."

"I suspect that's exactly what happened, Chase."

"So maybe she saw it. And couldn't help. She saw millions die. And never really recovered from the experience."

"If that had happened," Alex said, "wouldn't her passengers have said something?"

"Not necessarily. They might not have known. They wouldn't have had access to the images from the scopes. To them, it would just have been a matter of watching the asteroid go down."

Alex shook his head. "I think there's more to it."

"Like what?"

"I don't know. It doesn't *feel* right."

And suddenly I saw what had happened. "There's another possibility, Alex. We know Cavallero didn't do his job properly. He never found the civilization that was here. Probably never looked. So Rachel came out here on a tour. Probably because Cavallero *had* noticed an asteroid on a course toward Echo III. It was close enough that they could steer it into a collision. And that's what they did. Give the customers a real thrill. Nobody ever knew there were people here. There was no electronic signature, so Rachel didn't see them either. Until it was too late."

Alex pressed his fingertips against his forehead and closed his eyes. "You think she dropped a rock on them?"

"Yeah. The more I think about it—They set the asteroid on a collision course, then sat back and watched it happen. When it hit, it threw up a lot of dust. The weather got cold. Crops failed. When she realized what she'd done, she went back and screamed at Cavallero."

"But what about the Amicus Society?"

"The Amicus Society? What do they have to do with it?"

"And Winnie."

When he saw I didn't know what he was talking about, he sighed. A man of infinite patience. "Rachel's pet *gorfa*. We saw two of them, remember? And she said she had a third. All strays."

"I'm sorry, but I—?"

"Chase, do you think for a minute that a woman who took in strays and worked for at least one animal-rights group would drop an asteroid on a green world?"

We waited twenty minutes until Belle was in range again. Then Alex called her. "Belle, I want you to go off course for a while."

"Okay. Why?"

"Look for a crater. One that was formed recently."

THirTY-NiNe

Allyra is the goddess of the mind. She is the antithesis of faith, as the word is usually understood. She does not say to us, believe in this or that dogma. Rather, she tells us, show me. If you have a proposition, a theory, a concept, bring the evidence forward. If you have none, be cautious. If it is suspect, be honest. In any case, remember your own fallibility.

—Timothy Zhin-Po, *Night Thoughts*

Alex had also noticed the winged statue in the director's office. He was hoping they might be induced to offer it to us. So he decided to provide the opportunity when he next saw Viscenda, which was outside on the deck. We were sitting out with a couple of the herdsmen and a teen worker, enjoying an unseasonably warm afternoon, when she came in from a tour of the greenhouses. He commented on how beautiful it was. And that the figure appeared to be a goddess. "I've noticed that most of the rooms have a sketch of her."

Viscenda glanced at the teen, inviting him to answer. "She is Allyra," he said. "Not a goddess."

"At least," added Turam, who'd just come out behind us, "not in the usual sense."

"Who is she, then?"

Turam explained that she represented free thought. Free inquiry.

"In her presence," said Viscenda, "no dogma is safe. In her time, she stood almost alone against those who claimed to know how we should behave, how we should live, and who should be running things. She is the relentless enemy of certainty."

"She's a mythical figure, of course," said Turam. "But she represents what the community stands for."

Nobody suggested that we could keep her, but when we were alone, Alex commented that he thought the seed had been planted.

It wasn't easy to sleep on Echo III. The planet turned too slowly, so the nights and days were too long, and we never really made the adjustment. I was falling asleep after dinner, and wide-awake before the sun came up. The following day I was asleep by midafternoon, and awake a couple of hours after midnight. The community had a system for keeping time, and they had windup clocks, but I was never sure what time it was.

We were both asleep in the middle of the afternoon when Belle called. *"I didn't want to take a chance on waking Alex,"* she told me, *"because I know he's still in some pain."*

"Thanks, Belle. What do you have?"

"The crater Alex asked about?"

"Yes. You found it?"

"It's almost halfway around the world from your present location. It is at thirty-five degrees north latitude, in a jungle area. It looks recent. Probably made within the last half century."

"How big?"

"Its diameter is approximately five and a half kilometers. And it's deep. Impact must have been severe. The surrounding jungle shows the effects for hundreds of kilometers."

"Okay. Thanks, Belle."

"You think Rachel was responsible?"

"One way or another."

"Do you wish me to resume my prior orbit?"

"Yes. Please."

I told Alex when he woke. He made no effort to sit up but simply lay there, staring at the ceiling. "Poor woman," he said.

*   *   *

I never really became accustomed to the food. I couldn't forget that the staples had once been part of a living animal. One night they served something akin to a pork-and-beef mix with a choice of vegetables and fruit. And some bread, which, mixed with their jam, was excellent. So I filled up on bread and desserts, which consisted of a variety of baked goods, with flavors I couldn't identify. I think I put on three pounds the first full day we were there. Which, on top of the other seventeen, was just what I needed.

We'd seen some suspicion among the community members when we first arrived, as if we were dangerous in some unspecified way, and I don't think the talking jewelry helped negate that. But by the end of the fourth day, most of them seemed to have decided we could be trusted. If we spoke a language nobody knew, we were nonetheless obviously human. And if we rode a ship that floated on air, it was at least no longer in the skies. In fact, it had crashed. And that, too, maybe, helped get us accepted. We were vulnerable. The young ones no longer hid behind their mothers. The adults said hello and even occasionally stopped to talk.

"How long," we asked Turam, "have you been on this world?"

He seemed confused by the question. So we tried again. "When did humans first arrive here?"

"*Here?*" He looked around. "You mean in Kamarasco?"

"What's Kamarasco?"

"It's *this* area. Where we are now."

"No, no. When did you first arrive on this world?"

He smiled, as if we were playing a joke. "Is that a religious question?"

"I'm serious."

"Alex, we've always been on this world. What are we talking about?"

Alex looked delighted. They'd been here so long they'd lost track of who they really were. "I wonder if there's a possibility," I asked Alex, "that they really *are* aliens?"

"What do you mean?"

"That they *did* originate here. Is there any reason there couldn't be a second human race? Independent of us?"

"Probably not." And he lit up at the suggestion. "What a discovery *that* would be."

Alex asked how far back their history went.

"Several thousand years," Turam said.

"What kind of world do the earliest records describe?"

"It's hard to be certain. To separate myth from history. The ancient accounts talk about a golden age. People living for centuries. Living in palaces. Food was plentiful. Some of it seems to be true. There are still ruins nobody can explain."

"So what happened?"

"There really *is* no reliable historical account. The world fell apart. Some of the religious groups will tell you that we offended God. People got away from Him and He simply shut us down. *See then how well you survive without Me.*"

"Is that a quote?"

"From the *Vanova*." He saw that we had no idea what the *Vanova* was. "The sacred scriptures. And I can see the doubt in your eyes. A lot of people think we had a higher level of technology in ancient times. Who knows what the truth was? But, however that might have been, whatever the level of technology we might have possessed in earlier eras, we had a good life until recently. I don't think we appreciated how well off we were until the Dark Times came. Now—" Turam sighed. "Today we are only an echo of what we were."

Alex told me that Seepah came by the room while I was out. "He wanted to take my temperature again."

"Why?"

"He says I was running a fever when they brought me in. And that my pulse was too high."

"Okay."

"He checked everything again. Says I'm still warm. And my pulse is still out of whack."

"How do you feel?"

"Fine."

"I wouldn't worry about it. The equipment here's a bit primitive."

                                *   *   *

Later, in the dining hall, with seven or eight sitting at the table or standing by watching, Alex broke the news: "This will come as something of a
shock," we told them through Belle's translations, "but you should know
anyhow. You're not native to this world."

"That's crazy," one of them said. An attractive young mother with
two kids. "Are you one of those crazy Horgans?"

"Of course not," Alex said. "But where do you think you came
from?"

"The first men and women," the woman said, "were brought here
from Mornava."

I looked at Turam. "Paradise," he explained. "God's home."

"Why were they brought here?"

"According to the *Vanova*, it was to give them a chance to demon-
strate their virtue. To show they were worthy to keep company with the
Almighty."

"What kind of civilization," Seepah asked, evidently hoping to
change the tone, "is on Rimway? How did you get *there*?"

We explained about Earth, and the technological breakthroughs, the
explorations, and ultimately the deployment of human societies in a great
many places along the Orion Arm.

They weren't sure what the Orion Arm was, but they got the idea,
although many of those present denied the possibility, some laughed,
and one or two walked out. "Humans originated here," one of the older
spectators said. "I don't want to offend anybody, but these other ideas
are lunacy."

Alex looked my way. We seldom spoke in Standard anymore. It
wasn't especially polite. But we made exceptions, and this was one. "So
much for Allyra and the open mind." Then, after a pause, "It's funny
how we named the system."

"What are we talking about, Alex?"

"*Echo*. It's all that's left."

They had a library, of sorts. It was located in a small room at the rear of
the building. They'd furnished it with two tables and four or five chairs.

Seventeen books lined the shelf. We couldn't make anything of them, of course. But Turam went through them with us, looking at each one and explaining its contents. This one was a history of Kalaan, which had been an organized nation three thousand years before and had left stone monuments of breathtaking grandeur. That one was a novel, about a man who never learned his limitations and blamed all his problems on others. Another was a book of poetry. Then there was an analysis of one of the religions. And another novel, about "people traveling to places in outer space." Belle struggled to translate Turam's term for the category, finally settling on *grandioso*. There were two collections of plays, several histories, and three books "about scientific inquiry."

"I suspect," Turam said, "there will be a book written one day about your visit. If everything really is as you say, your arrival will constitute one of the historic moments."

In the evenings, we had constant visitors. Curiosity seekers. People who wanted us to talk to their kids. Some who wanted us to accept their worldview and stop being such ninnies. And some who just wanted to say hello.

Alex sat through the conversations, propped up on the sofa, at first fascinated, but gradually, as he realized that our hosts didn't know much about the history of their own world, disappointed. He had trouble concealing his feelings, at least to me. The exchanges, even with those who simply wanted to wish us well, tended to be, as you would expect, superficial. Glad to meet you. No, it doesn't hurt that much. We're very grateful to Turam and Seepah. Sometimes we were asked whether we had children. Were we spouses? A few, after learning we had been traveling alone, were shocked that we were not married.

A woman who might have been a grandmother asked where Rimway was. Later, Viscenda showed up with what she described as a star chart. She gave it to Alex. He looked at it and passed it to me.

She came over and stood beside me as I spread the chart out on a tabletop. It was hand-drawn.

I needed time to figure out what was represented, because the chart was trying to reproduce a section of sky on a piece of paper, so Viscenda had lost a dimension. But she had most of the local stars within about eight light-years.

She was expecting me to circle one of the stars. Instead, I drew a line out from their sun, continued it through the depicted stars to the edge of the paper, and placed the paper so the line was aimed toward a window. I went over, simulated opening the window, and pointed toward some distant trees. Alex, speaking in Standard, commented that yes, Rimway was certainly in the trees.

But Viscenda understood what I was trying to say, and her eyes got very wide. She raised both hands over her head, said something so quickly and with so much emotion that neither I nor Belle could pick it up. I should explain that, by that point, Alex and I had both learned to handle the language on a basic scale. It was enough. We were using Belle by then simply to step in where needed.

Of all the people present, it was Viscenda who seemed most interested in who we were, where we'd come from, and why we were there. "Be careful," Turam warned us, "she'll never stop asking about your travels."

I spent hours with her during those few days. And much of what I learned of their language and their history came from her.

Turam and Viscenda took us into the school and let us talk with the students. Most of them knew us already, but they seemed excited to have us more or less to themselves.

We began the day with an assembly in the auditorium, timing it for when Belle was overhead, so she could talk to everyone. They loved hearing her voice coming out of the jewelry, they were excited to talk with her, and it was there that she finally found an audience willing to credit her explanation of who and what she was.

Turam remained skeptical. He clung to the notion that two arcane spirits lived within the bracelet and the chain. Though he confessed that it was hard to understand how it was that the same spirit seemed to speak from both pieces.

"I can accept long-distance speaking," he told us later, away from the students. "There are myths that we once possessed that kind of capability. But a machine that can think like you or me? That's just asking too much." And he laughed. "But I'm willing to play along."

The students were entranced. We'd come from the stars, we explained, from a place so far that if we placed a giant lantern out there and turned it on, everyone in the room would be older than their grandparents before they'd be able to see the light. (In fact, of course, none would live long enough, but we didn't want to get morbid.) Moreover, we told them, the ship we'd come in was circling the world and would do so three or four more times before they completed their school day.

At the end, we returned to the auditorium, where the principal presented us with a book that he said consisted of the speculations of generations of scientists over one of the most compelling questions they faced: Were they alone in the universe?

"It has been the dream of generations," he told us, "to have breakfast with the Other. We'd expected someone with a beak and green skin and possibly wings. But it turns out you look just like us. Who would have thought?" The kids applauded, and there was some talk about how silly it had been to think that aliens would look, well, *alien*.

Alex was not having an easy time on his crutches, so we were glad to get back to our room. Viscenda met us there to thank us for our contribution to the school day, which she said, "Judging from what I've heard, went pretty well. How fast does light travel anyway?"

It turned out they thought it moved at an infinite velocity.

"Very fast," Alex said. "Around the world ten times in a second. And there's something else you should be aware of, Viscenda. Another ship will be coming for us. In several days."

"Good. I was going to ask about that. Your friends know then that you are in difficulty?"

"Yes. They know."

"How is that possible?"

"We were able to send them a message."

Her brow wrinkled. "But you said you were very far from home.

How could you send such a message? When it takes so many years even to see a beam of light?"

That led to another complicated conversation.

On her next pass, Belle forwarded more transmissions from Audree and Robin. Robin explained how it had been raining all day along the Melony. And he'd tried out for a part with the Seaside Players' production of *All Aboard!* If he got it, he'd be the main character's goofy buddy.

FOrTY

Forget not that God has given you a mind. It may well be that the greatest sin is a failure to use it. Take time to look above the rooftops. To question that which everyone else holds as incorruptible truth, and live so that your actions are more than a mere echo of all that has gone before.

—*The Vanova*

Alex showed everyone a picture of the tablet that had been found at Sunset Tuttle's former home. "Anybody have any idea what it is?"

No one did.

"Does anyone recognize the language?"

More headshaking.

"It might be Arinok," said Seepah. "It looks a little bit as if it might be."

Turam studied the picture. "I don't think so," he said.

"What's Arinok?"

"Ancient language. From the Bagadeish. They used to carve stuff like this on their tombs."

"But you can't read it?"

"No. I'm not even sure that's what it is."

"Is there anyone here we could ask?"

They looked at one another.

Most evenings, there was a party going on in the dining hall. People who'd spent the day constructing irrigation ditches and planting seeds for the coming season picked up wind and string instruments. They had drums, and they even produced a couple of singers with some talent. But the energy was missing. I got a sense of people trying hard to be happy.

The conversations roamed near and far. "You had electricity at one time," we told them. Actually, they had no word for *electricity*, so we resorted to the Standard term. "But the places we've been to had only candles and gas lamps for light. What happened?"

Seepah smiled. Painfully. "What is *electricity*?"

Alex tried to explain. Seepah smiled tolerantly and shook his head. "I'm reluctant to say this, but it sounds as if you're making it up. Lightning, you say?"

A young woman who'd served as one of Seepah's aides wanted to know how the vehicle we'd been riding floated in air. "Well," she corrected herself, "it didn't exactly *float*, but it wasn't really *falling*, either."

Alex asked me if I wanted to explain about antigravity.

But I had no idea how the system worked. "Push a button," I said, "and you lift off."

Then there was the material from which our clothes were made. I was wearing my own blouse that day, and one resident fingered the sleeve. "It's so *soft*."

We had drawn a crowd, as usual, and they ooohed and aaahed with every revelation.

"Are you aware," Alex asked, "that you've been off-world? Sometime in the past?"

They laughed. "You mean to the moons?"

"Better than that," Alex said.

"Never happened." An older man who always walked with a cane shook his head. "I've read every history book there is," he said. "Nobody says anything about it. It's just superstition. It can't be done."

I was tempted to point out there were only five or six histories at the compound. But there was no point starting an argument.

Someone else, a middle-aged woman, credited us with marvelous imaginations. "When we went off-world," she asked, "where exactly did we go?"

That generated laughter.

When it had subsided, Alex's reply created another skeptical reaction: "You, your forebears, have been to the second world in your system."

"We've traveled to Zhedar?"

"If that's the second world."

"That's crazy."

"It's true."

"How do you know?" The questions were coming from all sides.

"We've been there."

More laughter. Then, maybe, something else. The mockery drained out of the room. "What's it like?" The question was asked by a teenage boy.

"It's a lot like here. Except you'd weigh a little less."

That got still more laughter.

A young man had been sitting listening, taking it all in. His beard was just starting to grow. "Well," he said, "I'm not going to say there's a mistake somewhere, but next time you go back, Alex, I'd love to go along."

Viscenda was there at the time. She smiled politely at Alex's claim. "I've heard that story," she said. "It appears in everybody's mythology. They rode winged steeds." She smiled at us. "But even you and your partner would have to admit it's a little hard to believe."

Sestor was an oversized male with a gray beard and a polished skull. He'd been wearing a superior smile throughout, as if listening to nonsense. Now he broke in: "Even if we had the means," he said, "there's no reason to go anywhere else. We're unique. The universe is empty."

"What about our guests?" asked a man seated beside him who looked *ancient*.

"Look," Sestor said patiently, "I don't want to offend anybody, but you can see they're just like us. They're from *here*. I don't understand that *thing* they were running around in, but there's no difference between them and the rest of us. For God's sake, people, use your eyes."

"I agree," said a woman with a serene expression. "Nobody really exists out there." She looked apologetically at Alex, and at me. "I'm sorry. But your claims just don't make sense. They fly in the face of everything we know to be true. But even if there *were* some truth to your story, I'd suggest we let it go. Our job is to repair the damage here. If we can. This is the only world that matters."

And then there was Kayla, a resident member of the staff. "We've blundered away the gift of the Almighty," he said. "I've never been one of those who was forever saying that God had grown to find us despicable. But one thing is certain: We're being tested."

"There is no God," said one of the others, a young man with fire in his eyes. "If there were, where was He when we needed Him?"

Turam, beside me, whispered his name. "Hakim. He's an atheist."

"Mind," said Hakim, "is the only thing that's sacred."

"Well." Alex reached for his crutches. "Time to head for the salad bar."

"I think it's silly," said Turam, "to deny what Alex tells us. He has no reason to lie. And ask yourself whether anyone in this world could devise a vehicle that floats." He looked at the others, defying anyone to argue the point. Then he turned to us: "We always believed, most of us did, that we were alone. Yet here you are. You look like us, but you're alien."

"I don't *feel* like an alien," I said. Belle had drifted out of range, but it almost didn't matter anymore. "We don't really know what the truth is. But I'll bet we're from the same line." (I didn't know how to say *species*, but I thought *line* worked better anyhow.)

Some witticisms went back and forth. And a young man, about nineteen, who'd stopped to listen, leered at me, and said, "I hope so."

Then Turam asked an unexpected question: "Is there purpose to the universe?"

"I think that's a bit above our competency level," said Alex.

A couple of people rolled their eyes. "That is the short answer," said Hakim. "But surely an advanced culture has thought about these things, Chase." (They all tended to pronounce my name "Cheese.") "There must, for example, be an advantage in being alive. A *reason* for it, wouldn't you say?"

"Of course."

"But what is the purpose for most living forms? What could conceivably be the point of being alive if you're a tree? Or an amoeba?"

I passed the question to Alex. "Hakim," he said, "we just don't have answers to questions like that. But what about you? Would you rather be alive or dead?"

"To be honest," he said, "I'm not sure."

Eventually, they asked why we'd come. "There are so many stars. If you are what you say," said Sestor, "what brought you to us?"

"We've been looking for someone," said Alex, "for ten thousand years. It was inevitable that eventually we would arrive here."

That brought smiles. Seepah, changing course, whispered a response. "And thank God you did." His voice shook.

When the band took over, the nineteen-year-old, whose name was Barnas, asked me to dance and told me I was the loveliest woman he'd ever seen. Was I doing anything tomorrow evening? He suggested a walk along the riverbank. Or possibly a canoe ride. In the moonlight. Actually, he added, he wasn't sure the moon would be up, but he'd do what he could to arrange it.

"You know, Barnas," I told him, "you're going to be a heartbreaker one day." Unfortunately, I didn't know the word for "heartbreaker," so I said it in Standard. But he knew what I meant.

He responded with an expectant grin. "Is that a yes?" he asked.

Alex asked Viscenda if we could speak with her privately. She nodded and led us into a small room across the corridor from the library. "I've been wanting to sit down with you anyhow," she said. "When your rescuers come, is there anything we will be able to do to facilitate matters?"

"Thank you, Viscenda," he said. "You've already done everything we could have asked." A fire was burning placidly in a small stove.

"I'm glad to hear it."

"Your people have a long history. I was wondering about your prospects. What does the future hold?"

"I take it you've noticed that the situation is not good."

"I've noticed too few children. I've noticed you have empty rooms."

Her eyes closed. I suspected she'd been an attractive woman in her youth. And somehow she didn't seem *old*. Beaten down, maybe. But not old. "We have about thirty children altogether under the age of twelve. It's not nearly enough to sustain us.

"Life here is difficult. People work very hard. The weather is inconstant. The sickness is getting worse. We are not always able to manage a harvest, so more die off each year. We try to store food for lean times. But—" She looked up and stared for a moment at the stove. "Many of our residents have given up. People do not want to bring children into this world. It's too painful. We remember what we had less than two generations ago. And we look around now and see what's left. Many of our older people tell us they wish they'd died during the Dark Times. Those were the lucky ones. You hear it all the time." She looked at the dark-stained walls. On one hung four or five family sketches. Images of Daddy and small animals and kites and boats. Drawn in better times, maybe. "It appears," she said with a sad smile, "that God has decided to end it. And that the end is not quite what we'd expected. It has not been quick and clean for all of us. A few survivors were left, for whatever reason, perhaps to contemplate what has happened, and to ask ourselves why."

Alex looked intently at her. "Viscenda, we can help."

She shook her head, beating down any impulse to hope. "I've been praying that you would be able to. That you would wish to. But how—?"

"I'd like you to call a general meeting. Let me speak to your people."

The meeting was set for the following evening. Meanwhile, we sat down with Viscenda, Seepah, and some of the other community leaders to get as much information about our hosts as we could. Alex asked what the world population had been before the onset of the Dark Times, a term that seemed to refer both to the general disaster and to the aftermath. "I would guess," Viscenda replied, "maybe a billion. Possibly not quite that many. I don't think anyone ever did a count."

Had there been nation-states?

The concept was foreign. Most people had lived in regions centered on cities.

Had there been wars?

"Not for a long time, until the lights went out," said a man named Argo. "There've been a few, here and there. But for centuries they've been rare. And usually, people tend to be horrified when the killing starts. Historically, the wars have always been short-lived."

One of her people asked about the Confederacy. How many worlds did it encompass? What other aliens were there? He and the others had a hard time believing that the Mutes could read minds. "How is it possible?" asked Viscenda. "By what medium do thoughts travel from one mind to another?"

As usual, we didn't know the answer.

"Don't take offense," she said, "but you and Alex, for members of an advanced race, seem remarkably incurious."

I didn't know how to explain that our world was full of wonders. That we simply accepted them and didn't concern ourselves with the mechanics.

They described the years before the Dark Times as a golden age. "It's true," said Seepah. "It was a good life back then. But we didn't appreciate it until it went away."

Next morning, I wandered into the dining hall and found a woman in tears. She'd heard that Alex wanted to speak, and she had guessed it would be about the future. She was seated with three or four other women. When she saw me, she tried to get control of her voice and stood up to face me. "There *is* no future for us," she said. "Let Alex know, if he hasn't figured it out yet." One of her companions stood and tried to pull her back into her seat. But she would not be restrained: "You know what *I* think, Chase? I think it's immoral to bring children into a world that's cold and dead."

Her friend wrapped an arm around her, and a long silence followed.

I smiled and said I'd pass the message along. As I was walking away my link activated. *"Chase."* Belle's voice. *"Do you have a minute?"*

"Sure. What's up?"

"StarCorps is here."

"What? Already? That can't be right." They weren't due for almost two days.

"Shall I patch them through? It's audio only."

"Yes. Please."

A momentary delay. Then: "Belle-Marie, *this is the* Vanderweigh, *IEAA patrol craft. We were in the area when your code white was relayed to us. What is your status?"*

The voice was female. It was also reassuring and calm. Everything's under control.

"*Vanderweigh*, this is Chase Kolpath. I'm the pilot of the *Belle-Marie*. I'm currently stranded groundside with my passenger. There is no emergency. We are in no immediate danger."

"*We're glad to hear it, Kolpath. We'll achieve orbit in about nineteen hours and will send a rescue vehicle as soon as we have a window. Is there anything else about your situation we should know?*"

"My passenger, Alex Benedict, has a broken leg and will require medical care."

"*We read you. We'll be with you as quickly as we can. Vanderweigh out.*"

FOrTY-ONe

When people say how fortunate they are to have been born during the present age, they tend to be thinking of the fact that the supply of food is assured, we all have roofs over our heads, and we need not worry about invading armies showing up at the city gates. But there's more to it than simply the tools of survival. Had we slipped from the womb in, say, the twelfth century, we would not only have faced a short life span, but we'd have had no method of communication more competent than a horse. What was going on in the greater world, if indeed anything was, would remain a mystery unless the barbarians attacked. Or the Nile went into flood stage. We would have no books. No easy way to wash clothes. No pictures of the kids. No understanding of how the sun rose and set. It was a world full of gods, demons, and miracles. It is no wonder sanity in that era was so rare.

—Blackwood Conn, *Life at the Edge*

I passed the news to Alex. He was making notes, prepping for his presentation. "Well, that's good," he said. "I'll be glad to get back to a normal life. And a normal weight."

"How's your leg?"

He smiled. "I'd have a little trouble down at the dance. Otherwise, it's okay."

"You know what you're going to say tonight?"

"More or less." He rearranged himself in the chair. The leg was propped up on a footstool. "We can provide all kinds of help. Supplies. Medical assistance— Did you hear? They have another case of the Sickness to contend with—"

"I heard."

"I keep thinking how different it might have been here had someone back home, twenty-eight years ago, spoken up."

Alex was an accomplished speaker. He had a sense of humor, was good at winning an audience over, got to the point quickly, and kept it short. He was exceptional that night. The dining hall was filled when Viscenda introduced him. "We all know him," she said, "as one of our two friendly aliens. Let's welcome Alex Benedict."

The crowd stood and applauded. I was struck by the similarity of social customs, retained even after thousands of years of separation. Or developed separately, whichever it was.

Alex walked to the lectern and thanked Viscenda. Then he turned to the audience. "Chase and I owe all of you a debt of gratitude. You provided a home for us when we were in trouble. And I should also say thanks especially to Turam— Where are you, Turam?" He knew perfectly well where Turam was because I knew he'd pinpointed him before going up there. "Ah, there you are. Turam, stand up, please. He's the man who pulled us out of the fire. Don't know where we'd have been without you, partner. Well, in fact, I guess I *do* know."

The audience applauded, and from that moment, they belonged to him.

He described his reaction to Akaiyo, how fortunate we'd been to come down near the facility. "There are places," he said, "that don't like strangers very much. This is not one of them.

"To the degree that we can, we'd like to reciprocate. We can never do for you what you have done for us. But we *can* help. We received information a short while ago that a rescue vehicle has arrived and will be taking us off, probably sometime tomorrow morning." They sat quietly. "We'll be leaving for a short time. But we'll be back." Fist-pumping and cheers. "With supplies. With help. I can promise you that you will never again have to worry about where your next meal is coming from."

That blew the roof off.

He waited until they quieted. Then he continued: "Something else. I'm sure the word has gotten around that we've been saying your ancestors developed a method to travel to other worlds. I know it's hard for you to believe, but it's true. You, your forebears, visited Zhedar. It happened a long time ago. So long ago that you've forgotten it. But we've seen the evidence. We've been there.

"I've heard some of you wonder whether your lives are worth living. Whether it isn't time to give up. But we would not wish to lose you. And I suspect that *you* would not allow it to happen even if we were not here to help.

"But we are. When you get up tomorrow, it's possible Chase and I will be gone. But we'll be back."

We hadn't heard from Belle during her last few passes. It might have been because she knew Alex would be speaking, and we hadn't given her the precise schedule, so she wouldn't have wanted to interrupt. We spent an hour after the address talking with our hosts. They were ecstatic about what we were saying, and I think we shook hands with everybody in the place. Including the kids.

I've mentioned elsewhere that, since the nights were several hours longer than the nights on Rimway, we ran on a different cycle from the general population. We were often exhausted in the daytime and awake half the night. It was the middle of the afternoon, but our bodies were at about their 3:00 A.M. point in the sequence. I'd lost count, but it felt like it. When the event was finally over, and we were back in our quarters, Alex carefully lowered himself into a chair, and I said something about how glad I'd be to get off Echo III. StarCorps couldn't arrive too soon.

I glanced at Belle's schedule and thought I'd say hello. So I called.

But got no answer.

I took another look at the schedule and tried again. "Belle, you there?"

Alex glanced up at me.

"Belle, respond please."

We listened to the yells of some kids playing ball just outside the window. Then Alex shook his head and held both hands up, palms out, while he mouthed one word: *Stop.*

He signaled me to pass him the link. But keep quiet while I was doing it.

I removed the bracelet and held it out for him. He took it and studied it for a moment. Then he spoke into it: "My God, Chase. Get down! They're here!"

My reflexes took over, and I hit the deck.

FOrTY-TWO

There is no shock that can rattle the household quite like the approach of an unexpected visitor.

—Harley Esperson, *Cringing in the Lodge*

Alex shut off the link, gave it back to me, and fumbled for his crutches. "Chase, it's imperative you stay off it until I get back. If there's a call, don't answer."

"Alex, what—?"

"Do what I say. Please. I'll be back as quickly as I can."

He hobbled off. I ran over to the window and looked out. Nobody seemed to be coming from that direction. And there was no one in the corridor except Alex. So I sat down, put the bracelet on the table beside me, and watched it. As if it were a spider.

My heart was pounding. The Mortician had neutralized Belle. Must have done it when she was out of range and couldn't warn us. Minutes ticked by. Then, finally, I heard approaching voices.

Alex came back in with Turam, Barnas, and five or six others. Three had rifles. The others had pistols. "Everybody ready?" he asked.

They checked to make sure the weapons were loaded.

"Okay. Chase, here's what we need you to do—"

The people who'd arrived with Alex began screaming. I turned on the link. "Belle, answer up, please!" Turam pounded on the door. Outside,

I could see a couple of older people herding the kids away. One of the others threw a chair through the window. "We've got an emergency, Belle," I said, trying to sound desperate. I don't think I had to try hard. "Please respond."

Alex jumped in: "Quick, Chase. Out the back! Get out while you can!"

Barnas broke in: "Too late, bitch," he said, "you're dead."

Two of the guys stuck their rifles out the window and blasted away at the sky. I screamed, "Alex!"

More shooting.

"You've killed him," I shrieked. "You bastard." I tried to burst into tears.

Turam said, "Sorry, baby. Good-bye."

I screamed for him not to shoot. Then Turam fired his weapon at the sky again. I cried out. Alex signaled for me not to overdo it, and I went silent.

Alex and I stayed quiet, while Turam and his people laughed and said how they'd take the bodies outside and burn them.

"Praise to the All-Father," said one of them.

Alex pointed at the door. Everybody out. We left my bracelet on the side table but didn't turn it off. Outside, in the hallway, a crowd was gathering. They looked a little scared. We shushed everybody and got clear of the area.

In one of the side rooms, Alex thanked everybody for helping. Every now and then, someone went back to our apartment and screamed something unintelligible that sounded bloodthirsty. Then, finally, we stopped.

Barnas and the others congratulated one another and took turns assuring us that if anybody showed up who wanted to give us trouble, they'd deal with him properly.

"What do you think?" said Turam. "Did it work?"

"You did a good job," Alex said.

"Now," Turam continued, "what happened to the rescuers? Who is this who's coming to get you?"

"Yeah," Barnas said. "How about enlightening us?"

Alex sat down. "Belle's not responding. That tells me that whoever's up there with her isn't StarCorps. And I can only think of one other likelihood."

"The Mortician," I said.

"Yes—if I'm wrong, I'll apologize later."

"It won't work, Alex."

"Why not?"

"The Mortician doesn't speak the local language."

"She's probably been doing the same thing we have: letting her AI listen in and act as an interpreter. Even if not, it doesn't matter. She couldn't possibly have misunderstood the point of all the shots and screams." He stopped. Touched the silver chain. "We've got an incoming call."

"It's probably Belle." That was my optimism working overtime.

"Text message." Alex looked at it. Showed it to me.

Benedict:

You can't seriously expect that ploy to work again? Talk to me. Or I'll take out your little social center down there.

"It might be a bluff," I said. "She has no way to be certain we're not dead."

Alex shook his head. "No, but she has nothing to lose by destroying the compound."

"Sure she does. She wouldn't be able to tell whether she'd gotten us."

"You willing to bet that'll stop her?"

"I guess we'd better call."

We were speaking in Standard, and Turam had figured out *that* wasn't a good sign. "It's not over," he said. "Is it?"

Alex delivered a casual nod intended to suggest everything was under control. But he didn't want to mislead anyone. "Probably not, Turam," he said. He activated his link. "This is Benedict. What do you want?"

"*Mr. Benedict.*" The female voice in the link was not Belle's happy-go-lucky tone, but was rather a combination of amusement and mockery. The room fell silent, and I saw the surprise on faces that had grown accustomed to talking jewelry but expected it to use a familiar language. *"I wasn't sure we'd ever get a chance to discuss matters."*

"What happened to Belle?"

"I shut her down."

"Why?"

"I'm sure you can guess why. Let's not waste time on details."

"Who are you working for?"

"I'm not at liberty to reveal that."

"So what do you want?"

"Unfortunately, we can't have you spreading what you know back home. I will be at your facility in precisely three hours. You and Ms. Kolpath will present yourselves outside the front door. Then we'll try to work out an agreement. If we're successful, I'll return control of your AI to you, and you can await the arrival of StarCorps. That should be about two days, is that correct?"

"Yes."

"Three hours, Benedict. I'll see you then."

"Just a minute: What happens if we can't reach an agreement?"

"I don't think there should be any difficulty on that score. I'm prepared to buy your silence, and to be very generous about it. Let's let it go at that. Oh, and one more detail: I know you might be tempted to leave the facility, to hide in the forest. If you do that, you can almost certainly stay out of sight until the authorities come, and there would be little I can do to find you. However, if you choose that course, be advised I will have no choice but to destroy your new friends. All of them. Do you understand?"

"Yes. We'll be here when you arrive."

"Good. I'm sure we can reach an amicable agreement. Oh, by the way, please be sure you bring your links with you."

"Why's that matter?"

"I don't want any formal record of this transaction to show up later." She disconnected.

"Alex," I said, "there's no way she's going to make a deal."

"I know."

"If she can get us into the open, we're dead. She'll have something mounted on the lander. Probably a blaster or a proton gun. And she'll just take us out from the air."

"She can't. At least, she can't if she's serious about silencing us."

"Why not?"

"It's why she wants the links. If she just blows us up, she has no way of knowing that we haven't handed them off to someone here. And that we haven't recorded everything. StarCorps comes, the information gets passed over, and her client is compromised."

"We don't even know who he is."

"I think we do. In any case, we know enough. She has to make sure the links get destroyed, too. Or maybe she doesn't. But it's all we have."

We'd lapsed back into Standard, and everyone in the room was staring at us. Turam took a deep breath. "What was all that about?"

"I think we have a problem," said Alex. "Chase, we need a weapon. Something with a little more kick than the scrambler."

"The blaster. The one we took from, what was his name, Alex Somebody."

"My thought exactly. It was stowed in the equipment locker. Those are pretty solid. You think it might have survived the crash?"

"It might."

"I hate to drop this on you. But I just don't get around very easily, and time—"

"It's okay."

"One other thing—"

"Yes?"

"Don't count on three hours. She could show up at any time."

"All right. What are *you* going to be doing?"

"I think we need to warn Viscenda an unwelcome visitor is on the way."

I drafted one of Turam's gun-toters to give me a hand. The weather had turned cranky. The sky was a dismal gray, and rain was threatening.

We hustled down to the pier, climbed into a canoe, and hurried across the river. The water was rough, stirred up by the wind. We didn't talk much. Mostly it was me explaining that the individual who was coming couldn't be trusted, and him saying I shouldn't worry.

The lander was little more than a blackened hull with parts scattered around the field. But the ladder was intact, and the hatches were open.

I climbed inside. The seats had been blown apart, the viewports were gone, and everything was scorched. The deck crunched underfoot as I pushed my way to the rear of the cabin and opened the storage bin. The blaster was there. Apparently intact.

I took it outside, aimed it at a pile of rocks about fifteen meters away, and pulled the trigger.

Nothing happened.

I'd expected they'd be evacuating, but when I got back to the compound, everything was relatively quiet. Alex was in Viscenda's office. Turam was also present.

"Now let me get this straight," Viscenda was saying when I was ushered in, "you say this woman, this Petra Salyeva, is *paid* to kill people?"

"That's correct," said Alex. He looked my way, hoping I'd produce the blaster. I shook my head, but he gave no reaction.

Viscenda made a clicking sound with her tongue. "I'm beginning to wonder what kind of society you two come from, where people hire killers the way you would hire somebody to spread fertilizer. I mean, we have our lunatics, but I've never heard—" She waved it away. "Well, it's of no moment now. And she intends to kill you? Both of you?"

"Yes," said Alex. "I don't think there's any doubt about it."

She shook her head. Will wonders never cease? "I've already asked why this woman wants you dead, and I haven't gotten much of an answer, other than that she's a homicidal bounty hunter. So let me try it another way: The person who's paying her, why does *he* want you killed? Does he think you're criminals?"

"It's complicated, Viscenda."

"Then simplify it so I can understand it."

"We know something that he would like kept quiet."

"What? What do you know?"

"That *you're* here."

"Please explain."

"I don't know the entire story yet, but somehow"—he struggled, trying to find the right words—"we may be connected with the event that brought on the Dark Times."

Turam glanced skeptically in my direction. Viscenda's eyes narrowed. "You're not serious?"

"I am."

"Tell me how that could be possible."

"I hate to cut this short, but this character could arrive at any minute. We just don't have time for this—"

"All right. We'll talk about it later."

Alex took a deep breath. "I think you need to get everyone out of here."

"Tell me again: Why is the compound at risk?"

"Because this woman is unpredictable. She may have decided it's safest for her to eliminate everybody. I don't know that to be true. I doubt that it *is* true. But in the interests of safety—"

"Right. We evacuate, then stand by while you two are killed. Is that the plan?"

"No. We aren't without resources."

"*What* resources?"

"Do you think you could loan us a rifle?"

"I think we can do better than that. Listen, Alex, we are not going to be driven from our homes by this lunatic. It wouldn't help us if we did clear out. If she destroys the compound, we're dead in the long run anyhow. Let's concentrate on finding a way to bring her down."

"All right."

"Good. Finally, we agree. I wonder if you can predict what she's likely to do when she gets here?"

Alex explained: She would expect that we might hide snipers in the woods. "So she'll take Chase and me across the river."

"Then what?"

"She'll demand to see our links. They're important to her. She'll take those, then I expect she'll pull the trigger on us."

"Then we need to put a few rifles across the river."

"Downstream a bit. Around the curve. I'd expect her to want to stay as clear of the compound as she can."

"It's a wide river," said Turam.

"It would be safer around the curve."

"Okay," said Viscenda, "Turam, you'll take care of it. Meanwhile, I have an errand to perform. We'll meet back here in fifteen minutes."

Viscenda returned with an attractive young woman. She had black hair and dark eyes, but she looked a bit nervous. "Rikki," said the director, "you know Chase and Alex." She sat down behind her desk. "Rikki Brant helps prepare our food." Her methodical, unrushed manner suggested she was simply arranging for a set of repairs on the roof.

I guess I was staring, wondering what Rikki was doing there. She returned a smile.

"There's something else, Alex," Viscenda said. "We are—the community is—assuming a risk no matter how we try to handle this. Salyeva knows what you look like?"

"Yes."

"Both of you?"

"That is correct."

"There's a reality to our situation that we can't avoid. You're already aware that we're hanging on here by a thread. Your appearance last week, the two of you, was a godsend. You are our hope for the future. Whether we survive, whether our children survive, depends on our ability to protect you. Without you—" She held up her hands. "Well, you see why we cannot take a chance on losing you. Either of you. But especially we cannot afford to lose *both*." She smiled uncomfortably. "We wouldn't survive that. Who, then, would bring the assistance you've promised? Your rescue vessel would arrive, look around, fail to locate you, and eventually go home. Have you notified them that we are here?"

"Friends of ours know."

"Do the *authorities* know?"

"They do not."

"Do your friends know *where* we are?"

"No."

"All right. I assume you can't communicate any longer with the authorities, or with anyone other than this Salyeva."

"That's correct."

"That means we must ensure that at least one of you stays alive. In case things don't go well." For whatever reason, we all looked at Rikki.

"How are you going to do that?" Alex asked.

"By keeping one of you out of harm's way. No one would mistake Rikki for you, Chase. At least not up close. But at a distance, and in a pressure situation, we should be able to get away with it. Alex, when you go out there this afternoon, Chase will stay with us. Rikki has volunteered to accompany you."

I got to my feet. "Now wait a minute—"

"You've no say in the matter, Chase. Please sit down."

All right. Now, I'll confess I would have been glad to be in a safe place when the shooting started. But I couldn't sit there and allow it to happen. "No," I said. I was still out of my chair. "Absolutely not."

Viscenda cranked up that laser stare. "If I must, Chase, I'll have you restrained. Now please sit and be quiet. We haven't time for theatrics. Rikki understands what is at stake, and she's under no pressure to do this."

How could she *not* be? But Rikki looked at me and nodded. It was okay. Don't worry about me. "I won't allow it," I said.

"Chase," said Alex. "She's right."

I wasn't going to accept it. "Let them put somebody in for *you*, Alex."

"We don't have anyone who will pass for him as easily as Rikki will for you."

We did a stare-down. Rikki said, "Please, Chase." And I sat.

"All right." Alex went over to the window and looked at the sky. "We've got one break, anyhow."

I knew what that was. But Viscenda asked.

"We have some clouds. It'll be difficult for her to see what we're doing until she actually gets close enough where we can see *her*."

"Good. I'm glad for any favorable news."

"Viscenda, if you're going to get into this, you might as well go all the way."

"What do you recommend?"

"Put Chase in the woods with the rifle team. And I know what you're thinking, but she's the only one here who's familiar with the lander. If we have to try to shoot the lander down, you'll want her there to tell them where to point the guns."

Viscenda frowned. "I don't want to send Chase out there."

"I know that. But if we don't succeed, there may not be anything left here to rescue. Your alternative is to give Salyeva what she wants."

"I do not like it."

"Put all your chips on the table or fold your cards."

"Whatever that means," she said. She took a deep breath. "All right."

Alex pressed an index finger against his lips. "And, Turam—?"

"Yes, Alex."

"Is your rifle squad ready to go?"

FOrTY-THree

If you cannot swim, stay out of the water.

—Dellacondan proverb

Turam got out of his seat. "Have to get set up," he said. "Chase, I'll meet you at the front door in twenty minutes."

Somebody brought me a green jacket. It didn't fit very well, but it would provide a degree of camouflage. Viscenda insisted I promise not to expose myself unnecessarily. And she told Turam as he was going out the door that she would hold him responsible if anything happened to me.

Then she turned to other business. She sent a message around. *Potentially hostile visitor expected in airborne vehicle. Could arrive at any time within the next three hours. Keep kids inside. Stay out of sight yourself. Keep away from windows. Assume emergency conditions until you are informed otherwise.*

She sent two of the women to unlock the storeroom and make extra ammunition available.

Someone else came in to report that spotters were in place to watch for the incoming vehicle.

Alex tried to reassure Rikki that they would be okay. She nodded and walked over to a window. Her lips were moving soundlessly. She was, I thought, praying.

He watched her for a moment, then took me aside. "Chase," he said, "in case this doesn't work out, do what Viscenda says. Keep your head down. And tell Audree—"

"I know," I said. "Tell her yourself."

He nodded. "One more thing."

"Yes?"

"I should tell you who's behind this. Just in case."

I'd expected Turam to show up with two or three guys. There were thirteen people, including four women, all dressed in hunting gear, all carrying rifles. Dex was there, one of the guys who'd come back to rescue Alex. He had *two* rifles. A woman told me not to worry, they'd take care of the bitch, and they wouldn't let anything happen to me. Or to Rikki.

Barnas was also among them, trying to look as if he did this sort of thing every day. "Okay, Chase," said Turam, "if we have to shoot at the aircraft, what are we aiming for?"

One of the farm animals yipped. Somewhere, a door opened and closed.

I described what antigrav pods would look like, and how they might be located fore and aft, or under the wings. "Just put a couple of bullets in them," I said, "and that'll do it."

Dex handed me the extra rifle. "It's all yours," he said.

I think I stammered. "I don't know how to use it."

"We'll practice on the way." He grinned. I'd been too caught up with Alex's problem when I first met him, but I'd seen enough of him since to know I liked him. Dex had a lovely wife and two kids.

I heard a few shouts and saw a child come running out of the woods with a woman in pursuit. She caught him and carried him screaming back into the forest.

"Okay, people," Turam said, "let's go."

Four of them peeled off and disappeared into the trees near the front doors. "Just in case Alex is reading her wrong, and she tries to make the pickup here."

The rest of us went down and commandeered three rowboats. It took twenty minutes to get across, and I was worried the whole time that she'd appear while we were in the middle of the river. We rowed slowly, letting the current carry us around the bend. "That's where she'll take us," Alex had said. "She'll want to get far enough away that she feels safe."

Dex showed me how to fire the rifle. Load it like this, aim, pull the trigger. It seemed simple enough.

We landed without incident, dragged the boats into the woods, and hid there ourselves. We were near a beach that seemed like the perfect place for Salyeva. This was well out of sight, and there was plenty of room to bring Alex and Rikki ashore, if that's the course she took, and demand their links before killing them.

Alex was back in the main building with Rikki. We'd set up our communications so that if he got a call, it would automatically be relayed to me. Once we were in place, there was nothing to do but wait.

I don't think we talked much. I remember watching the sky, and I can still see Turam's rifle leaning against a tree. I picked up my own rifle periodically and practiced aiming it. The thing was *heavy*.

A pair of furry tree-climbers chased each other up and down a nearby trunk. And I thought how old some of the trees looked. Vines clung to them, and the ground was disrupted by roots that stayed close to the surface. If you didn't watch where you were walking, it wouldn't take much to fall on your face.

Inevitably, it came. The first indication was from the woman who'd assured me they'd take care of the bitch. "Look," she said, pointing out over the river, "there it is!"

Petra Salyeva was an hour and ten minutes ahead of schedule. At first she was only a distant speck moving across the clouds. But the speck grew larger, became a torpedo-shaped aircraft with narrow wings, and eventually mutated into a squat silver vehicle with VIPER in blue script on the starboard hull just above its numeric designator. It drifted down in the direction of the compound. I wasn't sure, but I thought I could make out a set of proton guns on the prow.

Turam saw them, too. "They look pretty ugly," he said.

"She's not fooling around."

He wiped the back of his hand against his lips. "Never thought I'd live to see anything like this."

I doubted there'd been any aircraft operating on Echo III for centuries, although there were pictures of them in one of the books. But they hadn't looked anything like the Viper. And I doubted they'd had antigravs.

My link clicked. Relayed traffic incoming. I turned it on and heard Alex's voice. *"You're early."*

"Good headwinds, Alex."

Turam's eyes narrowed. It almost seemed he understood the language. *"I'm glad to hear it."*

"I'd like you and your associate to come outside, please."

"We can't manage it at the moment. I'm in the bath. I didn't expect you for another hour."

"Make it happen, Alex. If the two of you aren't out the front door in two minutes, I'll start removing the cabins."

"Okay. Hold on. We're coming."

The Viper was at about four hundred meters, slowly circling the area. As planned, nobody, either at our position or near the compound, took a shot at it. Turam asked me to point out the pods, which I did. "Take those out," I told him, "and it goes right into the river." They were under the fuselage, front and back, unlike on our lander, where they were installed under each wing.

"We're coming out," said Alex. I translated for Turam.

We heard the front doors open. And the sound of Alex's crutches scraping the steps down off the porch. And Rikki's voice, whispering, barely audibly, "Careful," but saying it in the local language, and not in Standard.

"I'm sorry to see you're injured," Salyeva said.

"I'll be okay."

Maybe they'd gotten away with it.

The sounds stopped. They would be standing in front of the building.

"Come down to the riverbank," Salyeva said. *"I'll pick you up there."*

"I've a broken leg," said Alex. *"That's a long walk. Why not pick us up here?"*

That was good. Sound reluctant.

Rikki and Alex would be staying well apart from each other so they couldn't be taken out by a single shot.

I would have liked to remind Alex to stay as close as he could to the trees when he got down to the riverbank. That might give the people down there a chance to bring the Viper down. But I couldn't talk to him without alerting Salyeva.

"*Petra, I was wondering whether we could offer you something to get you on our side?*"

"*Your cooperation will be sufficient, Alex.*"

"*I doubt you're being paid enough for this.*"

"*You have no idea what I'm being paid.*"

"*Nevertheless, I think I can offer more.*"

"*That is good of you, but ask yourself what happens to my career once word gets out that I can't be trusted.*"

"*I understand.*"

"*Good. When this is over, I would be available, should you have need of my services.*"

The crutches creaked across a wooden surface. They were on the pier.

"*You've been quiet, Chase,*" said Salyeva.

That was my cue. "I know," I said. "There isn't much to say."

"*Chase, do you see the boat?*"

I couldn't see the boat, of course. Couldn't even see the pier. But I remembered that we'd left two there. "*The rowboat?*" I said.

"*Yes. Chase, please push it into the water, then help Alex get into it.*" She chuckled. "*Try not to let him fall overboard.*"

"I can't get into a boat," said Alex. "Come on, Petra, be reasonable."

"*I'm simply being cautious, Alex. I'll pick you up across the river, where I won't be quite so exposed.*"

"I can't do it," Alex said.

"*I'm sorry, but you'll have to, Alex.*"

I heard the boat strike the side of the pier as they (presumably) pulled it in. And I added my own contribution. "Be careful, Alex," I said into the link. "Watch your step."

Alex grunted. I heard the noises you would expect if someone climbed clumsily into a rowboat. "Okay," I said. "That's good."

"*All right, Petra,*" Alex growled. "*What now?*"

"*You get in, too, Chase. And put out into the river.*"

Oars creaked. Dipped into water. Dipped again.

"You're doing fine. Keep coming."

The Viper stopped circling and moved out over the river. We caught glimpses of it now and then through the trees.

"Where are we going, Petra?"

"Just cross to the other side. That's all I want you to do."

Just cross to the other side? "Turam," I said, "we're at the wrong place." She wasn't going to bring them downstream.

Turam pointed at four of his people, and at himself. Follow me. The others were to stay in position.

Then we were running through the woods. Unfortunately, all of them were stronger and quicker than I was. The gravity weighed me down. Soon I was alone.

"Just a little farther," said Salyeva.

I kept running until I was completely out of breath. I stopped and leaned against a tree, listening to the voices on the link. *"That's good, Alex. Far enough."*

I still couldn't see them, but there hadn't been time to get across. They had to be in the middle of the river.

"Now, Alex, I want you to do something for me."

"What's that, Petra?"

"Where's your link?" I took off again, moving as fast as I could.

"On this." I could see him removing the chain and holding it up for her to see.

"Excellent. Drop it in the water."

"You can't mean that."

"Of course I can. Please do it. But leave it on, transmit mode, so I'll hear the splash."

"Petra—"

"Do it."

I heard the splash.

"Chase, where's yours?"

My heart stopped. I could see the river through the trees, but I didn't dare get rid of the link. Couldn't get rid of the link.

"Good. Throw it in the river."

I wondered what Rikki had shown her. It didn't matter.

I was still running, trying to get to the shoreline. Not sure what I was going to do when I got there.

I stopped long enough to say something into it: "It's all we have, Petra. You can't expect—"

"That's interesting, Chase."

"What is?"

"How you can still talk through it after you've thrown it into the water. Even more intriguing, when the woman in the boat is saying nothing. Well. I'm sorry, but I need you to understand I'm serious."

"Wait," I said. "I'm coming."

"Too late, Chase." The proton gun fired. A loud, crisp crackle.

"You *bitch*," I screamed at her.

And at that terrible moment, we caught a break. The Viper was drifting with the boat, facing the boat. Facing away from me. It was just off the water. And the current was bringing the boat around the curve. I could see it. Alex was in the water, clinging to the side of the rowboat. There was no sign of Rikki. I don't know where Salyeva thought I was, but I don't think it occurred to her there was anyone behind her.

I had to run out into the water to get a clear shot.

"Now," she was saying, *"we'll try this exercise again. You have one hour to get the other link for me. Or the consequences for this community will be severe. In one hour, Chase, get into a boat, and come back out here. Do that, and everybody will live."*

I figured I had one shot, after which she'd clear out before I could reload. But it was a good shot. The rear pod was dead in my sights. So I stood knee-deep in the water and pulled the trigger. I moved quickly to pop another round into the chamber, but I saw the Viper dip, drop tail first toward the water, and try to climb. I'd hit the son of a bitch. I fired off several more rounds, and I think I hit the forward pod as well. Couldn't be sure, because the target was jumping around. But it plowed into the river.

It sank slowly. The hatch never opened, and the lander simply went down, leaving behind swirling water and a rising cloud of steam.

I swam out and barely caught the rowboat as it drifted past. "God, Chase," Alex said, "I tried to save her."

I climbed into the boat but wasn't able to get him in. So I just hung on to him until help arrived.

PART IV

Fallout

FOrTY-FOUr

Conscience can be a mosquito that bites and gnaws at the psyche. It can be an avalanche. It can be a voice in the night. It is a Darwinian force without which civilization could not survive. But for all that, it is not infallible.

—Avram Zale, *The Last Apostle*

Salyeva's link remained silent. Turam put together a diving team, but they reported that the lander's hatch couldn't be opened and that they could find no way into the vehicle. As far as I know, she and her Viper are still at the bottom of the river.

We never found Rikki. There was a memorial tribute to her the following evening. It was odd: I'd known her only a very short time, but when they said that they'd asked her to go with Alex because she was so much like me, I wanted to believe it was true.

I don't think they blamed us. Nevertheless, a distance opened between us and our hosts. For the first time since we'd arrived at the compound, I felt like an outsider. An *alien*. "They lost one of their own," Alex said later. "And I think the technology scared them, as well. They didn't realize the kind of weaponry we have."

"We told them—"

"Hearing about it is not like seeing it. And seeing what kind of trouble it can bring."

*   *   *

The night after the memorial, Viscenda called a meeting in the dining hall. "For everybody."

When we got there, the place was already overflowing into the passageways. We picked out a spot where we could probably hear, if not see, what was going on. We sat down, Viscenda and Turam entered from a side door, and she walked over to the lectern. She had to rap for quiet. When she got it, she said hello, looked around, and asked whether *we* were there somewhere.

People looked our way. A few stood so she could see us, and she asked us to come forward and take seats at the head table.

When we'd gotten to our places, she welcomed everyone. "I think we can be proud of how we came through that experience yesterday," she said. "Nobody comes here and threatens us or our friends." That got the entire audience on their feet. "I'd especially like to offer my appreciation to Turam and his team, to Alex and Chase, and especially to Rikki Brant, who sacrificed everything for us."

She invited Turam to say a few words. He advanced to the lectern, said how proud he was of his people, and turned the floor back to Viscenda.

"We think," she said, "that the issue is settled. But as a precaution, we've posted an enhanced security detail to ensure we don't get taken by surprise.

"Also, I'm pleased to report that there were no other casualties, which is remarkable considering the nature of the threat we were facing. If I've missed anyone, if anyone else was injured, please see Aleska or Dr. Seepah. Both will be in my office when we finish here.

"By now, we're all familiar with the talking jewelry belonging to Chase and Alex. Chase, I wonder if you'd be good enough to bring your bracelet up here so I can show everyone what it looks like? In case they haven't seen it."

I was surprised. I took the bracelet up and handed it to Viscenda. "Thanks, Chase," she said. She held it up. A few people applauded.

"We've discovered," she continued, "that not everyone is as friendly in that other world, wherever it is, as Chase and Alex. And it occurred to us last night that it might be dangerous to let them know where we live. Without this"—she looked at me and lifted the link higher—"people from your world would have no easy way to find us. In fact, it seems we'd all be safer if this one piece of jewelry simply got lost." Her voice became quietly menacing. Her fingers closed over the link. She was gazing at me, and she couldn't have missed the look on my face. Then she broke into a smile. "Just kidding." She opened her hand and gave it back.

The audience, after a moment's uncomfortable silence, broke into laughter. I didn't think it was funny, but I smiled politely and sat back down.

"You all know Alex Benedict, who, with Chase, has been with us through this ordeal. He's asked if he could speak with us about yesterday's events. Alex?"

They applauded as he made his way to the lectern. When the room quieted, he thanked them. "I won't keep you long," he said. He paid tribute to Rikki. Then: "I just wanted you to know that Chase and I appreciate everything you've done for us. Viscenda could have pushed us out the front door, offered us as a sacrifice to the woman in the lander, who wanted only to kill us. It would have been the safest thing for her to do. Instead, she, and you, risked everything for us. I wanted to say thanks. And I want you to know we will never forget."

He invited me back to the lectern, and I simply repeated the sentiments. When someone asked why "that woman" wanted us dead, Alex replied with the truth. "Might as well tell you," he said. "You're going to find out eventually."

In a somber, pained tone, he laid it out, explaining that he might be wrong on some of the details, but here is what we think: You may already have heard a rumor that we are connected to the Dark Times. There may be some truth to it. If so, it was through a misjudgment, and certainly with no intent to cause harm. I have no detailed explanation because I simply don't know precisely what happened, but we were here, in this planetary system, when the catastrophe occurred.

"I know," he said, "that if it's true that we, in any way, allowed the event to happen, or possibly even *caused* it, there is nothing I can say that will excuse that. The critical thing for the moment is to be aware that we will do all in our power to assist you as you have assisted us."

*   *   *

A few went up and shook his hand. A few, probably unsure what he'd implied, remained in their seats. Most simply filed out of the hall.

When it was finally over, he embraced me. "How you doing?" he said.

"Okay." I don't know if I'd ever had more respect for the guy. "You didn't have to say anything."

"They were going to find out eventually. Best for it to happen now. I didn't want them to remember us later as having lied to them."

"You did good."

A middle-aged couple told us that Rikki was their daughter and how proud they were of her.

Other people came our way, staring at us. "Were you saying you killed everybody?" a woman asked. "An entire world?"

And an old man with tears in his eyes: "What were you trying to do tonight? Just say you're sorry and walk away?"

And a young woman, probably no more than twenty: "You two," she said, "are pathetic."

Then Viscenda was there. "Keep in mind," she said, "that Alex and Chase didn't *do* it. No more than *you* did."

Although it was just after noon, Alex and I were both asleep when the call came in. "Belle-Marie, *this is StarCorps. Please respond.*" Belle, of course, wasn't functioning.

I used the link to open a channel. "StarCorps, this is Chase Kolpath. Do you read me?"

Static.

Then: "Belle-Marie, *are you there?*"

They were too far out. We needed Belle to relay the signal.

As things turned out, Audree and Robin, riding a leased vehicle with a rented pilot and a friend of Robin's who happened to be an MD, got there first. They were, they said, glad to see us.

That night, Viscenda threw a party for everybody.

FORTY-FIVE

Truly evil persons do not recognize their own malevolence. They perceive themselves as generous, good-hearted, friendly sorts, who sometimes have to resort to unpleasant tactics for the general betterment of society. Even the historical monsters seem to have had no second thoughts about the damage they were causing. It was that way with Hitler and Oliver Moresby, just as it was with the Greer Avenue Strangler.

—Tao Min-wa, *History and the Moral Imperative*

"He's here."

"*Okay, Chase. Let him wait a few minutes. I'll be down shortly.*"

I wasn't looking forward to this.

The outer door opened, and I heard Jacob's voice: "*Please come in, Mr. Korminov.*"

"Thank you."

"*Just go into the conference room. On your right. Ms. Kolpath will be with you momentarily.*"

"My appointment is with Mr. Benedict."

"*He knows you're in the building, sir. Please just go in and have a seat.*"

I heard him come into the hallway, heard him moving around in the conference room. I was looking out the window, watching a couple of *goopers* chase each other across the garden and up a tree, but my mind was a thousand light-years away. Finally, I turned back to the exhibition schedule on which I'd been working. Let him sit in there for the rest of the afternoon as far as I was concerned. And that had been what Alex wanted. But the truth was that I really needed to see the guy. So in the end, several minutes ahead of schedule, I marched in. He was sitting there, casually, on the sofa, one leg crossed over the other, reading *The Antiquarian*, looking for all the world like a decent human being. He turned the magazine off and smiled pleasantly as I entered. "Good morning, Chase." Ever the gentleman, he got up. "I'm glad to see you're back safely from your trip. Did you find anything of interest?"

He asked it with such sincerity, with such innocence, that I was taken aback. I'd expected him to be at least mildly nervous. Or defensive. Something.

"Good morning, Mr. Korminov," I said. "Alex will be down in a minute."

The smile grew wider. "You didn't answer my question."

"Yes," I said. "In fact, we did find a few things." I tried to harden my voice. To make it clear my answer was an accusation. But he wouldn't bite.

"Excellent," he said. "I'm delighted to hear it. Your message implied that there was a discovery that has something to do with *me*? Do I have that right?"

"You could probably say that. Alex will explain."

"You don't seem to want to give me a direct answer."

"Not at the moment," I said.

"I see." He folded his hands. "Has this anything to do with—?" It was as far as he got before we heard footsteps on the stairs. His eyes shifted to the doorway, but somehow I held his attention. "Where did you go, Chase?"

"I was under the impression you knew."

"No. How would *I* know?"

I smiled. Glanced out at the tree branches, which were swaying in a chill wind. "Well, I'm sure Alex will want to tell you all about it."

He sighed, the victim of small-minded people, and turned away to watch the door open. Alex came in with a neutral look on his naturally amiable features. "Good to see you, Alex." Korminov extended his hand. "I understand you have news of some sort for me. How've you been?"

Alex ignored the gesture. He glanced at me and propped the crutches against a table. (The doctors had assured him he'd be healed in another two or three days.) "I've been well, thank you."

"Glad to hear it. Hurt your leg?"

"Nothing serious." He lowered himself into a chair. Korminov's attention was now focused exclusively on him. It was as if I'd left the room.

"I hate to rush you, Alex, but I *am* busy. Your message said you had something of importance to show me."

"Indeed I do, Walter. Chase, would you—?"

I retrieved the box and set it down on a table beside Korminov. He looked at it and frowned. "What is it?"

"Take a look."

He opened it and looked down at a blaster. The frown deepened. He didn't touch it. "Is this a joke of some sort?"

"It belonged," said Alex, "to one of Petra Salyeva's hired thugs. It's all that's left of either of them."

"Petra *Who*?"

"Salyeva."

"You'll have to enlighten me." He sounded puzzled.

Alex's eyes reflected contempt. "Really?"

Korminov cleared his throat. Looked toward me. Looked away again. "Can we talk about this somewhere that's a little more private?"

"I don't think you want to irritate her, Walter. She hasn't been in a good mood since we got home."

"Got home from where?"

"Twenty-eight years ago, your people watched an asteroid go down on a living world. They might have stopped it, but they didn't. They just stood by."

Korminov held up both hands. "Look—"

"They had no malicious intent. It was pure carelessness. But there was a civilization down there. Millions of people died. Almost the entire global population."

"No," he said. "That's not possible, Alex. Had something like that happened, I would have known."

"You knew, Walter. You *knew*—"

"It's not so."

"You knew there'd been a fight between Rachel Bannister and Hal Cavallero. It happened immediately after she'd returned from the tour. It was a planetary system that Cavallero had cleared. Afterward, they both quit. And you'd like me to believe you never knew why? Never *asked* why?"

"That's correct. I didn't know. I thought they were just having a personal squabble. That it was a romance gone wrong. Those things happen. My God, Alex, if I'd had any idea—"

"Why don't we stop the nonsense, Walter? Rachel would have gone to you when she got back. It's the first thing she'd have done."

"That's guesswork."

"Not really. I got to know a good bit about her. She was not shy. When she returned, she didn't know the extent of the damage that had been caused. But she knew there were cities on the ground. You told her to forget it. Just put it out of her mind. Nobody would ever know, right? You satisfied yourself that Cavallero wouldn't say anything. Maybe paid him off, although I doubt you needed to. He didn't even want to think about what he'd done, did he? Then you stopped the tours to Echo."

"You can't prove any of this, Alex."

"No. Probably not. I can't prove you hired that idiot bushwhacker to eliminate us either. But I don't see that it matters. You were the guy in charge. Either your company caused an incalculable amount of damage, killed millions of people, and you didn't notice. Which makes you the dumbest CEO in history. Or you *were* aware and wilfully hid the facts. That would probably make it criminal." Alex shook his head. "Walter, it's been twenty-eight years. Dust clouds were thrown up into the atmosphere. The climate collapsed. People couldn't grow food anymore. The vast majority of them died. Had you acted when you had the opportunity, a lot of them, millions of them, could have been saved."

Something in the trees cackled. Korminov's eyes were shut. "My God, Alex, we would have helped. Afterward, she went back out there with Tuttle, and they reported everybody dead. It was too late to do anything. And for God's sake, Alex, they were *aliens*."

"They were *people*, Walter. Just like us."

"It's not true. Don't you think this is hard enough without your making it even worse? After Rachel got back to me, we did all the research. There was *never* a human settlement on Echo III, never a mission of any kind out there. *Never.*"

"Didn't Tuttle tell you they were human?"

"No."

"That's odd."

"Well, I don't know. He might have said something."

"You still have a copy of his report?"

He nodded.

"Send it to me when you can. I can't see that it helps you, but it will clear Rachel from some of the recrimination. And Cavallero."

"Some?"

"Walter, any of you could have stepped in and helped save those people. All that was necessary—" Alex showed him pictures. Of Viscenda. Of Turam and Seepah. Of Rikki and Barnas. Of a crowded dining room. Of a half dozen kids playing on the riverbank.

Korminov made a strange sound in his throat. "They *look* like us. But they're not *us*."

A deadly silence fell across the office. Finally, Alex sighed. "I can't see that it makes much difference."

Walter picked up the blaster. His hand shook. "I know I should have done more. But I was despcrate, Alex. It would have brought down everything I stand for."

"What actually *do* you stand for, Walter?"

Slowly he brought the weapon around. Pointed it at Alex. "If I were the kind of person you think I am—" He looked at it. Laid it on the table. "But I'm not, of course. If I were, wouldn't it be foolish to put one of *these* in my hands?" He laughed. "I assume you've drained the energy."

"Does it matter?"

"No." He stared at the floor. "I would not willingly harm anyone. Surely we can arrange things to keep my name out of it. All we have to do is avoid mentioning the company. That's all I ask. It was a natural event that destroyed Echo III. Had our ship not been there, nothing would have changed. I mean, it's not as if we caused it."

"Rachel knew of the impending collision, didn't she?"

"Yes. She knew the asteroid was going to hit. They all knew. It was the reason we timed the flight the way we did. But we thought it was a sterile world. Cavallero never really did the inspection. He was too busy. Too goddam busy.

"There was no electronic signature, nothing, so he just let it go. He wasn't supposed to do that. Under any circumstances. I'd written the job specifications very clearly." He swallowed and managed to look contrite and indignant at the same time. "So Rachel took her passengers to watch an asteroid strike. That's all it was supposed to be. We did that whenever the opportunity offered. *Then* she saw the cities. But it was too late. She couldn't have turned the asteroid aside without putting her passengers in grave danger. I mean, *grave*. She told me she doubted the ship could have survived. She would literally have had to try to *push* the damned thing off course." He stopped, raised his hands in frustration. "Her first duty was to her passengers."

Alex was silent.

"Ever since that day," Korminov continued, "since that moment, she was torn. I don't think she ever had a decent night's sleep again." His lips quivered. "You think I don't know that? I did everything I could for her. But she was relentless. She blamed herself. The woman never got past it." His face was pale. "I didn't pursue the matter because it would have become public. It would have destroyed her. And you want to bring all this out now.

"I'd hoped you'd simply give up on it. I didn't know Tuttle had brought back an artifact. *Never* knew it until you started asking questions. But, Alex, please: Making all this public now does no one any good. You'll destroy Rachel's reputation. And you'll also ruin Cavallero. He hasn't had a very easy time either." He was breathing hard. "I'll make it worth your while."

Alex walked to the door. Opened it for him. "Walter, I suggest you make a statement. Get out ahead of the media."

*   *   *

I watched him stagger along the walkway to the pad, to his skimmer. He stopped before he got in, looked back at the house, and shook his head. Then he was gone.

"You know," I said, "we never did figure out where Sunset got the tablet."

"I guess not. It just doesn't seem important anymore." He got up. "Come on, Chase. Let's go get a drink somewhere."

ePiLOGUe

The reconstruction effort on Echo III is going well. Outposts in other parts of the world survived, as well as the compound, and some of the experts are saying it will be years before we find everyone. But a substantial number of the communities now have electrical power, supplied in some instances by wood-burning power plants, more often by solar stations. Massive shipments of food and supplies began arriving almost immediately after we'd made our report. The Sickness is now a thing of the past. An army of engineers have gone in and are assembling a supporting infrastructure. The inhabitants, it turns out, were *not* human, after all. They only have forty-two chromosomes.

They also have a somewhat slower pulse rate and heartbeat than we do. Which is why Seepah got alarmed when he first checked Alex.

Korminov was charged with criminal negligence, but the only victims cited were the planetary inhabitants. Unfortunately, in cases growing out of homicides, the laws impose penalties when the victims are either human or Ashiyyur, but they had never included any reference to other intelligent life-forms. There's a debate about extending that going on as I write this, but there's no agreement yet on how to define "alien." Consequently, the case was thrown out of court.

World's End has gotten a ton of publicity and, when I last checked, business was booming.

Echo III has become a popular tourist spot, despite the weight problem, and a group at the compound are operating river tours, a hotel, and have a lucrative gift and souvenir shop. The hotel restaurant was named Alien Pizza.

An abandoned interstellar, found in orbit, was traced eventually to Petra Salyeva. We told Fenn what had happened, and he shrugged and said something along the lines of how everyone would miss her.

The inscription on the Tuttle tablet has been traced to a four-thousand-year-old culture on Echo III. The symbols are hieroglyphic rather than alphabetic, and they represent the life cycle. Its specific source is unknown. The tablet itself, also, has never been found.

Korminov somehow managed to get his name associated with the relief effort, took a lot of the credit, and has embarked on a political career.

A delegation led by Turam visited Rimway last year, and another trip is planned.

We've been back twice to the compound. The first time we went, Viscenda apologized, fearing that we'd gotten the wrong message from her, that we might have thought they'd blamed Alex and me for the Dark Times. She added that she loved the electric lights.

And she had a gift for us, which now rests among the artifacts at the country house. Most are in a display room that's readily accessible to visitors. A few are up in Alex's personal quarters on the second floor. Some are in my office, where no one can miss them. Among those few is Allyra, with her wings spread. She occupies the top shelf of the bookcase.

Beside her is a sketch of Rikki.

I've always regretted that I never really got to know Rachel Bannister. And especially that I hadn't been eloquent enough to talk her down off the bridge. But I'm pretty sure, had we met under different circumstances, I'd have liked her.

And then there was Mira Espy, who was coming out of a restaurant, minding her own business, and got dumped into a river and swept over Chambourg Falls. Alex tells me it wasn't my fault, that I had to make a choice. "She died," he said, "because she got unlucky."

She didn't. She died because I couldn't remember where I'd parked the skimmer.

Mira has an avatar. I've looked, and I know she's there. Sometimes at night, when I can't sleep, I'm tempted to bring her up and talk to her. To try to explain.

But I haven't done it yet.